# Highland Knight of Rapture

*Highland Dynasty Series—Book Four*

by

Amy Jarecki

~Scottish Historical Romance~

Rapture Books



Jarecki, Amy
Highland Knight of Rapture

ISBN: 978-1-942442-06-6
First Release: July, 2015

Book Cover Design by: Amy Jarecki
Edited by: Scott Mooreland

To all my wonderful Facebook friends. It is a joy to interact with you!

# Chapter One

*Mingary Castle, the Highlands. March, 1493*

Clenching every muscle in her body, Helen bore down with her remaining shreds of strength. She'd crossed the threshold of her endurance hours ago. Pain no longer mattered. After twenty-four hours of labor, she needed to expunge this bairn from her womb if it killed her, which may very well come about.

Her body shuddered as she shrieked through her grating voice box, pushing until her eyes bulged. "I…" she panted. "Cannot. Take. Anymore!"

"You can!" Glenda shouted. "Just a bit longer, m'lady."

Helen sucked in a gasp of air. If she weren't on the brink of death, she'd give her chambermaid a strong rebuttal. But before she could open her mouth, the blinding pain intensified. Panting, she gripped the bed linens and clenched her teeth so taut, they might just shatter. "Eeeeeeee," she screeched.

"I see the head, m'lady. Keep. Pushing!"

Helen loved Glenda, but by the saints, the woman had to be the spawn of the devil to encourage this mounting torture.

Straining so hard her skull throbbed, Helen gulped one more deep breath and pushed. This had to be the end. Swooning, she could take no more. Stars darted through her vision. Her insides ripped and tore. Many women died in childbirth.

Would she, too?

*Blessed Mother Mary, help me, I must survive.*

Then as if her prayer had been answered, the bairn slid out between her legs. Her pain subsided.

Helen collapsed against the pillows.

A slap resounded through the chamber. A wee cry sang out.

Helen's heart soared.

"'Tis a lass, m'lady."

She could have floated to the canopy above. Pushing the sweat-soaked hair from her brow, Helen smiled. "A wee lassie?" Joyful tears welled in her eyes. Suddenly, all the pain and agony seemed worthwhile as the infant's angelic voice gasped and cried. It was the most delightful sound she'd ever heard. She reached up. "I want to hold her."

"Let me finish cleansing her and then you can make the bond," Glenda said from across the chamber.

With a sigh, Helen gazed at the scarlet canopy above. She'd never been so elated, yet so exhausted.

Glenda came into view, a wide grin on her careworn face. She settled the bairn in Helen's waiting arms. "What will you call the lass, m'lady?"

Helen regarded the beet-red infant yawning at her. She had a tiny bow-shaped mouth, enormous blue eyes and a smattering of black curls atop her head. "You shall be named Margaret after my mother, but I shall call you Maggie, because you are the most adorable wee bairn I have ever seen." She kissed the top of her daughter's head. "And your second name shall be Alice after my younger sister. I like the sound of *Alice* ever so much."

With a fragrance as fresh as morning's dew, Maggie turned her head toward Helen's breast and nudged.

"She can smell your milk, m'lady." Glenda untied Helen's linen shift and opened the front. "Hold Maggie to your teat. She'll ken what to do."

Helen moved the bairn in place, and just as Glenda had said, Maggie started to suckle. But it burned. Alarmed, Helen gasped and shot a panicked look at her chambermaid.

"Do not worry, m'lady. It stings a bit at first, but eases as soon as your milk starts to flow."

Again, Glenda was right and the stinging lessened as quickly as it had come on.

Watching the miracle in her arms, Helen sighed. "I do not ken what I would do without you, Glenda. You are so wise with these things."

"Aye?" The chambermaid chuckled. "Having three bairns of my own gave me all the learning I needed, I suppose."

Helen stiffened when the door opened. Her husband strode into the chamber, his heavy boots clomping over the floorboards while the sword and dirk belted at his waist clanked against his iron hauberk. She would never grow accustomed to Aleck MacIain's harsh mien. With a bald head and black steely eyes, she'd yet to discover his compassionate side, despite five years of marriage. That the bulky man entered wearing his weapons, along with muddy boots, spoke volumes about his lack of respect for her.

Though Helen's skin crawled, she feigned a smile—the same one she always used to mask her fear. "Come meet your daughter, m'laird."

He stopped mid-stride and glared. "You mean to tell me that after five miserable years of waiting, you only manage to produce a lass?"

Helen tensed and glanced to Glenda. The chambermaid met her gaze with a frown, then snapped her attention to gathering the soiled linens. No one in the clan dared confront the Chieftain of Mingary, lest they be turned out to fend for themselves. A knot clamped in Helen's stomach. Aleck may be a tyrant toward her, but he would respect their daughter. "She is our firstborn—a lovely, healthy bairn. 'Tis not always a misfortune for a daughter to come first. We will have other children, of that I am certain."

He dropped his gaze to her exposed breast and frowned. "I have misgivings about your ability to be successful at bearing lads, given the length of time it took to conceive a lass." He grunted. "At least you've gained some shape to your udders, though I doubt they'll stay that way."

Helen turned her face away, heat prickling the back of her neck. Bless it, she'd just birthed *his* bairn and he hadn't a kind word to say? She bit back the tears threatening to well in her eyes. A long time ago, she'd vowed Aleck MacIain would not make her weep. She'd spent every day of the past five years trying to please him—looking at every insult as another chance to better herself. But her efforts had never been enough.

*If only I could do something to make him like me.*

She regarded the helpless bairn in her arms. Hit with an overwhelming urge to protect Maggie, she pulled the comforter over the lass to shield the child and her breast from Aleck's stare.

Glenda clapped her hands. "I'm afraid Lady Helen is very weak, m'laird. She has lost a great deal of blood and needs her rest."

Aleck's gaze darted to the chambermaid as if about to spit out a rebuke. But his lips formed a thin line and he nodded. With one last odious look at Helen, he turned on his heel and left.

Helen allowed herself to breathe.

Glenda dashed to the side of the bed. "I'm ever so sorry, m'lady."

"'Tis not your fault. I kent Sir Aleck wanted a lad." Helen smoothed her hand over Maggie's downy soft curls as the bairn continued to suckle. "He just doesn't ken how precious a lass can be."

"No, he does not. I doubt he ever will."

"Wheesht, Glenda," Helen admonished.

The woman crossed her arms. "I'll not pretend. I disprove of his boorishness, especially toward you, m'lady."

Her serving maid had never been quite so forthright. Helen should scold her further, but presently she hadn't the wherewithal to do so. At long last, she held Maggie in her arms and even Aleck MacIain could not quash the joy in her heart. Helen grinned. "She is beautiful, is she not?"

"A more precious bairn does not exist." Glenda reached in. "'Tis time for her to suckle on the other side."

***

After a fortnight living in solitude with her newborn cradled beside her bed, a bout of melancholy attacked Helen today. Aleck had ordered the bairn to be moved from Helen's chamber to the nursery. He'd cited the unbearable racket at all hours of the night screeching through his adjoining chamber walls. *Such is the affection of my husband.* The fortnight hidden away with Maggie had been a heavenly reprieve. But even Helen knew her bliss wouldn't last. Henceforth, Maggie's care would be entrusted to the nursemaid and Helen would resume her duties as lady of the keep.

Standing in front of her polished copper mirror, she clamped her hands to her waist and pushed in on her stays while Glenda laced her bodice. "I'm afraid I'll have to ask the tailor to alter all my gowns."

"You've slimmed down a great deal since Maggie was born."

Helen regarded her bosoms, now swelling above the neckline of her blue gown. At least she was more voluptuous. Aleck seemed to prefer women with more shape. Perhaps he would now look fondly upon her. The thought, however, turned Helen's stomach. She'd been married to Aleck long enough to shudder any time he suggested paying a visit to her bedchamber. In addition, by his frequent derisive comments, she suspected he wasn't overly fond of bedding her either.

Alas, arranged marriages often did not come with a silver lining…or love. But Helen had a duty to her clan, and now to Maggie, and she would see to everyone's care with forthright, if not stoic, dedication.

Glenda finished tying the bodice and gave it a pat. "How is that, m'lady?"

Helen released her grip and inhaled. Her head spun. "I must admit I haven't missed wearing stays during my confinement."

The chambermaid frowned, deepening the lines in her jowls. "These new contraptions are devices of torture if you ask me."

"True, but fashion dictates ladies must wear them."

"Aye?" Glenda placed a matching mantle of blue, adorned with gold threaded fleur de lis over Helen's shoulders. "Next the powers above will be convincing Scottish women that iron corsets are the style."

Helen laughed. "If that comes about, at least there will be no need for women's armor."

"Armor?" Glenda gaped, pinning Helen's silk veil in place. "Do not tell me the women at court wear armor?"

"Of course not, silly. But ladies might be a bit more secure if they did."

"Do you believe so?" The chambermaid brushed her hands along Helen's skirts. "But isn't that what menfolk are for?"

"Aye." Helen turned sideways and regarded her profile in the mirror. "Though perhaps we would gain a bit more freedom to move about if we were more self-reliant."

Glenda gestured toward the door. "Sometimes I think you live in a fanciful dream."

"I suppose I do." *I would have withered under Aleck's harsh nature by now if not for my vivid imagination.* Helen picked up her skirts with a sigh. "Besides, I like my stories. They help me escape, if only for a brief interlude, and I see no harm in it."

"Nor do I." Glenda opened the door and bowed her head. "Enjoy the evening meal, m'lady."

Helen smiled while her stomach squelched. She dreaded rejoining Aleck at the high table. But like the books she so loved to read, her time of solace had come to an end. She stood tall and headed to the stairwell. The voices below stairs rumbled with a familiar hum, reminding her of all the duties she must resume as lady of the keep—caring for the villagers of nearby Kilchoan, and menu preparation being at the top of her list.

The jumbled conversations grew stronger as did the aroma of rosemary herbed lamb. When she rounded the last few steps, she stood at the bottom of the stairwell and looked across the tapestry-lined hall. The tables, filled with her kin, were lined end-to-end forming two long rows. She nodded to those who noticed her, then focused on the dais.

Aleck presided over the throng from his oversized chair as usual, but Mary the widow sat in Helen's seat.

That the buxom woman had been invited to dine at the high table didn't surprise her, but the fact that the pair was being openly affectionate did. Upon Helen's confinement, Aleck had wasted no time finding a leman. Helen had felt slighted, of course, but he'd been reasonably discreet—aside from the lewd noises coming from his chamber at night. Fortunately, Helen was the only one privy to such a disturbance.

Mary wrapped her arms around Aleck and mashed her breast flush against him. In fact, the woman leaned so far forward, she not only gave Aleck a peek at her wares, the clan's highest ranking men seated at the high table could see as well. The scene was scandalous. Mary hadn't even respectably covered her brown tresses—she was, after all, a matron.

Something must have been inordinately funny because they laughed raucously, until Aleck looked up and spotted Helen. Then he puffed out his chest as if he was proud of consorting with his leman in front of the clan.

The rumble in the hall silenced.

Helen lifted her chin and affected a pleasant smile. All eyes fixated on her as she proceeded to the dais. The swishing of her skirts in concert with her footsteps echoed clear up to the rafters. Aleck shifted in his seat and glared with a look Helen knew well. She was to keep her mouth shut. Mary released his arm, but remained in Helen's chair.

*Lovely.*

"You're late," Aleck groused as she neared.

Ignoring him, Helen climbed onto the dais. Head held high, she strolled to the place reserved for the lady of the keep. "Good evening, Mistress Mary. My *husband* requested my presence in the hall this eve." In the folds of her skirts, she clenched her fists and forced a serene expression. "I believe 'tis time to remove your person from my chair."

Aleck inclined his head to the seat at his right. "Och, Helen. Mary has already portioned her trencher. It will not pain you to sit over here for a meal."

Heat flooded her cheeks, but she did not falter. How she'd expected *him* to support her assertion was beyond Helen. Clearly, he cared not about her humiliation upon arriving in the great hall to see a woman pressing her breast into her husband's arm. Then to be swatted aside with a "sit elsewhere" was almost more than Helen could bear.

She pursed her lips and slid into the chair at Aleck's right, then looked out over the hall. Stunned faces gaped back—faces of people she'd grown to love and she hoped had also developed a fondness for her. She spread her palms and offered a gracious smile. The banter resumed and a servant placed a tankard of mead in front of her.

Helen bowed her head in appreciation. "My thanks, Roderick."

On her other side, Grant, the MacIain henchman, dipped his head politely. "'Tis good to see your bonny face this eve, m'lady."

He'd learned his manners from Glenda, his ma. *Thank heavens all MacIain's are not brutes*. "I'm glad to be well enough to dine in the hall, though it was difficult to leave Miss Maggie."

"Och, the bairn will be right with Sarah. She's a fine nursemaid." Grant held up a trencher of bread and offered it to her.

"Aye, she is," Helen said, reaching in.

Before she could tear off a bit from the loaf, Aleck stretched in front of Helen and snatched the tray from Grant. "When I said it was time to return to your duties, I expected you to be attentive to the ram's horn announcing the evening meal."

Helen drew back her fingers and clutched her fist to her chest. "Forgive me. I had a bit of trouble fitting into my gown. The one I wore for my confinement is now too large and this one…" She gestured downward.

He arched a brow and glanced at her breasts. "I reckon a bit of fat on your bones is not a bad thing."

She pulled her mantle across her open neckline. "I was thinking of asking the tailor to let out one or two gowns to provide a bit more comfort."

His shoulder shrugged. "Do what you must."

When he started to turn toward Mary, Helen grasped his arm. "It would be ever so nice if you would pay a visit to Maggie, m'laird. She changes every day."

Aleck brushed her hand away and gave her a steely glare. "I'll not be visiting the nursery until there's a wee lad occupying it. I need a son to inherit my name, not a daughter. You'd best heal fast, wife, for I've no option but to visit your bed again soon."

She preferred not to have this conversation in the hall, but now that he'd mentioned the bedchamber, Helen would have her say. She leaned closer so only he could hear. "And once you return to my bed will you stop keeping company with the widow?"

"Wheesht and mind your own affairs." He grasped her hand under the table and squeezed. Hard. "I'll not have any lassie yapping in my ear like a bitch. I need your noble arse to bear my son and that's the last I'll hear of it."

Suddenly not hungry, Helen pulled her hand away and rubbed her fingers. How could her brute of a husband treat her with such disdain? And how in God's name was she to endure his boorishness for the rest of her life? Yes, her mother had always repeated the words: *that which cannot be helped must be endured.* But Da had treated Ma with respect, even in the beginning. Though Helen's parents had an arranged marriage, they'd grown to love each other, and in short order, too. Helen glanced at Aleck's bald head. She no longer harbored hope of love ever growing between them—tolerance was the best she could hope for.

*But I must try harder.*

The big oak doors at the far end of the great hall opened with a whoosh. A sentry wearing the king's surcoat emblazoned with an orange lion rampant stepped inside. "I've a missive for Sir Aleck MacIain."

The Chieftain stood and beckoned him. "Are you blind? Bring it here to the *high* table."

Helen huffed. Decorum would never be her husband's strong suit. Who on earth would not be aware the clan's chieftain sat at the high table? And flaunting the fact by being rude only served to promote discourse among those who paid fealty to him.

Aleck drummed his fingers while the man strode through the hall and climbed up to the dais with all eyes upon him. The room hummed as people mumbled, clearly impressed that a king's man had come all the way to Ardnamurchan to deliver a missive to their chieftain. Aleck snatched the velum from the man's fingertips and sliced his eating knife under the seal. Leaning toward the light of the enormous candelabra, Aleck knit his bushy eyebrows as he read.

Helen craned her neck in a futile attempt to see the writing. "What news, m'laird?"

With a frown, he shoved the missive into his doublet and looked to Grant, completely ignoring Helen's question. "The king has requested my presence at Stirling Castle. We must leave on the morrow."

"Stirling?" Helen clapped her hands together. "Oh it would be lovely to purchase some new fabric at the castle fete."

"Aye, but *you* will not be accompanying me."

Helen frowned. It was no use asking if he would bring back a bolt of gold damask. He wouldn't do it. And making such a request would only give him another opportunity to berate her.

Grant stood and bowed. "I'll ready the men." He looked to Aleck. "We'll take the galley to Dunstaffnage and ride from there as usual?"

"Aye."

Helen nearly melted when she heard the henchman say *Dunstaffnage.* She had many fond memories of that castle. It was only a short ride from Dunollie where her sister, Gyllis, lived with her husband, Sean MacDougall. If only she could stow away on Aleck's galley with Maggie. Helen could visit Gyllis and then travel east to Kilchurn Castle and see her mother. How wonderful such a holiday would be. She hadn't seen her kin in years.

Alas, Aleck would be in too much of a hurry to take her and Maggie to Dunollie—only four miles south of Dunstaffnage.

However, in her usual mien, Helen chose to see the positive side of this turn of events. Perhaps this journey would take Aleck away for an entire month. She smiled. Indeed, his absence was something she would welcome.

# Chapter Two

Eoin MacGregor, Chieftain of Clan Gregor, sat at the king's table. The gathering was a clandestine assembly, conducted in the king's antechamber, one doorway from his royal highness's bedchamber. The room was appointed with landscape tapestries woven with iridescent silk threads. The particularly rich greens made the scenes appear almost lifelike. The table itself was a work of art, hewn from walnut with carved lion's heads at each corner.

Eoin was flanked by Duncan Campbell, Lord of Glenorchy, and his brother, Sir Iain Campbell, who had recently been granted the title of Chieftain of Lawers.

Across from them, Eoin's good friends Sir Sean MacDougall and Sir Robert Struan completed this group of nobles who comprised the upper echelon of the king's enforcers. Each one a fierce warrior adept in weaponry, not even the English could stop their armies when united.

Seated at the head of the table was King James IV who, at the age of twenty, still looked like a lad with his brown shoulder-length tresses curling out from under a gold crown. But Eoin knew better than to underestimate his monarch. The king had risen to power five years earlier, having taken part in the rebellion against his father, the very unpopular King James III. Even though youthful, this James exuded authority with iron-clad confidence, and Eoin respected him as Scotland's sovereign.

Lord Duncan flicked a speck of lint from his velvet doublet. With a thick head of black hair combined with a neatly cropped beard, the baron could pass for a pirate on a sunny day. "Word has it the MacDonalds are rebelling to the north."

The king's eyebrows arched and disappeared beneath his gold crown. "'Tis why I summoned you. Now that I've stripped John MacDonald of the Lordship of the Isles, it appears his nephew, Alexander, has taken up his mantle and is raiding the entire west coast."

"Miserable, spineless dog," Sean MacDougall said from across the table. He had good reason for concern. His keep, Dunollie, sat on the western seaboard.

"Aye," the king agreed. "I'll not tolerate insurrection from any one of my subjects."

Duncan eyed each of his men—the inner circle of the Highland Enforcers. Though nobles and clan chieftains, each man was a sizeable warrior, every one willing to lay down his life for the other. "Spies report Alexander has made contact with all MacDonald Clans down the coast. He's planning a rebellion."

Eoin nodded. "Any idea when…or where?"

King James tapped his lips with his pointer finger. "My guess is he'll amass his army first."

Duncan studied the map on the table. It was dotted with red-inked circles and, leaning closer, Eoin realized each marked a MacDonald stronghold. Glenorchy pointed to the Isle of Islay. "They control this entire region. It makes no sense to mount an attack on the crown from the north. I'd wager they'll be building their forces at Dunyveig or Finlaggan."

The king ground his finger onto a cluster of red dots on the Isle of Skye. "Aye, but they also control the northwest. Do not underestimate the MacDonalds. They'll be marshalling their forces in the north as well as the south."

Duncan's lips thinned and he sat back. "The bastards."

"That is why we need the enforcers to lead sorties along the western seaboard." The king snapped his fingers at the sentry guarding the door, who swiftly exited. "I want three separate forces. Duncan, you and MacDougall will combine and train the troops at Dunstaffnage. Iain and Robert will lead my men at Tabert." His Grace looked to Eoin. "I want you to prepare the forces at Mingary in the north."

Eoin glanced from the king to Duncan and gulped. "Mingary, your Grace?"

Duncan spread his big palms to his sides. "'Tis a MacDonald keep."

The king ran his fingers over his smooth chin—yet to grow a full beard. "Aye, but Aleck MacIain MacDonald has stripped away the *MacDonald* name and has sworn fealty to the crown."

"I knew about the name, but can you trust him?" Duncan asked.

"You question me?" The king snorted. "God's teeth, he's your brother-in-law."

Duncan bowed his head. "Forgive me, your Grace."

King James leaned in, gesturing for the men to follow suit. Then he eyed Eoin. "'Tis why I chose Mingary. If you're based at MacIain's keep, the MacDonalds will be none the wiser, and you can watch the chieftain's every move."

"Then why are you not sending the Lord of Glenorchy up there rather than me?" Eoin would much prefer to be stationed at Dunstaffnage. There were a host of reasons why he'd do anything to avoid Mingary, not the least being its vulgar lord and master.

The king rapped his knuckles on the table. "Because I agree with Campbell. The greatest threat comes from the south where the bastards are closer to the throne. Glenorchy needs to be stationed at Dunstaffnage because he has the largest army at his disposal."

The door opened and in walked Aleck MacIain—the very man they had been discussing. He was a thick Highlander with a scraggly black beard. His beady eyes darted around the chamber until they rested on Eoin. Looking away, Eoin's upper lip curled. He didn't know Aleck well, but the few times he'd encountered the man, he hadn't been impressed. He was loud and gluttonous. Worse, he was Helen Campbell's husband. Aside from Aleck MacIain, the last person on earth Eoin wanted to see was Lady Helen.

Aleck bowed to their sovereign. "Your Grace."

"Sir Aleck." Duncan stood and offered his hand. "How is my sister?"

MacIain looked at Duncan's outstretched palm a bit too long before he shook it. "Birthed a bloody lass."

Eoin clenched his fist and ground his knuckles into his palm. *If the bastard utters a single insult about Lady Helen, I'll wring his unshaven neck—providing Duncan doesn't beat me to it.*

"Aye?" Duncan grimaced. "The good news hadn't yet reached me."

Aleck took a seat across from Eoin and shrugged. "Such is the tireless duty of a chieftain. I've not yet set quill to parchment."

"Gentlemen," said the king. "Allow me to apprise Sir Aleck of our plans."

Eoin regarded the black-bearded rogue across the table while the king talked. What Helen saw in the man, he had no idea. Other than being uglier than a hairy arse, she might be attracted to his size—though MacIain had a belly like a pregnant heifer.

Eoin again glanced to Duncan. Helen's marriage had been arranged by her elder brother. Though Eoin had never asked, he'd always wondered if the lass had encouraged it. He swiped a hand across his mouth. It didn't matter now. She'd been married for ages *and* she'd just given birth to a daughter. Eoin doubted Lady Helen would even remember him from their childhood.

When he was a lad, Helen's mother had asked him to stand in as an occasional partner for the lass's dancing lessons. Aye, he'd spent his youth as a squire for the Lord of Glenorchy, Duncan's da. Eoin smirked. Sitting across the table, Sean MacDougall had also attended those lessons. The Chieftain of Dunollie always managed to be partnered with Helen's elder sister, Gyllis, who happened to now be his wife of five years. *Lucky bastard.*

"How fast can you and your men relocate to Mingary?" the king asked.

Eoin looked to his sire and realized the question had been directed toward him. "Ah...If I leave for Glen Strae at first light, we should be in Ardnamurchan before the month's end." He turned to Aleck. "Have you cannons?"

"Bloody oath, I do," the braggart gloated. "Two black shiny barrels arrived from Portugal but two months ago."

"Good. We'll build a platform on your galley and turn it into a warship."

Aleck frowned. "Warship? I wouldn't want one of my cannons to sink—they're worth their weight in silver."

The king rapped the table with his knuckles. "You'd best change your thinking, Sir Aleck. The way to beat the MacDonald upstarts is to ensure we have bigger cannons, faster boats and better trained soldiers. Sir Eoin MacGregor is one of the best fighting men in Scotland.

He'll see your men become trained soldiers and make the best use of your guns."

Aleck glared across the table. Eoin folded his arms and raised his chin—not about to cower at the overblown boar's show of impudence.

The king appeared to ignore the exchange. "I'm famished. Shall we retire to the great hall?" When the monarch stood, all chairs scraped across the floorboards as the men rose and bowed.

After the king took his leave, Eoin adjusted his sword belt and headed for the door. Sir Aleck stepped behind him. "I give my men all the training they need."

Eoin made a show of glancing at the man's belly. "Well then, it should be easy work to quash the MacDonald uprising to the north."

"Aye, and then I will enjoy the spoils." MacIain grinned.

Eoin's jaw twitched. So that was why Aleck had opted to side with the king—not that it wasn't common for a chieftain to shift his loyalties with the promise of riches. It's just that Eoin MacGregor would never turn his back on his clansmen and thank God he was on the right side of this battle.

***

While Aleck was away, Helen found it necessary to jump back into assuming her duties a little faster than she would have liked, though she still spent every spare moment in the nursery with Maggie. Honestly, she welcomed the added work, regardless. Everything was so much more pleasant when Aleck was anywhere other than Mingary Castle.

This morning, she stood in the enormous kitchen with Peter the cook. Since she'd been a lass, the kitchen had always been one of Helen's favorite places in a keep, and Mingary's scullery was every bit as large as Kilchurn's had been. It was always so warm inside, even during the bitterest days of winter. At one end, a fire crackled endlessly in the giant hearth, with all manner of iron pots stewing over the grill at any given time.

Adding to the warmth was the bread oven. It, too, baked loaves upon loaves during the day to feed the many soldiers and their families who resided at the keep. Helen inhaled and filled her senses with the mouth-watering scent of baking bread while she stood at the board, reviewing a ledger of food stores with Peter. "I think we've enough flour to last through the first harvest."

He scratched his chin. Though Peter couldn't read, he was more familiar with the contents of the barrels in the cellar than she. "I think you're right, though it will be close."

"Should I order a barrel just to be certain?"

"I'd reckon so." He nodded. "And while you're at it, we could use two more barrels of oats."

"Very well." She made a note in the margin.

The outer door opened. "I've brought a basket of eggs. My hens have started laying like they've been sprinkled with fairy dust."

Helen turned. Though every muscle in her body tensed, she forced a smile.

Mary's eyes widened, then she quickly looked away. "M'lady. I didn't expect to see *you* in the kitchens."

"Oh?" Helen had no idea why. She had always spent a great deal of time working with Peter, from ensuring the stores were in good order to menu selection. She glanced to the basket. "Thank you for the eggs. It does look like your hens have been busy."

Mary arched an eyebrow and set the basket on the table. Then she regarded Helen with a defensive air. "Do you think Sir Aleck will return soon?"

A dozen retorts sprang to the tip of Helen's tongue. She wanted to shake her finger and accuse the woman of being an adulteress. But that would only serve to deepen the ill feelings between them. She was lady of the keep and she would maintain her poise and authority. In no way would she lower herself and engage in a discussion of Mary's lewd behavior—especially in front of Peter. "I imagine the galleys will return any day now." Helen plucked an egg from the basket. It was still warm.

Mary had the gall to jut out her chin. "Things around the castle are ever so dull when the chieftain's away."

The egg in Helen's palm cracked, sending yellow goo oozing through her fingers. *Has the woman no shame?*

Peter handed Helen a cloth. "Gratitude for the eggs, Mary. We'll see you at the evening meal." He inclined his head toward the door.

She gave Helen another look, her eyes as deceitful as a snake's. Mary drew in a breath as if she had something more to say, but she smirked, then turned with a huff and left.

"That windbag's head will be too fat to fit through the door soon," Peter said.

Helen chuckled and rubbed her hands clean. Gossip of Aleck's indiscretions would have run rampant through the castle like a brushfire. After all, he hadn't even tried to be secretive upon her appearance in the great hall. Even if that was his only slip, one act of carelessness was enough. It was human nature for everyone to love scandalous gossip—*everyone aside from me, that is.*

Hamish, one of the crofters, strode inside and dropped a massive mule deer stag across the table. "I've come to pay me rent, m'lady." He puffed out his chest and gestured toward the dead animal, blood encrusted around its nose. "He's an eight-point beauty."

Helen clapped. "My, that *is* an impressive animal."

Peter grabbed the basket of eggs from the table and clutched them to his chest. "Remove the beast from me board and go hang him in the cellar."

"Thank you, Hamish." Helen smiled. "I'll ensure the ledgers reflect your payment."

Peter put the eggs on the bench against the wall where they'd be less likely to be broken. "Mayhap I should set the boys to turning the spit on the morrow. That stag will keep us fed for days."

Helen watched the crofter disappear through the passageway. "The meat will be better after it cures for a bit and Sir Aleck will appreciate a meal of roasted venison upon his return."

Peter looked at her as if she'd lost her mind. "Aaaaye."

"You disagree?"

He scratched his greying head of hair. "Your affability never ceases to amaze me, m'lady."

Helen knew what he meant. She'd always catered to Aleck's whims and, though he didn't show appreciation for her efforts, he expected her to run the keep and see to his comfort. And she took pride in doing it well. At least that was one thing her husband was unable to take from her. She picked up the ledger. "I'll order the flour and oats and see to it everything else runs smoothly at Mingary." She turned and faced him. "Let no one say I've been remiss in my duties."

"Nary a soul would ever think that, m'lady. You're the one who keeps the castle in order."

She hesitated. It was pleasant to receive a compliment. A small patter of pride swelled in Helen's breast. "Thank you. 'Tis ever so nice so hear you say."

# Chapter Three

Helen sat in the rocking chair in the nursery and watched Maggie wrap her tiny hand around her pointer finger. “I cannot believe she is already five weeks of age.”

Having sent the nursemaid for a moment of respite, Glenda folded linen swaddling clothes near the window embrasure. “And I cannot believe how much she’s grown already, m’lady.”

“’Tis a pity Sir Aleck will not visit the nursery.” Helen sighed. “I do think even he would agree Maggie’s a healthy lass, and she’s so bonny, he’d truly fall in love with her.”

The chambermaid frowned over her shoulder. “He’s missing an opportunity to be a part of the greatest miracle of life, if I may be so bold as to say.”

Helen’s throat closed. But then Maggie cooed and grinned, snatching the lady from her sudden melancholy. “Oh my, look at that. She just made her first smile.”

Glenda hurried across the floor. “Honestly? I must see.”

“Have you another smile for me, lass.” Helen cooed and smacked her lips. “Come now, show us your wee grin.”

Maggie didn’t disappoint and squealed with an even larger smile. Glenda clasped her hands together. “Oh, m'lady. Doubtless, she will turn the heads of every laddie in the Highlands."

Helen cringed. "Let us delight in her infancy for a time. I hope not to see any lusty lads for twenty years or more."

"If I know Sir Aleck." Glenda shook her finger. "He'll marry her off as soon as her menses show."

For a moment, Helen could scarcely draw in a breath. *Not if I have any say in the matter*. She looked into her daughter's innocent eyes. "We shall see. Perhaps my next child will be a lad and Maggie will find favor with Sir Aleck at last."

A cynical sounding snort rumbled from the chambermaid's nose. "Do not count on the chieftain having a change of heart."

"Glenda," Helen chided.

The outspoken servant dipped her head in a bow. "Apologies, m'lady. I've never known anyone as hopeful as you. I'd wager most noblewomen would have given up by now and returned to their kin."

Helen wouldn't admit that she'd considered it. She'd even gone so far as to wonder if her brother, John, now Bishop of the Isles, would help her approach the Pope to enquire about an annulment. But such action would bring disgrace to the Campbells of Glenorchy. She had put the ghastly notion out of her mind and had tried not to think on it again.

The ram's horn sounded with three consecutive blasts. Glenda hastened to the window as voices rose from the courtyard. Helen stood and carried Maggie to the embrasure and squeezed in beside the chambermaid.

Fortunately, the nursery was on the fourth floor—an advantageous position from which to view the wall-walk surrounding the keep. Built of stone, Mingary was a sturdy fortress, sitting proudly atop a rocky promontory.

The castle presided over the region of Ardnamurchan, flanked by steep cliffs on three sides.

Helen peered down into the courtyard and then out over the sea. Her smile faded. Alas, her time of peace had come to an end.

"It looks as if the chieftain has returned," said Glenda. "And there's an additional galley in his wake."

"Look at that." Helen leaned further toward the window. "King's men?"

"You'd ken better than I, m'lady."

Though Helen couldn't make out the design on the pennant flapping in the wind, it was white and blue with no likeness to the king's yellow and orange colors. "Whoever they are, I suspect they'll be hungry." Peeking through the heavy clouds, the sun indicated the hour was late morning. She must make haste.

Glenda reached for Maggie. "I'll stay with the bairn until Sarah returns. Go meet the ships, m'lady."

Helen smiled. "Thank you." She quickly pattered through the stone passageway and down the stairwell. The great hall was empty, all except for Robert, the cruel guard who always seemed to be sharpening his weapons. With a scrape against the whetstone, he looked up and offered a yellow-toothed sneer. "M'lady," he said without the least bit of reverence in his voice.

Helen tried not to shudder, nodded, and hastened straight for the kitchens. Stepping inside the enormous chamber, the smell of onions and turnips filled the air. "Peter! Sir Aleck has returned with an additional galley in his wake and they've arrived just in time for their nooning."

The cook turned, four plucked chickens suspended from his fingers. "I heard the ram's horn."

She hastened across the flagstone floor. "What can we feed them?"

He tossed the fowl on the butchers block and snatched a cleaver. "I'll add these to the pottage I've set over the fire."

Helen regarded the raw meat—hardly enough for an army. But at least the enormous cast iron pot suspended above the hearth was boiling. "We'll need more than a few hens."

Peter attacked the chickens with violent hacks of the blade. "The maids are plucking a half-dozen more. I've bread and oatcakes aplenty, and cheese."

She chewed her bottom lip. "Sir Aleck won't like being met with such simple fare, but it will have to do at short notice." Helen pointed toward the cellar. "Set the lads to turning the venison on the spit."

The cook didn't look up from his work. "There's hardly enough time for that, m'lady."

Helen affected one of her pointed stares. "If they start now, the beast will be roasted through by the evening meal, and your chieftain will be happy."

Peter stopped chopping. "Right. I hadn't thought past the midday meal. I'll fetch the young fellas as soon as I've added these to the pottage."

"Very well." Helen smoothed her hand over her veil to ensure no tresses were loose. Then she pinched her cheeks and straightened her skirts and apron. Her appearance would have to do—not that Aleck ever noticed when she made an effort to look her best.

The incident in the great hall with Mary had her hackles up for the past month. Helen never considered herself unattractive, but it surely seemed as if she'd contracted a case of leprosy where Aleck was concerned. He made no secret of the fact he preferred larger women and Mary certainly fit that bill. The widow had enormous bosoms and a full body to support them. Forever seeing the logical side of things, Helen supposed Aleck's attraction to Mary made sense. After all, he was a large man.

Hastening ahead, she berated herself for always rationalizing everything. Blessed be the saints, Helen was Aleck MacIain's wife, and now that he had returned, she would do everything in her power to win his favor. She would never give up. He would visit her bed, and by God's grace, she would conceive immediately and bear a son. Then everything at Mingary would be pleasant.

Perhaps for the first time since she'd married him, Aleck would shed his gruff demeanor and be agreeable as well. *There's always hope.*

As she made her way to the sea gate, men and women followed, an excited hum rising from the crowd. Aleck's galley had sailed ashore and the guards were heaving her onto the beach. The boat behind was following suit, the crewmen hopping into the shallows, tugging the ship's ropes. None of the visiting Highlanders sported a royal surcoat, but they all wore hauberks and bits of armor. By the swords strapped to their backs, Helen had no doubt they were fighting men.

Wringing her hands, she watched Aleck jump over his galley's bow onto dry land—he'd stood at the stern of the boat while his men heaved it ashore.

With squeals grating in Helen's ears, Mary dashed up to him and threw her arms around his neck. Aleck kissed the widow on the mouth. It wasn't a peck. It was a vulgar clamping of the lips, their bodies crushed together in an obscene embrace.

Mortified, Helen covered her eyes, fearing they'd never pull away.

Her cheeks burned. Her throat ached like someone had taken a rasp to it. *There go my hopes of winning his favor. I wish I never had to speak to him again.*

Aleck slung his arm around Mary's waist and led her forward—straight toward Helen. She blinked. If only she could dash around the corner of the keep and hide. Helen glanced over her shoulder and considered a swift getaway. Blast, she would look the fool if she ran. Standing tall, she faced Aleck, unable to affect her usual serene smile.

But her husband grinned broadly. "You've forty hungry men to feed, wife," he bellowed. "You'd best go see to the preparations."

Mary leaned into him, grinning as if she were drunk. Helen had heard about whores in alehouses—Mary would blend right in to such a disreputable establishment.

Swallowing her urge to issue a dour retort, Helen refused to allow Aleck's behavior to degrade her in front of the clansmen. She regarded her husband with feigned indifference. "Who are your guests, m'laird?"

"The Chieftain of Clan Gregor and his band of upstarts. They'll be with us for a time." Aleck threw his thumb over his shoulder with a smirk. "King's business."

"The MacGregors? They are close allies with the Campbells of Glenorchy. It will be a pleasure to see to their comfort." Helen bowed her head. "Peter's making preparations for your nooning. I'll greet our guests and then oversee the kitchens."

Aleck didn't appear to have heard a word she'd said. He proceeded into the courtyard with that disgraceful widow still on his arm.

Helen cleared her throat and looked to the shore. She would act the proper lady. Never in her life would she demean herself by showing her revulsion at Aleck's behavior or letting on that it bothered her. Many great men took lemans. She would find a way to accept it.

With her resolution, she clasped her hands and focused on a sturdy man approaching from the stony shore. Water dripped from the quilted arming doublet beneath his hauberk and streamed down his well-muscled calves.

Recognition sparked deep in her stomach. Then her heart nearly thumped out of her chest.

To stifle her gasp, Helen clapped a hand over her mouth. When Aleck had referred to the Chieftain of Clan Gregor, she fully expected to see Sir Ewen MacGregor, but it wasn't the old grey-haired man who approached. The tall, rugged warrior was Sir Eoin—Ewen's son.

She took in yet another sharp inhale.

The tallest man in his retinue, Eoin hadn't changed in the past five years. If anything, his shoulders had grown broader. Flanked by his men, his muscular legs flexed with each step.

But to gaze upon a dear old friend was almost like traveling back in time—before she'd ever seen Mingary Castle or knew that Aleck MacIain existed.

Eoin wore his chestnut hair cropped short, a new and attractive fashion for him. His bold eyebrows hadn't changed. They formed two separate but angular lines over vivid sky-blue eyes. A straight nose, full lips—but the bottom lip was fuller. He even still had the wee scar on his chin.

A hundred childhood memories came flooding back when he grinned. Oh, how she'd enjoyed Eoin when they were children. *What a carefree time of life that had been.*

"M'lady." He stepped up and grasped her hand.

She hadn't remembered that he was so imposing or that he smelled like a vat of simmering cloves. "Sir Eoin." She maintained a properly serene smile. "What a pleasure to see you."

He bowed and pressed his lips to the back of her hand, then straightened and offered a controlled grin with a brotherly glint in his eye. "The pleasure is mine."

She clapped her fingers to her chest to quell her hammering heart. "When Sir Aleck mentioned the Chieftain of Clan Gregor was here, I expected to see your father." Goodness, it had been a long time since she'd seen anyone from her past.

He knit his brows. "Da's been gone three years now. I'm surprised word hasn't reached you."

Helen rubbed the back of her hand, wiping away the tingling sensation that remained from Eoin's brief peck. "Forgive me. Tucked away on this peninsula, I rarely ever receive news."

Eoin proceeded forward. "Not to worry, m'lady."

Helen followed, moving her feet quickly to keep up with his broad stride. "Aleck mentioned you would be staying for a time."

He glanced sideways at her, a dark eyebrow arching. "Aye, to keep an eye on the MacDonald uprising to the north."

"Oh no, how grave." She hadn't heard about the uprising either. "I hope 'tis nothing too serious."

"Me as well, m'lady, I'd hate to pose a burden to you and Sir Aleck and be forced to remain past my welcome."

"You could never be a burden." She raised her voice to be heard as they passed the blacksmith's shack. "It will be a pleasant change to have the MacGregors at Mingary. Besides, you must fill me in on all that's happened in the past five years."

His gaze trailed up the stone walls to the wall-walk—as if he had a great many things on his mind. "I'm afraid there's not much to tell."

She chuckled. "I doubt that."

Stopping beside the entrance to the kitchens, Helen beckoned a guard. "Mr. Keith, please show Sir Eoin to the guest chamber." She turned to the MacGregor Chieftain. "Your men are welcome to the hay loft. Nearly all the winter stores are gone. There's plenty of space for them to bed down."

"My thanks." He gave her a wink. "You needn't worry about us. My men can bed down anywhere they find a bit of straw."

"Very well, it has been a delight to see you again." She pointed to the kitchen door. "I'd best see to the midday meal. Your arrival was a surprise to the cook."

He bowed. "I do appreciate your gracious hospitality."

She stopped, not wanting to draw away so soon. "I shall see you in the great hall, then?"

"Aye, m'lady. My men and I will stow our gear and will be there anon."

Helen offered a smile and hastened toward the kitchen. What else had changed in the past five years? If Aleck had received word of the former MacGregor Chieftain's death, he certainly hadn't shared it with her. Had he sent condolences? What other news had her husband not shared? Scotland could have declared war and she would be none the wiser.

She pushed inside and suddenly felt lightheaded. Goodness, she'd nearly swooned when she watched the MacGregor Chieftain's bold stride as he made his way from the beach. Such an errant lack of propriety—even if only on the inside—mustn't ever happen again.

Patting her cheeks, she started for the hearth. As lady of the keep, Helen would be busy indeed, overseeing the meals and ensuring their guests were welcome. That, combined with caring for Maggie, would keep her occupied for certain.

***

After he watched Lady Helen disappear into the keep, Eoin dropped his things in the guest chamber, then headed to the stables to join his men. Satan's bones, he shouldn't have kissed her hand. He'd been in relative control of his faculties until then. Damnation, Helen hadn't lost an iota of her radiance. In fact, she was more beautiful than he'd remembered. With her hair hidden under a blue veil, she'd appeared matronly—but by no means plain. Her face was as pure as a painter's canvas—her expressive eyes the color of bluebells, her cheeks aglow like they'd been blessed by pink roses. As soon as he'd taken her palm in his, the silken softness of her skin ignited a flame deep in his belly. And when he bent to kiss it, he imagined himself in a garden filled with lilies.

He inhaled deeply.

*Lilies.*

Eoin couldn't remember the last time a woman's scent had practically brought him to his knees. And his lips still thrummed with a rhythmic pulse.

*Damnation.*

He swiped his arm across his mouth. Dragon's breath, he would not allow old emotions to boil to the surface. He was in Ardnamurchan for one purpose and that was to quash the MacDonald uprising. In no way would he lose sight of his mission. Eoin was one of the best fighting men in Scotland and Clan Gregor was renowned for their unsurpassed tactics. He and his men had kept the English out of Scotland when the truce with James III fell apart. And by God they would now ensure the MacDonalds crawled back to their stony keeps and kept their greedy fingers out of the king's coffers.

But this assignment to Mingary had to be the most miserable post of his life. Aside from being in the secluded region of Ardnamurchan, he rued being forced to be the guest of Aleck MacIain. The man hadn't impressed him in Stirling and traveling with the bastard for the past two weeks hadn't improved Eoin's opinion.

*And why the hell wasn't Sir Aleck standing beside Helen when I approached?*

That the man lacked manners was an understatement—and definitely none of Eoin's concern. He was there to focus on training and fighting, and that's exactly what he'd do. They'd be patrolling the northern waters as well. In fact, Eoin planned to spend more time sailing his galley than in the miserable guest chamber.

After climbing up the ladder to the stable loft, his feet crunched atop the straw strewn over the timber boards. The smell of musty hay filled his nostrils as he regarded his men. "Do not grow too comfortable. We'll be sailing north a few days hence."

Fergus, Eoin's second in command, stepped beside him. "Running sorties, will we?"

"Aye. We'll make a point of sailing past MacDonald lands flying the king's pennant. Let them know we've come to stay for a bit."

"And how long do you think that might be?"

"Who knows?" Eoin looped his thumbs into his belt. "With luck, the MacDonalds will realize they should be happy King James didn't rob them of *all* their lands."

Fergus smirked. "'Twill be a cold day in hell when that happens."

Eoin shrugged. "One day the MacDonalds will give up their feud and realize they cannot win a war against Scotland."

"Only after half of them are dead," said Willy, a skilled man with a mace and targe.

"Bloody oath," Fergus cursed. "They'd best not be taking us to Hades with them."

"Wheesht. 'Tis why we're the best fighting men in Scotland. We'll not be escorting the MacDonalds to hell. They can find the way on their own." Eoin drew his dirk and held it high. "But we'll be glad to show them the path."

"Och aye," the men bellowed, pumping their fists in the air.

"Let us see to our nooning, then we'll meet the bedraggled MacIain guard in the courtyard and determine if they ken how to handle their weapons."

# Chapter Four

With his arms crossed, Eoin stood beside the MacIain Chieftain in the courtyard, surrounded by thirty-foot curtain walls. During the midday meal, he'd opted to stop by the kitchens for a bit of bread and a hunk of cheese. He couldn't bring himself to step into the great hall and watch Aleck MacIain preside over the throng. Nor did he care to put himself in the middle of banter between young bucks flexing their muscles.

He turned his attention to the sparring warriors. As he'd thought, the MacIain men lacked in skill, though most were solid lads. If Eoin had a year, he just might be able to turn them into soldiers.

"Every one of my men is near fourteen stone," Aleck gloated.

Eoin kept his sights on the nearest pair, fighting with swords. "Aye, you've amassed yourself a great deal of meat."

The overstuffed chieftain puffed out his chest. "Brawn, mind you."

"Brawn?" Eoin raised his eyebrows and then cast his gaze to the clouds. "I'll give you that, they might even be good at slaying dragons."

"Watch yourself," MacIain growled.

Eoin inclined his chin toward the man sparring with Fergus. "Your man there is sizeable, but he wields his sword like he's chopping wood."

"Pardon me? Grant is my best warrior. He'd beat your man in a fight any day, hands down."

*He wouldn't.*

Eoin had a mind to place a wager on Aleck's claim. But he wasn't there to prove his men superior—the MacGregors already had distinguished themselves to king and country a hundred times over. The king asked Eoin to train and fight alongside the MacIains because of their reputation. He opted for middle ground. "Grant shows promise, but in general, your men lack discipline."

Aleck faced him. An edgy challenge reflected in his in his steely black eyes. Eoin didn't budge, in no way intimidated by a glare from an arrogant chieftain. "My men are the best in Ardnamurchan."

Eoin smirked. "I'd hope so."

Aleck circled his palm around the pommel of his dirk. "You're a smug bastard."

"I disagree." Eoin watched Aleck's hand with his side vision. If the cur drew his damned dirk, he'd be on his back before he could blink. "I'm simply better at fighting. So are my men." *Ballocks to the middle ground.*

MacIain turned beet red, his eyes bulging. "I've had enough of your gloating claim to greatness. You and the Campbells are tarred with the same brush. You all think you're superior to the rest of the fighting men Scotland."

An acerbic chuckle escaped Eoin's lips. He'd endured a fortnight of listening to MacIain's boasts and his ears could take no more. "Nay, we do not think it, we know it." Anticipating Aleck's swing, Eoin ducked and stepped forward while the big man stumbled with his dirk drawn. "I've not a mind to fight you this day. Let us agree to a wee demonstration."

"What do you have in mind?" MacIain growled, shoving his dirk back in its scabbard.

*Wise gesture.* Eoin's fingers itched to grab MacIain by the neck and smack his skull into the stone wall behind them. But he splayed his fingers instead. Perhaps he should have put up more of a fight when the king asked him to come to Mingary. Duncan and the others got the better end of the deal for certain.

"Fergus," Eoin beckoned his henchman. "Show Sir Grant how to take down a larger opponent."

Fergus grinned. "I thought we were supposed to go easy the first day."

"No one needs to go easy with my men," Aleck bellowed.

Eoin waived Fergus on, then leaned into Aleck. "Watch. This will not take long."

"Wheesht. I said to hold your tongue." The MacIain Chieftain practically had steam coming out his ears.

Eoin clapped a hand over his mouth and pulled his smile into a frown. It was easy piquing MacIain's ire and Eoin enjoyed this little rattling too much. They were supposed to be allies. *Once he realizes we can help him, the rivalry will settle.*

Fergus crouched, sword in one hand, targe in the other. "Come at me just like you've been doing."

Grant looked pretty good—better than the rest of the MacIain men around them. That's why Eoin knew this demonstration would prove his point.

Grant lunged in, wielding his great sword with both hands in a sideways hack. Sidestepping, Fergus defended with his targe, sending Grant tottering forward. Spinning around, the MacIain man regained his composure. Grant lunged again, this time with more force—but he missed Fergus by a wider margin than his first try. With a roar, Grant swung his sword over his head. It came down with a crashing blow that surely could have cracked Fergus's head, but the shorter man not only dodged the blade, his sword darted up and stopped short under Grant's chin, drawing a wee stream of blood.

Grant froze, his stunned gaze shooting to Aleck.

"That's enough," Eoin said.

Aleck stepped forward. "Your man was lucky."

"No." Eoin pointed. "Fergus used patience and watched Grant's hips. In an untrained man, the hips give away the angle of the attack every time."

"Hips?" Aleck batted his hand through the air. "Next you'll be fetching the piper and teaching my men a jig."

Eoin grinned. "Actually, that's not a bad idea. Dancing is exactly what fighting men need to maintain their balance and speed."

MacIain snorted like a hog. "And you're full of fairy shite."

"Well, you're either blind or the hair growing up your arse has addled your brain. I've had enough talk." Eoin moved into the center of the courtyard, more to step away from MacIain and his wafting stench than anything. "Gather round, men. Fergus and Grant—we need a demonstration on watching your opponent's hip movement."

The MacIain clansmen chuckled ruefully. However, by the end of Eoin's session they were all believers. All but one.

***

After the day's events, Eoin was a bit surprised when Aleck invited him to sit at the high table for the evening meal. Of course had he not been invited, MacIain would have acted against every code of decency in Christendom. Nonetheless, Eoin hadn't expected even one shred of decorum, given the pummeling the Ardnamurchan men took in the courtyard.

He was further taken aback when directed to sit at Lady Helen's left, but then, having her placed between Eoin and Aleck was good insurance against a brawl. Eoin was fairly certain he wouldn't allow MacIain to work him into a rage, but one never knew—especially if whisky was involved.

Wearing a scarlet gown of velvet, Lady Helen suited her role as lady ideally. The gown's feminine lace collar accentuated her neck, especially with her honeyed tresses drawn up under a conical hennin, with only a few wispy curls showing at her nape. She would have blended in well at the king's table and presently seemed out of place, considering her uncouth company.

Eoin smoothed his hands down the front of his doeskin doublet. He'd not thought to bring courtly attire on this journey, though he always carried this piece of finery in his traveling kit. One thing Helen's mother had taught him during his fostering at Kilchurn Castle, was the adage, *clothes maketh the man*, which was the only reason he carried the damned thing. Aside from its excellent craftsmanship, it was useless as an arming doublet and provided little warmth. He leaned back in his seat and regarded the Chieftain of Ardnamurchan. The lord of the keep looked slothful, wearing only a linen shirt over a pair of leather breeks. Worse, the shirt was unlaced at the collar—very slovenly indeed. Eoin puzzled. *Wouldn't Lady Helen have set him to rights above stairs, if not his valet?*

Aleck reached for a ewer of ale and poured for himself without a passing glance to his wife.

Lady Helen watched him with an unruffled expression.

*Something is amiss.*

Eoin swallowed his mouthful and leaned far enough forward to see that her tankard was empty. "Please excuse me." Eoin reached across for the ewer and held it up. "M'lady?"

Her eyes brightened with her smile. "Yes, that would be lovely, thank you."

"My pleasure." Eoin poured. "I understand you have a daughter."

"Aye, she's but six sennights old."

"She is a wee one indeed." His gaze slid down to her slender waist. "You are fit. No one would have any idea you'd recently birthed a bairn."

"How nice of you to say." Helen chuckled softly. "I named her Margaret for Mother and Alice for my younger sister."

"I am impressed. If the wee one grows up to be anything like Lady Margaret, she will be a woman to be reckoned with."

"I hope so." Helen daintily used her teeth to clip a bite of roast venison from her eating knife. "I call her Maggie. Margaret seems ever so serious for a bairn."

"Maggie? I like it." Eoin raised his tankard. "To Sir Aleck and Lady Helen for the birth of a healthy lass. May she grow up to be as bonny as her mother."

Aleck slowly picked up his tankard, a sneer stretching one corner of his mouth. "The bairn should have been a lad."

Eoin shrugged. "Aye, but the world needs lassies as well as lads—and she's only your first."

"It took five miserable years for Maggie to come about." Aleck slammed his tankard onto the table and glared at Helen.

Folding her hands in her lap, she fixated on her trencher, her face nearly as red as her gown. Eoin averted his gaze and shoveled a bite of food in his mouth. He had no business worrying about Lady Helen's domestic issues. MacIain was irritated that she'd birthed a lass? The bastard had best get his arse above stairs and start working on the next bairn, which Eoin prayed would be a lad—not for Sir Aleck, but for Lady Helen's sake.

Eoin tore off a bit of bread and slathered it with butter while watching Helen out of the corner of his eye. She'd always been mindful of her manners, but her motions seemed exact, as if she were making a conscious attempt to be perfect. Her back was erect, her chin level—she was the picture of a well-bred woman. The only problem was she appeared too stiff. Was she trying to hide something? Come to think of it, since Eoin had taken his seat, Sir Aleck had hardly given his wife a nod.

"The venison is delicious." Eoin tested the waters. "I commend your excellent skill with the menu, considering you had little notice of such an immense gathering of guests."

Helen beamed with a radiant smile.

"Cook has it well in hand," Aleck said, his mouth so full, he spat food across the table. "Lady Helen had little to do with it."

The lady's lips disappeared into a thin line and that rigid spine somehow inched a bit straighter. Eoin couldn't help but lean toward her ear and whisper, "My guess is your husband's quite mistaken."

She dabbed the corner of her mouth with a delicate finger. "Actually," she said loud enough for Aleck to hear. "Had I not stopped by the kitchen on my way out to welcome you, we might be dining on bread and cheese this eve."

Aleck reached for the ewer, then slammed it down with overzealous force. "Bring me some whisky!"

Helen jolted and clapped a hand to her chest.

*Married five years and her husband's raucous behavior still makes her jump? Dear Helen, what mess have you made of your life?*

Eoin raked his fingers through his hair and looked away. How many times must he remind himself Lady Helen's plight was not his worry? She hadn't asked him for help. In fact, aside from Sir Aleck's ribbing, she appeared to be healthy—coping quite well.

After a servant brought a flagon of whisky, Aleck poured for himself then shoved it past Helen where it nearly toppled over in front of Eoin. "Join me in a tot?"

"My…ah…thanks." Eoin would have preferred to tell the lout he was about as chivalrous as a moray eel.

Aleck took a swig. "Play us a tune, wife."

Helen regarded him. "I don't think our guests—"

"Bloody hell, woman. I want to hear some music—playing the lute is about all you're useful for around my keep." He flicked his wrist. "Go on."

Eoin had heard enough. He pushed back his chair and stood.

Helen did as well, but grasped his arm. "Leave it be," she said in a low tone.

Eoin glared at Aleck—the bastard had remained seated when his wife stood. "Did you not see the lady rise?"

The chieftain looked up with an irritated glare. "Pardon me?"

"Your wife." Controlling his rage, Eoin opted for restraint rather than inviting the ruffian out to the courtyard. "Aside from being the lady of the keep and a wife of one of Scotland's noble chieftains, she's the daughter of a baron. Do you not show her a knight's courtesy when she stands?"

MacIain's eyes grew wide while he gaped at Eoin, but his surprise was soon replaced by a black-hearted scowl. "She would have earned her respect had she birthed a lad." He gestured to the empty seat. "I suggest you mind your own affairs whilst you're a guest in *my* castle."

Eoin paused for a moment. If only MacIain would lose his temper and blurt out a threat. He'd welcome any excuse to take the bastard to the courtyard and teach him a lesson in chivalry. But aside from a smoldering fire in his eyes, the chieftain managed to control his ire. Eoin bowed to Lady Helen, took his seat, and turned his attention to her performance.

As he'd remembered from his years at Kilchurn Castle, Helen had a magical talent with the lute.

She sat on a stool and tuned her instrument. While Eoin watched, he tried to recall her age. If he remembered correctly, she was seven years his younger. That would make her five and twenty—still young and certainly able to produce an heir for MacIain several times over.

Taking in a deep breath, Helen began to strum a familiar tune, a ballad he could accompany her with on the pipes. The music floated on the air as if carried on butterfly wings. Aye, her proficiency rivaled the king's minstrels. And when she opened her mouth, her voice was soft, though clear as a lark. But it held a sultry sadness Eoin hadn't remembered.

A buxom woman climbed the dais stairs, clutching a flagon. She had a handsome face and ample hips made for child-bearing. She grinned at Aleck. Eoin had seen that look on a woman's face many times before. There was no mistaking what she had on her mind as she sauntered around the table. Aleck slapped her bottom, then held his hand there.

Eoin looked to Helen. Her tone had grown softer. The lady shifted upon her stool and projected her song out to the hall. The crowd listened appreciatively, but all eyes were on the chieftain. With Helen's back now turned, MacIain pulled the woman onto his lap.

Eoin stared, mouth agape while Aleck devoured the wench with a lascivious kiss that made no bones about his intentions.

Lady Helen's voice trembled as if she had eyes in the back of her head.

"I'll see you anon." Aleck lifted the woman from his lap and gave her a hearty smack on the behind. She giggled and flashed a cheeky smile as she scurried away.

Any misgivings Eoin had about Helen's happiness were now amplified ten times over. Aleck MacIain had not only taken a leman, he was openly demonstrative about it. No wonder Helen's voice sounded woeful.

The lady finished the tune with a strum that made chills run up Eoin's spine. She smiled and bowed her head to Aleck and then to Eoin. "If you gentlemen will excuse me, I must bid goodnight to Miss Maggie."

Her husband dismissed her with another flick of his wrist.

Eoin stood and hastened after her. "Lady Helen."

She stopped before descending the dais steps, staring at the floor.

"Thank you." Eoin reached for her elbow, but snatched his hand away before he touched her. Such a gesture might be seen as unseemly. "I enjoyed listening to your performance. It brought back fond memories." He gulped. Satan's bones, he sounded like a milksop. If only he could speak to her without an audience and enquire as to her happiness.

She emitted a chuckle that had an edge to it. "Memories of a fairytale life from long ago." She dipped her head. "Please excuse me."

He bowed. "M'lady."

Eoin glanced to the table. MacIain had turned his attention to the man sitting to his right—completely unperturbed that Eoin had ventured to speak to his wife.

*I've had enough.* He bowed because that was what was expected of any knight when taking his leave. "If you would pardon me, I've things to attend."

He didn't wait to see if Aleck acknowledged him or not. After watching this eve's twisted state of affairs unfold, Eoin needed air. God, how he wanted to climb into his galley and sail back to Argyllshire. Eoin had never hoped for a battle before, but he wished the MacDonalds were planning something rash so he could chase them up and down the western coast of Scotland—anything to take him away from Mingary Castle and its quagmire of shite.

***

Helen hastened to the nursery while she bit back her urge to cry. Her mortification had been exacerbated by Eoin's presence in the great hall. It was bad enough for Aleck to be openly brazen when amongst their clansmen and women, but her husband's actions this night were deplorable. She pushed through the nursery door.

Sarah looked up and smiled.

Taking a deep breath, Helen quickly regained her composure. "Good eve. How is my darling?"

The nursemaid gathered Maggie in her arms. Helen still hadn't grown accustomed to seeing her bairn cared for by another, but Sarah was the ideal nursemaid. She never left Maggie unattended or wanting for anything. "I was just about to put her down for the night, m'lady." She held the bairn out.

Helen gathered the wee bundle in her arms. "Have you eaten, Miss Sarah?"

"Not yet."

"Go on now, I'll care for Maggie."

She curtseyed. "Thank you, m'lady."

After the door closed, Helen carried the bairn to the rocker. "Have you been giving Miss Sarah any difficulty?"

Maggie gave a gummy grin.

"I'm sure you have. 'Tis your duty to make a fuss."

The wee lass squealed.

"That's exactly what I say. Do you remember when I told you an old friend had come to Mingary?" Helen arched her brow expectantly. Thank heavens Maggie hadn't a clue what she was saying. "Sir Eoin, to my surprise, hasn't lost his manners. If anything he's become more chivalrous." She turned her head away. "And decidedly more handsome than I'd remembered."

Helen rocked the babe for a while and hummed, losing herself in her thoughts. Maggie's eyelids grew heavy, yet Helen continued to rock rather than place the bairn in her cradle.

"I loathe being embarrassed in front of the clan—and now outsiders. If only I could stay in the nursery with you. Nothing in the world seems to matter when one is inside a nursery." Helen chuckled. "Can I stay in here at least until Sir Eoin and his men take their leave?" She glanced down at Maggie's face. Her eyes were closed now, her wee mouth slightly open. In slumber she looked like an angel from heaven.

Helen touched her lips to her daughter's forehead. "I shall never approve of an arranged marriage for you, lass. I swear it on my father's grave. You shall have your choice of any knight in the realm."

Helen rocked and rocked, humming whilst she allowed the quiet solitude to revive her soul. Perhaps she could spend more time with Maggie—or feign an illness so she wouldn't have to see Sir Eoin again. How poorly he must have apprised her after Aleck slobbered that kiss all over Mary.

An anchor sank to the pit of Helen's stomach. She couldn't remember Aleck ever kissing *her* like that. Worse, she definitely could not imagine him ever doing so. In the past, her husband's kisses had been brusque pecks. He'd never been overly affectionate. In fact, his ever increasing disdain for Helen oft had her doubting he harbored any affection for her at all. Aye, she'd tried to act the ideal wife, always seeing that things ran smoothly in the keep—always trying to make Aleck happy. If only he would show appreciation for her efforts.

Helen closed her eyes to rest them for a bit. And as the hour grew later, her eyelids became ever so heavy. She leaned her head back and allowed sleep to take her mind away.

She woke with a start when Sarah tapped her shoulder. "M'lady?"

Helen rubbed a hand over here face. "Sarah? You've returned already?"

"I was afraid you'd be cross with me for staying away too long."

"Not at all." Helen stood and gently rested Maggie in her cradle. "Is the hour late?"

"Aye. Everyone has gone to bed. The lamps and candles in the hall have been snuffed."

"Oh my, you were away for a time."

"Forgive me." Sarah blushed.

Helen figured there might be a lad who'd caught her eye. After all, nursemaids were allowed a bit of fun from time to time. She patted Sarah's shoulder. "Not to worry. Maggie and I were fine. But I'd best find my bed. I fear tomorrow will be busy with a stable loft full of warriors."

"Och, aye." Sarah grinned. "Will they be here for long?"

"I sincerely hope not." Helen gave her a wink. "But their chieftain is a childhood friend of mine, if you'd like me to put in a good word on your behalf."

Sarah's cheeks grew redder. "I'm sure that will not be necessary, m'lady."

"You could do far worse than a MacGregor lad."

"Aye?" Sarah curtseyed. "Thank you, m'lady."

Helen collected a candle and opened the door. "I shall see you on the morrow."

Making her way through the dimly lit stone passage, she sighed. If only things had been different for her. True, her brother had made a good alliance with her betrothal, but Helen hadn't seen Duncan in years.

Once inside her chamber, she set the candle on the bedside table. Unlacing her gown took effort, but she didn't want to wake Glenda. When she finally shook out her linen shift and climbed into bed, noise from the adjoining chamber startled her.

"Your bosoms make my cock harder than forged iron," Aleck's voice rumbled through the walls, followed by a woman's chuckle.

"I want you to suckle me." No question, it was Mary's voice.

Aleck's growl rattled the wall.

Helen tensed and clamped her fingers around the linens.

The bed on the other side of the wall creaked. Louder and louder the disgusting noises of passion grew. Mary moaned and begged for more, her mewls growing faster.

Helen clapped her hands over her ears, but the bed thudding into the wall was too loud. On and on the bed creaked. Aleck bellowed a gut-wrenching roar. Every muscle in Helen's body tensed. She sat upright for a moment, ready to flee. But just when Helen thought it would never end, all went quiet.

She moved her trembling hands over her face and coughed out a sob. *God in heaven, I can take this no longer.*

# Chapter Five

By the next morning, Helen had made up her mind. She would confront Aleck and let her feelings be known. After dressing and breaking her fast, she gathered her wits and proceeded to the second floor solar. Along the way, she reminded herself of the important points—things that had kept her awake all night. Her first concern, of course, was Maggie. Helen would protect her daughter no matter what, but she would also speak her peace. She'd done nothing but serve and bow to her husband for the past five years. He owed her a modicum of respect.

It was time she made some demands of her own. But still, as she proceeded down the winding tower stairs, unease gripped her insides.

The bottom further dropped from her stomach when she arrived at her husband's solar door. Summoning her fortitude, she knocked softly. When there was no answer, Helen stood a bit taller and gave two firm raps.

"Come." The foreboding timber of Aleck's voice was enough to make most lassies tremble.

Though Helen wanted to crack open the door and peer in like a mouse, she stepped inside and closed it with a deep, empowering inhale. "We must talk."

Aleck looked up from the ledger. His black eyes narrowed with his disapproving frown. "Well? Out with it. I've things to attend," he said, drumming his fingers to further make his impatience clear.

She clasped her palms together and stepped forward. There was no use trying to soothe him with flowery language. That had never worked in the past. "I request that you send Maggie and me to Iona."

Aleck glared, the color of his face flushed like he'd held a fire to it. "Pardon?"

She'd seen that heated stare before and this time she would not allow him to intimidate her. "As you are aware, my brother, John, is Bishop of the Isles and resides at the abbey. He could help us secure a place in the nunnery. I would retire into the service of our Lord and raise our daughter with sound Christian values."

"A nunnery? Have you lost your mind?" Aleck leaned forward in his seat, his scowl taking on a deadly glint. "No, wife. You'll not be going anywhere, especially with *my* daughter."

Beneath her heavy skirts, Helen clenched her bottom muscles and stared him in the eye. "Why ever not? You openly disdain me and you haven't seen Maggie since the day she was born."

"How dare you question me? What are you thinking with that feeble, female mind of yours? A nunnery?" Aleck braced his palms on the table and stood, leveraging his size for further intimidation. "You and the bairn are *mine*. *My property*. I'll *never* allow either of you to leave Mingary."

Her mind raced. She'd expected his refusal—had rehearsed her argument. "We could keep it quiet." She spread her hands to her sides and took a bold step forward. "I simply ask to reside in a nunnery where I will no longer cause you consternation—or give you excuses to taunt me."

He growled, but Helen continued before he had a chance to spew another rebuttal. "I'd hoped you might see reason after bashing the bed against the wall with Mary half the night. I-I understood when you took a leman upon my confinement. But if you persist—"

"So now you're threatening *me*?" He scoffed and sauntered toward her. "My God, you are a foolhardy woman."

This time, his insult made the hackles at the back of her neck stand on end. "Why is it that every time I confront you, you manage to completely avoid the issue and try to make me out the bumbling idiot?"

"Because—"

"No." Clenching her fists, Helen took another step toward him. They were finally behind closed doors and she would confront him. "I shall tell you why. Because you have *never* cared for me. You haven't given me an iota of respect since the day I came to Mingary. Last eve you couldn't even pay me a compliment for ensuring the meal was prepared and plentiful for forty unexpected men."

"You overstep your bounds." His gravelly voice deepened.

She allowed his threatening tenor to embolden her. "Do I? Am I never allowed my say?"

Aleck's eyes growing darker, he sauntered forward like a man bent on violence. Her husband had never struck her before—would he now?

Though Helen trembled from head to toe, she refused to flee. "I've kept this keep in good order for five years and I've never once heard a word of thanks from you. And yet you have the audacity to call me foolhardy." Her chin ticked up. "I daresay, I'm not the foolish party in this room."

"Watch yourself—you will push me too far." He stepped within a hand's breadth, towering over her small frame.

Her heart hammered so hard her temples throbbed. "There you go, using your size to threaten me. Isn't that always the way?" Helen met his gaze. "You will not coerce me into submission this day. You claim you want a son? I have healed from birthing Maggie and am again ready to conceive." The thought of lying with the brute turned her stomach sour.

His hand darted out and clamped on to her shoulder and he regarded her with a menacing glare. "Would you like me to bend you over the table now?"

"Och, aye?" she taunted with a sneer of her own, calling his bluff. "You choose to treat your wife like a whore?" Helen twisted from under his grasp and skittered backward. "You find Mary so much more attractive than I? What is it you prefer about that woman? Her *enormous* breasts? Her *gargantuan* backside?"

Aleck's eyes narrowed. "Curb your vulgar tongue, woman!" Faster than the strike of an asp, he slapped her face.

Reeling back, Helen drew her fingers over the stinging cheek, blinking in rapid succession to clear her vision. "How dare you raise your hand against me?" Gracious, he'd hit her so hard, her teeth wouldn't meet as if he'd knocked her jaw out of alignment.

He closed the gap. Helen turned to flee, but his arm clamped around her midsection. He tugged up her skirts. "I'll show you who is lord and master in this castle."

Shrieking, Helen twisted and fought to flee, but he held her in a viselike grip. The arm around her waist clenched so taut, she could scarcely draw a breath. With a gasp she threw all her weight against him. "You think I am daft?" she screamed.

He grunted against her writhing attempts to burst free. But that did nothing to allay his powerful grip around her waist while he savagely tugged up her skirts.

Regardless of his oafish brutality, her tongue would not be quelled. Helen would speak her mind and damn the consequences. She twisted enough to manage a deep breath. "You would prefer to be whoring with a vindictive, immoral wench?"

Alex dropped her skirt. Fastening his fingers around her jaw, he twisted her head to face him. He pressed his lips to her ear. "Mary was my leman long before you arrived at Mingary." His tone took on a deadly growl. "You have no right to speak ill of her. The widow went through hell after she lost her husband."

Hit with the ominous shock of the depth of her plight, Helen stopped struggling. Her head swooned. "You have been intimate with that woman throughout the duration of our marriage?"

He released his arm and spun her around, sinking his fingers in to her shoulders. "That is none of your concern."

By his deadpan glare, Helen knew he had never been faithful to their marriage bed. He sickened her. Though her face throbbed from his slap and his unyielding fingers dug into her flesh, she could not refrain from her tirade. "Even though I am able to conceive again, you've chosen to consort with that whore rather than your wife." She stamped her foot. "Worse, you openly show your lust for that woman. Do you know how much your actions humiliate me? And yet you refuse my request to retire to a nunnery?"

His grip clamped tighter. "Must I repeat?" He shook her until her teeth rattled. "You are *mine*. I will use you as I please and you *will* be staying at Mingary."

*I hate him.*

Helen closed her eyes and forced her mind to go to a place of serenity. "The position you have placed me in has become untenable," she uttered in a low voice. "If you cannot at least make your advances toward your *leman* subtle, I'll have no recourse but to take Maggie and head to the sanctuary of Iona."

She didn't even see the next slap coming, it was delivered with such vehement force. Her face instantly hot, pain seared across her face and Helen blinked in rapid succession as tears stung her eyes.

"You will not threaten me. I've an alliance to make with the lass," he growled, giving her another teeth rattling shake. "If you attempt to take my daughter from Mingary, I will hunt you down and kill you."

Helen's tongue slipped to the corner of her mouth, met with the iron taste of blood. He had not only broken the code of chivalry, he was the vilest man she could imagine. *So now he threatens murder?* She shuddered.

He leaned into her with a sickly sneer stretching his lips. "But it won't be an easy death. I'll make sure you suffer for a very long time."

A sense of calm precluded her panic. She looked from his right hand to his left. "Release me." Her voice was lower than she'd ever heard it. "Lest you give me cause to seek an annulment—"

"A *woman*, appeal to the Pope?" he bellowed with a hideous laugh, but his grip eased.

Helen jolted from his steely fingers and darted for the door. "Guard! Help!" She flung it wide and hurtled into the passageway.

Grant ran toward her, his sword drawn. "M'lady—"

"Do not let him touch me." Helen picked up her skirts and dashed past the guard.

"You were brought to Mingary to increase my wealth and to produce my heir! And you've woefully failed on the second account." Aleck's voice resounded through the stone passageway. Then he bellowed another taunting laugh. "After all this time, do you still have imaginings of love and sailing off into sunsets, like the stories in those ridiculous books you read?"

Helen clapped her hands over her ears to block Aleck's tirade and ran for the solace of the beach. She ran to the only place in God forsaken Ardnamurchan where she could be alone. Once outside the bailey walls, a brisk wind cut through her gown, but Helen could scarcely feel the cold. The entire time she'd been in Aleck's solar, she'd maintained her composure, but now, free from his brutality, she couldn't stop her tears as sobs wracked her body.

***

Eoin rubbed his hand over the worn timbers of his galley. The boat was in need of a good refit. At the very least, he and his men must patch the joins with pitch to ensure they had no problems when they sailed north. He walked around the outer hull, making a mental note of weak spots that could possibly give them trouble. There was nothing more damning than a bloody leak in the midst of a squall in the North Sea.

He straightened at the sound of a woman's wail sailing past on the wind—an eerie sound. Most likely it was a seagull, but Eoin stooped and peered beneath the curve of galley's stern, looking in the direction of the noise. Lady Helen ran across the stony beach with her hands clapped to her face. Then she climbed a small outcropping and disappeared behind the rocks.

*What the devil?*

It didn't surprise him that she was upset. Any man would have challenged Sir Aleck to a brawl had they been insulted in the way Lady Helen had endured last eve. Eoin straightened and swiped a hand across his mouth. He had no business meddling. The lady had made her decision long ago. She'd broken his heart once and seeing her again only served to open the old wound.

Her wail howled on the wind.

Eoin's heart twisted. They had been good friends once. His memory returned with clarity. Of the four sisters, Helen had always been the most well-mannered—not that any of Duncan's sisters were audacious. But why had Lady Helen married a rogue?

Pushing aside his unfounded concern, he continued with his inspection of the hull.

The wail came again. This time the agony in the lady's tone cut through to his gut.

Before he allowed himself another thought, he strode toward Lady Helen's hiding place. The rocks were sharp and slick with mist. *She could have fallen.*

Arriving at the outcropping where she'd disappeared, Eoin looked down. The hem of her blue kirtle peeked from under the stony shelf.

As he descended, Helen's stuttered breaths swelled up to him. Her voice filled with incredible agony, the woefulness of it wrapped tendrils around his heart.

Jumping down, Eoin landed upon smooth sand.

With another gasp, her hem disappeared further into the cavern.

"Lady Helen?"

"Leave me." Her voice trembled.

*I really ought to take her advice.* Eoin crouched down and peered inside. As his eyes adjusted to the dim light, he realized she had a bruise forming under her eye.

*I could kill the bastard.*

He crawled beside her and kneeled. "You've been hit." She had another, larger bruise on the right side of her jaw. "More than once."

"I am fine." She snapped a hand to her chest, sucking in sharp inhales as if she were trying to regain control.

Reaching out, he brushed the bruise near her eye with the back of his finger.

She flinched.

"Did Sir Aleck do this?" Honestly, he needn't ask.

She pursed her lips and nodded, the anguish in her eyes unmistakable. Eoin wished he'd been the one on the receiving end of that strike. Aleck MacIain would think twice before he lashed out at a woman again.

"I-I-I…" Drawing the corners of her mouth into a tortured frown, she turned as red as a ripe apple. She hid her face in her hands, breathing like she'd just run a footrace.

Eoin slid onto his haunches and smoothed his arm over her shoulders. "Easy, lass. There's no need to say a word."

She leaned into him as if craving compassion. "I'm sorry."

Wishing to give her comfort, to do anything to take away her agony, he rubbed his palm on her shoulder in a circular motion. "There's nothing to forgive. Just have a good cry and everything will feel better."

Gently he rocked her, realizing Helen wore no veil covering her hair. Her locks were the color of burnt honey and smelled of lilies and rain. How anyone could raise a hand against such perfection, Eoin would never know.

Her breaths grew short—like hiccups. Eoin encircled her with his free hand and continued to sway, back and forth in a hypnotic rhythm. "It will be all right," he whispered into her temple. He hoped to God it would. *Why did she marry that brutish maggot of a husband?*

"It will *never* be all right." Her voice was as bitter as bile.

Not once had Eoin ever heard such defeat come from another living soul. His tongue twisted—spewing curses about Aleck MacIain wouldn't help the lady. If he hadn't witnessed the bastard's behavior last eve, he never would have believed a woman as genteel as Helen could be so openly scorned by a man who had taken a solemn marriage vow to love and protect his wife. But to see the lady battered made Eoin want to march into the keep and show Aleck MacIain exactly what it was like to take a beating.

He bowed his chin to Helen's silken tresses and kissed the top of her head. "I do not take kindly to any man who strikes a woman, no matter the cause."

She sighed deeply and shook her head. "I suppose I deserved his ire."

He blinked. "Why on earth would you say that?"

"I tried to confront him about Mary and asked…"

When she stopped herself, curiosity needled at the back of his neck. "What did you ask?"

"It doesn't matter. He'll never allow me to leave Mingary. And I cannot flee without my daughter."

Eoin pursed his lips. He'd want to run too—had he been in Helen's position. "Aye, you've a bairn who needs you."

She leaned into him, her hands clutched under her chin. "I fear more for Maggie than for myself."

Eoin's gut roiled. "Don't tell me he's turned his hand against the wee lass."

"Nay, but he plans to make an alliance with her marriage—far before she's ready." Helen tensed in his arms. "I swear on my father's grave, I'll not see her in a miserable marriage. 'Tis no life without happiness."

Heaven help him, the woefulness in her voice tore his heart to shreds. "No, lass. It is not."

Helen's breathing grew steadier, but she remained nestled into him as if afraid to let go. Eoin's heart swelled. Lady Helen needed someone to care for her—to stand up for her. Whom could he appoint? By the end of summer he would return to his clan and then he'd be of no use to her at all. But holy Mother Mary, it had been a long time since he'd wrapped his arms around a woman—even longer since he'd embraced a lass without seeking a kiss.

She seemed content to remain in his arms for a time. Oddly, Eoin could think of no other place he should be presently. There were probably a host of things requiring his attention, but his mind blanked. Only Lady Helen filled his senses as his rocking motion brought on a peacefulness he hadn't a mind to end.

He thought back to the years he'd spent as a squire at Kilchurn Castle. Helen had been such a darling child, but he was older—seven years was a great deal to a young lad. He'd never thought of her romantically until…*hmm…she must have been about ten and five the first time I realized she was stunning. Though I wanted to, I couldn't do much about my desires at the time. Even at two and twenty I was still trying to earn my place as a knight.*

He smiled at the memories his thoughts rekindled. Helen wasn't as tall as Gyllis, her elder sister by one year. She was fairer and more fine-boned—quieter, but by the intelligence reflected in her eyes, Helen was aware of everything that happened around her. He chuckled.

Helen pulled away a little. "Why are you laughing?"

Eoin didn't want to release her yet. He smoothed his hand along her outer arm, akin to comforting a fond pet, and she eased back against him. "Do you remember the time your mother blamed you and your sisters for pinching the Yule log?"

She tapped her fingers to her mouth and blew out a burst of air—not a laugh, but almost. "Aye—why on earth would you remember that?"

"Duncan and I used it the night before for a bonfire—sort of a rite of passage ceremony we dreamed up." He inclined his cheek against her hair. "We didn't realize what we'd done until the next day. Holy Moses, your mother was furious."

"And you allowed her to believe we girls took it?"

Eoin absently smoothed his hand over her tresses. "Duncan made me swear a vow of silence—said we'd not eat a decent meal in a month if Lady Margaret discovered we'd used her masterpiece."

"Do you realize that without a guard, Ma took us into the forest—whilst it was snowing, mind you—and each of us chopped until blisters formed. Then she made us drag the heavy thing all the way back to the keep."

Eoin grimaced. He hadn't been aware of the severity of their punishment. "I'm sorry we made you go to so much trouble. I never should have kept mum."

Helen turned her face up to him. "And go against your vow to my brother?"

God in heaven, he'd never realized her eyes were so incredibly blue. "That would have caused some consternation," Eoin said, his voice husky.

"I'll say." Helen smiled, ever so innocently. "Knowing Duncan, he still wouldn't have forgiven you to this day."

# Chapter Six

Aleck trudged toward Mary's cottage, a trek he'd made many times before. He'd done a good job of keeping his affair with Mary a secret up until Helen gave birth to a bloody bitch. Christ, he'd waited so goddamned long for Campbell's sister to bear his son, the birth of a daughter pushed him over the edge of his tolerance. Any *reasonable* man would feel the same.

If only Mary had been the daughter of a knight, he would have been able to marry the widow. He'd been in love with her even before her husband passed. But she was the daughter of a common crofter. An alliance with her would bring no riches. Lady Helen Campbell had come with an impressive bloodline as well as a healthy dowry, not to mention the alliance with her family served him well at court.

The problem was the lady herself. How on earth Colin Campbell, the great Black Knight of Rome could have sired a mouse like Lady Helen was beyond Aleck's comprehension. He'd expected and preferred a robust woman who brazenly spoke her mind and presided over the keep with a firm hand. Helen was too bloody nice for a noblewoman. Aleck couldn't imagine Lord Campbell ever allowing servants to be friendly. They were provided by God to serve the gentry and perform a duty for their maintenance.

Aye, bringing Helen to Mingary had been a mistake. She was so demure—hadn't a backbone in her body. Aleck stopped and scratched his chin. Her behavior in the solar this morn had been quite out of character for her. She'd never confronted him with such passion. He'd wanted to take his dagger and slit that slender neck of hers. *Seek an annulment? Take Maggie away? The bitch finally gives me a bairn and she's suddenly found her grit? Well, she will not leave me until I've interred her rotting corpse into the family crypt.*

He pulled out his dirk and ran his thumb over the flat edge as he continued along the path. The thought of Helen meeting her end tempted him. But that wouldn't solve his problems in the short term. He needed an heir from Helen first. After she birthed a son, Aleck would be free to dispose of her as he saw fit.

But he must visit her bed again soon. The very idea repulsed him. He'd never enjoyed swivving with his wife. She provided him no sport whatsoever. Worse, with small breasts and a tight arse, she looked more like a lad than a lass. But Mary? Aleck could bury himself in her mountainous breasts along with his cock in her...

He moaned and rubbed his crotch. Christ, just thinking about that woman made his seed dribble in his breeks.

He rapped on Mary's door and entered the small cottage. It smelled of tallow candles—a scent to which he'd grown fond. It reminded him of Mary's practicality and made him hungry for her.

Seated at her loom, the woman glanced over her shoulder and stood with a smile. "I'm surprised to see you m'laird."

"Oh?" He crossed the floor and pulled her into his arms. "And why wouldn't I visit my leman in the middle of the day, as well as after dark, or any time that suits my fancy?"

"Leman," she grumbled. "I hate that word."

"But you are." He nuzzled into her hair. "And so much more."

She pushed away and strolled toward the hearth. "Tell me, why is Sir Eoin MacGregor here?"

Aleck unfastened his sword belt and tossed his weapons on the table. "King's orders—his royal highness thinks the bastard can help us quell the MacDonalds to the north."

"Aye?" Mary faced him. "I do not like the way he looks at me—or you for that matter."

Aleck's gut clenched. "You don't say? I've always thought that man always sported a disagreeable scowl."

"Mayhap, but he's got dagger-eyes for you, m'laird."

Aleck was well aware Eoin was close to Helen's brother, Duncan. He didn't give a rat's arse if the knight disapproved of his behavior. But Eoin could cause a stir with the Lord of Glenorchy. Not that Aleck thought anything would come of it…still, it was always better to avoid tempting potential dragons. "Perhaps it would be best if we kept our rendezvous secret whilst he's here."

"But I've been ever so happy now it is no longer necessary to sneak around that woman's back." Mary groaned. "Why can you not push the wench out an upper window and marry me?"

Chuckling, he reached for her, but she snatched her hand away. Aleck wouldn't let her little outburst dissuade him. "We've been over that many times. I need Helen to produce an heir. After that..." He dipped his chin and waggled his dark eyebrows—a look that always made

Mary damp between the legs. "Any matter of ills could befall her."

Mary took a step back, appearing more distraught than usual. "*I* should be your lady. You love me, not *her*—I cannot bear the thought of your visiting her bed to produce your *heir*."

"Och, Mary." He grasped her hand firmly and this time she didn't pull away. "I do not like the idea any better than you."

She stepped into him and twirled his shirt laces around his finger. She rubbed her mons across his crotch. "Get me with child. I'll give you a son, I'm certain of it."

With Mary so close, Aleck couldn't think straight. For years he'd fought his urge to see Mary birth his bairn. The thought tempted him. Would the king allow him to legitimize a bastard? Perhaps if Helen had an unfortunate end. *Eventually*. And he'd need to ensure he received credit for any battles they won against Clan MacDonald and not that sniveling maggot, Eoin MacGregor.

Mary opened his shirt and slid her hand over his chest. "Stay away from that woman's bed and have faith in my ability to produce an heir."

***

A sennight had passed since Eoin had comforted Lady Helen in the stone cavern. Since then, he'd hardly seen her. Even at meals, she'd rarely made an appearance. He suspected her absence was because of the bruising on her face. Even with a wimple, the purple surrounding her eye was noticeable.

He'd tried to push thoughts of Helen from his mind and focus on the task at hand—after all, he was there on the king's orders and quashing the MacDonald uprising was a task not to be taken lightly.

Today he strode down a line of men, all sparring with various weapons. Each warrior was paired according to skill. Eoin stopped to watch Fergus and Grant—MacGregor's finest against MacIain's best, just as they'd been paired on the first day. He wouldn't have believed it a sennight ago, but Grant looked as if he'd make a fine knight one day…until Fergus darted in with an upward strike of his battleax and the sword flew from Grant's hand.

The soldier groaned and grimaced, appearing as if he could slam his fist into the stone wall.

Eoin stepped forward. "You were looking good right up until you took your eyes off Fergus's weapon."

Grant opened his mouth as if he were about to deny his error, but Eoin held up his hand. "I saw you, lad."

Grant's expression softened and he nodded.

Eoin stooped to retrieve the sword. "When your opponent is coming over the top with an ax, spin away and counter with a backward thrust like this." He demonstrated how to swivel his grip and maneuver the weapon backward while securing it with both hands rotating at his left hip to ensure a kill straight to the gut. Eoin would have stepped in and sparred with the guard, but he'd opted against wearing his hauberk this day—*no sense in chancing an injury when Fergus is outfitted for a fight.*

The corner of Grant's mouth turned up. "That's bloody brilliant."

"'Tis just good swordsmanship, lad." Eoin slapped the soldier on the shoulder and handed him the weapon. "Go on, give it a try."

With a few practice moves, Grant had mastered the maneuver. *Perhaps I should ask him to join Clan Gregor.* Eoin chuckled at the consternation such an offer would bring Aleck MacIain.

No sooner had he thought about the braggart when Aleck strode into the courtyard. It was about time the beef-witted chieftain showed his face during the training.

MacIain mostly steered clear of the daily sparing sessions. Eoin gestured to the line of sparring soldiers. "Your men are showing promise."

MacIain frowned, his dark eyes squinting in the sunlight. "My men were well-trained before you arrived." He pointed to Grant. "Look there, my henchman just out-maneuvered yours."

A smirking blast of air trumpeted through Eoin's nose. It would be useless to try to explain what had happened to the clueless buffoon. Instead, he opted to focus on the positive. "Now you've got it, Grant. Give Fergus a good run and make him earn his keep."

MacIain scowled. "You think you're so bloody superior. If you put my army against yours, my men would stand together and come out the victors."

That stopped Eoin short. "You reckon?"

"I don't reckon. I ken."

Eoin smoothed his hand over his chin and eyed the man's belly—it was nearly as big as the man's bravado. Then a picture of Helen's bruised face came to mind. "Seems to me you'd prefer to fight with the lassies than come out here with the men." He waggled his brows. Mayhap he'd rile MacIain enough to make him take a swing.

Aleck shoved Eoin's shoulder with the heel of his hand. "You'd best watch your mouth, else someone might opt to cut out your flapping tongue."

"Aye, oh, *great* chieftain?" Eoin would have liked to see him try. He stepped within an inch of the braggart's nose. "Why have you been hiding in your miserable keep—or do you let your men fight your battles for you?"

With a growl MacIain shuffled away and drew his sword. "I'll show you a thing or two, you bloody bastard." The big man advanced, hacking his weapon like he was wielding a meat cleaver.

Anticipating the assault, Eoin had snatched his sword from its scabbard. He defended the attack with swift counter moves. What Aleck lacked in finesse, he made up for in brute strength. Eoin suspected the chieftain would tire quickly—he hadn't seen MacIain lift a finger in the past sennight. No warrior could withstand a good fight without honing his stamina daily.

Eoin darted from side to side, eluding the brutish strikes while patiently waiting for the big oaf to tire. "Tell me, how did Lady Helen end up with a blackened eye?"

The thug bellowed as he hacked his blade with herculean thrusts. "That is none of your concern."

*Och, but I'm making it my concern.* Eoin played along with Aleck's display of brawn, deflecting every bone-jarring blow, biding his time until the brute made a critical mistake. Deep down, Eoin wanted to match MacIain stroke for stroke—to drive him to the wall and hold his blade against Aleck's neck and demand he never raise a hand against Lady Helen again. But first, he would wear him down.

"Do you know what I think?" Eoin asked casually as if he were out for a noonday stroll.

"I don't give a rat's arse," Aleck growled, sucking in deep gasps of air. "You can take your thoughts and sail back to Argyllshire."

"That would be my pleasure," Eoin seethed through gritted teeth. "If we didn't have our beloved *Scotland* to defend." Eoin circled, watching and waiting for Aleck to make his next move. "I think," he said, not caring whether Aleck wanted to hear his opinion or nay. "You struck *Duncan Campbell's* sister—a noblewoman, for one, and a lady who has no means to defend herself against an oaf as large as you."

Aleck's toe caught on a cobblestone and he stumbled toward Eoin. Hopping aside, MacGregor let the swine crash into the wall.

Eoin tapped his foot and waited while MacIain regained his composure. Clearly, Aleck wasn't concerned about raising the ire of the Lord of Glenorchy. Eoin blew a scoff out the side of his mouth. "I'm surprised Lady Helen hasn't informed her brother of your brutish behavior toward her."

"A man has a right to maintain order in his castle." Bellowing, Aleck charged like an incensed bull.

*Mistake.*

Clamping an arm around MacIain's neck, Eoin used the brute's momentum to pull him into a stranglehold and angled his blade to the bastard's throat. "No respectable knight would ever raise his hand against a woman," he growled. Aleck squirmed and bared his teeth, but one errant move and he'd be a dead man.

Eoin clamped his arm so taut, he all but crushed the man's voice box. "If you strike the lady again, I'll show you no quarter. Even after I've sailed back to Argyllshire. If I hear rumor of your brutality…one word from *any* source, I'll come upon you in the dead of night and cut out your heart."

"Did you hear that men?" Aleck bucked against Eoin's chest. "He threatened to *murder* me."

"Aye, I promised it—should he raise his hand against Lady Helen." Eoin pushed the sniveling maggot into the crowd.

Aleck scrambled for his sword and held it up in challenge. "Oh no, this isn't over."

Eoin loosened the buckle of his sword belt and let it clatter to the cobblestones. "All right then. Let's have a real fight—no weapons—man to man." He held up his fists.

Chuckling, MacIain passed his blade to Grant. "I'll turn the backstabber's face to pulp," he gloated.

"My coin's on MacGregor," someone hollered from the crowd.

The men surrounded them in a circle, raucous shouts echoing between the bailey walls.

Eoin studied the behemoth facing him. Looking like a Highland bull ready to charge, MacIain could have blown steam out his nose.

Braying a battle cry, Aleck barreled toward Eoin—exactly what he anticipated. Steeling his nerves, he stood firm. One step before impact, Eoin lunged aside, too late for MacIain to change his course. The chieftain stumbled face first to the cobblestones.

Grunting, Aleck pushed up with his palms, shaking his bulbous head. When he rose, blood streamed from his nose, his face crimson. "You're a backstabber, you are."

"I think not." Eoin raised his fists. "Come again."

This time, Aleck approached with more caution, ready to strike.

Breathing deeply, Eoin waited for the cur to make the first move. Aye, rage tore at his gut, but he'd not let it control him as Aleck did. With a roar, Aleck swung his fist toward Eoin's jaw. Ducking, Eoin slammed a punch to MacIain's gut. The wind wheezed from the maggot's lungs, but it wasn't enough to stop him from jabbing his elbow into Eoin's sternum.

He reeled back at the bone-crunching thud. Something cracked, but he could feel no pain. Rage swelled inside his chest. Advancing with relentless pummeling of his fists, Eoin drove the bastard backward. The blood oozing from his nose turned to a stream of red. But Eoin didn't stop. Faster and faster he threw his fists until he could scarcely make out MacIain's face through the mass of blood.

Shouts from the crowd grew louder, driving Eoin deeper into the frenzy of attack. A fist connected with his jaw, but he didn't even feel it.

Aleck stumbled and dropped to his knees.

Eoin advanced.

Someone caught him by the elbows.

"Enough," Fergus growled in his ear.

Eoin blinked, suddenly aware of the beating he'd unleashed. Rarely did he lose control. He nodded and took in a calming breath. Fergus was right. They were allies. It was time to stop.

Eoin held out his hand. "Shall we call it a draw, Sir Aleck?"

MacIain eyed him, blood oozing around his teeth and from the jagged cuts on his face, then he grasped Eoin's palm. "No one makes me look the fool," he said with a low snarl.

Eoin should have expected a traitorous move.

Before he could pull away, MacIain swung at him with a dagger. Bending backward, the blade sliced across Eoin's abdomen. Hot blood oozed down his gut. Nostrils flaring, Eoin advanced and pulled the dagger hidden in his sleeve. Hands clamped around his arms. He fought to break away, throwing his left, then right. "Release me you mongrel varmints."

"I'll murder the bastard," MacIain bellowed from across the circle. He too was being pulled away by his men.

"He's nay worth the king's ire," Fergus hissed in Eoin's ear.

"What is this commotion about?" Lady Helen dashed into the midst of the mayhem.

"Get back into the keep woman," Aleck bellowed.

When Helen shifted her gaze to Eoin, he stopped struggling and froze. What would she think of him now that he'd started a brawl with her husband?

# Chapter Seven

When Helen saw Eoin bleeding across his midsection, her heart beat so fast, it nearly hammered out of her chest. She ignored Aleck's command to go back inside and raced toward the MacGregor Chieftain. "My God, what happened?"

Eoin shrugged away from his men's grasp. "'Tis a scratch."

Fergus shook his head. "Laird MacIain drew his knife—'twas after Sir Eoin had offered his hand."

Helen spun to Aleck. "Is this true?"

He wiped his bloody nose on his sleeve. "What of it?" He gestured to the cuts on his face and rising bruises. "I swear the bastard broke my nose."

Helen stepped up and examined him. It wouldn't be the first broken nose she'd seen on her husband's roughhewn face—but there was little that could be done for it—or for the bruises she imagined Eoin had inflicted. After careful inspection, she determined Aleck's injuries were superficial. "And so you pulled a dagger in a fair fight?" Yes, she'd seen and heard enough of the encounter from the kitchen window.

"Wheesht, woman. I told you to return to the keep."

Helen turned and pointed at the MacGregor men. "Take Sir Eoin to the antechamber off the kitchen. I'll fetch my medicine bundle and meet him momentarily."

She started for the keep when Aleck stepped in front of her. "You're off to tend that miserable cur when I'm bleeding like a stuck pig?"

She stopped and dabbed beneath his nose with her kerchief. "The bleeding's mostly ebbed." She rose up on her toes and inclined her lips to his ear, whispering, "Perhaps you should wander up the hill and have Mary ply it with a bit of ointment."

He snapped his hand back, but Grant caught his arm. "Och, m'laird. Do you not think we've had enough beating for one day?"

Helen didn't wait to hear the outcome of that interchange. Under her breath, she prayed Aleck wouldn't start another brawl with the brave henchman. By the looks of her husband's face, he'd certainly received his due—though his injuries were nothing compared to the quantity of blood staining Eoin's shirt.

It took Helen no time to retrieve the basket with her healing essences and salves—something no respectable wife would be without. She hastened to the antechamber where she'd sent Eoin. The room was close to the courtyard and had a stone floor which would be easy to clean. She would have preferred to have sent him to his chamber above stairs, but it might be seen as scandalous. She also feared Aleck would balk. As it was, he might tell her she couldn't tend Eoin—though his wound appeared far worse.

She bustled through the kitchen and Peter gave her a look of earnest solemnity. "The sparring got a bit serious today."

She shook her head. "I ken and Sir Aleck had to be in the center of it."

"As well as the MacGregor Chieftain." Peter followed her across to the passage that led to the small chamber mostly used for drying herbs.

"Whatever the cause, I wish they'd behave like grown men rather than a pack of heathens."

Peter scoffed. "Now that's asking a bit much, m'lady."

Helen pushed into the chamber filled with men who stank as if they'd been a month or longer without a bath. She flicked her hand through the air. "Shoo, the lot of you, and go find a basin of water and a bar of soap."

"Bloody hell, I had a bath last year." The cheeky lad slipped past before Helen had a chance to scold him.

As the men cleared, she found Eoin sitting on a stool. He gave her a sheepish smile. "Apologies, m'lady. I'll see the men take a dip in the sea. That'll fix them up."

"My thanks." She stood awkwardly. Now that the room had emptied, she realized they were alone—*together alone*—just like they'd been when he'd consoled her on the beach. Her palms perspired. Oh how heavenly it would be if she were able to offer him the same soothing embrace right now. But that would be improper and impertinent. Realizing she'd been staring, Helen drew in a breath and turned to set the basket on the table. "Why were you not wearing your hauberk?"

"I've been training all this time and wasn't planning on doing any fighting. Moreover, the day was warm." The deep hum of his voice eased her tension. She could listen to him recite passages from the Book of Job all day and remain completely enthralled.

Helen swallowed and regarded him over her shoulder. "I surmise you'll think again before you make such a blunder."

"Aye." Eoin glanced down. "Had I been wearing my mail, I wouldn't have felt so much as a pin prick."

She agreed. It wasn't like Eoin to be careless. "Your shirt is ruined."

He held it out and examined the gaping hole and the stain. "I suppose it would look a bit odd with a seam across the middle, even if the blood did wash out."

"Do you have another?"

"I've one in my kit."

She gestured with her upturned palm. "Then you'd best give this one to me and I'll see what I can do to mend it."

"All right." He pulled the shirt over his head and held it out.

Helen drew in a stuttered breath. She'd seen him shirtless often, but that was years ago when she and Gyllis used to watch the knights sparring from the battlements at Kilchurn Castle. And she'd never been this close. His arms were sculpted with thick, undulating muscles. The one holding the shirt flexed, defining perfection. His chest was as broad as a horse's hindquarters with hard muscle beneath embossing each masculine breast. She ached to press her fingers against his flesh to discover if he were made of iron. Her eyes drank him in, then dipped lower. Well defined muscle rippled over his abdomen, but that's where she stopped. Helen clapped a hand to her chest and gasped.

He shook the shirt. "Should I set it on the table?"

Her mouth suddenly turned as arid as a hot pan with no water. She licked her lips and plucked the clothing from his grasp. "I'll do it." She turned her back to him on the pretense of folding the shirt. *You are here to tend his wound and that is all.* She steeled her nerves with a deep inhale. "Tell me what happened." After she pulled a cloth from her basket, she swathed his wound. It was still weeping, but thankfully the heavy bleeding had stopped.

"I suppose it was my fault." Eoin held up his palms and shrugged. "Sir Aleck came into the courtyard and I needled him a bit for not being present for our training sessions. It turned into a challenge and, the next thing I knew, we were throwing fists."

"And he pulled a dagger." She pushed against his belly to see how deep the injury went. A hand's breadth long, it wasn't the worst she'd seen, but the cut needed to be tended for certain.

He hissed. "Aye. I should have been expecting him to pull a blade."

"Why? I heard the part where you said no weapons."

He hesitated and pursed his lips, but Helen gave him her inquisitive eye—it worked on everyone but Aleck.

Eoin gave her a lopsided grin. "Some people don't like to play fair."

"That would be Aleck MacIain."

"Aye, m'lady," he whispered, a touch of color flooded to his cheeks as if he were embarrassed to admit to it.

She fished in her basket for a bone needle and thread. "It needn't bother you to speak the truth."

"No, m'lady." His voice rasped.

"Your wound must be stitched." Helen held up a needle and threaded it.

"I can think of no gentler hands to tend me."

She regarded him over her shoulder. His chin was slightly lowered and he looked up to meet her gaze. There was a hunger in that crystal-blue stare, fringed by long, dark lashes. It was Helen's turn to flush. From the heat spreading across her cheeks, she knew she must be as red as a berry. *If he asks, I'll say the room is overwarm.*

She stepped into him. "Shall I call for some whisky?"

He continued to stare. "Nay, it'll be fine."

Helen swallowed and ignored those piercing blues, at least tried to make a pretense of doing so. "S-sir Aleck always ensures he has plenty of drink before being stitched."

"Do you stitch him often?"

"I did once, but now he has…someone else tend to his ills."

Eoin's gaze narrowed and he looked at her with a concerned expression. Then he grasped her chin and examined the bruising around her eye. "It has almost completely faded."

She turned her head away so he couldn't see the eye. "I've been trying to keep it hidden."

He smoothed his hand over her cheek—the one without the bruise. His fingers, though rough, were gentle—so unlike Aleck's. If only things had been different for her.

"I'm sorry you've been unhappy," he said, making her heart skip a beat.

She smiled and knelt, holding up the needle. "Are you ready?" Heaven help her, he smelled of the sea on a warm summer's day.

"Aye." And his deep burr curled off his tongue like a lazy wave.

Helen forced herself to focus on the task at hand, lest she hurt him. She carefully used her thumb and pointer finger to pinch Eoin's flesh together, trying to keep her hands steady. "Things are not half so lonely now that I have Maggie."

He chuckled. "How *is* the bairn?"

"She's healthy. Growing too fast." She made the first suture.

Eoin didn't even hiss. "Wee ones have a way of doing that."

"I suppose they do, though this is the only time I've had the opportunity to see it first-hand." She tied off the second suture.

He tugged a strand of hair from beneath her veil and twirled it around his finger. "Does she have honeyed locks like her mother?"

Helen almost didn't want to say. "'Tis black with silken curls." Helen whipped two more stitches. "She'll be a bonny lass, for certain." Then her face fell with thoughts of the miserable life her daughter might endure because of her beauty.

Eoin released her hair. "Why so glum?" The MacGregor Chieftain was too perceptive and too disconcerting.

Helen couldn't help but heave a sigh. "Aleck aims to make an alliance by marrying Maggie off as soon as her menses show."

She must have stabbed Eoin with the next stitch because the muscles across his abdomen contracted. He let out a grunt. "I'll wager you're not happy with the prospect of seeing her married so young."

Helen tied the last knot. "I would do anything to keep her from an unhappy marriage."

She snipped the thread and Eoin took in a deep breath. "At least you have a dozen years or more before you must worry about that."

"Aye." *I'll have a dozen years to keep her away from Aleck's lash, too.*

"I'd like to see her," Eoin said as if he cared not if the bairn was a lass or lad.

Something warm flickered within Helen's breast. "You would?"

He puzzled. "Why have you not brought her to the great hall? Everyone is fond of a glimpse at a wee bairn."

Another deep sigh slid through her lips. "Everyone except Sir Aleck, I'm afraid."

"I don't understand." Eoin knit his brows, looking rather dangerous. "True, he wanted a lad, but he has a lass to love until a boy is born."

Helen's throat closed. If only Aleck could be half as sensible as Eoin. She fished in her basket and pulled out a small stoneware pot. "This salve has avens oil to help you heal." She couldn't bring herself to apply it. Smoothing her fingers over his warm and banded flesh was more than she could bear.

He took the pot and his finger brushed hers. It was as if he'd taken a feather and teased her with it. She wrapped her hand around the finger to staunch the tingling. Why on earth did Eoin MacGregor disarm her with a simple touch? Yes, it had been an eternity since she'd had such a friendly conversation with a man, but must a mere brush of his fingertip send her insides into a maelstrom of fluttering butterflies? Helen picked up her basket and dipped into a curtsey. "You'd best find that shirt before you catch your death." *Or you make all the women in the castle swoon into a heap of worthless mush.*

***

Eoin let out a long breath as he watched Helen stroll out of the antechamber. Holy Mother Mary and all the saints, whether coming or going, the lady was a vision to behold. *A married vision nonetheless.* He still couldn't believe he sat there and wrapped a lock of her hair around his finger. Then it was all he could do not to hold it to his nose and inhale.

Devil's bones, he'd acted like a lovesick fool. He wasn't in love. Even if he were—which he definitely was not—the lady embodied the metaphor of forbidden fruit. Worse, she had to be married to the most insufferable arse in the Highlands. Without a doubt, this was the most god-awful assignment Eoin had endured since he'd joined with the Campbells and the Highland Enforcers.

Christ, his gut hurt worse now than it had after MacIain sliced his dagger across it. *The miserable backstabber. That'll teach me. I should have been wearing an arming doublet and hauberk.*

Eoin glanced at his belly. Helen had tied off a half-dozen stitches, each one perfectly exact in a row just below his navel. Funny, he hadn't felt any pain whilst she was stitching, but as soon as she left the room, the wound throbbed and ached as if he'd been gutted. Bloody oath, he could use a healthy swig of that whisky now. He pulled the stopper out of the pot, hit by a strong clove-like aroma. Spreading it over his wound, he let out a grunt. It stung and, holy hell, his eyes watered.

Truth be told, he'd wanted Helen to apply the salve with her deft fingers—wished she'd do it. He'd even closed his eyes and prayed she could hear his thoughts. *Please. Smooth in the ointment. I need to feel your lithe fingertips upon my skin just once more.*

He understood why she'd handed him the pot. He must have made the lady damn uncomfortable when he touched her hair…and her cheek…and examined her eye. God, he was daft.

If anything, the confrontation with MacIain, gave him the impetus to make up his mind. They hadn't heard any news from the spies posted up the coast. It was about time someone paid them a visit. He and his men needed time for respite and a few days at sea would serve to ferry them away from Mingary for a bit. Besides, they could also do some spying of their own and discover more about what Alexander MacDonald was up to. The chieftain controlled a great deal of land around Skye—and his northern lands were far away from the scrutiny of the crown.

Eoin pushed the stopper into the pot and stood just as Fergus walked through the archway.

The henchman held out a shirt. "I fetched this from your kit—thought you might need it." He glanced from side to side as if expecting to see Lady Helen. It was a good thing she hadn't tarried. Eoin wouldn't want the castle astir with any gossip about her, no matter how unfounded.

"My thanks." Eoin took the shirt and pulled it over his head. "Tell the men we'll be sailing at dawn on the morrow."

"Had enough of the MacIain scoundrels have you?"

"Of sorts." Eoin wouldn't divulge the extent of his ire to one of his men. He supported King James's cause, and that was all they needed to know. "Moreover we need to run a sortie to the north to discover what the MacDonald scallywags are up to."

"After Aleck cut you today." Fergus lowered his voice. "I cannot see why we don't just sail back to Argyllshire."

"Because that's not what the king ordered." Eoin picked up his weapons and headed out with his henchman on his heels. "If we tuck tail and head for home, MacIain could side with the MacDonalds, and then we'd have no foothold on the northwestern shore." And Eoin wasn't about to release his hold on Mingary for any length of time until he knew Helen would be safe. Aye, she'd survived Aleck's brutality for the past five years, but something wasn't right, and Eoin had a mind to fix it—somehow.

Fergus fell in beside him. "Are you coming with me to tell the men?"

"Nay, I'm off to find the chieftain of this keep and let him know our plans." Eoin gave his henchman a wink. "Wouldn't want him to gloat, thinking he'd scared us away."

"Good luck with that." Fergus chuckled. "Better you than me."

Eoin gave him a jab with his elbow. "Aye, and kiss my arse while you're at it."

# *Chapter Eight*

Helen sat in a beam of light shining through the narrow window in the nursery painstakingly making tiny stitches as she repaired Eoin's linen shirt. Maggie napped in her cradle. Glenda and Sarah tended their needlepoint beside the hearth.

"You'll go blind holding that shirt so close to your face," Glenda said.

Helen looked up. "I'm trying to make it appear as if it weren't slashed open. Sir Eoin told me he had only one to spare. And I feel responsible since Sir Aleck was the one who ruined it."

"Sir Eoin is fortunate. Most soldiers have the clothing on their backs and that is all," Sarah said as if she possessed a great deal of knowledge on the subject.

Helen pushed in her needle for another careful stitch. "Aye, but Eoin is a chieftain. I'd expect him to be a bit different."

Glenda rose and crossed the floor. "Let me have a look."

Helen held up the shirt. "I'm nearly finished."

The chambermaid grasped the edges and pulled it taut. "You've done a fine job, m'lady. You can only see the join if you look closely."

Sarah stepped beside her. "And no one will see it at all if he's wearing a doublet atop."

Helen regarded the shirt with a sigh. "Well, at least you scrubbed out the blood stain, Glenda."

"Perhaps you should have made him a new shirt," Sarah suggested.

Honestly, Helen had thought about it, but decided she might raise Aleck's ire if she gave the Chieftain of Clan Gregor a new shirt that she'd handcrafted. "Mayhap, but Sir Aleck is still maddened about their disagreement in the courtyard. I wouldn't want to upset him further"

"The men are saying the chieftain shouldn't have lashed out at Sir Eoin after he'd offered a fair handshake." Her eyes popping wide as if she'd just made a grand faux pas, Sarah pressed praying fingers to her lips. "Forgive me for being so bold, m'lady."

Though Helen would never speak ill of her husband to the servants, she nodded. "I'm afraid you could be right in this instance." She took in a deep inhale and smiled. "Perhaps Sir Aleck and Sir Eoin will agree to put their differences behind them once the MacGregor Chieftain returns."

Glenda coughed. "You must be the most optimistic person I know, m'lady."

Helen pursed her lips and returned her attention to her sewing. She didn't care to have Glenda speak out in subtle disagreement. True, Helen always tried to find the good in every situation, but lately, her kindheartedness had been pushed to the ragged edge.

Sarah brushed a wisp of hair from her face. "When do you think the MacGregor men will return?"

Helen frowned. She had hoped they would have come back by now. The return trip up around the northwestern islands should have only taken a couple of days and they'd been away an entire sennight. "I'm sure they've a great many things to attend," she replied as indifferently as she could manage.

As the women returned to their needlepoint, the chamber grew quiet, the crackling of the fire in the hearth the only sound.

After Helen tied off the last stitch, the ram's horn sounded, piercing through the silence. The suddenness of the blast nearly made her heart hammer out of her chest.

Sarah's gaze brightened with her grin. "I'll wager 'tis them."

Helen waved her toward the window. "Go have a look." She made one more knot for good measure and snipped it with the shears. If Sir Eoin had indeed arrived, she could return his shirt this very day.

"'Tis the MacGregor men," Sarah announced, her voice squeaking with excitement.

Why Helen's insides were fluttering, she had no idea. Perhaps the lass's exuberance was contagious.

Glenda gestured to the door. "I'll stay here with Maggie if you'd like to greet them."

Sarah curtseyed. "Thank you, ta." She bit her lip and cast a hopeful gaze toward Helen. "If that meets with your approval, m'lady."

Helen stood and draped the shirt over her arm. "Of course. We'll go together."

While they proceeded down the tower stairs, Helen paused at an arrow slit and looked to the north. Stepping out the door of Mary's cottage, Aleck was fastening his sword belt. She glanced over her shoulder to see if Sarah had seen him. The woeful expression on the maid's face confirmed she had.

Helen pretended nothing was amiss and clapped a hand to her chest. "Thank heavens Peter has plenty of meat hanging in the cellar."

"'Tis a good thing indeed, m'lady," Sarah agreed.

Though Helen tried not to think of it, she suspected the entire clan avoided speaking of Aleck and Mary in her presence. She breathed in deeply through her nose. She would hold her chin high and maintain her poise just as she always had.

When they stepped into the courtyard, noisy activity echoed between the bailey walls with a refreshing air of excitement. The blacksmith shack clanged and guardsmen were all jesting amongst themselves about their surprise that the MacGregors had bothered to return after their chieftain "bested" Sir Eoin in the sparring ring. Helen wanted to issue a sharp retort. Was she the only person who'd seen Aleck lash out after Eoin had offered his hand? Or had a sennight and whisky faded their memories? Then again, by the way they were laughing and blurting yarns filled with hyperbole, she realized most were genuinely happy Sir Eoin and his men had returned.

Helen glanced at the nursemaid who anxiously strained to see beyond the open sea gate. "Do you fancy one of the MacGregor lads?"

Sarah clapped her hands to her cheeks. "Is it that obvious?"

Walking across the courtyard, Helen grasped her arm. "If you had wings, I do not believe your toes would touch ground at all." She waved Sarah forward. "Go on then."

The nursemaid giggled and dashed ahead, straight into the outstretched arms of a MacGregor man. Helen chewed the inside of her cheek. Would she need to find a new maid for Maggie soon?

Her thoughts were interrupted when Eoin hopped over the hull of his galley and splashed into knee-deep water. Helen shivered, well aware the North Sea was never anything but icy cold. She stood at the top of the incline, as customary. It would have been entirely inappropriate had she raced down to shore to greet the men. After all, she was lady over the lands of Ardnamurchan, a post held by a woman born into nobility. *Unlike Mary the widow.*

Eoin waded through the surf nodding greetings to the MacIain guards. The men all surrounded him with welcoming claps on the back and ribs about the length of time he'd been away. It appeared some had appreciated their sennights of sparring lessons with the big warrior. Laughing, he seemed not to notice the wet hem of his surcoat, dripping from beneath his hauberk—or the water sloshing from his boots. As he neared, he looked up the incline. His gaze met Helen's and he grinned while the others chortled around him. He surged ahead of his retinue and strode straight toward her.

Helen's heart fluttered.

"Lady Helen." He stepped in and grasped her hand. Though he'd just been walking through the icy surf and sailing in a chilly May breeze, the fingers surrounding hers were ever so warm and welcoming.

Her breath caught, but she maintained her poise. With the current between their gazes connecting them like lightning to the earth, her insides fluttered in an alarming rhythm she would never reveal through her expression.

Time stilled. Everything surrounding them faded into oblivion, as if they were the only two people on the shore. Her every breath rushed with the sound of waves hitting the beach.

Eoin's eyes twinkled, reflecting a glint of sunlight. His lips parted in a broad grin, revealing a row of straight, healthy white teeth. A dark beard had grown in during their absence. If anything, it made his eyes bluer, his teeth whiter. She chuckled to herself. The black hair shadowing his face gave him a devilish look.

Blinking, Helen realized he was staring at her, as if expecting her to say something. "Sir Eoin, we thought you and your men would have returned days ago," she managed in a higher pitch than normal.

With a halfcocked grin, he lowered his gaze, shading his eyes with dark lashes—far too long to belong to a man. "We had a bit of fun following a pair of MacDonald galleys down the coast." He plied the back of her hand with a kiss, so warm it scorched.

Certain his lips had left a mark, Helen glanced at her hand. "How is your wound?"

Eoin pressed his hand to his ribs to the side of the injury. "'Tis coming good. I had Fergus take out the stitches a couple days past."

Recalling the undulating muscles over his abdomen, Helen's gaze drifted down. With a start, she remembered the shirt in her hand—the one he hadn't kissed. She held it up. "I mended this for you."

His eyes brightened. "That's *my* shirt?"

"Aye. I stitched it trying to mirror the weave. 'Tis not perfect. I'm afraid my eyesight isn't as keen as it once was."

"I'm impressed." He peered closely at the seam. "It looks as good as new. Thank you, m'lady."

When Aleck moved in beside them, Helen took a step back. She feigned her usual demure expression. "Sir Eoin has returned, m'laird."

"I see." Aleck frowned and regarded Eoin's wet boots. "What took you so long, MacGregor? Can you not navigate?"

A muscle in Eoin's jaw twitched. He motioned toward the sea gate. "I've news."

Following the men into the courtyard, Helen half expected Eoin to finish his sentence with a scoffing comment akin to, "you daft Highlander." She'd often heard the MacGregor Chieftain and her brother rib each other with such remarks, but that had all been in fun.

Perhaps, Eoin was wary about pushing back when Aleck MacIain issued an insult. Unfortunate, she would have enjoyed hearing how he'd really wanted to respond—but then again, such a rebuttal could have set off another inordinately-serious courtyard sparring session.

Aleck stopped by the well and crossed his arms. "My spies reported seeing MacDonald galleys on the move—said they appear to be transporting items south."

Helen had no idea her husband had dispatched spies.

Eoin nodded and pointed his thumb over his shoulder. "The galleys were indeed heading south. We followed them all the way to the Isle of Colonsay."

"Close to the Isle of Islay—MacDonald's greatest holdings in southern waters." Aleck scratched his whiskers. "The king's concerns about a stir to the south must be founded."

"Aye. That's what took me so long. I sailed to Dunstaffnage to alert Lord Duncan and dispatch a missive to the king."

"We must set sail and join them," Aleck said, spreading his arms wide.

"Not yet." Eoin held up his palm. "I counted fifty-two galleys moored alongside Dunskeath in Sleat."

Aleck nodded as if he actually paid heed to the MacGregor Chieftain's words. "'Tis a good place to hide if you're building an army."

"My thoughts as well." Eoin narrowed his gaze. "You ken Clan Donald. My gut is telling me they're planning a siege along the entire west coast. Where would you guess they'd strike to the north?"

Aleck tugged on his beard. "They're sworn enemies with the MacKenzie—none too friendly with the MacLeods either."

"Agreed, and I'd also wager Alexander MacDonald wouldn't have been pleased after the king granted *you* Sunart lands."

"He'd never cross me." Aleck planted his fists on his hips. "If the bastard is so bold as to attack my lands, I'll murder him—set fire to his castles and put his family under my blade."

"Pardon? There is a lady present." Eoin flashed an apologetic glance at Helen—as if he were responsible for Aleck's vulgar tongue in front of a lady. "We need to be ready—ensure any battles remain far away from the womenfolk."

Helen tapped her fingers to her mouth and stifled her gasp. "Heavens, they wouldn't lay siege to Mingary, would they?"

"I'll not take anything for granted." Eoin started toward the keep. "I want to review where we've posted the spies."

Aleck threw up his hands and surged ahead. "We've stared at that map a hundred times."

"And we need to study it again. We've new information to process," Eoin said with an edge to his voice. "Unless you want Clan Donald scaling Mingary's walls."

With a deep grumble, Aleck shoved through the big double doors.

Helen hastened beside Eoin as they followed Aleck inside. "Do you think we're in imminent danger?"

He stopped and almost reached for her shoulders, but snatched his fingers away hastily. "We should be safe for the time being, but we must be careful. If you leave the castle, ensure you do so with a guard."

She wrung her hands. "Sir Grant or Mr. Keith always accompanies me regardless." She glanced over her shoulder. Aleck watched them from the stairwell with his arms crossed over his chest.

"I'd thought no less, but it is important to exercise additional caution. No one knows where they'll choose to strike next." Eoin's gaze also flickered toward Aleck.

Helen stepped nearer—but not improperly close. "B-but when do you *think* they'll attack?"

"I still believe the greater threat is to the south, but *if* they threaten Ardnamurchan lands, it will be before summer's end for certain."

"Soon, then?"

"Aye, I fear things are afoot." He grasped her hand and held it snugly between his warm palms. "Do not worry. Our spies will see them coming hours before they reach the castle."

"But Maggie—"

"Are you planning to stand there and cosset my wife all day?" Aleck bellowed from the stairwell.

Eoin gave her a squeeze and drew his hands away. "The bairn will be my first concern should there be any threat," he whispered.

"Thank you." Helen bowed her head, then clutched her fists to her chest and watched him disappear up the stairwell. Aleck followed, but not before he gave her an evil glare.

Helen threw her fists to her sides. *Curses to him. If only Aleck could show a modicum of concern for the bairn—and me for that matter. I received far more information from exchanging a few words with Sir Eoin than I have for the past year from my own husband.*

***

Eoin led the way to the chieftain's solar. He'd hoped the time apart had helped to assuage Aleck's ill will, but he should have realized MacIain liked being disagreeable. Eoin had seen similar behavior before and usually tried to steer clear of such unsavory characters. The only problem was he couldn't avoid Aleck MacIain on this mission. Mingary was the arse-licking boar's keep and Ardnamurchan his lands. Eoin was merely there to direct the army—a fact the miserable chieftain had seemed to have forgotten, or refused to accept.

Aleck marched in behind him and closed the door. "Why did you not stop here before proceeding to Dunstaffnage?"

Eoin strode to the oblong table and rotated the map to face him. "We practically had to sail past the castle on our return trip. It didn't make sense to double back and waste a day of sailing."

Aleck placed both hands on the table and leaned in. "I would have liked to have met with Campbell and heard what my brother-in-law had to say."

Eoin's shrugged. "I'll keep that in mind the next time I follow a pair of suspicious galleys sailing south."

"Do not patronize me," Aleck said with a shake of his finger.

Eoin pretended to study the map, but his jaw set tighter than a trigger for a snare. "I wouldn't dream of it." He'd rather challenge MacIain to a fair fight—though the chieftain had already proved he didn't understand the meaning of the word *fair*.

Aleck sauntered to the sideboard. "What is your interest in my wife?"

"Lady Helen?" Eoin tensed. What was the bastard up to now?

"I do not believe I've wedded any other woman," Aleck said while reaching for a flagon of whisky.

Eoin choked back the words on the tip of his tongue: it wasn't clear to whom Sir Aleck was wedded by his behavior with the widow. If only he could indeed follow such a remark by saying Aleck's indiscretions provided much gossip for the clan—ugly rumors were never good for the health of the men and women who served a chieftain. But Eoin opted to humor the dimwitted boar this time. "Lady Helen and I have been friends since childhood. You're aware her father fostered me? I consider her a sister, especially since I never had one, myself."

Aleck poured only one goblet. Eoin licked his lips, his mouth was dry, but he didn't expect MacIain to offer him a drink. Christ, he'd known more affable enemies. The cur took a sip and eyed Eoin. "I don't want to see you touch her again."

Eoin's fingers itched to ball a fist to slam across that smug chin. How many times in the past sennights had Aleck touched Lady Helen with tenderness? If only it were Eoin's place to ask. Rather than reply, he turned his attention to the map. "Lord Campbell increased the guard at Ornonsay Priory to keep an eye on MacDonald keeps on Colonsay and Islay, so we've no need to worry about anything to the south. The king has ten times the troops watching them there."

Aleck moved to the table and stood beside him. "I'd assume the same."

*MacIain is actually listening this time?* Eoin pointed. "Our spies are posted on Eigg, The Kyle of Lochalsh and on the northern point of Ardnamurchan." He moved his finger south and west past Mingary. "I think you need a lookout here in northern Sunart. We should be prepared for an overland attack."

"Have you got your head up your arse?" Aleck shook his skull with a tsk of his tongue. "MacDonald will not attack by land."

"No?" Eoin moved his finger a bit further north. "It wouldn't take much effort to march an army south from Tioram Castle."

Aleck threw back his whisky and swallowed. "I don't like the idea of splitting our forces."

"Agreed there—we're stronger if we stay together." Eoin tapped his finger on the region of Sunart—land recently acquired by MacIain—land he wouldn't want to forfeit to the marauding MacDonald. "Station a watch—three men with fast horses. Where's the highest point?"

"Beinn Resipol." Aleck scratched his beard. "It overlooks Loch Sunart to the south and Loch Schiel to the north."

"Excellent. Have them notify the local crofters to be on the lookout for MacDonald men. If they attack us from behind we'll be ready."

Aleck's expression grew dark. "I'm still not convinced we should waste our time covering our arses in the east. MacDonald wants the Lordship of the Isles back, not *my* lands."

"You think not?" Eoin met the belligerent man's stare. "As I recall, Sunart used to be under control of the Lord of the Isles—as was Mingary. You may very well be his first target on his way down the coast."

"'Tis possible that they try, but no one crosses me. Though Sunart was bequeathed to me by the king after I agreed to renounce the MacDonald name, my ancestors have been the Chieftains of Ardnamurchan for a good long time. No other clan within a hundred miles would try to attack me and my men. I have the king's backing and MacDonald knows it. If he attacks, I'll show him no quarter."

Eoin listened, but Aleck's bravado changed nothing. "Would you like to stand before the king with your bonnet in hand and explain why you allowed Clan Donald to take your lands?"

MacIain slammed his fist on the table. "That will never happen. I'll not allow it, and I'll not tolerate your coming into my keep, placing your soiled hands on my wife and telling me how to manage my men."

Eoin sauntered forward until he was within a hand's breadth of the bastard. Then he folded his arms and met the man eye-to-eye. Though Aleck was probably four stone heavier, they were the same height. "I'm here because our king requested my presence. As soon as this business is over, I'll gladly take my leave." Eoin's ire boiled too near the surface to hold his tongue any longer. "And as for your wife? If you'd pay a mind to your own bed rather to that of the merry widow, Lady Helen just might birth the son you've a yen for."

Gnashing his teeth, Aleck drew his fist back. But Eoin was faster. Before MacIain could follow through, Eoin clamped his fingers at the base of Aleck's neck—a maneuver he'd learned from the Black Knight—one that would cause excruciating pain.

MacIain grimaced and tried to twist away, but Eoin held the miserable buffoon in a viselike grip. "The king has ordered us together whether you like it or nay," he growled through clenched teeth. "I will see to the safety of this keep and the women and children within regardless of your bull-brained overconfidence."

Aleck dropped to his knees, sweat beading his brow.

Eoin tightened his fingers. "The next time we're in public together you *will* give me due respect, just as I pay to you."

With a push, he released his hold and strode out of the solar without a backward glance.

# Chapter Nine

Eoin stood beside Fergus while they supervised the construction of the platform on the Ardnamurchan galley. His men, Samuel and Willy walked past, carrying a stack of wooden planks.

"How much more timber do we need?" Eoin asked.

"I reckon one more load ought to do it," Samuel said, as he and Willy continued up the ramp of the MacIain galley.

"Look at us working like servants for bloody MacIain." Fergus folded his arms and spat. "I still think we should climb aboard our boat and head for home."

Eoin could barely hear him over the hammering. "I must admit the thought has crossed my mind more than once."

"Then why are we still here while the Lord of Glenorchy and the others rally their armies at Dunstaffnage? My oath, our men are doing the lion's share of the work."

"We'll be on our way soon enough. Just set your mind to the task at hand and remember we're fighting for the king, not the mule-brained Chieftain of Ardnamurchan."

"What's that you say, MacGregor?" Aleck grumbled from behind. If nothing else, MacIain had impeccable timing.

Eoin bristled and faced the cur. "Fergus and I were just discussing how nice it would be if your men joined us whilst we build the platform on *your* galley."

The laggard planted his fists on his hips like he owned all of Scotland. "You'd best not be doing anything to make her less seaworthy. That boat has sailed up and down the west coast of the Highlands with nary an issue."

"Aye," Eoin cocked his head and made a show of examining at the galley's hull. "By the looks of the mollusks adhered to your timbers, I'd say she's well past due for a refit. If you don't clean her up, you'll be lucky not to sink the next time you take her out, and the new cannon platform will not be the cause."

Aleck stepped closer to the boat and squinted. "There's nothing wrong with her."

Eoin shrugged. "She's your vessel."

"When will the deck be ready to mount the cannon?"

*Och aye, the lazy scoundrel would be interested once the hard labor is completed.* "Today with luck."

"Send someone to fetch me when she's aboard." He pointed up the curtain wall. "In the meantime, I'll be training my men to fire the big gun atop the battlements."

Eoin glanced up to the black cannon sticking though the crenel notch directly above them. "Just ensure you don't misfire that damned thing and hit one of us—or my galley."

Aleck stepped a wee bit too close. "Boar's ballocks, do you think I'm incompetent?"

*Aye, I ken you are.* Not about to be intimidated, Eoin leaned in. "If you've any experience with those newfangled guns, you'll know that they can misfire. Aim your sights out to the open sea and no one will end up dead."

"Bloody insolent milksop," Aleck grumbled as he turned and marched toward the keep.

"MacIain," Eoin called after him.

The man stopped and turned his ear.

"If you hit my galley, I'll expect you to pay for the reparations."

***

One of Helen's favorite pastimes was collecting shells along the Mingary beach. The melodic sound of waves rolling to and from shore soothed her. And as of late, her mind had been troubled. Aleck's clear disdain for her had grown much worse since Maggie's birth. Worse, his open affection for Mary was an affront that insulted Helen to her very core. The tactics she'd used in the past to seek congenial ground and subdue Aleck's temper seemed to be no longer effective. He'd grown more belligerent, negative and spiteful. She had no idea how she could live up to his expectations. It was as if he wanted her to fail.

She'd always tried so hard to maintain kinship and goodwill at Mingary—to ensure that Aleck and all of the clansmen and women lived harmoniously, but since Sir Eoin had arrived, there was an underlying tone of angst amongst everyone. Not that there was anything wrong with the Chieftain of Clan Gregor. Simply put, Aleck was jealous of Eoin, and resented his presence.

*Regrettably, that resentment has put an even greater strain on our relationship than there was before.*

Helen bent down to pick up a sea sponge, then held it up. *My, this is a large specimen. Glenda will be impressed for certain.* She placed it in her basket beside the flame shells she'd found earlier.

Overhead, a flock of black guillemots squawked. Helen watched the seabirds land on a rocky outcropping, the white feathers under their black wings flashing with their every flap. It reminded her of a ship's signal from across the sea.

At least spending an hour or two alone on the beach brought her peace and a welcomed respite from her worries.

Aside from Aleck's increased pugnaciousness, Helen enjoyed having Eoin at Mingary. He, too, could bring a moment's enjoyment simply with a smile, or a kind remark.

Eying a conical snail shell, she stooped to retrieve it.

*Boom!*

A blast from atop the battlements shook the ground. Helen's heart flew to her throat. Her entire body startled with a jolt. Before she could exhale, a high-pitched whistle soared through the air, growing increasingly louder.

She froze.

*It's heading straight for me.*

Before Helen could run, the cannonball thundered into the beach. Rocks and sand hurled into the air.

Flinging her hands over her head, Helen did her best to protect herself from the flying debris. She shrieked as stones and sand slammed into her body with such force she stumbled to the ground. Something hit her head, her arm, her shoulder. Everything hurt. She crumpled into a heap and wailed. Had she become so much of a failure, Aleck had decided to fire a cannonball at her?

"Lady Helen!" Eoin roared, sprinting along the beach.

She swiped a hand over her crown only to be met with warm moisture. Holding her palm in front of her face, it was covered with blood.

"My God." Eoin dropped to his knees beside her. "You've been hit."

"M-my head's bleeding." The world spun.

"Christ almighty, you've blood streaming down your face." He used the cuff of his shirt to dab it.

She hissed, her hands trembling out of control. "T-the cannon ball…ouch…and I didn't h-have time…and rocks h-hit me. And—"

"I know, lass. Where else does it hurt?"

Her mind raced. "Everywhere."

"Can you move your arms and legs?"

"I-I don't know."

Another blast boomed and whistled overhead.

"Get down, m'lady!" Eoin flung his body atop Helen, shoving her into the stony shore.

Her heart hammered so hard, it nearly burst from her chest. But Eoin protected her from another pummeling. The lead ball hit the surf this time, showering them with a spray of saltwater.

"Stop firing, you bastards!" Eoin yelled, rising to his knees and waving his arms over his head.

The men working on the galley all started hollering in a chorus to stop.

Eoin gathered Helen into his arms and stood. "I must carry you out of harm's way, then we'll see to your injuries."

He raced toward the sea gate. "Forgive…me for…being so familiar…m'lady," he said while sucking in deep breaths.

"'Tis all right." With her fists under her chin, she curled into him. "Thank you for coming to my aid, m'laird."

Another cannon shot boomed from the bailey wall.

Eoin nodded at his henchman. "Fergus, run up there and tell them Lady Helen has been injured. And tell them to look where they're aiming before they fire that blasted thing again."

He pushed into the courtyard and regarded her face. "I'd best see you inside, m'lady."

*If I allow him to carry me further, Aleck will launch into a rage*. "I think I can walk."

"Are you certain? You've had an awful blow to your head."

"Let me try."

Eoin carefully set Helen on her feet.

The courtyard spun and she wobbled. He grasped her elbow.

"Ow." She pulled her arm away and rubbed.

His eyebrows drew together with a concerned expression. "Your arm is hurt too?"

"Just bruised, I think."

He pressed his fingers to the edge of her hairline. "You're still bleeding and there's a nasty knot."

"Why the bloody hell are you touching my wife?" Aleck cupped his hands around his mouth and yelled from atop the wall-walk.

"You nearly killed her with your cannon fire," Eoin bellowed back at him.

Up on the battlements, Fergus trotted up to MacIain, flailing his arms and pointing in the direction the cannon fire.

Aleck threw up his hands and glared down at Helen. "Stay off the beach the next time we fire the cannons, you mindless wench!"

Wiping more blood from her forehead, Helen wanted to melt into the cobblestones and die. *Can I do nothing right?*

Eoin placed his palm in the small of her back. "Come, m'lady. We must apply a cloth to your head to staunch the bleeding."

Nodding, she couldn't bring herself to look up. Aleck had fired a cannon in her direction and then had berated her in front of everyone for being in the way? She tested her legs—at least nothing hurt so much she couldn't walk.

"Bring a bowl of water," Eoin ordered and grabbed a cloth from the kitchen workbench as he led her to the same antechamber where she had stitched up his wound. He pulled out a chair. "Please sit, m'lady."

Helen did as asked and buried her face in her hands. "I had no idea Aleck was planning to test the cannon today." Another boom ricocheted so loudly the entire chamber shuddered. She pressed her fingers against her temples. "My heavens, that thing is going to make the castle walls crumble."

Eoin chuckled. "I doubt it will. Mingary walls were built to withstand attacks by battering ram and catapult. I doubt the recoil from a cannon will do more than loosen a few masonry stones." He touched the cloth to her head.

"Sssss." Helen pulled back. "That hurts."

Peter came in with the water. "What on earth happened?"

"Lady Helen was thrashed by a cannon shot," Eoin replied, peering closely at her wound.

The cook set the bowl on the table beside them. "Do they not look and take aim before they fire that hideous contraption?"

Eoin dunked the cloth in the water. "Apparently not around these parts." He wrung it out. "This might sting a bit, but I must cleanse away the blood so I can see how bad the cut is."

"Very well." Helen remained very still while he carefully dabbed her head. "Is it bad?"

He leaned forward and looked closer. "'Tis nowhere near as bad as I thought. Cuts to the head can bleed something fierce." He looked at her eyes. "Does your head hurt?"

"'Tis throbbing a bit. Perhaps I should have Peter bring in some willow bark tea."

"Once you're situated in your rooms I'll ask him to send some up with chamomile added to calm your wits. You had quite a fright."

She clapped a hand over her mouth and blinked back her tears. "Aye." But her humiliation dove far deeper than the initial fear she'd felt on the beach. "Why could he not utter one word of apology?"

Eoin's lips formed a straight line and he shifted his gaze aside, as if there were a great deal he wanted to say but chose to hold his tongue. Helen wasn't sure she wanted to hear it—most likely, he pitied her. *Oh poor, forlorn Helen whose husband is a roguish beast. Too bad she was sent to Mingary for an arranged marriage and ended up an unhappy matron.* Well, she needed no one's pity.

She started to stand, but Eoin put his hand on her shoulder. "Sometimes people do things that are nonsensical. In my opinion, your husband has acted abominably and should apologize profusely."

She drew in a sharp breath. "Oh no, you mustn't approach Aleck and ask him to apologize to me. It would put him in an unimaginably foul mood. He'd lash out at you for certain." Then she looked away. "And me," she whispered, praying Eoin wouldn't think less of her for such an admission.

"I do not fear anything Aleck MacIain can dole out, but if he were to further raise a hand against you on account of this incident, I'd…I'd kill him."

"Please, Sir Eoin, promise me you'll not confront him. I will check with the guard before I take a walk on the beach to ensure they won't be firing the cannons."

He flung his arm in the direction of the courtyard. "But—"

"Please let it lie."

He regarded her for a moment with a hard line forming along his jaw. "If that is what you wish."

Daring to reach out, she lightly brushed her fingers over his heart. "It is. No good can come of calling him out. No good at all."

# Chapter Ten

Helen hummed while she wrapped Maggie in linen swaddling clothes. She'd embroidered this set with a border of yellow primroses during her confinement. "I have decided 'tis time the lass was introduced to the clan." *Regardless of what Aleck thinks.*

Sarah twirled Maggie's black tresses around her finger. The bairn's hair had grown just long enough to make a darling curl atop her head. "You chose a good day for it with the minstrels coming—twill be a grand gathering."

Maggie wiggled with a darling squeal. She raised her head twice as if she wanted to be picked up. Helen's heart squeezed. After she tucked in the end of the swaddle to secure it, she gathered the babe into her arms. "Hopefully the extra bit of cloth we've stuffed between her legs will keep her from piddling through the fabric."

Sarah chuckled. "I do not think you can count on it, m'lady. Piddling is what wee ones do best."

Maggie laughed. The joy in her tiny infant voice tickled Helen's insides and she chuckled. Oh, how this little one could warm her heart.

Helen gaped at the nursemaid with a wide-mouthed smile. "I think she agrees with you."

Holding out her arms, Sarah inclined her head to the bairn. "We'd better haste to the great hall. You wouldn't want to be late and upset the chieftain."

Helen placed Maggie in the nursemaid's arms, then straightened her red silk veil. "We do not want to do *anything* to raise Sir Aleck's ire."

"Not to worry, m'lady." Sarah started for the door. "As soon as Sir Aleck sees Miss Maggie, his heart will melt."

Helen opened the door and followed the nursemaid out. "I hope you are right."

"Who wouldn't instantly fall in love with such a darling face? Her blue eyes and black curls will enchant everyone in the hall."

"I do like your exuberance." Helen followed Sarah down the stairwell. "Now remember—we're to parade her around the hall and then take Maggie to the dais. We don't want to overdo her premier appearance. At the first sign of fussiness, spirit her back to the nursery."

"All right, m'lady."

"And we mustn't whirl around the hall like we're dancing a reel. Wait for me at the bottom of the stairwell." Goodness, Helen shouldn't be this nervous. As they descended the wheel-stairs, the noise from the crowd grew louder. She drew in a calming breath just as she rounded the last few steps. "Let us wait at the back of the hall until they notice us."

"Aye, m'lady." Sarah grinned. "They'll be overcome with ooh's and ah's any moment."

Helen grasped Sarah's elbow and together they stepped into the great hall. As usual on the third Friday of the month, there was excitement in the air. The men told their stories with more animation and the women laughed with a hearty fullness in their voices. Yes, everyone knew the minstrels would play and there would be dancing and drink aplenty.

Looking out over the hall, the servants noticed them first. They stood at attention, gazing Helen's way. Gradually, the hum of voices ebbed. Upon the dais, Aleck pushed back his chair and stood. Eoin followed suit.

When Aleck planted his fists on his hips, Helen gulped. But it was time. Miss Maggie would not be imprisoned in the nursery for the duration of her childhood. Helen gestured to the bairn and smiled. "Please allow me to introduce Miss Margaret Alice MacIain."

As if on cue, the bairn squealed while Sarah raised her elbow so the crowd could better see Maggie's face. Everyone audibly sighed at once.

"She's a handsome bairn for certain," someone called from the crowd.

"She has the chieftain's tresses."

"Aye but her mother's beauty."

Indeed, the clansmen and women gushed with admiration.

Helen gestured to Sarah and together they proceeded through the center aisle slowly so everyone could take a good look at Maggie. As they neared the dais, Aleck's fists remained on his hips, his face unreadable.

*I will not allow him to intimidate me.*

Raising her skirts to her ankles, Helen ascended the stairs with Sarah following. Aleck strode to her side, but didn't offer his hand. Instead he pressed his lips to Helen's ear. "I told you I didn't want to see the bairn."

Helen turned to the crowd and spread her arms to address them. "I thought there would be no better time than a gathering with music and dancing to introduce Maggie to the clan."

Sarah held the bairn to Aleck, giving him no option but to reach out and cradle her. He looked up with a forced smile. "What the clan needs is a lad," Aleck growled, none too softly.

"You'd best head above stairs and make one, m'laird," a male voice bellowed from the crowd.

All went silent.

Helen could have withered where she stood. *Please let there not be a scene*. She clapped a hand over her mouth and scanned the faces to see who had uttered such a bold remark, but no one stood out.

"Mind your own affairs," Aleck groused.

Maggie's face grew red and she launched into an ear-splitting wail.

Aleck thrust the babe toward Sarah. "Take the brat back up to the nursery. She has no business in the hall until she can sit at the table and hold a knife in her hand."

Shrieking at the top of her lungs, Maggie didn't settle. Sarah shot Helen a panicked grimace, as if she'd just been scolded by a humongous troll.

Helen stepped in, smoothed a hand over her daughter's crown. She would see that Maggie's first appearance ended on a positive note. "Thank you, dear Sarah," she said so all could hear. "Maggie made quite an impression for her first appearance and I am ever so happy to have your assistance. I believe it is time for her to retire now."

Sarah dipped into a brisk curtsey. "As you wish, m'lady."

Helen affixed her regal smile while Sarah proceeded to the stairwell with the howling Maggie. Honestly, the wee cry was music to a mother's ears. The clansmen and women also watched and applauded appreciatively. Besides, no one ever expected a bairn to be silent.

When Helen turned to the high table, Aleck had resumed his seat, but Eoin remained standing. In two strides, he took her hand and led her to the lady's chair. Helen recalled her father had paid such a courtesy to her mother often.

"Miss Maggie is delightful, m'lady." Eoin grinned as if nothing were amiss—as if it were a common occurrence for the chieftain to shun his daughter and ignore his wife. "Thank you for bringing her for an introduction."

Helen took her seat. "I'm ever so glad you approve, Sir Eoin."

Aleck gestured to the empty chair with his knife. "Sit your arse down, MacGregor, and stop acting like you're groveling to the Queen of Scotland."

Eoin's pleasant exterior waned. "This is a well anticipated gathering is it not?"

"Aye, everyone enjoys the minstrels when they come." Aleck poured himself a tankard of whisky. Evidently, he'd decided ale wasn't strong enough this eve.

Eoin reached for the bread. "I, too, enjoy music and dancing."

Aleck snorted. "You seem like the type who would prefer to kick up your heels and rub elbows with the lassies rather than take part in more manly pursuits."

Stopping mid-chew, Eoin rolled his eyes toward the chieftain. "Let us say I enjoy all manner of pursuits."

Aleck took a long draw from his tankard. "Do you enjoy swivving buxom lassies?"

*How utterly inappropriate*. Helen's face burned. If only she could slide under the table and hide, but she could never do that, and chiding Aleck would only serve to rouse him further.

Without a modicum of emotion etched on his face, Eoin reached for the ewer of ale and filled his cup. "With all due respect, this is not suitable conversation for mixed company."

"So you consider it appropriate banter for an alehouse, do you?" Aleck threw his head back and laughed.

*Could things grow worse?* Helen glanced at the faces of the clansmen at the table. Every single face appeared uncomfortable and not a one looked her way.

Suddenly not hungry, she pushed her food around her trencher to the sound of idle chatter from the crowd. Still, no one on the dais uttered a word. When she at last looked up, Aleck eyed her from behind his tankard. She tensed as he leaned forward to speak. "If you continue to disobey me, I'll have no recourse but to lock you in your chamber."

She drew away from his foul-smelling breath. "You wouldn't."

Aleck scowled. "Now that you've asked to go to Iona, how will I know you will not run?"

"Mayhap I'd already be away if I had."

A tic twitched under his eye. "Do not use an insolent tone with me."

Helen pursed her lips and stared down at her lap. *Must he grow more disagreeable by the day?* She glanced at Eoin. He offered an apologetic shrug of his shoulders.

"What about hunting?" she asked, blurting out the first thing that came to mind. "I enjoy a good hunt with a bow and arrow."

Eoin appeared to appreciate the change in subject. "As I recall, your marksmanship is admirable."

She smiled.

"We could put her atop the bailey walls if there was a siege." Aleck swayed in his chair and laughed at his ill-placed humor.

*How much whisky has he consumed?*

"I'll pray that will not be necessary," Eoin said, but he glared at Helen's husband like the Chieftain of Ardnamurchan must be completely daft.

Aleck picked beneath his thumbnail with his eating knife. "You're soft, MacGregor."

*Heaven help Sir Eoin to maintain his calm.*

Her prayers were dashed when she shifted her gaze his way. Helen had seen the look on Sir Eoin's face once—right before he and her brother launched into a real fight—one stopped only by six armed guards. She couldn't even remember why the two friends had attacked each other with such ferocity. Though the reason no longer mattered, she knew Eoin to be deadly when provoked. Every muscle in her body tensed while the dais filled with silence.

Across the hall, the music started.

*Thank the good Lord.*

Helen clapped her hands, praying the minstrels would pull Aleck from his foul mood.

Eoin raised his tankard, his jaw set. "Do you enjoy dancing, Sir Aleck, or does that not appeal to your bull-brained audaciousness."

Helen froze. *God save us, there'll be a brawl for certain.*

Aleck squinted. "Are you in…" He belched. "…sulting me?"

"Insult the generous chieftain of this fine keep?" Eoin spread his arms wide. "Nay, nay. I'd never consider such an offense."

Aleck shook his eating knife as he swayed in his seat. "You'd best not."

"I see you've musicians this eve." Eoin changed the topic and sat a bit straighter. "It would be ever so enjoyable to watch you give your wife a turn on the dance floor."

Helen tightly clasped her hands under her chin. "Oh no, Sir Aleck doesn't care to dance."

Her husband guzzled more whisky, the tankard weaving before he set it down. "Dancing is for lasses before they marry. A young buck has no need to strut like a preening peacock after he's bedded a woman."

Helen gaped, completely horrified at his remark. Yes, Aleck had always been brazen, but his behavior this eve topped all tasteless babble.

That deadly glint return to Eoin's eyes. "I strongly disagree. I've watched women—er—people of all ages enjoy a good reel." He stood, bowed and offered his hand. "May I have this dance, Lady Helen?"

She risked a startled glance at Aleck. He rolled his hand through the air. "Go on. If you want to kick up your heels like an alehouse tart, don't let me be the one to stop you."

Helen pushed back her chair and stood. "I beg your pardon? I have *never* set foot inside an alehouse." Before Aleck could make another snide remark that would embarrass her to her toes, she snatched Eoin's hand and pulled him to the dais steps. "I will enjoy this dance if it slays me."

The MacGregor Chieftain chuckled. "'Tis good to hear, m'lady." He offered his elbow. "No woman dressed in such style should be required sit idle while dancing music plays."

"My sentiments exactly." Helen had a great deal of difficulty maintaining her serene countenance. By the saints, Aleck had irritated her. Why couldn't he have commented on Maggie's beauty? Why did he sit on the dais and brood, pouring whisky down his gullet? Did he hate her? Surely he did and, if so, why had he not allowed her to retire to Iona? The man reveled in making other people uncomfortable or unhappy and he'd only grown worse since Eoin MacGregor had arrived with his army.

*'Tis bittersweet to see an old friend. On one hand, I've ever so enjoyed having him as a guest, but I believe it would be best if the MacDonald uprising were quashed soon. The longer Sir Eoin remains, the more likely there will be a serious confrontation between the two chieftains.*

Eoin led her to the line of women and took the place across from her in the line of men. He looked dashing, wearing a plaid, shirt and leather doublet. Sarah had been right—the patchwork in his shirt wouldn't be noticeable, especially when covered by a doublet.

He grinned.

Merciful heavens, Aleck had never grinned at her like that. When Helen met her husband, it had been their wedding night, and that was disastrous. He'd soused himself with whisky and bumbled through copulation, which completely mortified her. Helen had been embarrassed to show her face in the great hall for an entire season. Fortunately, he only visited her chamber a few times a year. Doubtless, such an arrangement exceeded the bounds of the ordinary. After all, she wasn't completely ignorant of the world. There were clansmen and women—married folk—who seemed to enjoy coupling. And she'd happened upon more than one guard with a moaning woman in his arms.

Helen never moaned—gritted her teeth and bore Aleck's brutal thrusts, was more like it. Perhaps she was just one of those "frigid" women who would never enjoy copulation. She'd heard about that, too. Oh, the many things a lady of the keep overhears when supervising a bevy of servants.

She locked arms with Eoin and skipped in a circle.

"Are you all right, m'lady?"

"Of course." She feigned a smile. "Why would you ask?"

"I thought for a moment you might be unhappy with the prospect of dancing with me." He pointed to his feet. "As I recall, you were ten and six when you told me I'd never learn my left from my right."

She laughed out loud—only Eoin MacGregor could pull her from melancholy and make her chuckle. "Oh my heavens, I was the most atrocious lass at ten and six. I acted as if I were the Queen of Sheba."

"Not at all. You were right and I spent a fortnight practicing before I allowed your mother to talk me into partnering in your dancing lessons again."

Oh, how many fond memories his words brought. "Dearest Mother. She always had a way of bending you lads to her will."

"That she did." They parted and continued to their respective lines. When they once again faced each other, he hadn't lost his jovial grin. "You were about ten and six when I really first noticed you."

"Honestly?" Helen thought back. "But hadn't you started partnering with us years before that?"

He stepped in and clasped her hands. "Aye." The look in his eyes grew dark.

She watched his face while they sashayed through the tunnel of dancers. Her mouth suddenly went dry and her midsection was attacked by a swarm of fluttering dragonflies. They had to be dragonflies rather than butterflies because the sensation was completely unnatural. She dare not question him about his meaning.

*He hadn't noticed me before I'd turned ten and six?*

They exited the tunnel and parted. Helen clapped a hand over her mouth, the full significance of his words dawning on her.

All this time she'd believed the looks of longing across the hall were frivolous one-sided yens of a silly maiden. Had he actually returned her affections—even a little? Not that it mattered now, but to know they'd once shared something deeper than mere friendship. Helen's heart thrummed. Perhaps that would make tolerating Aleck's abuse a wee bit more palatable.

When she rejoined the line and faced Eoin, she didn't have to feign her smile. Nothing in all of Christendom could wipe the grin off her face.

Again they joined elbows. "I believe dancing agrees with you," Eoin said.

She took in a refreshing breath. "I think you are right. I'd forgotten how much I enjoyed it."

He smiled down at her with eyes shining, just as she'd remembered him doing years ago. "I meant what I said. People of all ages should dance. 'Tis invigorating—makes the heart rush and one's breathing speed. I think 'tis good for the soul."

When the music ended, all of the dancers laughed and clapped. Helen held her hands out to the minstrels. "May we have another reel, please?"

The fiddler bowed. "Certainly, m'lady."

She clasped her hands together and faced Eoin. "Do you think your heart can withstand another lively dance?"

"There's no question about the power of my heart." He grinned ever so warmly. "But are you up to another?"

"Me? Why I'm only getting started."

He tugged at her veil. "Perhaps this time your matronly head covering might fly away in a spin."

She touched her hands to her veil. "You jest." She stole a glance to the dais. The chieftain wasn't paying the slightest bit of attention while he nuzzled into Mary's ear—and the widow had again moved to Helen's chair.

*Why am I fretting about what he thinks?*

She tugged the suffocating veil from her head and cast it to a nearby table. "There. Now we no longer need to worry about it."

"Bravo, a woman with your beauty certainly needs no head covering." Eoin's gaze darted to the dais as well. He growled before he returned his attention to Helen. But this time, they danced in silence. Helen's emotion ran the gamut—first to humiliation and anger that her husband was up on the dais fawning over his leman—then to exhilaration that she was dancing with unabashed fervor for the first time since she arrived at Mingary Castle. At last, she opted to revel in the moment. With her hair unbound and brushing her hips, she felt free and unfettered. It reminded her of the days when Helen and her sister, Gyllis, were still maids, running up the Kilchurn tower stairs and watching the guard spar in the courtyard while the wind blew through their long tresses.

Eoin had been one of the knights in the courtyard, as had Sean MacDougall, Gyllis's husband.

When the music stopped, Eoin took her hand. "You look deep in thought."

"Aye." She sighed. "Just remembering the years at Kilchurn."

The minstrels began a slow almain. Eoin grasped her hand, leading her in the stately dance as if it were second nature for him. "Fond memories?"

"Very much so. I miss my sisters. Gyllis especially."

"Ah yes, the two of you were very close." The rough pads of Eoin's fingertips plied her hand while they danced in a circle. Step-hop, step-hop.

She smiled at him. "I love this dance."

"Aye, it can be very stimulating with the right partner."

She stopped. "I hope I am not keeping you from seeking out a more *entertaining* lass."

He reached for her hand and pulled her step-hopping in the other direction. "Nay, m'lady. There is no other person with whom I'd rather be dancing this night."

*No?* "Why have you not married after all these years?"

He chuckled. "Because either the king or your brother has me running sorties all over Scotland. I've scarcely had the time to think about it."

"But you've been to court."

"Aye."

"I think we should find you a wife."

He shot her a wee frown. "Pray Lady Helen, I'd prefer to find my own wife."

The food churned in her stomach. "Have you someone in mind?"

"Not yet."

She knew she shouldn't press, but couldn't help but ask. "Not ever?"

He shrugged. "No one who ever stuck."

*Good Lord, what did he mean by that?*

They danced through one song after another and Helen never tired. At the end of a high-steeping reel, she dipped into a curtsey and fanned her face.

"Are you enjoying dancing with my wife, MacGregor?" Aleck groused from behind Helen.

Her back tensed as if someone had just run a block of ice along her spine.

Eoin straightened from his bow. "You would have been welcome to cut in at any moment."

The two men regarded each other with leery eyes, but Aleck swayed—and smelled pickled. He faced the thinning crowd and clapped his hands while swaying in place. "The hour is late. Good m-morrow."

*He's in his cups for certain.*

Helen searched for Mary. The nasty widow was still sitting in Helen's chair, watching them as if a spectator at the Highland games.

"Come, Helen," Aleck said loudly as he clamped his fingers around her wrist. "You've frolicked with Sir Eoin enough for one night."

The stragglers in the hall stared.

Helen cast an apologetic look at Eoin. "Thank you for dancing with me. It was most invigorating."

The muscles in Eoin's jaw tightened and his eyes grew dark—deadly. But he smiled at her and bowed his head. "The pleasure was mine, m'lady."

"Bloody frivolities," Aleck grumbled as he pulled her to the stairwell. Helen tried to yank her wrist from his grasp, but he tightened his grip. She could never imagine Aleck gently holding her hand in an almain. She couldn't imagine him dancing with her at all. *If he did, it would be with a grudging scowl on his face.*

She hastened her step to keep from being dragged. "Why do you not dance with me?"

He continued up the steps. "I don't care for dancing."

"But I do."

"Mayhap that's why I allowed that sniveling maggot to fawn all over you." He exited the stairwell and pulled Helen to her chamber door.

*Surely he isn't planning to go inside.* "Are you well m'lord?"

"I'm bloody fine." He opened the door and pushed her in. "You dishonored me with your making merry." He held up her discarded veil. "You are a married woman and yet you bared your tresses in front of the entire clan."

Her face grew hot. "You dare criticize me?" Clenching her fists, Helen refused to look away from his angry stare. She didn't care if he towered over her by a foot and looked like an overstuffed black boar. She would not tolerate his scorn behind closed doors. "I have watched you fawn all over that woman, *that whore*, for ages, and you have the audacity to confront me about dancing at a gathering?"

"Your place is not to question me but to obey."

"Is it now? I am to remain taciturn and non-communicative in infinitum whilst you spend your days within Mary's cottage? And presently you do not even try to be secretive about your infidelity."

His eyes had taken on a red hue, but that only served to make him appear more hideous. He grabbed her fingers and squeezed while he leaned forward, his sour breath oozing over Helen's face. "Mary is my business and you will *never* speak ill of her." Though his words slurred a bit, he'd been perfectly clear, especially with his bone-breaking grip.

But Helen ground her teeth and bore the pain. "Is that so? Do you know how humiliating it is to be gazing out the window with Sarah while you're adjusting yourself when leaving Mary's cottage?"

He stepped in with a deadly glint in his eye. "I—"

"No. I'll not listen to another overbearing word." Helen snatched her hand away and skittered from his unpredictable right-handed slap. "What about slinging your arm around Mary's shoulder and kissing her after disembarking from your galley? Bless it, Aleck. The entire clan watched you."

He sauntered forward, swaying a bit. "You are a bitter shrew." As he neared, her nostrils filled with the stench of distilled spirit mingled with sour male sweat. "I ought to still your tongue with the iron branks and lock you in the dungeon."

Helen inched backward until she bumped into the table. Three years past, he'd imprisoned her in the iron branks for a whole day. Every time she swallowed, the metal contraption holding her tongue cut a little deeper. No, she shouldn't have held forth so boldly, but so much angst had built up of late, she had no recourse but to confront him.

"No." She shook her head, trying to keep her tears at bay. "N-no..." She couldn't lose her courage now.

With a mean growl, Aleck lunged and snatched her arm.

Helen tried to yank away. He raised his palm. With a screech, she recoiled, but his slap connected with stinging force. Reeling backward, Helen stumbled into the table, grasping it to maintain her balance. Her fingers wrapped around a candlestick.

Aleck grabbed her by the hair and yanked her into the center of the floor. "You *will* obey me."

Before she could twist away, he latched a hand around her throat. Helen couldn't breathe. His torturous fingers dug into her voice box. She screamed, but only emitted a choking croak. The room spun. With a surge of courage, Helen swung the candlestick with all her might, twisting enough to bash him in the temple.

He released his grasp and tottered backward.

"Help!" Helen shrieked, praying someone might hear. She stood square and faced him, brandishing her makeshift weapon with both hands, prepared to defend herself against another strike. Aleck's red eyes grew wide as if stunned. Then they rolled up. Toppling backward, he thudded to the floor with a resounding boom.

Helen gasped, clutching the candlestick for dear life, her entire body trembling. *Merciful father, what have I done?* She looked at the weapon in her hands. *I didn't think I hit him that hard.*

The door opened. Her candlestick clattered to the floorboards as Helen's gaze snapped up. Glenda led Sir Eoin into the chamber and quickly shut the door.

A tear dribbled from Helen's eye as she gestured toward Aleck's body. "I-I didn't mean to hurt…" She clutched her throat. "H-he was choking me—and then I-I."

Eoin knelt and patted Aleck's face. The big man moaned and licked his lips. "He's drunk."

Standing with her back to the door, Glenda clapped her hands together. "Thank heavens. Forgive me for intruding, m'lady, but when I heard the commotion, I ran to fetch Grant, but Sir Eoin was the first man I saw…"

Eoin stood. "Thank you for alerting me, matron. You may return to your quarters. I'll see to it Sir Aleck makes it to his bed."

"Aye." She curtseyed and looked to Helen. "If you do not need me for anything else, m'lady?"

"N-no."

Eoin held the door. "Please keep this incident in your confidence. I wouldn't want anyone bearing false witness against your lady. Sir Aleck fell because he is in his cups."

"Of course. I'll not tell a soul." She leaned forward. "'Tis about time Lady Helen stood up to him. I'll own to that fact even if it earns me a month in the dungeon."

"You are a good woman." Eoin patted her shoulder. "Good morrow."

"Are you certain you don't need me, m'lady?" Glenda cast a worried look to Helen.

"I'll be fine." At least Helen's breathing had returned to normal, though her hands still shook. "I'll see you on the morrow."

After he showed Glenda out, Eoin closed the door and faced Helen, but his expression had changed. His expressive eyes reflected the same myriad of emotions churning in Helen's breast.

Needing to explain, she spread her arms. "I—"

Before she blinked, Eoin enveloped her in a sheltering embrace.

# Chapter Eleven

Eoin shouldn't have run to Lady Helen and gathered her in his arms, but she looked so vulnerable standing there trembling, her face stricken. However, now that his arms surrounded her, he couldn't bring himself to let go.

She huddled into him, still shaking like a frightened kitten. "I do not know what came over me, b-but he slapped my face, and I fell into the table. And then he-he-he wrapped his fingers around my neck. And-and I don't know how I ended up with the candlestick, but I swung it at him to make him stop cho-k-ing meeeee."

Sobs racked her body, and he held her tighter, wishing to God Glenda had fetched him sooner. If Aleck wanted a fight, Eoin would have been a more apt opponent.

"There, there," he soothed, pressing his lips to the top of her head and closing his eyes. Who in their right mind would raise a finger against lovely Lady Helen? Beautiful, gentle, unpretentious Helen. Her fragrance alone was sweeter than an entire meadow abloom with heather. A willowy woman, she seemed so frail in his embrace. If he squeezed too taut, she might snap. This precious jewel of a noblewoman needed to be put on a pedestal, protected and admired.

She coughed. "My throat still hurts."

Forcing himself to release his embrace, he cupped her face. Helen winced. Knitting his brows, Eoin examined her. She had a red mark along her cheek bone, with purple spreading beneath. *The monster.* "It looks like you'll have another bruise."

"Not again," she groaned.

Eoin's gaze trailed downward and he hissed. "Sir Aleck's fingerprints have left bruises on your neck as well."

She covered her throat with her hand. "Is it bad?"

"'Tis a bloody outrage if you ask me. A knight takes an oath to protect women—to honor them. This is a disgrace against you and against the code of chivalry. I ought to—"

"But Aleck will severely punish anyone who tries to stand up to him." Her voice warbled with fear. "He's lord of these lands."

"Aye, but he's not lord over Scotland, nor is he God's emissary on earth."

She pressed her fingertips to her lips. "Whatever do you mean?"

"The Pope, m'lady. No woman should be forced to suffer the brutish hand of her husband and only the Pope can free you from this unbearable marriage."

She swayed in place, covering her mouth with her hand. "An annulment?" she uttered the abomination in a whisper.

He reached out and brushed away the lock of hair covering her eye. "Aye."

"Aleck would kill me first—he said so himself."

"Not if you had my protection."

She stepped away from him and paced, clutching her arms around her stomach. "But I have Maggie to think of. I can *never* leave Mingary without my daughter. I am the only person who will look out for her."

"No one would expect you to give up your child to a tyrant." Eoin grasped her hand. "Please. Allow me to help you."

Uncertainty and fear shadowed her eyes as she cast her gaze to the brute still flat on his back.

Aleck moaned and snorted.

Eoin hastened to MacIain's side. Good, he hadn't roused from his drunken stupor.

Helen stepped beside him. "Are you sure he'll be all right?"

"With a bull's head like his? The only thing that will be ailing him come morn is a nasty ache in his skull caused by guzzling too much whisky."

"Oh dear, that'll make him angrier than a badger." Helen grimaced. "And I'll wager he'll blame me."

Eoin, kicked the bottom of Aleck's foot with no result. "Perhaps not if we spirit him to his bed. When he wakes, he'll have no idea how he arrived there."

"But he'll suspect I had something to do with it."

"He mightn't even remember what happened."

"I hope you are right." She didn't appear to be convinced, but Eoin needed to move Aleck out of her chamber. If the bastard awoke on her floor, she'd be punished for certain.

"Is there a door between your chambers?"

She pointed. "Nay—his chamber is the next one along the passageway."

Eoin scratched his chin. "Unfortunate."

Helen tapped her fingers to her lips. "He mustn't stay here. You are right about that. If we can slip out quietly, no one will be the wiser. Aleck only posts a guard at the stairwell."

"The one I walked past on my way up here?"

"Aye, most likely."

"A great deal of protection he'll provide. He was slumped over and sound asleep."

Eoin grasped Aleck's arm and pulled him to a sitting position. The chieftain's head dropped forward and he snored. *Such a display of exemplary boorishness.*

Helen clapped a hand to her chest. "How do you think you'll lift him? Sir Aleck's an awfully large man."

Eoin grinned. "After years of rescuing your brother from every peril imaginable, I think I can carry this bear to the next room." *But it's damn near going to break my back.* Eoin planted his feet and heaved, swallowing his urge to bellow as he lifted.

Once Aleck's body was up, Eoin crouched and slid his shoulder under him. "Go," he strained through gritted teeth.

*God's teeth, the bastard must weigh twenty stone.*

Helen pattered ahead and opened the doors. The sinews in Eoin's neck strained. He either was going soft or Aleck MacIain was the heaviest blighter he'd ever carried.

Once inside the chieftain's chamber, Eoin staggered to the bed and unfolded MacIain onto the mattress.

Helen lifted the man's legs and pushed them onto the bed.

Watching her touch the overstuffed codfish made his gut clench. He didn't care if MacIain was Helen's husband, the bastard hadn't earned the right to be tended by her loving hands.

She removed his shoes and covered him with the plaid from the end of the bed. "I don't suppose there's much else we can do for him."

"Nay. The best thing for him is sleep."

Again she wrapped her arms around her midriff, then turned full circle as if looking at the chieftain's chamber for the first time. Lit only by the fire in the hearth and a candle flickering on the mantel, she shuddered. "I hate it in here."

Eoin didn't need to ask why. He placed his palm in the small of her back and ushered her through the passageway to the lady's chamber door.

Helen placed her hand on the latch but hesitated. "I do not know how to thank you, Sir Eoin. Your kindness has exceeded all bounds."

He brushed the back of his finger along her smooth, unbruised cheek. "If only I could do more."

She caught his fingers and brushed her lips over them. Then with a squeeze, she released his hand. "Sleep well."

He bowed. "I shall see you on the morrow, m'lady."

He waited until she slipped inside. Then he raised the hand she'd kissed and pressed it to his lips. The lady mightn't ever end up wrapped in his arms again, but after this eve's events, Eoin vowed to henceforth protect her.

***

Helen awoke when Glenda drew aside the window furs. A cock crowed and Helen pulled a pillow over her head. "It cannot possibly be morning." Helen's throat hurt and her voice rasped.

"'Tis time to break your fast m'lady," the chambermaid said with too much enthusiasm.

With a groan, Helen sat up and pushed the bedclothes aside. "Brr. There's a cold wind coming from the window."

"Aye, it looks like it might rain." Glenda held up Helen's dressing gown. "Are you still planning to go to the village today, m'lady? You sound like you might be coming down with a sore throat."

"I'm fine." Yes, her voice was a tad gravelly, but it was Saturday. Helen visited the village with food and her medicine basket every Saturday. "Everyone would miss me if I didn't go. Besides, I'd like to spend a day away from Mingary." *If only I could tell her how much I'd like to get away.* Helen donned the dressing gown and then grimaced, tapping her fingers to her tender jaw.

"Are you hurt, m'lady?"

"I'll come good in a day or two."

Glenda placed her palms either side of Helen's face. "Let me have a look."

Helen flicked up the neckline of the robe to cover her neck. No use causing a stir about the fingerprint bruises as well.

"Lord in heaven, he's given you another bruise."

Helen pulled away. "'Twas just a slap."

"Just? Pardon me for speaking my mind, m'lady, but Sir Aleck should never raise a hand against you. 'Tis just not right."

Helen looked to the tray with a bowl of porridge and a cup of mead awaiting her on the table by the hearth. "I'll set to eating if you could brush out my blue kirtle and cloak."

Glenda didn't budge. "I do not understand why you always pretend nothing is wrong. From the noise coming from this chamber last eve, I was afraid Sir Aleck was going to do more than slap you."

Helen sat and stared at her porridge. "It was that bad?"

"Why else would I barge in with an armed knight in my wake?"

"Thank you." Helen sighed and looked her chambermaid in the eye. "I have no idea what I would have done…" *Devil's bones, I'll not start weeping again.*

"I believe Sir Aleck has grown more short-tempered since Miss Maggie was born."

Helen picked up her spoon and nodded. Glenda was right, but there wasn't anything Helen could do about it.

"Mayhap 'tis the MacGregor army." *He must feel threatened as well.*

"Who knows?" Glenda held up her finger. "But I'll say it was fortunate Sir Eoin was about last eve."

"It was," Helen said, doing her best to be vague. Even Glenda could make a slip, inciting unwanted rumors.

"What happened after he sent me away?" she persisted.

Helen pretended to flick a bit of lint from her sleeve. "We took Sir Aleck to his chamber and put him to bed."

"Heavens." The chambermaid fanned her face with a brisk wave of her hand. "If only Sir Eoin were our chieftain."

Helen looked up, affecting disdain. "Glenda, what a horrible thing to say." Though Helen admonished her maid, she couldn't deny she felt the same. Still, some thoughts should *never* be uttered.

"Apologies for speaking out of turn, m'lady." She opened the trunk and held up the kirtle. "Come, 'tis time to dress."

Helen took one last swallow from her cup of mead and stood.

Glenda gasped and stared directly at Helen's neck. "My heaven's m'lady, you've hand prints on your throat."

*Curses, the blasted dressing gown slipped.* Helen moved to the looking glass and examined the purple bruises. "Only high-collared gowns for the next fortnight." She tried to sound jovial.

Glenda harrumphed. "How you can be so unconcerned about nearly being choked to death is beyond me."

Helen was very concerned. She was beside herself. Aleck actually had tried to choke her. What *would* have happened if Glenda hadn't intervened? A Cold chill slithered up her spine. What might happen if he struck out against Maggie? She hated to think of it.

After pulling off Helen's dressing gown, Glenda eyed her expectantly. In no way would it be proper for Helen to share her feelings, so she opted for the adage her mother had always used. "That which we cannot help must be endured."

The chambermaid held up a set of stays. "I'm not sure how much more enduring you can do, m'lady."

Helen held out her arms and stood patiently while Glenda transformed her into the Lady of Ardnamurchan, the picture of the woman the crofters and patrons had grown to love and respect. After covering her head and neck with a grey wimple, Helen regarded herself in the polished copper mirror. "With a dab of lime, no one will even notice the bruise on my cheek."

***

After she bid good morn to Maggie, Helen gathered her wits and proceeded to the second floor where she rapped on Aleck's solar door. Though he would be aware of her usual Saturday trip to the village, she'd always given him the courtesy of letting him know before she set off. Though she would have preferred to avoid him altogether, it was best to maintain her regular routine, lest she create further discourse. When there was no answer, she pulled down on the blackened iron latch and peered inside.

*Odd, Aleck always spends his mornings in here. Where has he gone? Is he still abed?*

She let out a long breath. At least she wouldn't have to face him. Only heaven knew how he'd respond after last evening's events. And he'd most definitely find a way to make the candlestick incident appear to be her fault. In the five years of their marriage, Aleck had proven an expert at passing the blame, not only to her, but to anyone who disagreed with him.

She headed to the courtyard to look for Grant. Surprised to find it unusually quiet, she found no guardsmen whatsoever. The blacksmith shack clanged with the sound of iron striking iron, the piglets in the pen by the stables squealed, roosters crowed, but aside from the few sentries patrolling the wall-walk above, the MacIain guard was not training with weapons as expected. *Where are Eoin and his men? Are they gone as well?*

Perplexed, she headed out the main gate to the stables. At last she discovered the MacGregor guard busy at work honing their weapons. Every man wielded a rasp, working blades of swords, dirks and battleaxes into deadly sharp weapons.

Eoin made an imposing sight, supervising with his fists on his hips. When he spotted her, he smiled and hastened her way. "Good morrow, m'lady, I hope you are well." He peered closely at the bruised cheek, now concealed by a layer of powdered lime.

Bless him for not saying a word about last eve's blunder in front of the men. Helen still held on to a thread of hope the *argument* hadn't wormed its way through the castle gossips. "I am feeling very well, thank you." *Aside from the throbbing on the right side of my face and my gravelly voice.* She held up her basket. "I usually visit the villagers in Kilchoan on Saturdays, but I cannot find Sir Grant anywhere."

"Are you looking for him to provide an escort?"

"Aye."

Eoin's angled brows drew together. "Did you not know Sir Grant and most of the MacIain men sailed north for a sortie at dawn—ah—with your husband?"

Helen glanced up at the elderly guard on the wall-walk. "Aleck is away?" They always left the older sentries at the castle.

"Gone up to Sleat to inspect a report of suspicious activity."

"That sounds rather dangerous," she said absently, wondering whom else she would ask to escort her to town.

"No more so than sparring in the courtyard every day." He pointed to his men. "My lads are taking a moment's respite to sharpen their weapons."

"Is that not a daily necessity?"

"Aye it is, especially to keep a man's sword and dirk from rusting, however, pikes and battleaxes do not always receive the same care."

She looked beyond Eoin to ensure they were out of earshot of his men. "Did you speak to Sir Aleck this morn?" she whispered.

His blue eyes squinted a little in the morning light. "For a brief moment. After a messenger arrived, he hastened away."

"And said nothing about…" She rolled her eyes toward the keep.

"Nary a word." He grinned. Blast, how his grin could unravel her wits. "Though I doubt he'd confide anything to me."

"Fortunate, I suppose." With a nod, Helen spotted Mr. Keith up on the wall-walk and waved to catch his attention.

"Ah," Eoin's deep voice rumbled behind her, oddly making gooseflesh rise on her skin. "If it would please your ladyship, I'd enjoy escorting you to the village this day."

Mr. Keith waved. She cupped her hands around her mouth. "Is all well?"

"Aye, m'lady," he hollered.

Normally Helen would never raise her voice, but she'd needed to act quickly. She returned her attention to Sir Eoin. "Why thank you. It would be an honor to be accompanied by the Chieftain of Clan Gregor. I'm sure the townsfolk would be very impressed indeed."

He gestured forward with that handsome grin. "If you are ready, may I carry your basket?"

"My thanks." Not even Sir Grant had offered to carry her basket on their many trips to the village.

Helen led the way along the path she'd traveled countless times. When sufficiently far enough away from the castle gates, she glanced over her shoulder to ensure no one else had followed. "What is the suspicious activity that was reported?"

"Nothing too alarming, just undue movement of galleys, similar to that which I saw with my men on our last sortie."

"I do hope everyone will be all right."

He ambled beside her with an easy stride. "I doubt there'll be any altercation at all, m'lady. Sir Aleck wanted to see things for himself."

Helen cringed at the mention of her husband. After last eve, she shuddered at what Sir Eoin must think of her.

They walked for a bit and he shifted the basket to his far arm. "I didn't want to say anything in front of my men, but would you mind if I had a look at your bruises?"

Stopping, she clapped her hands either side of her linen wimple. She and Glenda had chosen it because silk would have been too sheer. "I wouldn't want to take this off. Without my chambermaid, it would be difficult to secure it back in place."

He smoothed his fingers atop the back of her hands. "We don't need to take it off. I just would like to see the marks now that we're in the light."

"But why?" she asked. "Looking at them will not make them fade any faster."

"No." His eyebrows pinched as if he were very concerned. "However, there may come a time when I need to bear witness to Aleck's treachery."

That made her mouth go dry. Helen nodded and lowered her hands. Yes, people at the castle had made offhand remarks, but no one had ever alluded to helping her. The thought was rather terrifying, yet liberating. "Glenda said I looked awful."

He examined the linen appreciatively. "She did a wonderful job with your wimple. No one will know." He pulled out the right side and encouraged her to angle her face toward the sun. "Devil's bones, it does look far worse than it did last eve." He tried to tug on the neck cloth, but it was wound too tight.

Helen dropped her gaze to her toes. "'Tis humiliating."

"Does it hurt you?"

"Aye, but only when I smile."

He raised her chin with the crook of his finger until their gazes met. "'Tis a folly, for you are most beautiful when you smile."

Mercy, must Eoin look so fetching when saying something as nice as that? Didn't he know Helen wasn't accustomed to praise of any sort? She cast her gaze to the path and patted her wimple where he'd mussed it. "We should keep going."

# *Chapter Twelve*

Eoin enjoyed the fresh air and walking through the pastoral countryside with Helen more than he should have. The leaves on the trees shimmered, alive with a bright verdant color only seen in the Highlands in spring. The season must have enlivened his very soul, because he felt like humming—not because he'd just examined Helen's bruise—the fact that Aleck had struck her abhorred him. But walking beside the lovely lady made him a bit giddy. Who wouldn't want to hum with birds singing while puffs of clouds gently sailed above? The mere idea made him thank the stars his men weren't there to give him a good ribbing.

*Perhaps that's why the old hens call it spring fever.*

If only he could talk to Helen more about last night's incident with Aleck, but she seemed so reluctant and embarrassed. Bloody hell, he hated seeing bruises on her porcelain skin. What had Eoin concerned the most, however, was her future safety. When Glenda had found him last eve, she'd told him Aleck had grown more abrasive since the birth of their daughter. What if, God forbid, Helen gave birth to yet another lass? What reprehensible acts would MacIain resort to then?

Lady Helen might have the will of a warrior woman, but in stature, she was fragile. In no way could she withstand beatings from that barbarian. Not that any woman should ever be forced to endure Aleck MacIain's ire.

Helen pointed ahead. "I always stop at Mistress Cate's cottage on the way into town. She's an elderly lady and cannot move about all that well."

"Does she live alone?"

"Aye, but her son and daughter-in-law till her lands. They live in the village and check on her every day."

Eoin followed Helen up an overgrown path to a small lime-washed cottage with a thatched roof.

"Mistress Cate?" Helen rapped on the door. "I've brought you some cheese today."

Eoin grinned. Lady Helen might be married to the Devil's spawn, but *she* was certainly an angel. It was good to see her carrying out charitable activities on behalf of the clan. That was an important role of the chieftain—to provide safety and support for his people. *Unfortunate not all chieftains remember that fact.*

"A moment," a voice called from inside. When the door opened, a haggard face framed by grey hair, crinkled more by a toothless grin. "Good morrow, Lady Helen." The woman's gaze inspected Eoin with a hint of unease. "And where is Sir Grant today?"

Helen graciously introduced Sir Eoin as her dear friend from Glen Orchy. And when she rattled off his title, Mistress Cate's apprehension spread into an adoring grin. Stepping aside, she promptly invited them inside. The stone-walled cottage comprised one room with a bed on one end and a cooking hearth on the other with a table and benches in between.

The elderly woman ambled toward the hearth. "I've some onion broth over the fire. You will stay and have a bowl with me?"

"Of course we will." Helen sat and motioned for Eoin to do the same. "And how is your rheumatism?"

Mistress Cate bent down and picked up an iron ladle. "Coming good now the weather is warming."

Helen nodded with a warm smile. "Och, I am happy to hear it."

"And how long will you be visiting Mingary, Sir Eoin?" Cate asked.

"A month, mayhap two." He didn't want to alarm the poor crofter with the reason for his visit.

The elderly woman placed a wooden bowl of broth with one sliver of onion in front of him. "Do you think those MacDonalds will leave us be?"

Evidently the rumor mill was as alive and healthy in Kilchoan as it was in every other Highland village. Eoin cleared his throat. "I hope so, mistress."

Helen lifted her wooden spoon. "Sir Aleck sailed this morning to inspect the MacDonald lands in Sleat. Are you aware Alexander MacDonald threatened the king?"

"Aye. 'Tis disgraceful if you ask me." Mistress Cate tottered over with a bowl for herself and lumbered onto the bench beside Eoin. "Times are changing. The Highlands are now part of Scotland just like Edinburgh or Glasgow or Inverness—No more *Lord of the Isles* ruling over us."

Helen dabbed her lips. "Aye, and the young King James has done much to bring us together."

"Unfortunately the MacDonalds do not see it that way," Eoin said. "And I suppose Clan Donald has lost the most, though they have no grounds for complaint. Their lands are vast."

"Too vast if you ask me." Cate spread her arms wide. "All I need is this cottage and a wee parcel of land to till. Why a man needs a dozen castles is beyond my imagination, even if he is an earl—or a king for that matter."

The old woman certainly was sharp for her advanced age. Eoin watched Mistress Cate hold forth while Helen listened, thoughtfully eating his abominable broth—it hadn't a lick of salt, though that commodity was worth its weight in gold.

After Helen had eaten every last drop, she stood. "As always, I want to thank you for your gracious hospitality."

The old woman rose, wringing her hands. "Must you leave so soon?"

Helen patted Cate's shoulder. "I've many others to see today, but I'll come around again in a sennight."

"Will you bring Sir Eoin with you?" She batted her eyelashes at him with her endearing toothless grin.

Helen glanced at Eoin and blushed. His stomach made some sort of irregular jumping motion that must have been caused by the broth. Why on earth would such a question make Helen turn red? But the lady maintained her poise. "I'll wager Sir Grant will be back from their sortie by then," she said.

"Well then." Mistress Cate grasped Eoin's hand and squeezed. "'Tis not every day a Highland chieftain comes to call." She then clasped his upper arm. "And by the size of you, you're a good fighting man as well."

He bowed. "I do what I can m'lady."

After picking up her basket, Helen headed for the door. "Hopefully Sir Eoin will return to Glen Orchy without having to wield his sword."

Eoin wished it would be so, though with every passing day, war became more eminent.

Not long after they resumed their journey down the path, the village children came running, calling Lady Helen's name. Her visage instantly brightened. "Hello everyone." She crouched to be on eye-level with the littlest one. They all had a barrage of questions from, where is the bairn, to how old is the bairn, to can you bring Maggie to play with us. Helen answered every question as if it were of the utmost importance. Then she fished in that basket of hers and gave each child a coin before she sent them on their way.

"They adore you," Eoin said.

"They are all very special to me. I think visiting the village is my favorite part of being lady of the keep."

Eoin cringed inside. Indeed he was a chieftain with lands, but his clan was armigerous to the Campbells. The MacGregors were governors of Campbell lands, but Eoin had no castle of his own. His clan lived in a village of long houses, which by rights were as functional as a keep. However, though his rooms were spacious, it wasn't a castle akin to that which Lady Helen had been accustomed her entire life. Truly, she would frown upon such meager living quarters as he possessed in Glen Strae.

Walking through the muddy lane, a beggar hailed them. "Lady Helen, have you a tot of whisky for me today?"

"Nay, Hamish, but I do have a parcel of food for you." She handed him a leather-wrapped bundle.

He took it and pulled the thong. "I'd be a mite bit happier if you brought me whisky."

She held up her finger. "Now you know I cannot bring you spirit."

He grinned pinching a bit of chicken with grimy fingers. "Och, but I can keep asking, m'lady."

Spending the afternoon with Lady Helen was like watching a saint flit about—one who wasn't entirely aware of the effect she had on others. Everyone she touched smiled at her with their face aglow. It was as if she'd strolled into the village illuminated by her own ray of sunshine. She handed out tinctures for cough and a salve for a burn, and by afternoon, her basket was nearly empty.

Eoin took note of dark clouds rolling in from the west and pointed. "Are you nearly finished, m'lady? It looks like we could be seeing some rain."

"Oh my." She pressed her gloved fingers over her bow-shaped lips. "We'd best be heading back."

Eoin took Helen's basket and led her out of the village and past the turn to Cate's cottage. They'd nearly traveled a mile when a sloppy raindrop splashed Eoin's cheek. "We may have left a bit late."

She walked briskly beside him. "If we hurry we might make it."

A streak of lightning fingered across the sky, followed by a thundering clap. In the blink of an eye, the skies opened with a deluge.

"Ack!" Helen lifted her hem and hastened her pace.

The rain came down in sheets and they hadn't even traveled halfway to the castle. Worse, Mistress Cate's cottage was a good half-mile back.

Eoin peered left then right—searching for anything that could provide shelter. Nestled against a hill was an old lean-to. Eoin grasped Helen's elbow. "Come." He tucked her beneath his arm and held his cloak over her head. "'Tis not much, but it will do until the downpour eases."

She leaned into him. "I hope this squall doesn't last long."

He helped her step over a fallen tree. "The clouds are thick, but I've never seen a torrent like this last for more than an hour or so."

When he led her inside, Helen shivered. "Brr, I'm soaked clean through already." Her wimple had been pushed from her hair and her mantle draped flush against her shoulders like wet bed linens.

Eoin removed his cloak. Though it had been oiled, it was too wet to be of any use in warming her. He hung it on a nail. "Take off your mantle and I'll hang it beside mine."

"I doubt they'll dry." She handed him the garment.

"But you'll catch a chill if you remain wrapped in wet garments."

She smoothed her hands across her face and over her exposed tresses. "I'm afraid that cannot be helped."

Eoin's gaze dipped to her chest. Though wearing a high collared neckline, her wet gown clung to her breasts like a second skin. A twinge of yearning hit him deep in the gut. His gaze dipping lower, her nipples stood erect through the woolen fabric.

Devil's bones, his cock came alive like a waking dragon.

Helen pulled her arms across her body, her teeth chattering. "Unfortunate we've no hearth and flint."

Eoin placed his hands on her shoulders. "Allow me to warm you, m'lady."

Her lips parted and she drew in a sharp breath as if she were going to issue a rebuttal. But she offered a shy nod.

Cautiously, he slid his palms around her back. , wet woman molded to his chest, her breasts plying him. The points of her nipples teased as if begging him to untie her kirtle and suckle them. Eoin stiffened when her mons brushed his cock. Not a maid, she would be aware of his arousal.

Helen suddenly stood very still. She did not pull away, nor did she push into his erection. When she slid her hands around his waist, Eoin gasped. Damnation, the lass felt better than any woman he'd ever held in his arms before. His heart thrummed, his cock ached to push into her and rub. But this was Lady Helen. He couldn't force himself upon her and take advantage of his best friend's sister, a woman he'd known since he was four and ten—a woman who was…*married*.

*Jesus strike me dead now.*

She rested her head against his chest, yet still said nothing.

Eoin inhaled and tightened his embrace, settling his cheek atop Helen's head. She smelled purer than a newborn lamb. God, he'd do anything to turn back time and offer for her hand.

When her fingers pressed into his back, Eoin almost moaned for the soothing caress of her touch. But he controlled his longings and held absolutely still. He even kept his breathing shallow.

Ever so gently, she plied his lower back with deft fingers. How long had it been since he'd felt a woman's gentle touch. *Too long.* And Helen's fingers were caressing him so lightly—like a timid kitten.

Eoin pressed his lips into her silken hair and closed his eyes. Drinking her in, he wanted to savor this moment. Fate had led them into this rickety shelter and, by the grace of God, the only woman he'd ever loved was wrapped in his embrace.

Ever so slightly, Helen relaxed into him.

Had he imagined it?

Her hands slid up his spine, fingers massaging as they slid back down.

He shivered.

*Good God.*

Insatiable hunger stirred in Eoin's lower belly, his heart swelled in his chest. The tip of his tongue snuck out from between his lips. Taking his time, he trailed kisses from Helen's temple to her ear, then down the side of her long, feminine neck.

Helen sighed—a high pitched, breathy sound that told Eoin she wanted him. Needing no more encouragement, his heart took over. His hand slid up and cupped her face as he gently plied her lips with a lingering kiss.

Her heartbeat drummed an intoxicating rhythm that carried to the tip of that bow-shaped mouth.

Sliding his fingers under her wimple and through her tresses, he brushed his tongue across her lips and coaxed them open. Once inside her mouth, she ensnared him, and all the gold in Scotland would not be payment enough to entice Eoin to pull away. She tasted fresh as the rain dripping from the eaves, but warm and soothing like a blast from a brazier. Opposed to the cold air surrounding them, her silken mouth welcomed him. Eoin's legs weakened with the stirring of desire in his groin. He tightened his thigh muscles to regain a modicum of control.

She returned his kiss with another intoxicating sigh. Deeper his tongue probed while she ignited a bone-melting fire that thrummed through his blood. Though Eoin wanted to rush, to unlace her kirtle and fill his palms with Helen's breasts, he was lucid enough to realize that attacking Lady Helen with such wild abandon would be folly. Taking his time, he controlled the pace with languid strokes of his tongue.

Helen swooned in Eoin's arms. Overwhelmed by the tenderness of his touch, she was so lightheaded she couldn't breathe…or stop.

*Mm.*

Aleck had never kissed her with his tongue—never turned her body to molten honey. And that's how Eoin tasted—warmed, *raw*, delicious honey.

She'd been aware of Eoin's manhood pressing into her nether parts since he first wrapped her in his embrace.

She had stood very still for a moment, not wanting to encourage him, but not wanting to pull away either. His body felt so exquisitely warm, so powerful. For the first time in five years she knew sanctuary. A man with a caring heart like Eoin's would protect his own. He was trained to be a knight by Helen's father. Deeply-seated within his soul was the sense of right and honor.

*Honor.*

Helen's entire body tensed. She forced herself to ease away from his kiss. It didn't matter how much she wanted this man. He was not hers to covet. "We cannot."

He tightened his grip and pressed his lips against her temple. "Forgive me."

She chuckled. "I should thank you."

"Why?" he whispered, his voice strained.

It was difficult to admit she'd never been kissed like that before. How could she put it? Her cheeks prickled with heat and she lowered her gaze.

The rough pads of his fingertips brushed along her jaw. "Are you all right?"

"Aye," Helen said hoarsely. She looked directly at the lips that had just plied hers so reverently. They were slightly pursed, full and, by the stars, she wanted to kiss them again. "I've never…" She released her grasp and turned away. It was too humiliating to tell him.

She heard his quick inhale as he stepped behind her. Placing his hands on her shoulders, Eoin's simple touch filled her with warmth. How could anyone sap her resolve with a mere touch? *I should step away.*

But Eoin's breath caressed her cheek. "My guess is he is not tender with you."

She glanced over her shoulder. Eoin looked at her with such deep care reflected in his eyes, she could not deny the truth. "You can read me too well."

For a moment she thought—hoped he would kiss her neck, but instead, he nudged her tresses and wimple aside with his chin, his warm breath making gooseflesh rise along her shoulders. “It doesn’t take a seer to realize you’re being mistreated.”

Clapping a hand over her mouth, Helen closed her eyes and ground her teeth against her urge to cry. What a mess she’d made of her life. But she would not again break down in front of Eoin MacGregor. She needed no man’s sympathy. She must be strong.

“I cannot bear…” Eoin removed his hands from her shoulders.

Cold chills coursed across her skin. If only she hadn’t turned away, his arms would still be surrounding her. She faced him. “You cannot bear?”

“I-I’ve always held the sanctity of marriage in high esteem, yet I cannot bear to watch you suffer under the hands of that *tyrant*.”

Helen should admonish such a slander against her husband. But Eoin was not a servant. He was the only person in Ardnamurchan who knew about her past—about who she was at her core. “Duncan considered it a good alliance for the Campbell Clan. Mingary gives him a base from which to spy on the MacDonalds.” She didn’t need to tell Eoin about the centuries-long feud between their clans.

“I suspect the alliance had something to do with Sir Aleck’s separation from Clan Donald.”

She huffed. “Sir Aleck will be loyal to whomever offers him the greatest prize.”

A shadow passed over Eoin’s face. “I feared as much. He cannot be trusted.”

“You shouldn’t say that.” Helen clapped a hand over her mouth. Though Eoin was right, she’d trained herself to stand up for her husband.

"You, more than anyone, should realize the truth."

She crossed her arms and rubbed the outside of her shoulders with a subtle nod.

"Come here," he beckoned her. "I promise I will not try to kiss you again."

To her surprise, a twinge of disappointment squeezed her heart. "You're as damp as I, yet so warm."

He chuckled and Helen again relaxed into his embrace. Thunder cracked overhead as the downpour continued.

*Odd, the torrent is ever so soothing.*

"Lady Helen?"

She loved how her name rolled off his tongue. "Aye?"

His hand rubbed her back in a circular motion. "I think I should talk to your brother about asking the Pope for an annulment."

Every muscle in her body tensed and she pushed away from his arms. "You cannot be serious."

Eoin groaned and released her. "I've thought of nothing else since I found you in the alcove on the beach. John Campbell is the Bishop of the Isles. He has the Pope's ear."

A cold shiver twitched through her body. "But Aleck has sworn he'll murder me. If I'm deceased, Maggie will have no one to protect her."

"I will protect you. I vow it." Eoin combed his fingers through his damp tresses. "That did not come out as genteel as I would have liked." He inhaled deeply and gazed at her eyes intently. "I also promise I will not approach your brother unless you give your consent. Please, Lady Helen. Think about this for a moment. Remaining at Mingary is not a viable solution for you *or* the bairn."

Arms folded, Helen paced in a circle, her mind abuzz with all the reasons she should not listen. "What you suggest is madness."

"Just hear me."

She moved to the edge of the crude shelter and stared at the driving rain. She would never do anything to compromise Maggie's safety. "I cannot abandon my daughter."

"Of course no one would ever expect that of you. She's a part of you and deserves your love. Aleck has proved he has no capacity to care for the babe."

Helen folded her arms tighter. All the tension in her body returned tenfold. Aye, things were bad with Aleck, terrible, even. But seeking an annulment could purchase more trouble than she'd ever experienced in her life—and Maggie could end up in the midst of the worst of it.

"If you scribe a letter to your brother, I will deliver the missive without Aleck ever being aware." Eoin stepped behind her, his presence radiating like a furnace, but his words so extremely disconcerting. "If the Pope grants the annulment, Aleck doesn't need to know about it until you and Maggie have been safely spirited away from Mingary."

Again she tensed. "Aye? And then what? Aleck will come after me. He sees Maggie as his mark for bargaining, and if it weren't for the feud he'd cause with the Campbell Clan, he'd sooner see me dead."

"Your words ring true," Eoin agreed. "But you and Miss Maggie would have the protection of Clan Gregor *and* Clan Campbell. On that you have my vow."

Too many warring consequences muddled her mind. "Please. This is too terrifying to consider. What if my missive were intercepted? What if the Pope rejects my plea appeals directly to Aleck?"

Eoin clapped his hand over his heart. "I will have words with John to ensure that does not happen. Once your brother knows of your situation, I am certain your protection will be paramount to the family."

If only she could believe him. If only she could be sure she and Maggie would be free from Aleck's retribution. But Helen could not take such a risk. She plucked her cloak from the peg and slung it round her shoulders. "Please, take me back. This talk of annulment is too disconcerting."

She caught the look on Eoin's face before he turned to retrieve his mantle. His frown forlorn, he looked as if he'd just received notice of the passing of a loved one. Did he care for her that much? If he helped her and was discovered, Aleck would not only kill her, the Chieftain of Ardnamurchan would not rest until Eoin was dead too.

She could never put so much at risk.

Could she?

# *Chapter Thirteen*

The rain had stopped, though every stitch of Eoin's clothing was still soaked clear through.

As they approached Mingary Castle, the hair at Eoin's nape stood on end. He had a hunch something had happened and knew better than to ignore his instincts. All was quiet. *Too quiet.* There wasn't even a sentry upon the wall-walk.

He drew his sword and motioned for Lady Helen to move behind him.

"What is it?"

"Just a feeling, but there's no guard above." He glanced over his shoulder. "Stay behind me."

Voices echoed from behind the man door. He recognized Fergus's voice. Eoin pounded his pommel on the hard oak. "'Tis Lady Helen and Sir Eoin."

The door opened straight away to Fergus's wide-eyed stare. "Thank heavens you've returned, m'laird."

Eoin ushered Helen forward. "What the blazes is going on?"

"William's arrived from Sunart with news. The MacDonalds are marching overland."

"'Tis the truth." A MacIain man stepped forward. "And they've already burnt out Gilles's cottage. We saw the smoke first."

"Are you William?" Eoin asked the man.

"Aye."

"Did the other men from your post come with you?"

"Nay." William inclined his head eastward. "They've stayed to keep an eye on the Donald's whereabouts."

"Good." Eoin looked between the men. "How much time do we have before they cross into Ardnamurchan?"

"A day, mayhap two," William surmised. "Depends on how intent they are on pillaging poor crofters."

Damn, there was no time to wait for MacIain to return with his best fighting men. *I told Sir Aleck the greater threat was Sunart, but the bastard wouldn't listen.* Forced to make a snap decision, Eoin pointed to the stables. "Ready the men for battle. We'll ride at once."

Helen grasped his arm. "What can I do to help?"

"Keep everyone calm." Eoin patted her fingers. "Ensure you have enough food and water within the walls in case there is a siege."

"A *siege*? I thought you said they wouldn't march on Mingary."

"I aim to see that they do not, but you must prepare for the worst." Eoin grasped her hand. "We shall leave the remaining Mingary guardsmen here. With luck, Sir Aleck and his men should return soon and provide reinforcements." He pointed to an elderly sentry sporting a bow and arrow—one who clearly had left his post atop the wall-walk, having left it unguarded. "Resume your station immediately. There must be at least three sentries on the battlements at all times. No question."

"Yes, m'laird." The man bowed his head and hastened off.

With her chin raised, Helen looked Eoin in the eye. "I will make certain we secure the fortress." Though she was a small woman, her stature exuded confidence—

something absolutely necessary in a leader. By God, she was Colin Campbell's daughter.

"It is up to you to rally the Mingary forces in the absence of Sir Aleck. Your word is law. Do not forget that, m'lady." He pulled her aside. "The attack on Sunart might be a ploy to pull us away from Mingary. When Sir Aleck returns, tell him to prepare for an attack by sea. With the MacGregors protecting your back and the MacIains covering the sea gate, all should be well."

***

As Helen watched Eoin take charge, she wanted to throw her arms around his neck and beg him to stay. He could be killed in the fighting—or injured. He'd sworn to protect her and now he planned to ride off and face a band of pillaging rogues. She clasped her hands together to stop herself from embracing him. *I mustn't fear. Eoin has ridden into far worse. He's a king's enforcer. If anyone can stop Clan Donald, it is he.*

But watching him ride through the gate, clad and equipped for battle without so much as being able to give him her kerchief, tied Helen's stomach in knots. *Dear Lord, please watch over Sir Eoin and his men and bring them back to Mingary safely.*

The gates closed behind the mounted warriors with a resounding boom.

Her nerves jumped across her skin.

*What on earth should I do now?*

Blinking, she recalled how Eoin took charge, and how her brother managed his men. Her father had been a legendary commander in The Crusades. Squaring her shoulders, Helen knew what she must do. Casting misgivings about her gender aside, she turned in a circle. She'd been left with the elder guardsmen—every man sported greying locks, if they still had hair. Presently, they all stared at her—even Peter the cook had come into the courtyard with an expectant gaze.

Snapping a hand to her hip, Helen pointed in the direction of the east paddock. "Bring a dozen head of sheep into the courtyard and three times as many hens. Have the lads fill every spare barrel with water."

No one moved.

She clapped her hands. "Quickly. Work together. I want all this done and the gate bolted before the evening meal."

She turned to the nearest guard—Mr. Keith. "Do you have enough men to maintain three lookouts in a scheduled rotation?"

"Aye, m'lady. 'Tis what Sir Aleck ordered afore he set sail."

"Very good." At least she didn't have to worry about organizing the guard. She'd assumed as much, but presently she was in charge and needed to know exactly when and where to expect her guards. "I want a weapons report. Pikes, swords, number of arrows, and number of fighting men remaining at the castle."

Mr. Keith bowed. "I'll fetch that for you straight away, m'lady."

"Tell the men we are on full alert until Sir Eoin returns."

"Very well, m'lady."

He hesitated for a moment. Helen looked at him directly. "Was there something else you needed?"

He scratched his head. "I don't believe so."

She shooed him away with a flick of her wrist. "Then get to it. We must ensure we have plenty of arrows to defend the keep and provisions to ensure we are all fed."

Glenda hastened to Helen's side. "I just heard the news. 'Tis terrible Sir Aleck is away whilst we are under attack."

Helen held up her finger. "We are preparing for an attack that may not come. The important thing is that we are ready should such an incidence arise." As people scattered, she eyed Thomas, the stable hand. "Send a runner to the village. Tell the crofters they must take refuge within the castle walls immediately."

The boy gaped. "'Tis that bad?"

"Nay," Helen reassured him. "But I'll not wait until the Donald is upon us to open the gates to our kin."

The ram's horn sounded from the wall-walk. Helen's heart lurched. She peered up at the lookout.

He cupped his hands to his mouth. "A galley flying the MacIain pennant."

*Aleck has returned.*

Though the fighting men were needed, Helen could not assuage the tightening in her chest. Heaving a heavy sigh, she grasped Glenda's hands. "I haven't seen Miss Maggie since before I left for the village this morning. How is she?"

"A happy bairn. Do not worry, Sarah has the lass's care in hand."

Helen she pressed her palms against her abdomen. "I will be up to check on her as soon as I am able. Go help Peter with the provisions. I must hasten to face the dragon."

Glenda snorted out a howling laugh.

Helen bit the inside of her cheek and turned away. She'd never made such a derogatory remark about Aleck to the chambermaid. Reminding herself she mustn't ever reveal her true feelings about her husband, no matter what, she let out a heavy sigh. Helen must be careful not to slip again. Gathering her composure, she headed for the sea gate.

Men furled the galley's sail while others took up the oars and guided the boat toward the shore. The men's voices echoed on the breeze as they sang a seafaring ditty to the rhythm of their rowing. Aleck stood astern, manning the rudder. The sight of the clansmen sailing home always brought an air of triumph and the castle courtyard buzzed with excitement.

Helen often stood beneath the archway of the sea gate and watched Clan MacIain approach—usually from a day of fishing. Typically she watched with an emotionless gaze, but today her insides jumped with restlessness.

After Aleck hopped over the side of the galley, Helen hastened toward him. "Urgent news m'laird."

He smirked, hardly regarding her. "What is it now?"

Helen didn't allow his gruff demeanor to dissuade her. Eoin had put her in charge. She would not shirk from any duty required of her. "A sentry reported the MacDonalds have burned out the Gilles's cottage in Sunart. Sir Eoin and his men have ridden to intercept them before they march into Ardnamurchan."

Aleck jammed his fists into his hips, leaning in so he towered over her. "He's ridden without me?"

Helen mirrored his pose. "Aye—and not too long ago."

"You stupid woman, why did you not tell him to wait?"

She blinked in rapid succession, willing away his insult. *I have a duty to the clan.* "We had no idea when to expect your return, m'laird. With news of the raid, Sir Eoin hadn't any choice but to make haste."

Aleck lashed out with a swift backhand. Flinching, Helen tried to duck, but he clipped the side of her cheek with his fingernails. Stumbling backward, she touched a hand to her face.

"Sir Eoin?" Aleck said. "I've had a gut full of that cur coming into my keep and giving orders as if he were lord and master."

Helen looked at her palm. Blood streaked across her fingers. She touched her tongue to the corner of her mouth. The iron taste of blood swilled across it while every muscle in her body clenched. She was no pigeon for Aleck to strike whenever he pleased.

"Ready the horses," he bellowed.

Thomas stepped into view, wringing his hands. "So sorry, m'laird. Sir Eoin and his men took most of the horses. We've only a couple of nags left." The lad's gaze shifted to Helen's bleeding mouth.

"He bloody what?" Aleck looked as if he were going to wallop poor Thomas. But he growled instead. "Saddle those that remain and fetch my battle armor." He beckoned Grant. "You and I will ride ahead—the rest of the men will follow on foot."

Holding a kerchief against her wound, Helen hastened toward him, but kept enough distance to avoid another strike. "What if the MacDonalds should attack by sea, m'laird?" she asked, careful not to mention Sir Eoin's name this time—though he had been the one who suspected a dual strike.

Aleck glared. "Do you not have something to embroider? My God, had Duncan Campbell told me how utterly daft you were, I'd not have signed my name to the marriage contract."

"Nor would you have received my dower lands." Helen shuffled back in anticipation of an angry strike for her impertinence.

"Watch your mouth." Aleck stepped in, but didn't raise a hand this time. "We've just returned from a sortie to the north. The MacDonald galleys are still sailing back and forth between Colonsay and Sleat. They've much bigger fish to fry—and I am to see they do not succeed."

Grant strode forward, leading the horses. "Right after we stop them in Sleat, aye, m'laird?"

"Too right." Aleck circled his hand over his head. "Come men, there'll be no rest. We'll not be letting Clan Gregor fight our battles."

Helen watched as the MacIain army marched out the gate behind Aleck and Grant. All looked worn from their three-day stint at sea. They carried every manner of weapons from poleaxes, bows and arrows to dirks and swords. She could only pray that Aleck had been right—there was no threat from the sea. Once again she'd be left with Mr. Keith and the aged guardsmen. Nonetheless, not a pleasant thought, given Eoin's warning.

Helen whispered a silent prayer for their safety and headed into the keep to cleanse the blood from her face.

Mary stood propped against the kitchen doorway, watching Helen as she passed. The widow's arms were folded and she had a smirk across her mouth as if she enjoyed seeing Helen receive a slap from Sir Aleck.

Helen stopped short. *I am in charge. I am the lady of this keep.* "Mary, see to it you keep the sheep and chickens out of the garden."

The woman's jaw dropped. "Me?"

"Aye, and while you're at it, you can give Master Thomas a hand with the pig's feed." Helen didn't wait for a response. Rather, she proceeded through the great hall and up the stairwell. With things set in motion to secure and provision the castle, she would clean her face and then see to Maggie's safety.

*Pray the MacDonalds continue their business between Colonsay and Sleat for another sennight at least.*

# Chapter Fourteen

It was dark when Eoin and his men arrived on the summit of Beinn Resipol. William led them directly to the lookout sight and introduced the other two MacIain men as Malcolm and Rob. Though their hands were sooty and their fingernails caked with dirt, Eoin shook their hands. "Good work spotting the MacDonalds straight away."

"It wasn't too hard, given the black smoke billowing from the north," Rob said while Malcolm nodded.

Eoin scanned the terrain below, but could only see blackness. "Where are they now?"

Malcolm threw his thumb over his shoulder. "Headed southeast, I wager they aim to pillage their way to Mingary."

Eoin instantly thought of Helen and prayed Aleck had already arrived to defend the keep. Since the MacDonalds were heading south, it now made even more sense to sail a patrol galley through Loch Sunart. Thank heavens he'd thought to have Helen pass along the message. "How many are there?" he asked.

"Forty, near enough," said Rob.

"All mounted?"

"Aye. I reckon they rode down from Tioram."

Eoin looked at the sky and shook his head. The news was just as he'd predicted. If only Aleck MacIain had a brain the size of his cods, they might have stopped the invasion before it began. Now a poor crofter was out of a home, his farm burned.

"Have they set up camp for the night?"

"Aye." Malcolm pointed to a range of craggy hills, a darker black against the cloudy sky. "Behind them crags."

"Gather round, men," Eoin said, beckoning the group in a huddle. "We'll eat and camp here for the night. I want the watch changed every hour. Before dawn, we'll ride to the southeast and set a trap in the ravine." He looked to William. "What say you, how long will it take us to ride to the base of the hill, yonder?"

"An hour. If we head out afore the birds start chirping, we'll be there by dawn for certain."

"Very well." Eoin looked at the expectant faces staring at him. "That'll be the plan then. Get some rest. I guarantee we'll have a nasty battle to face on the morrow."

***

"Get up you laggards!" Eoin had no sooner found a comfortable patch of grass when Aleck MacIain's irritating voice brayed across the campsite. "What the hell are you doing making camp, you miserable flea-bitten swine?"

"M-m'laird." William immediately sprang to his feet. "Sir Eoin gave us orders to rest afore we head off the MacDonald."

"Sir Eoin, aye?" Aleck panned his glare around the camp until he found Eoin. "Why haven't we attacked?"

Rubbing the back of his neck, Eoin stood and sauntered forward. "Why are you not protecting Mingary's sea gate? I left word with Lady Helen—"

"A woman will *never* give me orders. And you're wrong. The MacDonalds have nearly moved all their men to Colonsay."

"Aye?" Eoin leveled his stare with MacIain's. "That's only a half-day's sailing from Mingary at most. I wouldn't put it past them to double back. Och aye, they're uniting."

"And I aim to stop them right here in Sunart." Aleck shoved Eoin's shoulder. "I asked you to tell me why we have not yet attacked."

Grinding his back molars, it took every bit of self-control Eoin possessed to explain his plan while MacIain glared at him with those beady black eyes. Satan's bones, Eoin wanted to slap the bastard—not only slap him, wrap his fingers around his neck and squeeze until he dropped—Aleck would be a whole lot more use if he were unconscious.

When Eoin finished, Aleck snorted with an arrogant smirk. "That's the poorest idea I've ever heard. And from you, a king's enforcer? My mother was a better strategist."

*Enough.*

Before he blinked, Eoin's hand darted out and clutched MacIain's throat. The big man's eyes bulged. Aleck tried to pull away, making choking gasps, but with his every move, Eoin clamped his grip harder while his gut churned with bile. "You might play the *almighty chieftain* to a lesser man," Eoin hissed in a low growl. "But if you ever try to belittle me again, especially in front of the men, I'll reach down your throat and cut that flippant tongue out."

Aleck gurgled and clawed at Eoin's hand. It was a matter of heartbeats before the bastard would drop from lack of air.

"Do. You. Understand?" Eoin demanded.

MacIain gave an eye rolling nod—at least as much of a nod as he could manage. Eoin shoved Aleck away. The dull-witted toad launched into a coughing fit, clutching his hands around his neck.

"He tried to kill me," MacIain coughed out. "D-did you see that? He nearly c-committed the abominable sin of *murder*!"

Eoin gave him an emotionless stare. "If I'd wanted to kill you, you'd be dead, you daft Highlander." He backed away and stood between Fergus and Samuel. As far as he was concerned this battle of wills was over, but he didn't trust MacIain to let it rest. "Now, I'd like to get some sleep afore I ride into battle."

The firelight was bright enough for Eoin to see the faces of Aleck's men. They were unshaven and haggard—each one looked like he hadn't had a decent night's sleep in a sennight. Not that this night would be restful. "You all look like shite."

"The MacIain Clan can withstand a night without sleep," Aleck rasped. "And I will not take orders from a MacGregor." He pointed to the horses tied at the edge of camp. "We'll be collecting our horses and we will beat back the MacDonalds without the likes of you."

Fergus stepped beside Eoin, gripping the hilt of his sword. Eoin sliced his palm through the air. "Let them go."

"You're serious?" The henchman dropped his hand.

"Aye."

After Aleck had ridden off with the horses, neither Eoin nor his men could sleep. They all sat around the small campfire staring at the flames as if mesmerized.

"Why didn't we fight them?" Fergus asked.

"You want to spill blood for naught?" Eoin studied the faces of his men. They all questioned him as Fergus had. "Over the past month have you found MacIain's men disagreeable?"

"Nay, just their leader," said Samuel.

"Exactly." Eoin shrugged. "Let them venture down to meet the MacDonalds. The grade is steep and it won't be any faster going with horses than on foot. We'll wake as planned and we'll cover their backs…if they need us."

Fergus chuckled. "Oh, I'll wager they bloody will need us and in short order."

Eoin stood and headed toward his patch of grass. "As MacIain said, let them fight their own battles. Besides, while Clan Donald is toying with the chieftain, they're not threatening the king at the moment. And that's the reason we're here—to subvert any action against the crown."

He flopped down and pulled his plaid over his shoulders. The only problem with Eoin's current plan was that he was too far away from Mingary. He could hardly believe Aleck hadn't at least left a few seasoned soldiers to guard the keep.

He lay on his back and a rock poked straight into his spine. Worse, every time he closed his eyes, he saw Helen. No matter how much he wanted to be there to protect her, it wasn't his place, dammit. And blast her for refusing to pursue an annulment.

From the outset, he knew the king shouldn't have sent him to Ardnamurchan. He was doomed the day he arrived. The first person he saw when his galley sailed ashore was Helen Campbell and, ever since, he'd been able to think of little else.

Even worse, he'd had no recourse but to bite his tongue and witness MacIain's deplorable treatment of the lady. And she was so frail. When she was young, she was smaller and more delicate than her sisters. Lady Helen needed someone to revere and protect her—not issue a slap at every disagreement.

Eoin slapped a hand to his forehead. *Ballocks*. Did he have to kiss her after they'd found shelter from the rain? What the hell had he been thinking? But, God almighty, she felt like heaven in his arms. What was a single man to do when a soaking wet woman's succulent body was pressed against him? *Protect her you stupid lout.*

But Lady Helen wasn't going to make it easy for him to safeguard her. Oh no, and Eoin didn't blame the woman. She was right to worry about her daughter. What Eoin feared the most was as soon as the bairn reached an age where she would be playing about the castle, her father would behave like a tyrant. MacIain had already proved he had no qualms about striking a woman. What reprehensible things would he do to a child?

Eoin didn't want to find out.

And when the time came, he didn't want to leave Lady Helen alone to endure her miserable marriage. But he couldn't force her to seek an annulment…and she was right. If Aleck MacIain discovered she'd even thought about approaching the Pope, he'd lash out at her. She'd said he'd already threatened to kill her.

Eoin tried to adjust to a more comfortable position. *Why the bloody hell did the king send me here?*

***

Eoin did eventually fall asleep, because after Fergus stirred him awake, he could have sworn someone had bludgeoned him between the eyes. But once the men were up and on the trail, the pounding in his head ebbed.

God, he loved the Highlands. The crisp morning air filled his lungs with vitality, as the frost-kissed grass crunched beneath his feet. The men headed down the mountain at a steady jog, Eoin's legs brushing the heather. Though it would be a month or so before it was in bloom, brilliant green grass peeked everywhere. At one with nature, this was Eoin's favorite part of his membership in the Highland Enforcers. He was meant to live off the land and sleep under the stars. Breathing the fresh clean air away from the stench of humanity revived his soul.

As the sun rose, the path ahead grew clearer and the men sped their pace. Eoin and his band of warriors could continue all day, only stopping for water and food.

They'd traversed about six miles when the orange glow completely receded from the wisps of clouds above and the sun fully illuminated the path ahead. Eoin estimated they'd nearly reached the place where he'd planned to set a trap for the MacDonald reivers.

Ahead, voices rose in a battle cry. Had Aleck opted to wait until daylight? *Most likely, the witless Highlander.*

"It looks as if you'll have your fight after all," Eoin said, taking a deep breath.

Fergus chuckled. "At least…they'll wear them down first."

With any luck, the MacIains would send the MacDonalds running for their mothers.

But when they ran atop the ridge, Eoin's wishes were dashed. Blood splattered everywhere. Some horses were down along with their riders. Clad in a full set of battle armor, MacIain spun his mount in the middle of the mayhem, bellowing curses as he wielded his sword like he was hacking with an ax.

*The sheep-headed maggot is going to get himself killed.* What the chieftain lacked in skill, he made up for with the pure aggression reflected in his technique. But no one could last long, brandishing a sword as vigorously as MacIain with such little effect. The men attacking him on either side dodged Aleck's enormous blade each time it swung their way. As predictable as the tide, the chieftain didn't even bother to change the cadence or direction of his swings. Above all, he could have benefitted from a bit of training in the courtyard.

Eoin motioned for his men to fan out. "It looks as if the MacDonalds have the upper hand. We'll not let them keep it."

Bellowing their battle cry, the MacGregor warriors pounced like phantoms from the hills. If there was one good thing about Aleck's dull-witted decision to ride ahead, it gave Eoin and Clan Gregor the element of surprise.

When the MacDonald men realized they'd been surrounded by yet another army, Eoin caught the panic in their eyes. Their movement became more urgent, exerting desperate strikes while they fought to gain any advantage.

Aleck remained mounted in the center of the fight, roaring like a wounded bull. Clearly tiring, he wielded his weapon with sluggish hacks. The two men attacking him on either side grew more daring. If Eoin didn't reach him quickly, the MacIain Chieftain would be dead. *But why am I saving his arse?* Eoin battled his way toward Aleck. *Because that's what King James expects of me.*

Mayhap if Eoin saved his arse, Aleck would be more humble—develop some respect for Clan Gregor. Eoin reached the chieftain just as a MacDonald drew back for a killing thrust of his sword. Eoin caught the assailant's arm and used its momentum to throw the varmint to the ground.

"I do not need your help, MacGregor!" Aleck bellowed.

"Aye? Then stop chopping wood and bury that sword in someone's gut." Eoin spun and faced the man he'd sent to the dirt. With a bellow, the warrior charged—straight onto the point of Eoin's razor-sharp sword. With a grimace, Eoin kicked him back and yanked his blade from the dying man's flesh.

Aleck's horse reared. Shrieking, the chieftain flew from the saddle, then crashed to the ground in a heap. A MacDonald man sprang over the MacIain with a high-pitched wail. Lunging, Eoin swung his sword up in time to deflect the man's deadly blow.

The guard regarded Eoin with a grating chuckle.

The two circled, their eyes assessing one another. The MacDonald man sucked in heavy gasps, while he bled from the nose. "Ye come to be killed?"

"Nay. But you did." Eoin sprang forward. Years of perfecting his trade had turned him into a lethal killing machine, and he quickly dispatched the man, and the next, and the next. When blood changed the dirt from brown to red, the MacDonalds turned tail and ran for home.

Eoin knelt beside Aleck and removed the big man's helm. He was out cold, but still breathing. Eoin had seen far too much of the bastard whilst out cold—though he preferred comatose to the usual braggart. Beneath the lower vambrace plate, MacIain's arm rested at an awkward angle. Aye, he'd broken the limb during his fall no doubt.

Eoin inclined his head toward his henchman. "Fergus, bring me a couple sturdy sticks. I must fashion a splint." He then tore a bit of cloth from his shirt. The same one Lady Helen had recently stitched for him. He hated to do it, but Aleck's arm needed to be set straight away. Eoin unbuckled the armor guard from Aleck's forearm.

Fergus came over with the sticks. "Jesus, that's a nasty break."

"Aye. Good thing the varlet's unconscious, otherwise setting it would hurt like hell." Eoin motioned for Fergus to move beside him. "I'll do what I can to straighten the arm out, then you slide the splints in place."

Fergus nodded.

Eoin glanced at a pair of onlookers. "You men, hold him down just in case he wakes."

Eoin grasped either side of the break and tugged. Then using all his strength he used the heel of his hand to force the bone back in place.

Aleck bucked and bellowed. "Bleeding, bloody, pox-ridden ballocks!"

"Quickly. The splints!" Eoin yelled.

Fergus clapped the sticks in place and held them firm while Eoin tightly wrapped the bandage.

Aleck bellowed like a bull in the castrating pen. "Are you trying to kill me?"

"Nay," Eoin said, tying the bandage. "Just saving your arm, you ungrateful boar."

"I didn't ask for your help."

Eoin smirked. "Mayhap next time I should let them kill you."

Aleck hissed through gritted teeth. "I was wearing them down, you smug bastard—I always win in the end."

Eoin clenched his fist around the bandage, close to smashing his knuckles into the bastard's face just to shut him up again. "Och, you would have been run through after you fell from your horse and were out cold."

"Aye," Grant said with a hint of admiration in his voice. "I've never seen a man move so fast. Sir Eoin arrived in the nick of time. Any later and you would have been skewered for certain, m'laird."

Aleck turned a shade of green as if he'd swallowed a vile tonic.

Biting his bottom lip, Eoin choked back a laugh while he finished securing the splint. Once he'd tied off the bandage, he stood and looked to Grant. "Any dead?"

"Three of ours. Six of theirs."

"Only six?" Eoin asked, a little surprised. He'd killed four of them. "And the injured?"

"Scrapes and cuts—the usual," said Samuel.

"Any injured men ride the horses. I ken you're all tired, but we cannot leave the keep guarded by a handful of aging soldiers."

He prayed there would be no more surprises. Though he was a trained killer, every time he took a life, a piece of his heart tore away. After many a battle, Eoin had taken to the seclusion of the Highland mountains just to be alone with his demons. He saw every face in his dreams. Men all looked the same when they faced certain death—stunned and terrified until their eyes turned vacant.

# Chapter Fifteen

Helen cradled Maggie in her arms and sat in the rocker while humming a madrigal. The bairn cooed and gurgled as if she wanted to sing with Helen too. Reaching up, Maggie grasped at Helen's linen wimple, her eyes wide as if the bairn liked the feel of the cloth.

"'Tis soft, is it not?" Helen took the bairn's hand and guided her fingers over her woolen kirtle. Maggie's eyes rounded with surprise and she laughed. "You like the different textures?"

The babe reached up and tugged Helen's veil until it nearly came off. "And you're a strong lassie if I've ever seen one."

"Aye she is," Sarah said from her perch in front of the hearth. "And almost as bonny as her mother."

"How sweet of you to say." Helen smoothed her hand over Maggie's curly black locks and gazed at her daughter with warmth filling her heart. "I daresay this little one will be far more beautiful. Who could possibly resist those enormous blue eyes?" As soon as the words came out, Helen could think of only one person who wouldn't be entranced by Maggie's eyes, and that was the bairn's father. *If only that man would take the time to simply look at her. He would fall in love just like everyone else.*

The back of Helen's neck pricked. It shamed her to think about the incident with Eoin in the shed. *I never should have allowed him to kiss me*. Even after a day, her lips still tingled…her senses still filled with his woodsy scent.

Helen instinctively cradled Maggie tighter to her breast. Aleck had struck her three times now. There was no longer any doubt his animosity toward her was growing worse. She touched the bruise on her jaw, still tender from his slap. What if he took out his anger on their daughter? He'd already said he'd use Maggie to foster an alliance—garner more lands for himself. Of course that was the way of things…but could Helen trust Aleck to act in their child's best interest rather than his own?

Deep down, she knew the answer to her questions. And that realization tied her stomach in knots.

The ram's horn sounded. Helen held her breath as her gaze shot to Sarah.

It sounded twice more.

"Dear Lord, no." She sprung from the rocker and carried Maggie to the window. A lead ball sank to the pit of her stomach. Two galleys rounded the point of Ardnamurchan.

Sarah stepped in behind her. "Are those MacDonald ships?"

"I've no reason to think they're not." Helen turned. "Take Maggie and bolt the door behind me. Do not open it for a soul until I return."

"They're aiming to attack?"

Helen grasped her skirts and headed toward the door. "They burnt out the Gilles's croft in Sunart. Why should they be sailing to Mingary on a goodwill sortie?"

Sarah drew in a sharp gasp. "Lord Jesus, help us."

Before opening the door, Helen faced the nursemaid. "I am leaving my daughter in your care. She is *the* one person in this world I love most. Protect her with your life." Blinking to recover her wits, Helen raced for the top of the battlements.

With only a skeleton crew of aged fighting men, this would be a harrowing day indeed. Regardless of the odds, she would defend Mingary and fight until she drew her last breath. *May God have mercy on our souls.*

***

Atop the wall-walk facing the sea, Helen stared at the black cannon Aleck had brought in from Portugal. It was an ugly thing that looked like death. She glanced at Mr. Keith, the old guard who'd been left in charge of safeguarding the castle. "Do you know how this contraption works?"

"I've had a bit of training with it. 'Tis not too hard. You ladle in the black powder, tamp it down, then drop in the ball and set your sights, light the slow match and pray."

Helen definitely would hold up her end with praying. "Do you have enough of those lead balls to sink both the MacDonald galleys?"

He gazed out to sea and shuddered. "God, I hope so."

The galleys had sailed close enough that she could see the colors of their pennants. *MacDonald for certain.*

Mr. Keith pointed toward the stairwell. "You'd best go inside, m'lady."

Helen crossed her arms. "I will do no such thing. In the absence of Sir Aleck, I shall direct this battle, and pray it does not turn into a siege." *Where in Heaven's name are the men? Aleck left me here alone with a handful of old guards and had the gall to call me daft? I shall never forgive him for this.*

Archers approached carrying barrels of arrows. Helen dashed toward them. "Have you lit the brazier?"

"You want us to fire flaming arrows?" Torquil asked as if she'd sailed down from the moon.

"Aye." She held up a finger. "Let them make the first move. If they're hostile, we shall show no mercy, and flaming arrows will set their boats afire. My father always said the most dangerous thing for a galley ship is a fire." Thank heavens she'd listened to Da's tales of fighting in The Crusades.

Every muscle in her body clenched while she marched back and forth atop the wall-walk, watching the MacDonalds sail nearer. Never in her life had a sailing ship appeared to take such a long time with its approach. Jitters twitched along her skin.

The men set two braziers burning with peat—one on either side of the sea-facing wall.

Mr. Keith grasped Helen's arm. "I mean it. You must go inside, m'lady. They'll be firing arrows soon and you haven't even a hauberk or a helmet."

Nor did she have a cloak—and an icy gale blew relentlessly from the sea. "I'll not leave."

"Then at least seek shelter behind a merlon."

The MacDonald galleys were now near enough she could see the warriors lined on one side with bows and arrows ready to fire. She ducked behind the safety of the stone and raised her arm. "They're preparing to fire. Light your arrows!"

The men stared as if they'd never been in a battle before—or perhaps they'd never been commanded by a woman before.

Sucking in a stuttering breath, she peeked beyond the stone and out to sea. Arrows soared toward them. "Now!" she screamed, covering her eyes.

"In coming!" someone yelled from down the wall-walk.

The men all ducked behind the safety of the four-foot stone walls as arrows hissed overhead and smacked against the stone battlements. Helen dared look. No one had fallen. "Fire!" she shrieked.

She peered around the stone merlon and watched the MacIain arrows fly. Some hit the nearest ship, but they'd need more. Clenching her fists, she mustered her strength. "The only way to keep them at bay is to beat them. We have the power to hold them off, but every single man on this wall must shoot straight and hit your mark!"

The men reloaded their bows with trembling hands.

Helen bolstered her resolve. Cowering behind the stone wall was no place for a woman who must instill confidence in her soldiers. Keeping her head down, she hastened around to the back side of the cannon. "Set your sights Mr. Keith, and sink those two galleys." She marched down the row of elderly men, now firing their arrows at will. "They think they can attack Mingary? I assure you, it will take a great deal more than two galleys filled with fighting men to conquer us. We have five-foot thick walls and a grand gun from Portugal on our side."

The cannon boomed. Helen jumped so high, she nearly fell off the wall-walk. She coughed at the acrid smoke burning her throat. And while the haze cleared, her ears took on a high-pitched hum. She peered through a crenel notch and strained until she could again see the galleys. Curses, the cannonball missed its mark, but flames leapt above the hull on one of the galleys.

Helen's heart skipped a beat.

They'd made their first gain.

She raced toward Mr. Keith. "Can you make an adjustment and actually hit one of those galleys?" The words rattled from her tongue in an anxious high pitch.

"That's what I'm trying to accomplish." Sweat dripped from his brow as he turned the crank. "I cannot believe I actually got the blasted thing to fire."

She gave a sharp nod. "You're doing well. But we must stop them from reaching the sea gate."

Baring his teeth, he strained with one more crank. "Stand back, m'lady."

She stared at the long black gun as if it were about to explode and take down the wall. The thing nearly killed her when she strolled on the beach. Would it now be her salvation? *'Tis time to make the gun worth its while.*

At the chilling sound of a man's anguished shriek, Helen whipped around. "Oh, no." She sprinted to the far end of the wall-walk. Torquil lay writhing on the stony floor, gasping and grunting from an arrow shot to the shoulder.

Helen dropped to her knees beside him. "Hold on and we'll set you to rights." She glanced over her shoulder. Every able-bodied man was needed to defend the keep from the pillagers below. And she knew better than to try to pull the arrow out now—but there must be a way to help him endure the pain. "Have you any whisky?"

"I-I-I've a flask in me sporran," he managed through panting breaths.

Finding it, she held the spirit to his lips. "Drink it all."

He guzzled greedily.

"They're coming ashore, m'lady," Mr. Keith hollered.

She stoppered the flask and set it beside him. "Hold on, sir. We'll see to your comfort as soon as we are able."

Torquil's weathered face ashen, he nodded.

Helen picked up the man's bow and ignited an arrow tip. The MacDonald men were jumping over the side of their galleys and splashing through the water toward the sea gate. A row of men carried a pole as thick as a tree trunk—a battering ram for certain. *Heaven help us, they aim to smash through the gate.*

She trained an arrow straight down on a man. She'd hunted deer and rabbits, though had never killed a human being—but these men were attacking her home. Holding her breath, she released. Her arrow fell short. She must raise her sights to account for the distance.

She pulled a second arrow from the barrel and lit the tip.

The cannon boomed.

This time Helen didn't flinch. With the ringing in her ears intensifying, she focused on another MacDonald raider and let her arrow fly. Smoke and the stench of burning sulfur stung her eyes as she lined up her sights. She hit her mark and the man fell to the ground, writhing and clutching at the arrow.

Her insides squelched like she was about to vomit.

Ahead, the whistling cannonball smashed the stern of a MacDonald galley—though it wasn't enough to sink the boat, Mr. Keith had done some damage.

But there was no time to celebrate. The battering ram boomed as it slammed against the sea gate. The bailey walls shook. Stones crumbled. It was a matter of time before the MacDonalds breached the walls.

Nonetheless, Helen and her crew of grey-haired warriors fought while the cannon blasted and the battering ram blow thudded, cracking timbers with each strike.

Helen fired arrows until her fingertips grew raw from the bowstring. Beyond the sea gate, the MacDonald men were chanting a cadence of heave-ho with every thundering impact from the battering ram.

Unable to find a clear shot, Helen closed her eyes and prayed. *Dear God in heaven, please save us*. Her eyes flew open when a bellowing roar erupted from the courtyard.

Eoin and the men poured in from the forward gate, weapons drawn.

With a horrible crash, the sea gate gave way. Spurring to action, Helen pulled back her bow. She shifted from side to side, looking for a shot. Before her eyes, mayhem erupted while MacDonalds collided with MacGregors and MacIains. If she fired now, she could kill one of her own. Holding her bow at the ready, blades flickered in the sunlight in a brutal battle.

Helen had always thought watching men spar was like a dance, but this was nowhere near the same. Ugly, brutal, vicious, the men attacked. Iron clashed with screeching scrapes of metal on metal. Blood curdling screams made chills slither over Helen's skin.

Helpless to fight from the battlements, she and the archers watched in horror as blood spurted and the cries of men echoed between the inner bailey walls. Helen had never been witness to a battle in her own home. If the men failed, there would be little hope for survival. They might even try to ravish *her*…or…

She shuddered in concert with another blast from the cannon.

*I will die before one of them places his filthy hands on my daughter.*

Directly beneath her, Eoin fought two at once. By the saints, he was quick on his feet. His deadly sharp sword whipped through the air so fast, Helen only saw a silver blur swinging in arcs around him while he defended every blow. Just when he cut one down, another stepped up.

On and on the battle raged with terrors far worse than the stories Helen had heard—and no one ever described such raw violence—uglier and more brutal than anything she could have imagined. *War truly embodies hell on earth.*

"To the boats!" a loud bellow boomed over the throng.

Before Helen could make out who'd given the order, the MacDonald men ran for their galleys. Helen raced to the other side of the wall-walk. Mr. Keith's cannonballs had sunk one of their galleys. Eoin and his men gave chase while the surviving MacDonalds climbed over the hull and took up their oars.

Mr. Keith stepped in beside her. "Should I fire the cannon at them, m'lady?"

She'd seen enough bloodshed to last her lifetime. "I think not. Besides, if that noisy thing misfired, the men down on the shore could be injured." She had first-hand experience with that.

He grinned at her, stretching his weathered features. "My thoughts as well."

Eoin stood on the beach and watched the galley sail pick up the wind. It didn't look so proud with a torn pennant and the tip of its stern blown off. But Eoin looked magnificent with his sword in one hand, dirk in the other. Drawing in deep breaths, his shoulders rose and fell in a slow rhythm. He stood with his feet apart, braced as if he were ready for another attack.

A sunbeam broke through the clouds and illuminated him.

*A warrior sent from heaven.*

After the galley disappeared around the point of Ardnamurchan, Eoin turned and looked directly up at Helen. Her heart swelled in her chest. Time slowed for a moment while their gazes locked. Even if Helen had wanted to, she couldn't turn away.

*If only I could race down to the beach and fall into those brawny arms.*

Then Helen realized Aleck hadn't been involved in the battle at all.

Keith tapped her shoulder. "They're leading Sir Aleck into the keep."

She clapped a hand over her mouth and dashed to the other side. "Oh my heavens." Aleck was walking, but his shoulders stooped, and he held his arm close to his body.

Helen rushed to the stairwell and pattered down three flights until she met Aleck and his men at the second-floor landing. "What happened m'laird?"

"Broke my arm fighting in Sunart." From the looks of the purple bruise spreading from his forehead and around his eye, he'd nearly broken his head as well.

"We must tend it directly." She reached for the elbow not in a sling. "Please allow me to assist you to your chamber."

He jerked away. "I need neither your sympathy nor your help. Send Mary up with a flagon of whisky."

"M'laird." Helen looked over her shoulder at the stunned faces of the guard. Eoin stepped behind them. "At least allow me to see to your comfort and then—"

"Be gone with you and do as I say." He raised his hand as if to deliver a slap, but the wallop stopped midair.

Eoin's big hand wrapped around Aleck's wrist. "The lady just held your keep against Alexander MacDonald and your thanks is to strike her?" Eoin's voice seethed, as if he could snap Aleck's arm in two.

Sir Aleck faced the MacGregor Chieftain and snarled. "If I weren't waylaid, I'd finish this now."

"Aye?" Eoin emitted a spiteful chuckle. "Backstab the man who saved you in Sunart?"

Aleck jutted his face so close to Eoin's, their noses almost touched. "I told you I didn't need saving."

"Too right," Eoin growled. "I should have let the MacDonald bastard run you through."

"You sicken me. Have you not a beloved sword to sharpen?" Aleck turned his shoulder and limped toward his chamber. "Send Mary up with my whisky and leave me be."

After the door closed behind him, Helen clapped her hands to her cheeks and ran. Must her husband now humiliate her every time she saw him? So, their first born was a lass. They weren't the only couple in the world who had produced a female child first. Did Aleck want a boy so he could cast her aside and never have to perform the vile act of consummation with her again?

Worse, did Eoin MacGregor have to ascend the stairs just as Aleck was issuing his retort? And would she have ended up with yet another blackened eye had Eoin not intervened? Helen gasped. Would Aleck seek retribution against her dear friend and ally? Undoubtedly he would. He could not withstand any man who made him appear weak.

Tears dribbled down her cheeks as Helen reached the far stairwell and started up toward the nursery.

"Lady Helen," Eoin called after her. "Please wait."

She shook her head. "Go away."

Starting up, she hoped he'd turn around, take his men and sail back to Argyllshire. But his hand wrapped around her wrist. He grasped her firmly, but not so hard his fingers would leave a bruise. "Please stop. I'd like to talk—to thank you for all you have done."

Helen backed down the step, swiping a hand across her face. She didn't want him to see her crying yet again. "Pardon me?"

He placed his palm on the wall near her head. "I saw enough. You stood beside the men on the battlements and fought off the MacDonalds—my, you are quite a markswoman."

She smirked. "Aye, though all would have been lost had you not arrived when you did."

He casually leaned toward her. "But you wore the enemy down. Made our job easy. It would be an honor to have you in Clan Gregor any time."

If only that had been the way of things from the outset of her miserable adulthood. But no, she was married to Satan, and had been forced to act as a warrior woman due to circumstances, not because she was courageous or a great tactician. She'd had no other choice. She'd taken part in killing—and no matter how necessary it was to defend her home, her mind couldn't rationalize it. "I am most certainly not proud of this day."

She must have missed a tear, because he brushed the pad of his thumb over the corner of her eye. "'Tis because you have a kind heart. You should not have been forced to defend Mingary."

"But I did, and then Aleck—" She clapped her hands over her face. Her heart twisted in knots. She must stop seeking pity from Sir Eoin. So her husband hated her—had no qualms about embarrassing her in front of the entire clan or outsiders. There was nothing she could do about it now—not with Maggie tucked away in the nursery and Aleck threatening vile acts of vengeance.

Eoin grasped her hand between palms that had no right to be so warm. "My lady, no woman should be forced to endure the humiliation I witnessed today."

She tugged her fingers away. "Eoin, I know you have only the best intentions, but I must ask you to ignore Sir Aleck's gruff treatment of my person. After all, he is my husband. An alliance was made upon our betrothal and witnessed in the eyes of God. When he is ready, he will come to me to produce the heir he needs to continue the MacIain name. It is my duty to see it done." The words sank like lead all the way down to her toes.

His face fell as if he'd just lost a battle. "As you wish, m'lady." He took a step back and bowed. "But know this. I will sail for Dunstaffnage and then Iona on the morrow. If you should want me to carry missives to either of your brothers, I would be happy to personally deliver them on your behalf."

"I cannot."

He narrowed his gaze and his lips formed a straight line. "If not for yourself, think of your daughter. If he can raise a hand against you, what will he do to Miss Maggie once she starts laughing and running and playing? Do you want her to live in fear as you do?"

"I-I…" Pins and needles bristling across her skin, Helen curtseyed and fled up the tower stairs.

# Chapter Sixteen

After Helen had spent most of the evening holding Maggie to her breast, trying to protect her child from the MacDonald pillagers who had already sailed, Sarah had finally moved in beside her and held out her hands. Helen ignored the nursemaid for a moment. She didn't want to let go. She couldn't stop thinking about what could have happed if Eoin and his men hadn't arrived in time. Would the MacDonalds have killed her and the bairn? Helen never wanted to release Maggie from her arms.

"My heavens, you need your rest, m'lady." Sarah reached in for the sleeping bairn. "I'll put her down. You should go find something to eat and then your bed."

Helen wanted to tell the nursemaid to mind her own affairs. But she relented. As soon as she released Maggie, a cold chill washed over her. She wanted to stay. Only she could protect her daughter. And it seemed the world was against them.

Helen stared as Sarah rested the bairn in the cradle. She'd replayed Eoin's words over and over in her head: *If not for yourself think of your daughter. If he can raise a hand against you, what will he do to her once Miss Maggie starts laughing and running and playing? Do you want her to live in fear as you do?*

What would Helen do once Eoin was gone and no one remained who could stand up to the likes of Aleck MacIain?

Numb, she headed down the passageway. She couldn't eat. On top of everything else, she had killed a man. Her hands shook violently every time she pictured him clutching at the arrow and falling to the ground. *No wonder men drink so much whisky*. She needed a tot herself just to calm her tremors. Perhaps after a dram she might even be capable of thinking straight.

Helen roamed the passageways of Mingary without direction. Walking invigorated her and she sped her pace. As she paced, her mind honed. She had taken charge of affairs this day because there had been no other choice. And striding through the draughty passageways, she realized she'd achieved one good thing from today's experience. Confidence.

*If I do not take action to gain control over my life, no one will.*

Arriving at her bedchamber door, she knew exactly what she must do.

Upon entering, something thudded against the wall. *Aleck's bed.*

At first, Helen considered checking on him, but when a woman's voice moaned, the lady of the keep's stomach churned.

*Let Aleck while away his time with his leman. I will stand for his mistreatment no longer.*

She took a seat at the writing table, reached for a clean sheet of velum and inked her quill.

*My dearest brother John, His Worship, Bishop of the Isles,*

*It is with great heartache that I write to you this somber eve, but as Sir Eoin can attest, my situation at Mingary has become untenable…*

She omitted nothing, belied nothing. In doing this, she was, in effect, committing treason against her marriage vows and had no illusions that her story must be so infallible, neither her brother nor the Pope would question her plea. She had no doubt that if Aleck discovered she'd written this missive, he would either kill her or lock her in the dungeon until she died. If she were caught, she wouldn't be alive to protect Maggie, but if she did nothing, both she and her daughter would suffer under Aleck's yoke of tyranny.

After she signed her name, she sanded the parchment, then folded it and held a red wax wafer to the candle flame. Once she sealed the missive with the Campbell crest that she'd brought with her from Glen Orchy, she stared at the velum as if at any moment it would be set alight by God's own hand.

Helen stood and paced. *How can I take the missive to Eoin without anyone knowing?* If she stole away to his chamber, it would be scandalous. But as this late hour, it would also be unlikely she'd be seen by anyone.

The vulgar noises coming from the laird's chamber had been replaced by Aleck's rumbling snores. Was Mary sleeping wrapped by his good arm, or had she returned to her cottage? Helen hadn't heard the door.

She chewed her thumbnail and paced. Every time she passed the table, she shuddered. Sleep would be impossible with that missive on the table.

***

After serving the king and Duncan Campbell for years, Eoin had learned to sleep lightly. A knight made enemies enforcing the king's laws, a fact never far from Eoin's mind. No one had to tell him he couldn't be too careful and, as a result, he always slept on his side, facing the door.

The hinges must have been well oiled, because it made not a sound when the door opened and someone slipped inside. Instantly awake, Eoin made no move, and waited for the backstabber to attack. The man kept to the shadows, but the outline of his form was too small to be Aleck MacIain. Eoin wouldn't have been surprised if that man tried to slit his throat whilst he slept.

Even the intruder's breathing was inaudible as he hugged the walls, still as a statue.

The orange glow of coals from the hearth cast eerie amber light, shrouded and heavy with nocturnal shadows. But Eoin didn't fear the dark. He used it to his advantage.

He palmed the dirk under his pillow and waited. Let the intruder make the first move—it would be his last. There could only be one reason for someone to steal into Eoin's chamber—Aleck MacIain wanted him dead. The vainglorious chieftain had no integrity. Clearly, he saw the fact that Eoin had saved his life as a slight to his masculinity.

*Sending someone to murder me? This is the last straw.*

In his mind's eye, Eoin pictured how the culprit would sneak across the floorboards and attack. But the intruder made not a move. Squinting, Eoin peered through the dim light. Crouched in the shadows, he couldn't make out the stature of the man. Not that it mattered. As soon as the varlet crept toward the bed, Eoin would run his blade across his neck, and then he'd gather his men and make a damning report to the king. Attempting to murder a king's enforcer? Doubtless, such an act would prove Aleck MacIain a traitor. His lands would be forfeit to the king and Aleck would be declared an outlaw just like the MacDonalds who'd attacked this day.

Eoin waited.

Scarcely breathing, the intruder remained still for what seemed like an eternity.

*This is a very patient man indeed—or terrified—and so he should be. Fear, aye? Perhaps the bastard needs an invitation.*

Eoin sprang from the bed, landing in a crouch, dirk at the ready. "What manner of murderer is it who enters my chamber and hides in the shadows?"

"Eoin?" A woman's voice trembled. "Y-y-you're awake?"

Shocked as if he'd been smacked between the eyes, Eoin lowered his weapon. "Lady Helen?"

"Aye." She stepped from the darkness, shielding her eyes from him.

Eoin looked down. Without a stich of clothing, he must have frightened the wits out of the poor woman. He tossed his dirk on the pillow and snatched the plaid from his bed, tying it around his waist. "Forgive me. I thought you were an intruder."

"Oh?" She emitted a deep chuckle, as if not entirely repulsed by what she'd seen. "Is it not every night you lie abed, waiting for the lady of the keep to spirit into your chamber?"

He laughed as well, scratching his head. "'Tis good to hear you're in good humor, m'lady."

She sighed and moved further into the room, her gaze fixated on his stomach. "I wish it were so. But since we last met, I've not been able to think of anything other than your words."

Eoin's muscles clenched as he held his breath. Was she saying she agreed with him? "It wasn't my place to be so forward. Forgive me."

"There's nothing to forgive." Her gaze skimmed up his torso and met his. By the stars, the amber from the coals made her eyes shimmer like the North Sea on a clear day. "I needed a good jolt to make me realize that by remaining at Mingary, I am putting my daughter's future at risk. And as you said, my brother, John, is the only person I know who's in a position to help."

"I am glad you have reconsidered." Eoin's heart thumped against his chest. He gestured to the table. "Would you sit, m'lady? I'll light a candle."

"I mustn't stay long." She moved to the seat and Eoin swiftly stepped behind her and held the chair. She placed a sealed missive atop the table.

Eoin wanted to wrap his arms around her and tell her how courageous she'd been. But he busied himself with lighting a candle. "I've nothing but a tot of whisky to offer you."

She tapped dainty fingers over her lips. "I never drink it." Glancing up with a spark in her eyes he hadn't seen since she was a lass, she arched her eyebrows. "However, after the events of this day, mayhap a wee sip would be permissible."

"Straight away." Once he poured two small tots, Eoin sat opposite her. He glanced at the velum. "I take it this is for your brother, John?"

"Aye." She looked up with worry filling her eyes. "Are you still willing to act as messenger?"

He smoothed his finger around the wax seal. "I would be honored for you to entrust such a sensitive matter to my care."

Helen's breath caught and she stared at him for a moment. She needed not utter a word. This act of liberation scared her to death. It would scare anyone. Her trembling fingers lightly tapped the table and Eoin moved his hand atop hers for comfort. "'Tis a very brave thing you've done."

She nodded. "I couldn't sleep."

"'Tis not surprising." Her pulse beat a fierce rhythm beneath his palm. But this simple touch made his heart swell. If only he could tell her how much she meant to him. "I'm proud of you," he said, his voice husky.

She bit her bottom lip. "I-I feel numb."

"However nervous this may make you, I believe you should celebrate your decision." He forced himself to remove his hand and raise his cup. "Slainté."

"Slainté" She sipped and then coughed. "My, that is potent."

"It is." Eoin tapped the missive with his pointer finger. "You described your oppression…including Sir Aleck's infidelity?"

Helen nodded then took another dainty sip.

"What changed your mind?" Eoin asked.

"This day was so terrifying. Never before have I feared for my life, and you helped me realize that if anything happened to me, Maggie would be at Aleck's mercy." She covered her mouth and a high-pitched cry slipped between her fingers. "And Aleck has become more abusive toward me by the day." She fanned her face and took in a deep inhale. "I fear neither of us will be safe if we remain here."

Eoin shoved back his chair and knelt at Helen's side, grasping her hands between his palms. "You have made the right decision."

She cringed. "What if John refuses to appeal to the Pope on my behalf?"

"He won't. I promise." Eoin swallowed. If John did not offer his assistance, Eoin would take Helen's missive to the Pope himself.

Her breath stuttered. "I'm so afraid."

Eoin took her hands and pressed her palms to his heart. "You can do this. I saw you act with more courage today than I've witnessed in many men."

"But what if Aleck discovers I've written the missive?"

"I swear on my father's grave I will tell no one. Whilst I am away, go about your affairs as if nothing were any different."

She leaned forward and buried her face in his shoulder. "I shudder to think what Aleck will do if the Pope *does* approve the annulment."

Eoin smoothed a hand over her back. "When the time comes, you will have my protection. I've vowed it before and I will stand by my word no matter what." Eoin closed his eyes and pressed his lips to Helen's temple. If only he could hold her in his arms all night and whisper that everything would work out for the better. But such an act would be folly. If they were caught together, Aleck would severely punish Helen. He took in a deep breath. "In the meantime, try not to worry."

She wrapped her arms around his shoulders and clung tight. "I shall pray for your safety and swift return."

By the grace of God, her embrace felt heavenly. How much he wanted to kiss her again—to taste her succulent lips and mold her body to his.

But he steeled his resolve. "Allow me to escort you back to your chamber."

"I think not." She straightened and shook her head. "If anyone were to see us there would be a scandal—and that would make Aleck suspicious that I am up to something."

Eoin nodded. Of course she was right, but it didn't sit well with him that she would have to traverse the cold passageways alone.

He walked her to the door and placed his palm upon her cheek. "Sleep well m'lady." She looked up at him, her lips red as rose petals, her eyes so filled with emotion. Leaning forward, Eoin had no inclination to stop himself. His tongue slipped out and moistened his bottom lip while he dipped his head and covered her mouth.

His entire body ignited with unquenchable desire. He deepened his kiss and Helen matched his fervor. They bonded like a raging wildfire—two lost souls joining in the darkest hours of the night. The incredible softness of her unbound breasts plied his chest.

God, he wanted her.

The bed was only a few short paces behind them. But heaven strike him dead, he would not sully Lady Helen's virtue. She'd already taken a great risk by visiting his chamber. It took every ounce of control Eoin possessed to pull away and catch his breath. "I'll peer into the hall first. Once I'm sure 'tis clear, you must haste back to your chamber."

# Chapter Seventeen

"Iona ahead, m'laird," Fergus bellowed from the stern of the galley.

"Furl the sail," Eoin replied. He'd opted to sail to Iona before meeting with Duncan Campbell at Dunstaffnage. Eoin had known the Lord of Glenorchy most of his life. Delivering news of the MacDonald raids in Sunart and Ardnamurchan would cause consternation. Duncan would want to act swiftly, which might prevent Eoin from delivering Helen's missive with haste.

Honestly, Eoin knew he should rush to Dunstaffnage, but a quick detour to Iona would only set him back a day. Besides, they'd beaten the MacDonalds by land and by sea. Alexander and his kin would need time to lick their wounds before they tried another foolish attempt to regain their forfeited lands.

As the men heaved on the oars, heading toward Iona's white sands, he thought about how Aleck MacIain would react when he discovered Eoin and his men had sailed to make a full report. Eoin had purposefully asked his men rise at dawn and set sail before MacIain had broken his fast. He couldn't take a chance on the bastard insisting on sailing with them, even though Eoin would have been able to argue that Aleck's arm needed time to heal. Eoin couldn't give a rat's arse about upsetting the damn

Chieftain of Ardnamurchan, but if the moth-brained codpiece ever again released his ire on Lady Helen, Eoin would sooner kill him.

When the galley ran aground on the white sands of Iona, Eoin jumped over the side behind Fergus. "Keep the men near. I've some business at the abbey. We sail for Dunstaffnage as soon as I return."

Nuns wearing black habits hastened along the path beside the nunnery as Eoin made his way toward Iona Abbey. He removed his helm and bowed his head respectfully, but the women hardly noticed him and continued on their way.

The cloistered world of nuns and monks was foreign to him. He couldn't imagine taking a vow of poverty, chastity and obedience and then hiding from the world, praying at all hours—godly and ungodly.

When the path curved toward abbey, Eoin sped his pace. He was met at the cloister gates by a pair of sentries dressed in the uniforms of the Knights Hospitallers, with red crucifixes emblazoned in the middle of their white surcoats. They crossed their poleaxes in front of the door.

"Eoin MacGregor, Chieftain of Clan Gregor, here to see Sir John Campbell, Bishop of the Isles."

"State your purpose," said one.

Eoin thumped his cloak over the spot where he'd secured the missive. "I bear an urgent message from the bishop's family." He dared not allude to Lady Helen in any way.

"The bishop is seeing no visitors this day."

Eoin sauntered forward, smoothing his fingers over the hilt of his sword. "Did you not hear me? Sir John's family needs his attention straight away. Find someone to notify him of my presence before I summon my men and burn this gate to a cinder." He eyed each man with a deadly squint. "And neither of you will live to see it."

One nodded to the other. “Go, fetch the brother.”

In short order, an unarmed monk ushered Eoin through the gate. “The Bishop is a very busy man.” The man’s ring of brown locks shook with his head. “I’m not certain he’ll be able to see you today.”

Wearing a hauberk, helm, dirk and broadsword, Eoin was a tad over-armed for hallowed halls. “Just tell him who I am. We were good friends before Sir John joined the priesthood.”

“You may refer to him as His Worship, or Bishop Campbell,” the monk corrected, sniffing through his upturned nose. When they entered a square cloister surrounding a well-manicured courtyard, the man pointed to a bench. “Wait here whilst I inform the bishop of your presence.”

“Very well.” Sitting, Eoin glanced at the masonry of the uniform archways. He’d been in the vast nave of the church, but never in this courtyard. A mourning dove soared down and sat atop a bronze statue in the center of the courtyard. Its wings whooshed. Eoin heard the bird’s movement so clearly, he sensed that he’d stepped away from the world for a moment. Through the quiet, he could hear his own heartbeat—yet his senses weren’t heightened as they were before he stepped into danger.

He chuckled. *Mayhap I should be a bit uneasy, given the message I bring.*

Footsteps clattered through the adjoining passage, interrupting the ethereal tranquility. The monk stepped into view. “The bishop will see you now. You must be an important man, indeed.”

Eoin stood. “’Tis good to know Sir John isn’t too busy to visit with an old friend.”

“Please try to remember to address him as Bishop Campbell, m’laird.” The monk led Eoin to a large oak door and pulled on the blackened iron latch. The stone passageway had been rather stark, but the chamber beyond the door gleamed, alive with rich red tapestries trimmed with gold.

*John has done quite well for himself. Clearly, the Bishop of the Isles is a man of abundant wealth.*

Seated in a great upholstered chair, *His Worship* looked as if he could have been the Pope. He wore a brilliant red velvet chasuble trimmed with gold over a long purple dalmatic, and atop his head he wore a matching mitre. More affluent clothing had not the king.

Seeing him, the bishop stood and held out his arms. "Sir Eoin. My word, what a surprise."

Eoin took John's hand and kissed it. Every finger was bejeweled with rings bearing enormous stones. "'Tis good to see you, Bishop Campbell."

"Please, old friend. Call me John."

Eoin gave him a pointed look. "Not 'Your Worship'?"

As expected, John turned red. Aside from his garb, he remained the same humble man Eoin knew well. "'Tis a moniker I abhor and a dear friend from my past will not refer to me thus." He gestured to a smaller chair. "You are fortunate to find me at home. I'm leaving for Rome on the morrow."

Eoin grinned and removed Helen's missive from beneath his cloak. He did have impeccable timing. "How very fortuitous, indeed."

"And what brings you to Iona?"

Since leaving Mingary, Eoin had thought about how he'd broach the subject of Helen's plight with John. This was a matter not to be blurted in an outpouring, but needed careful depiction. He began by explaining the MacDonald uprising, which came as no surprise to the bishop—Duncan had ensured the Abbey was on alert as well—thus the heightened interrogation by the guard upon Eoin's arrival. Then he went on about how, much to his chagrin, he was assigned to Mingary and Aleck MacIain.

"How is my sister enjoying being lady of the keep in Ardnamurchan?" John rubbed his hands with a broad smile.

Eoin met John's expression by frowning and placed the missive on the small table between them. "Lady Helen is the reason for my visit."

John picked up the letter and examined the seal. "You haven't read this, I see."

"No, the lady entrusted it to me in utmost confidence." Eoin leaned forward. "Her situation is unbearable. I've seen swine treated better than your sister."

"Helen? Mistreated?" A deep crease formed between John's brows. "How preposterous."

Eoin's lips thinned. "I would have had the same reaction if I'd not witnessed her husband strike her." Then he jammed his finger into the table for added effect. "And I've seen telltale signs of further abuse as well."

John ran his thumb under the seal. "Who in their right mind would raise a hand against Helen? Of all my sisters she is the most genteel."

"True, and Lady Helen is frail as a lark. Though she has the heart of a lion." Eoin launched into a detailed description about how Helen held Mingary with a handful of aged warriors during the MacDonald attack.

John perused the missive, his frown growing deeper.

When Eoin described the part about Aleck humiliating Helen by insisting he be tended by his leman, Mary, the bishop held up his hand and asked for silence. His eyes reflected alarm. "This also says she fears for her daughter. I was not aware she'd birthed a bairn."

"Aye, Maggie—she named the lassie Margaret after your mother."

"'Tis a good name." Scratching his beard, John looked toward the window as if deep in thought. "Do you honestly think Aleck MacIain would threaten the life of his own daughter?"

"I believe so." Eoin nodded. "He's refused to see the bairn because he wanted a son—has told Lady Helen he'll marry Maggie off as soon as her menses show."

The crease between John's brows pinched. "'Tis not unusual to make an alliance when a lass reaches such an age."

"True." Eoin pointed to the missive. "*If* Maggie should survive that long. And if Lady Helen births another lass, I'm afraid MacIain will stop at nothing to snuff your sister out."

John shook his head. "Few annulments are granted—even fewer when requested by the wife."

"But surely, with your sister's life in danger…there could be an exception. You have the power of the church behind you. How could you force her to remain in a marriage where she is being beaten?"

"She could retire to the nunnery right here on Iona. I would guarantee her sanctuary."

"Helen has already asked to be sent to Iona with the bairn." Eoin looked John directly in the eye. "Sir Aleck told her he would kill her first."

John again held up a hand. Eoin pictured the bishop doing this often when considering a grave decision. Again John read the missive. "I cannot believe Helen has been mistreated so."

"With all due respect, I would not be here if I hadn't witnessed such abomination myself. Jesus, John, you know me, and moreover are aware I would not speak falsely to you or any man of God." Eoin spread his palms. "Can you not appeal to the Pope on this matter?"

The bishop folded the velum and slapped it in his palm. "If it is in the best interest of my sister, I will present her supplication to the Pope. This news is disturbing and I believe we should make haste. I fear for her safety and that of my niece."

Eoin attempted to mask his relief with a frown. "As do I."

"Do what you can to protect her until I send word."

"I shall. I must meet with Lord Duncan and then plan to return to Mingary forthwith."

John stood and ran his hand down his beard. "Before you go, I must ask one thing."

Eoin quickly rose as well. "By all means."

"As I recall during your fostering, you fancied Lady Helen. Ah…you haven't committed a sin?" John drew out the word sin with a suggestive lilt.

Though he should have expected this question, it still took him aback. Eoin shook his head with vehemence. "Never. Neither I nor the lady would stoop to such a disgrace."

John patted Eoin's shoulder. "I thought no less, but it was a question that needed asking. If an annulment is to be considered at all, there must be no errant behavior on Lady Helen's behalf, else she could end up tied to the stake and burned."

Eoin shuddered. He couldn't deny he hadn't thought about Helen in that way. But John's words drove home the need for saintly behavior. "When can I expect word?"

"I will request an audience with His Holiness as soon as I arrive in Rome, but traveling across the channel can be treacherous, no matter the time of year. Two months is my best estimate."

Bowing, Eoin thanked the heavens this detour to Iona hadn't been in vain. "I wish you a safe journey."

***

He didn't usually lie abed when injured, but Aleck's arm bloody hurt. He blamed Eoin MacGregor for that. The bastard had been none too gentle when he'd applied the splints. Aleck growled. He'd wager MacGregor took great pleasure in setting the bone.

The bastard again set sail without saying a word. *At least I no longer have to put up with his stench.*

Mary offered him a tonic. "This will help with the pain, m'laird."

Aleck scowled. "Does it have whisky in it?"

"'Tis willow bark steeped with valerian."

He pushed it away. "I'll not take another one of your concoctions without a healthy tot of whisky."

"Are you planning to continue to act like a milksop, m'laird?" Mary huffed.

"Pardon me?"

She placed the cup on the bedside table. "In all seriousness. You allow Lady Helen to force me to tend the pigs and then you refuse a wee bitter brew because it hasn't a dram of spirit?" She chuckled and squeezed his upper arm. "You still *feel* like a brawny Highlander."

He batted her hand away. "Silence." He grabbed the cup from the table and threw it back, forcing himself not to make a sour face. "What is this you say? Helen made you tend the pigs?"

She sat beside him and smoothed her fingers over the plaid. "Did you not command it?"

He shifted against the pillows. "Of course I would do no such thing. When did this occur?"

"After Sir Eoin left for Sunart, Lady Helen took charge as if she were lord of the castle." Mary thumped the bed. "She shouted orders to everyone, and then she pointed at me and gave me the lowliest duty of all."

Aleck frowned. It came as no surprise that Helen acted out against his leman, now that she knew the truth.

Though Helen had never shown she possessed a backbone. Regardless, it was a relief he no longer needed to pretend. Before Helen had birthed the worthless female bairn, Aleck had felt compelled to keep his affair hidden from his wife—but now he cared no more.

He'd never been attracted to Helen. First of all, she had no figure whatsoever. If she bound her breasts, she could pass for an adolescent boy. He hated her demureness, always trying to make everything right, always doing things to compensate for his *gruff miens*, as she'd referred to them. She had no idea how to handle the affairs in Ardnamurchan. If he showed the slightest inkling of compassion, his clansmen would start taking advantage. Aye, a chieftain had no recourse but to rule with an iron fist, lest he lose his lands and his castle to someone closer to home than Alexander MacDonald.

"What are you going to do about it?" Mary cut through his thoughts.

"As soon as I can use this arm, I'll hunt down Alexander MacDonald and send him to hell."

Mary frowned. "I meant, will you allow Lady Helen to treat me like a stable hand? Do I mean so little to you that you'll allow *her* to command *me* to tend pigs?" The tenor of Mary's voice rose with every word until she sounded on the verge of hysterics.

Aleck was in no mood to hear supplications even if they were from the woman he loved. But when the flicker of ire in Mary's eye softened into a seductive glint, his heart squeezed. Truly, he could never allow Helen to mistreat his leman. If Helen had done her duty and had grown pregnant when they'd first married—and birthed a son—Aleck would not be in this predicament.

Helen would be dead.

He reached out and grasped Mary's hand. "Ask Sir Grant to bring Lady Helen to me and I will see to her priorities."

Mary turned his hand over and swirled her middle finger around his palm. "But I've something to tell you first." Her words were pensive. It wasn't like Mary to be shy about anything.

But her touch soothed him. He waggled his brows. "What is it?"

"I'm with child."

***

Tending the wounded in the great hall, Helen applied a cool cloth to Torquil's forehead, then pulled away the bandage and examined the arrow wound in his shoulder. Yellow puss oozed from it. She bit her bottom lip and offered a silent prayer that he'd survive the fever. So many MacIain men had been injured during the fighting. Most sported cuts that would soon heal, but Torquil and Roy could very well succumb to their now putrid wounds.

Sir Grant entered the hall and stopped beside her. "How is he?"

"I'm afraid no better."

"Sir Aleck has asked to see you."

Helen glanced at Torquil and wondered why her husband would care to see her now. Above stairs, he had Mary to give him everything he needed. "How is his arm?" she asked.

"I haven't seen him." Sir Grant shrugged. "Mistress Mary fetched me."

*Why on earth wouldn't she just come tell me? This situation grows worse by the day*. Helen wiped her hands on her apron and stood. "Perhaps the chieftain wishes to listen to a merry tune. I haven't played my lute for him in some time."

The guard bowed and gestured to the stairwell. "M'lady."

Grant accompanied her to Aleck's chamber, which was a quandary. *Mayhap he's concerned for the safety of Mingary whilst Aleck's abed. I certainly would be if I were he.*

Aleck sat propped up against the pillows, his arm in a sling across his waist. The chieftain frowned when they entered—looked directly at Helen and narrowed his eyes.

She glanced toward Grant. *Now what have I done?*

"Exactly why did you command Mistress Mary to tend the pigs?" Aleck drove straight to the point.

Helen rolled her eyes to the ceiling. *For goodness sake.* Was she to be reprimanded for taking charge when it was her duty to do so? Of course her husband would give no accolades for her work in holding the castle after he'd abandoned her and ridden east.

She sighed. "I assigned duties to everyone. Mistress Mary was idle and the livestock needed tending. After all, she manages her chickens. I saw no harm in asking her to tend the pigs as well."

"It was demeaning for her."

Something inside Helen's heart snapped while a flash of heat seared across the back of her neck. "You are serious? And you think rejecting me in front of the clan and bellowing for your leman does nothing to subjugate *my* honor?"

"I knew it." Aleck slammed his fist into the mattress. "You lashed out at Mistress Mary in a jealous rage because I prefer the widow in my bed."

"I did no such thing." She pointed toward the door. "Ask Mr. Keith. He was there. I was simply preparing to defend the keep against attack. Which, by the way, I managed to do whilst you were breaking your arm in Sunart."

"Hold your tongue, you wicked shrew." Aleck pulled his dagger from beneath his pillow and pointed it at her.

With her heart thundering in her chest, Helen skittered toward the door. He'd never threatened her with a weapon before.

"You are fortunate I am abed, else I would take great pleasure in cutting out your barbed tongue."

Helen clapped a hand over her mouth. From the evil glare in his eyes, she didn't doubt he could do it. Trembling, she scuffled aside. How dare he threaten her for speaking out against a woman who had lowered herself to that of a whore? Her eyes rimmed with tears.

Sir Grant stepped forward. "M'laird. I think Lady Helen acted with the courage of a warrior. She managed to keep the MacDonalds at bay until we arrived—"

"Oh really? And who pays your wages, you irreverent beef-witted codpiece? As I recall, Alexander MacDonald was bashing through the sea gate with a battering ram when we arrived. Lady Helen did nothing but issue orders and fire a few paltry arrows as I've heard it reported."

She threw her fists to her hips. "We sank one of the MacDonald galleys!"

He slashed his dagger through the air. "You nearly destroyed my brand new cannon."

"Preposterous!" Helen's mind raced. Who would deceive her thus? Or would Aleck twist the truth so he didn't appear incompetent? By all the saints, she dare not utter another word, else Aleck would make good on his threat.

He pointed the ridiculous dagger at Sir Grant. "Take her to the dungeon. Allow her to see no one—especially that shrieking little brat she birthed." Then he glowered at Helen. "Whilst you rot, think about your station here and about what *I* care for. Your role is to please me and provide my heir."

Every muscle in her body clenched. She had to say it, though the thought made ice course through her blood. "How can I fulfill my duty if you will not return to my bed?"

Throwing the dagger at the floor, Aleck barely missed Helen's feet. She skittered into Sir Grant.

Her husband's steely eyes filled with hate. "Your place is not to question me."

Grant seized her arm. "Come, m'lady."

"No!" She struggled to wrench her arm free from the henchman's grasp. "My place is not to be locked in the dungeon when I have committed *no* crime. I am a *Campbell*, daughter of the legendary Lord of Glenorchy. My father was Scotland's hero."

Aleck sneered. "Unfortunate you are not more like him."

*I am my father's daughter and you can never take that away from me.*

Grant again tugged on her arm and pulled her into the passageway.

Helen stumbled over her skirts. "I am no common criminal!"

"You are and have always been a thorn in my side!" Aleck's hateful bellow echoed through the stony corridor.

# Chapter Eighteen

On the second floor of Dunstaffnage Castle, Eoin sat with Lord Duncan and King James in the king's solar and stared at the map on the table in front of them. They'd gone over the plan so many times, the topography of the west coast of Scotland was permanently emblazoned upon Eoin's mind. Worse, as he feared, as soon as he'd arrived at Dunstaffnage, he'd been embroiled in meetings about the MacDonald raids up and down the seaboard. At least he'd learned the attack on Ardnamurchan lands had been a part of many raids the MacDonalds had staged to wreak havoc against the king.

Lord Duncan hit the table with his fist. "We cannot allow them to further build their forces. We must attack at once."

The king ran his fingers down to the point of his brown beard, making his frown look graver and far older than his twenty years. "We shall not fail this time. I will have Alexander MacDonald's head. I gave him quarter once. It shan't happen again."

Eoin hid his smirk behind a cough. "If Aleck MacIain doesn't kill him first. The Chieftain of Ardnamurchan is hell bent on seeking revenge."

The Lord of Glenorchy gave Eoin a stern glare. "Given only two galleys attacked, I'd wager Alexander was only toying with MacIain—giving him a warning. If MacDonald wanted to sack Mingary, she would have fallen."

*How easy it is for a man to surmise, when he wasn't even there.*

Duncan moved one of the wooden markers carved in the shape of a galley and positioned it in front of the stronghold of Dunyveig on the Isle of Islay. "Spies report Alexander is preparing to defend our attack here. If we move now, as I recommend, he'll be out-muscled, out-maneuvered and out-smarted. I'd wager my first born he'll fall right into the king's hands. Sir Aleck will have to settle on a win for Scotland, rather than avenging his feud."

Eoin had to agree—after all, they'd been sitting in this stifling chamber, planning this siege for an entire sennight. He pushed back his chair and stood. "I'll sail for Ardnamurchan at dawn." *Finally, I'll have the opportunity to inform Helen about my visit with her brother.*

"No need." Duncan moved the wooden figurine of the MacIain galley through the sound and placed it in front of Dunstaffnage on the Firth of Lorn. "I've already sent a messenger to summon Sir Aleck and his army. I expect them within a sennight."

Eoin gaped. Perhaps he should have informed Duncan of Helen's plight, but this was not the place. He most certainly couldn't mention it in the king's presence. Besides, Eoin had been reluctant to say anything to Duncan because one never knew how the baron would react. He'd made an alliance with Aleck MacIain with his sister's marriage, and to learn that she was planning an annulment could cause Duncan to confront Aleck directly. Eoin feared such a move would put Lady Helen's very life in danger.

He grumbled under his breath. He'd wanted to return to Mingary to ensure Lady Helen's safety. Aleck behaved unpredictably. Even in the short time he'd been at

Mingary, the chieftain had grown more hostile toward his wife.

*At least she'll be safe if Aleck is sailing here.* Eoin's gut roiled. *But will he sail with his men given his arm is in a sling?* "You do recall he broke his arm fighting in Sunart?"

"Aye, but a man doesn't need two arms to stand at the helm of a galley and shout commands," Duncan said, gesturing for Eoin to resume his seat.

"And I disagree with you, Glenorchy. Now is not the time to attack. We'll let them think we've lost interest first." The king snapped his fingers and motioned for the valet to refill his goblet. "But I do agree 'tis time to unite our armies, though not here where we are in plain sight."

"What do you suggest?" Duncan asked.

The king smiled. "Tabert."

"How long will we sit on our laurels at that old keep?" Eoin mumbled, casting his gaze to the fire crackling in the hearth. The heat sweltering around the room was suffocating. *It would be best to keep MacIain away from Helen for as long as possible until word arrives the annulment has been granted. Mayhap the king's idea has merit.*

The only problem with this change in plans was that Eoin had no idea when he'd see Lady Helen again. Nor could he send her a missive advising of his meeting with John. Putting news of such sensitivity in writing would be too dangerous.

Duncan whacked him on the shoulder. "What the devil is under your skin? You've been on edge since you arrived a sennight ago."

Eoin knitted his brows, feigning an addled expression. "I've no idea to what you're referring." He spread his palms for added effect. "We've a madman trying to reclaim the Hebrides and the northwest of Scotland and revert it to Norse rule. Forgive me if I'm a bit concerned."

"You ken as well as I we'll quash the rebellion." Duncan shrugged. "But it isn't like you to worry. Usually you're the first man to take up his sword."

"That is precisely why I'm irritated. I've been sitting in this solar for too long talking about what we plan to do. I was ready to sail into battle three days past."

The king chuckled. "'Tis settled then. If my nobles are growing impatient, I can only imagine how tempers are flaring in the ranks. I agree with Sir Eoin, we shall move our base to Tabert and create a ruse. We'll give them time—make the MacDonalds think we've given up on their petty scheme and then we'll attack when they least expect it."

Eoin didn't like that either. *Tabert?* He was sailing further away from Lady Helen by the day.

***

Nearly a fortnight had passed while Aleck enjoyed feigning illness and allowed Mary to cater to his every whim. But the duties of a chieftain prevented him from remaining idle, especially when King James requested his services. As soon as Mary finished buckling his breast plate over his hauberk, he and his men would set sail—and when he returned, he'd impale Alexander MacDonald's head on a spike above the Mingary gate.

"I wish you didn't have to go," she said.

He flexed his arm in its sling. The damned thing still hurt. "I'm sure I will not be long. I'll have my revenge—and then I'll be free to think about you and the bairn." Aside from his insatiable desire to murder the MacDonald bastard who'd tried to seize his lands, Aleck had thought of nothing else but the infant growing in her belly. It gave him renewed hope for an heir and now he'd devised the perfect scheme so no one would ever know the child was a bastard.

He cupped Mary's face. "You are already showing, my dear."

"Aye." Her cheeks turned red. "I left it as long as I could afore I told you, m'laird."

"You've known for a time?"

She nodded.

He didn't blame her for hiding it from him. Anything could have happened, but having his son arrive sooner than later would only be a benefit, given his scheme. "When do you expect…ah…"

She gave him a knowing smile. "Three months give or take. Around St. Crispin's day, I expect."

A giddy flutter tickled his stomach. "Excellent. I shall send you to my Uncle's stronghold in Duntulm. No one will recognize you there."

She covered her mouth with her palm and stepped away. "You desire to be rid of me?"

"Not at all. I desire only for you to birth the bairn in secret." He chuckled at his ingenuity. "Henceforth, I'll allow no one to see Lady Helen. Once I receive word that you've birthed my son, I'll send for you."

"And what of your wife?"

He chuckled. "She'll remain locked in the dungeon and receive her meals under the door. No one will know whether her belly is growing or not." He eyed Mary. She was the only person to whom he could entrust his plan. "After I fetch you with my son, Helen will perish from birthing the bairn in her cell. I've the whole thing planned."

A delightfully wicked grin spread across Mary's face.

***

Helen had lost track of how long she'd been incarcerated in the dank dungeon. When the sentry came with her meals, a ray of torchlight would flicker from beneath the door, but otherwise she'd been in darkness with no idea whether it was day or night.

If only they would allow her some light, she might be able to read or embroider to allay the endless boredom. But no, the most malevolent guard in all of Mingary was her jailer.

Aleck had assigned Robert to her care. And Helen had no doubt her husband contrived to put her under a guard who had no sympathy for human life. When he wasn't acting as a guard, Robert spent his days in the great hall sitting alone, sharpening his weapons. Helen had once caught him in the courtyard, pulling the claws from a kitten. He'd put the poor thing in a burlap sack, holding one paw through the opening. Helen wouldn't have known he had the kitten until it yowled in pain as Robert tortured it with a pair of iron tongs. She'd given him a firm lashing with her tongue and snatched the poor, trembling kitten from his grasp.

Of course, Aleck had found the whole incident amusing and Robert never did receive a reprimand. After that, the sadistic guard would sit in the hall and glare at her whilst sharpening his dirk. She could have sworn, the whetstone would screech louder when she passed through the hall. It always made her skin prickle.

For the past several days, she crouched in the corner, rubbing her outer arms. The cell was always cold. On the far wall, a stream of water trickled tirelessly. With no privy closet, she'd used that side to relieve herself. Helen hated how miserably disgusting her life had become. Living in the dark, she'd lost all sense of time. She could have been imprisoned for a sennight or a month. Time simply blurred. With her mouth riddled with sores, her hair matted, she had been reduced to a subhuman troll living in purgatory.

Aside from the lack of a chamber pot, she had no ewer and bowl for bathing. She had no comb, no cloak and no blanket. She slept on a musty bit of straw, which she imagined had been there for years. She wouldn't allow herself to think about who else may have used it or what they might have used it for.

*How could Aleck do this to me?*

Helen's anger had transformed into a numbness that consumed her. She'd never thought she could hate anyone, but now she realized exactly how much she hated Aleck MacIain, and it tore at the inside of her gullet like the iron tines of a rake claw into the earth. The only thing that kept her remotely sane was her driving need to protect Maggie.

Would Sir Eoin help her?

Did he know she was there? Surely he had returned by now. Did Aleck discover she'd sent the missive to John? Had Aleck killed Eoin?

*My God, the possibilities are horrendous. Will no one come to my aid?* Bile burned her throat. *Why on earth did I scribe that missive to John?*

The door above creaked as it always did when Robert descended the narrow steps to the dungeon with a bit of food. Prisoner's fare she'd grown to expect. A bit of bread. A half a cup of ale—broth if she was lucky.

Heavy footsteps slapped the stone steps and stopped outside her door.

Helen crawled to the gap and held her hand to the light now shining through the three-inch space.

"Are you there, m'lady?"

Her heartbeat quickened. "Mr. Keith?"

"Aye. I've a trencher for you."

He slid the wooden platter under the door. Helen nearly swooned at the heady smell of roast lamb and onions. With a trembling hand, she grabbed a piece of meat and shoved it into her mouth. The sores hurt like someone pierced her gums with knives, but she salivated at the stimulating juices and her eyes rolled back.

"Mm."

When she swallowed, she realized Mr. Keith hadn't yet ascended the stairs. The light still shone from beneath the door. "Thank you for bringing me something other than bread."

"I cannot bear to see you in here, m'lady. 'Twas the least I could do."

"Where is Robert?"

"He sailed with Sir Aleck. The chieftain received a summons from the king."

"Whom did Sir Aleck leave behind to tend the keep?"

"Just the grey-haired warriors. Much the same as usual."

She reached her hand under the door as if she could touch the light. "Have you seen Sir Eoin?"

"Not in some time. Come to think on it, not since you…"

*Not since before Aleck threw me into the dungeon. Dear Lord in heaven, what on earth happened to him?* "How is Miss Maggie? Have you seen her?"

"I believe she's well. Miss Sarah has orders to keep the bairn above stairs."

"Could you…" She had to ask. After all, Mr. Keith was loyal to her—at least a little. "Could you please bring her to see me?"

"Oh no, m'lady. I shouldn't even be speaking with you. We've all strict orders to stay away. I took a risk bringing you a good meal—if it weren't for Peter's insistence, you would have ended up with your ration of bread and ale."

Helen wasn't about to stop. Deploringly, she pushed her hand under the door as far as it would go. "Please.

I've not seen a soul in God knows how long. I need to hold my bairn in my arms. You cannot know how devastating it is to be locked in blackness for days on end."

"I-I'm ever so sorry, m'lady, but Sir Aleck threatened to hang anyone who dared help you."

"I'm not asking for help. I'm merely asking to see my bairn. Please. Talk to Glenda. She'll ken how to spirit Maggie here with no one the wiser."

"You do not ken what you ask. These walls have eyes." His feet shuffled. "I'd best be getting back to the patrol, m'lady."

"Mr. Keith," Helen raised her voice, her pulse racing. "Please. Fetch Glenda. You can bring Maggie—"

Footsteps clapped. The light faded.

"I *need* to see my daughter!"

The door above boomed, snuffing the light.

"I must see her!" Helen screamed at the top of her lungs. Over and over she shrieked and pounded her fists on the door. "Please, please, please, pleeeeaaaasssse. I will die if I cannot see her."

Kicking the trencher aside, Helen crumpled onto the musty straw and bawled. Her voice box grated as she shrieked.

"I have done nothing wrong!"

She howled into the crux of her arm.

"I am innocent, yet I am being treated as horribly as the most heinous criminal. Is there no one who will stand up to Aleck MacIain?"

Tears burned her eyes as her throat closed.

*My God, my God. Will I never again see the light of day? Will I never again rest my gaze upon my beautiful child?*

# Chapter Nineteen

Helen's eyes snapped open when the lock clicked. She sat up with a jolt and rubbed her neck. The awkward angle in which she had been sleeping gave her a needling pain running from the base of her head all the way down her spine.

An eerie light drifted from under the door.

A wee voice cooed.

"Maggie?" Helen managed to choke out while a lump formed in her throat. The door opened, rendering her completely blind.

"Aye, m'lady." Glenda's voice rose above the creaking of the door. "I've your daughter and a satchel with your things."

Helen barely heard the end of Glenda's sentence. Blinking rapidly so to gain her sight, she braced her hand against the wall and stood. Goodness, her legs were trembling. She locked her knees and reached out her hands. "Please. I would like to hold her."

Glenda's ghostly outline became clearer as she stepped forward. "She has missed you, m'lady. I'm sure of it."

A tear streamed from Helen's eye when Glenda placed the wee bairn in her arms. Maggie's tiny fists were curled under her chin as she slept without a care. "Praise to the heavens. I cannot tell you how much this means to me." Sniffing, she touched her lips against Maggie's forehead.

Someone in the corridor moved. "We mustn't tarry."

Helen glanced up at the sound of Mr. Keith's voice. "Please. Allow me more time."

"Nay, m'lady." He gestured up the stairs. "'Tis the witching hour and the castle is quiet. I've a skiff waiting to ferry you away from here."

She clutched Maggie to her breast. Surely she must have misunderstood. "Y-you're helping me escape?"

"'Tis the only way. I wish I had time to brush your tresses and help you wash." Glenda tucked a lock of hair behind Helen's ear. "I overheard the chieftain when I was dusting your chamber. I could not make out every word, but plain as the nose on my face, I did hear him say you would perish in your cell whilst birthing a bairn. Are you with child, m'lady?"

Helen looked from Keith to Glenda and coughed. "Not unless the Lord in heaven has seen fit to grace me with an immaculate conception."

Glenda clapped her hand over her mouth. "Then I fear the worst for you. You must go with Mr. Keith."

"But what will you do once Sir Aleck discovers I'm away?"

"Me?" Glenda chuckled. "Why, how would I know you escaped from the dungeon? I'm a sound sleeper if there ever was one. Besides, I doubt even the chieftain would punish the mother of his henchman."

"I do not trust him," Helen said, shaking her head.

Glenda grasped her hand. "I can watch out for myself and I have Grant to protect me."

From the intensity of Glenda's stare, Helen knew she'd not be able to persuade her chambermaid to go with them. She shifted her gaze to the guard. Helen would see no one sent to the gallows for her escape. "And you, Mr. Keith. You've been assigned to guard me. Sir Aleck will punish you for certain—you said yourself you'd be sent to the gallows for helping me."

He dipped his chin and raised his brows. "If it please your lady, I should be honored if you would appoint me your man-at-arms."

"It would be my honor, but…" Cradling Maggie with one arm, she reached out and grasped his shoulder. "You do realize you will never be able to return to Mingary?"

"Aye, m'lady. I cannot stand idle and watch you be treated like a common criminal. I heard your cries earlier this day and you are right. You are innocent and the laird is..." Keith glanced over his shoulder as if he feared someone might be listening. "He has gone too far this time."

Helen's bottom lip trembled and she dropped her gaze to Maggie. Mr. Keith was offering her a chance at freedom and the protection of his sword. He was giving her a gift she could not refuse. Not when she had this precious bairn to protect. "I will see that you are safeguarded by my family. The Campbells are one of the most powerful clans in all of Scotland."

He bowed. "I thank you m'lady."

"Quickly," Glenda said, holding up Helen's sealskin cloak. "I've brought your mantle to keep you warm." She draped it across Helen's shoulders. "Pull the hood low over your head. Hold Maggie close and keep her quiet."

"We shall spirit through the shadows, m'lady. I've left the sea gate ajar. No one will realize we're gone…hopefully for days."

Helen situated the bairn beneath the cloak and pulled the hood over her brow as Glenda suggested. "I cannot tell either of you how thankful I am."

Glenda drew her into an embrace. "Slip away and never come back. You are too refined a woman to put up with the likes of Aleck MacIain."

Helen took in a stuttered breath. Would she ever again set eyes on her loyal servant?

Keith swung the satchel over his shoulder. "We must make haste."

"I shall miss you most of all." Helen kissed Glenda's careworn cheek, then followed the guard up the steps. There was no time to consider the consequences. She was fleeing her home and Aleck MacIain must never find her.

***

Mr. Keith doused the torch before they stepped into the courtyard. "This way, m'lady."

Helen cradled Maggie as tightly as she dared and followed the guard into the shadows. Her heart beat a fierce rhythm, thundering in her ears while they made their way to the sea gate. She couldn't recall ever being so afraid in her life, sneaking away from her home as if she were a criminal.

*Blast Aleck for forcing me to this.*

For a moment, her blood turned to ice. *What if the Pope does not approve the annulment?*

She stopped dead, but Mr. Keith grasped her elbow and pulled her along. "This way," he whispered.

*I cannot allow thoughts of doom to cloud my mind.*

Once beyond the gate, Mr. Keith led her around the rocky outcropping to a skiff sitting askew on the stony beach where it was out of sight from the castle battlements. He placed the satchel in the boat. "Climb aboard and I'll cast off."

She did as told, her arms aching from maintaining the tight hold on her daughter. She sat on a bench toward the stern and arranged Maggie in her lap. The bairn launched into a wail that cut though the cold night air like a siren.

"Ballocks," Keith grumbled while pushing the skiff into the surf.

Helen cradled the babe to her breast. "There, there. Wheesht, little one."

Maggie's cries softened to whimpers, but the damage had already been done. Shouts rang out from atop the wall-walk. Helen watched the guards assemble in the light of the blazing braziers while Keith heaved on the oars.

"Do you think they'll come after us?" she asked.

"And leave Mingary unprotected?" He shook his head. "Besides, I made certain there were no boats nearby."

"You put a great deal of thought into my rescue."

"Aye, m'lady. I suppose I did."

"I am indebted to you for my very life."

"You are my lord and master…och, I mean my lady and mistress. I will see to your protection as long as you should need me." He steered the skiff through the heavy swells of Loch Sunart. "Once we cross into Argyllshire, we'll hug the coast to avoid being capsized should the sea decide to turn angry." He pointed to the dark outline of the far shore. "After we traverse the Firth of Lorn, I reckon we should row through Loch Etive until we reach Taynult. 'Tis but a day's hike to Kilchurn Castle from there."

Helen couldn't imagine hiking through the rugged Highlands along the River Awe with a bairn in her arms. Besides, that would be dangerous. "Kilchurn is the first place Sir Aleck will look, and if I know Duncan, he'll be so irate with me, he'll bow to Aleck's claims before I've had a chance to explain."

Mr. Keith stopped rowing. "What do you recommend, m'lady?"

"After we pass through the Sound of Mull, head across the Firth of Lorn for Dunollie. My sister Gyllis will help us—and we'll not have so far to row."

He again pulled on the wooden oars, taking them further from Mingary. "She must be the one married to Sir Sean MacDougall."

"Aye, she is. And I would trust her with our lives." Helen shivered as the skiff rocked and bobbed in the swells. *Dear God, please keep us afloat.* "How long will it take to pass through the Sound of Mull?"

"Once we enter the narrows, the current will help. I'd reckon we'll reach Dunollie by midday on the morrow."

Helen groaned. "That will be a terrible strain for you. If only we had a sail."

"Not to worry, m'lady. There'll be plenty of time to rest once I am content you are safely away from Mingary."

***

The king's move to Tabert Castle on Kintyre enabled him to amass a secret fleet of loyal clans. Situated at the mouth of Loch Fyne, deep in Campbell territory, there would be no opportunity for Clan Donald to spy on the king and his ever-growing forces.

Before Aleck MacIain joined them, Eoin and his men sailed daily in and out of the Firth of Clyde. They posed as merchant seafarers, running goods up through the Sound of Jura. They were, in fact, spying on the heightened activities of the MacDonalds on the Isle of Islay.

Normally, Eoin had patience for surveillance, but the daily sorties had him on edge. He couldn't stop thinking about the missive the Bishop of the Isles was carrying to Rome. *What if the Pope refuses to grant Lady Helen the annulment? What in God's name will I do then?*

His mind had run the gamut. The only thing he hadn't considered was walking away. He should have let the MacDonald warrior kill Aleck in Sunart, but Eoin wouldn't have been able to live with himself if he hadn't stepped in. His code of honor would never allow such malfeasance. Unfortunately, Aleck MacIain would have to see to his own ruination.

"Ruination," Eoin said aloud, mulling the word over in his mind. Though he'd welcome MacIain's ruination, he needed to safeguard Lady Helen's reputation to ensure she remained in good standing.

"Bloody oath." Fergus gripped the rail of the galley beside him. "We'll see to the ruination of Clan Donald before this war has ended."

Eoin nodded at his henchman, not letting on to why he'd uttered the word. He took in a deep breath of salty air. What more could he do to protect Lady Helen? She was as fragile as fine blown glass. What Duncan had been thinking when he'd arranged her marriage to that bombastic swine, Eoin couldn't fathom. If he'd been the suitor who'd won her hand, she would have all the luxuries life could afford.

A dark chasm spread through his chest. Again, he reminded himself that he was lord over lands with a stone longhouse, not a castle. *Helen has lived her entire life in a keep, her every need catered, as it should be for such a delicate flower.* Eoin's wealth was a pittance compared to the Campbells of Glenorchy or the miserable Clan MacIain of Ardnamurchan.

The galley sailed around the Mull of Kyntire for what seemed like the hundredth time. Fergus pointed toward Dunyveig Castle on the southern shore of Islay. "Well, I'll be damned."

Eoin chuckled. "They've decided to show their hand, have they?" At least thirty galleys moored in the shallows, and though it was too far to see, Eoin didn't have to guess that they were all flying the MacDonald colors. He circled his hand over his head. "Tack to starboard. Set a course for Tabert. I've no doubt this news will interest the king."

# Chapter Twenty

By the time Helen and Mr. Keith had rowed through the Sound of Mull, Maggie could not be comforted. The bairn's high pitched wails rattled in Helen's skull, giving her a royal headache, and she had no doubt the poor guard suffered as well. "If only I had some milk for her."

Mr. Keith dragged the oars through the swells like a man ready to drop from exhaustion. "There're some oatcakes in the satchel. Try chewing up a bit and feeding it to her."

Helen reached for the satchel and did as he suggested. Cradling the babe in her arm, she swiped a bit of the paste from her tongue with her finger. "Here you are, darling."

Maggie howled and thrashed her head from side to side until Helen shoved her finger in the bairn's mouth. Within the blink of an eye, Maggie sucked the paste from Helen's finger. Helen worked quickly to feed her more, then grinned up at Mr. Keith. "Did you have children?"

"Not me." He grunted with another heavy pull on the oars. "I'm a confirmed bachelor, but I was the eldest of twelve."

"Twelve? Bless your mother."

"Aye, she was a saintly woman."

The bairn continued to eat and suckle from Helen's finger while the waves tossed the boat. Gazing at her daughter's cherubic face, Helen counted her blessings. Aye, her life was in a shambles, but she had a brave guard willing to row all the way to Dunollie, and praise the heavens, she cradled her daughter in her arms. Better, somewhere out there Sir Eoin MacGregor worked to help her appeal for an annulment.

Helen looked at her attire and sniffed. With matted hair, her gown caked with filth, Gyllis would hardly recognize her.

Mr. Keith rested the oars on the sides of the skiff. "Are you all right m'lady?"

"Aye, just struck by a moment of reflection." She glanced at him. "I lost track of time. How long was I in the dungeon?"

"About a fortnight."

"That long?"

"I regret that I was unable to aid in your escape sooner," Mr. Keith said, wiping his forehead with his shirtsleeve.

Helen took in a stuttered breath. "I thank the Lord for your generous kindness."

"I could watch you suffer no longer."

She knew he referred to far more than the past fortnight. The clansmen and women had watched her take Aleck's abuse for years, but things had grown worse in the past several months.

Mr. Keith blew on his palms and resumed rowing. "At least we're sailing with the current."

"Perhaps you should rest while we coast toward the shore." She glanced over her shoulder. The eastern sky had taken on a cobalt hue with the promise of a new day. She made out the contour of the mainland, though it seemed ever so far away. "Why not let me row for a while?"

"Nay m'lady." He chuckled. "I could never allow that."

Maggie yawned and stretched, and Helen wrapped the bairn in her cloak, her eyelids growing ever so heavy. The crossing of the Firth of Lorn seemed to take an eternity as Mr. Keith labored to row the tiny skiff through the swells, his movement becoming more sluggish by the hour.

Helen must have curled over and dozed for a bit, because she startled at the sound of Mr. Keith's voice. "We're nearly there."

Sitting upright, she yawned and looked over her shoulder. A quick stuttering of her heart lifted her spirits. Indeed, the outline of Dunollie Castle loomed above the verdant trees on the shore. "I'm certain I could row the remaining distance." She grinned. "I used to row a skiff on Loch Awe with my sisters."

He smiled with clenched teeth making him looked like he grimaced. "Aye, but Loch Awe is inland. She's not subject to the currents of the sea."

"But you must be exhausted." Helen moved Maggie, cradling the bairn's head to her shoulder and patted her back, as they rocked with the erratic sway of the boat.

With a nod of his head, Mr. Keith gestured to the shore ahead. "I'll rest once you're safely delivered into your sister's arms."

"You are truly a saint." She kissed Maggie's temple. "See, lassie, we are nearly there."

Then, Helen situated her cloak's hood to cover her matted hair.

The strength of the current proved to be far stronger than Loch Awe. They reached the shore far sooner than Helen anticipated. *Thank heavens!*

A Dunollie guardsman met them at the embankment and offered his hand. "Did you row all the way across the Firth of Lorn?"

She entrusted Maggie into Mr. Keith's strong hands, and let the guard help her alight, careful to keep her mantle closed to hide her filthy kirtle. "My man-at-arms rowed all the way from—" She stopped herself from saying anything about Mingary. "A very long way. I am Lady Campbell and I've come to visit my sister, Lady Gyllis." With two other sisters, Helen wasn't the only Lady Campbell—and it would be impertinent of the guard to ask.

The guard examined her sealskin cloak from head to toe. Thank goodness Glenda had thought to bring Helen this one piece of finery. "Well then, let us away to the keep. I'm sure Lady Gyllis will be delighted to see you." He turned to a guard standing with a poleax at the sea gate. "Run ahead and tell her ladyship her sister has arrived—quickly, now."

After Mr. Keith retuned Maggie to her arms, they proceeded up the embankment. Though exhausted, Helen took in a deep breath and strode with renewed hope filling her heart. Dunollie had never looked so grand with ivy growing up her stone walls. The guard ushered them through the sea gate and up the steep path to Dunollie's inner courtyard. By the time they reached the keep, her legs were a bit unsteady. Bone-weary beyond anything she'd ever experienced in her life, Helen grew woozy at the prospect of seeing her sister.

The door to the keep burst open. A lad stood beside Gyllis, with a toddler peeking out from behind her skirts. Helen's sister grinned wide enough to see her back molars, but as soon as she looked at Helen, a grimace of concern quickly turned down her exuberant smile. Gyllis spread her arms wide. "My heavens, what on earth has happened? You look as if you've sailed through the bowels of hell."

Helen fell into her sister's embrace. "Indeed, I have." Inhaling the familiar lavender fragrance, a load as heavy as stones lifted from Helen's shoulders.

Gyllis squeezed tight. "Why did you not send word?"

"There wasn't time." Between them, Maggie fussed. Helen pulled back far enough to give the bairn room to breathe. "I've much to tell you."

Gyllis looked down and her eyes popped. "Oh my. Is this Margaret? I received your missive some two months ago."

Helen raised her elbow to show off the babe. "Aye, I call her Maggie."

Grasping the lad and the lass beside her by the wrists, Gyllis grinned. "This is Zander and Anna—meet your Auntie Helen and your wee cousin."

Helen knelt down so the children could get a good look at the bairn. "I am very pleased to make your acquaintance."

Anna shoved her finger in her mouth. "Can she talk yet?" The words came out a bit garbled due to the finger, but Helen understood well enough.

"Not yet. She's but four months of age."

"I'm two-and-a-half." The darling looked awfully proud of herself—already standing like a well-bred lass with chestnut locks.

Helen chuckled. "My, you are a young lady nearly grown."

Zander, a good head taller, nudged Anna aside with his shoulder. "I'm almost five and my da says I'm to be a knight."

"I'm certain you will be a fine knight indeed." Helen scrubbed her fingers into his sandy hair. "You're already a brawny lad. I'll wager you take good care of your sister. That is what knights do. They protect women and children."

The lad twisted his mouth and gave Anna a sideways glance. "Och, you mean I have ta protect *her*?"

"Aye," Helen offered a stern nod. "Without hesitation, a man defends his family first—"

Maggie launched into a wail. Evidently the soggy oatcakes had run their course.

Gyllis offered her hand and pulled Helen up. "Forgive my impertinence, but you look like you've spent a month in purgatory."

Helen stood with a woeful glance at her gown. She parted her cloak enough to show her sister the extent of the filth. "I have."

With a gasp, Gyllis cringed. "I cannot believe my eyes. My sister would never be seen in public clad thus. For the love of all that is holy, your plight must be inordinately grave." Gyllis gestured inside. "Come above stairs and we'll set you to rights straight away."

"I'd like nothing more, but first may I ask for some warm milk for Maggie, and food and a bed for Mr. Keith? He nearly broke his back rowing a skiff all the way from Mingary Castle."

"Rowing a wee skiff?" Gyllis's jaw dropped. "I'll see it done." She clapped her hands and faced a woman who'd been standing in the kitchen doorway. "Jinny, please see to all Helen has requested."

The matron curtseyed. "Straight away, m'lady. And I'll fetch the nursemaid for Anna and Zander."

"You'd best fetch the milk for the bairn first," Keith said with a bow. "She's been howling since daylight broke."

Gyllis knit her brows. "Goodness, your circumstances sound graver and graver."

Helen inclined her head toward the stairwell. "You shall not believe how dire things have become." She again parted her cloak. "May I request a bath as well?"

"Of course." Gyllis slipped her arm around Helen's shoulders. "You shall be treated as royalty whilst you're at Dunollie."

As they proceeded toward the stairwell, Gyllis's limp was barely noticeable. Helen's sister had suffered from a bout of paralysis before she had married Sir Sean MacDougall. The disease could have left her abed for the rest of her days, but Gyllis had been determined to walk again. Only through her determination and perseverance did she recover. Helen maintained the utmost respect for her sister—she proved herself the strongest of all the Campbell lasses. With hope, Helen had inherited some of that strength as well—no doubt she'd need it.

Once in the lady's solar, Jinny arrived with Maggie's milk in no time. Helen accepted the bowl and spoon. "Thank you ever so much."

"My pleasure, m'lady. The lads will bring up the bath barrel and buckets as soon as the water has warmed."

"Lovely, again, I cannot thank you enough."

Jinny curtseyed and left them.

Helen cradled Maggie on her lap and spooned the milk in the bairn's mouth. The wee one lapped it up like a greedy puppy.

Gyllis sat in the overstuffed chair opposite. "She has Aleck's coloring."

"Aye, but she's fine-boned like me." Helen tried not to show her irritation. She didn't want Maggie to resemble Aleck in the slightest, but the lass did have black hair.

"Hmm." Gyllis pursed her lips. "I can tell by your frown, my remark displeases you."

Helen bowed her head. "Aye," she whispered.

"Tell me why you're here looking like a guttersnipe. Truly, Helen, your news must be deplorable." Gyllis drew her eyebrows together. "What of Sir Aleck?"

Closing her eyes, Helen took in a deep breath. Where should she start? She gave Maggie another spoon of milk. There was no way to soften the news. "I have appealed to the Pope for an annulment."

With a gasp, Gyllis slapped both hands over her heart. "Oh dear God in heaven, 'tis that grave?"

"I'm afraid so," Helen said, blinking to allay her urge to cry. She stood and rested the bairn in the cradle. "I've been forced to flee my home with nothing but the rags I am wearing and my child."

After Helen returned to her seat, Gyllis quietly listened while Helen divulged every sordid detail of her twisted marriage. It wasn't usually like Gyllis to keep silent. Helen was the sister who always listened and consoled the others. But this time, Helen needed an impartial ear, and her dear sister rose to the occasion.

She omitted nothing. The disdain, the violence, her decision to send Eoin to Iona with her missive, her wrongful incarceration in that abominable dungeon, and further vile treatment whilst she remained locked in complete darkness.

When Helen finished, she pressed her face against her palms. "If it weren't for Mr. Keith and Glenda, I'd still be rotting in the dungeon."

Eyes wide, Gyllis looked completely stunned. "Your suffering is inconceivable. I cannot believe you endured his hostility for so long."

"'Tis like I'm floating in a dream right now. I cannot believe I am finally free from him."

"We must assure we remain discreet. Have you received word from the Pope?"

Helen rubbed her aching eyes. "Nay, and I've not heard from Sir Eoin since he sailed for Iona. He promised to bring me word, and now that I have run away, he'll never find me even if the Pope does grant my annulment."

"Oh, my heavens, you poor dear." Gyllis crossed the floor and took Helen's hands between her palms. "Your plight is far worse than anything I could have imagined."

"I need a place to hide and, somehow, I must send word to Eoin MacGregor without anyone the wiser, especially anyone connected with the MacIain Clan."

"Of course, of course. We shall see to everything." Gyllis rubbed her fingers atop the back of Helen's hand. "And what about the elderly guard who accompanied you here? Mr. Keith, is it?"

"Aye." Helen nodded. "He can never return to Mingary. I owe him my life."

"Rowing all that way? God bless him. He is a loyal soul, indeed."

"There is none more so—he's been incredibly kind. I promised him the protection of the Campbell Clan."

"He'll have the protection of the MacDougalls as well."

"You are a jewel." Though she wanted to sink into the overstuffed chair and close her eyes, another thing needed to be said. "I did not tell the guard my given name. I think 'tis best your servants remain unaware of which sister has come to call."

"On that you needn't worry. I shall ensure everyone thinks you to be Alice." Gyllis laughed. "With our sister living in Perthshire, no one will have a clue as to her identity."

"You are so clever. I still cannot believe I am here." Allowing herself to smile, Helen peered into her sister's caring blue eyes. "Oh, Gyllis I knew it was right to come to you."

Reaching out, the Lady of Dunollie patted Helen's shoulder. "We shall see you're fed, bathed and have a good night's rest. But I think we must hide you away from a Campbell keep."

Helen didn't like the sound of that at all. "Do you think it necessary?"

"I do. When Sir Aleck discovers you're missing, there will be hell to pay, and the first place he'll look is here and Kilchurn."

"I hate this." Wringing her hands, Helen clenched her teeth. "Where will I go?"

"I have just the place." Gyllis held up a finger and waggled her brows. "On the morrow, I shall spirit you and Maggie to Sean's hunting cottage in Fearnoch Forest. No one will ever find you there—and 'tis well provisioned for the season. There you can stay and await word from the Pope."

"A hunting cottage?" Helen allowed herself to hope. "It sounds ideal."

"'Tis a tad rustic, but you should want for nothing. And I can visit you often." Gyllis chuckled. "When Sean first became chieftain, the forest was riddled with outlaws, but no longer."

For the first time in years, the tightness in Helen's chest eased. It was hard to believe that she and Maggie would be free at last. "I'd like to pen a missive to Sir Eoin. Are they still stationed at Dunstaffnage?"

"Unfortunately, nay. The king is amassing his army at Tabert." Gyllis covered her mouth with a sharp inhale. "'Tis a big secret. My husband would be very upset to know I'd told you so freely."

Helen's heart sank—Dunstaffnage was only four miles north of Dunollie where it would be ever so easy to dispatch a message. If only Eoin were there. "Curses, if I didn't have rotten luck, I'd have no luck at all. Tabert is quite far." She knew of it only because the castle lay on Clan Campbell lands.

"But not for a galley." Gyllis grinned, the same mischievous smile she'd had as a child. "A small crew could set sail in the morning."

Helen gasped. "Honestly? Would they be able to take Mr. Keith with them? I would entrust a verbal message only to his care. I will not even venture to put quill to parchment."

Gyllis patted her hand with a reassuring glint in her eyes. "Then we shall make it so."

***

In the guest chamber, a wooden tub filled with warm water had been placed in front of the hearth, which already crackled with a hearty fire. Helen pulled the lace on her kirtle, untying the bow. "I cannot wait to be rid of this gown. It smells worse than a swine's bog."

"I shall have the maids clean it and bring you a fresh change of clothes." Gyllis stood back and eyed her. "I've a kirtle that's a wee bit too short. It ought to fit."

"Thank you ever so much. I hope that one day I will be able to repay your kindness."

"No my dearest." Gyllis cupped Helen's face with her palm. "We are family. Campbells take care of their own."

"'Tis music to a lady's ears."

"Shall I ask Jinny to assist you?"

Helen glanced at the tub. It looked so inviting. "Honestly, I'd prefer to be left alone. I am ever so tired."

"Very well," Gyllis agreed. "I shall send up a tray later—and worry not about the bairn. The nursemaid will take good care of her until the morrow."

"Are you sure?" A tightness gripped Helen's chest. Though tired to her bones, she didn't like being separated from Maggie all night. "Perhaps we should bring a cradle in here."

"Let me help you this once." Gyllis pulled Helen's cloak from her shoulders and draped it over a chair. "You need a good rest before we head for the cottage. I'll see to it plenty of stores are loaded on a pack mule and we shall haste away after we break our fast. Does that meet with your approval?"

"I don't know what to say." Helen clasped her hands together. "Thank you ever so much for your gracious generosity."

"You are my dearest sister. If someone asked me to give you my right arm, I wouldn't hesitate."

Helen let out a lightheaded chuckle. "I hope we never have to go to such extremes."

Stepping in, Gyllis grasped her elbow. "Are you certain you do not need assistance? You're looking a bit pale."

That didn't surprise Helen in the slightest. "I'm sure my head will stop swooning just as soon as I can immerse myself in the tub."

"Very well." Her sister pointed. "If you should want for anything, my chamber is straight down the passageway."

"Thank you."

Helen waited until Gyllis left, then peeled off her dirty clothes and piled them in a heap in the privy closet. As far as she was concerned, that's the only place where they belonged.

Stepping into the basin, the warm water instantly soothed her. Gradually, she lowered herself in the heavenly tub until she sat with her knees tucked under her chin. The chambermaid had left a cake of soap, a comb and a drying cloth on a small table, and across the room, a dressing gown had been laid out on the bed.

Holding the soap to her nose, Helen inhaled. "Sugared lavender." Mother's concoction, the scent would always remind her of home. *Home. Such a comforting thought.*

With languid strokes, she washed every inch of her body and lathered soap in her hair. Once clean, Helen closed her eyes and leaned back. Oh, how the warmth buoyed her woes and took them floating away. How long had it been since she'd allowed herself to be at ease? Peaceful, she cleared her mind and focused on sunshine. The sun's rays started inside her midriff and radiated out through her limbs. She stretched her fingers and toes and the radiance of the sun shot through the tips of each, until the sense of complete weightlessness flooded her entire body.

Helen rested there, suspended in complete tranquility. Only when the water grew cold did she open her eyes.

***

"With all due respect, I do not like the idea of abandoning Lady Helen in a hunting cottage in the midst of the forest," Mr. Keith said, riding a grey gelding alongside Helen's bay and pulling a pack mule behind.

"I agree. I would not allow it if the forest were not entirely safe," Gyllis replied as she led the way, sitting sidesaddle atop a sorrel Galloway. "Dunollie guards patrol Fearnoch daily. Make no bones about it, I assure you my sister will be secure."

"I'm sure I will be fine," Helen agreed. Maggie rode in a sling suspended around her neck, and seemed to be quite enjoying the horse's movement. "If Lady Gyllis is confident, then so am I."

After a good night's sleep and a morning meal of oats, bacon and eggs, Helen felt like a new woman. With two borrowed kirtles, and a pack mule loaded with enough stores to see her through Yule, she was excited about this new adventure. *How a modicum of independence enlivens one's soul.*

"There it is." Gyllis pointed through the trees.

Helen leaned aside to look around her. Sure enough, a stone cottage was practically hidden by the dense forest. She instantly adored it. "Oh, 'tis quaint."

"'Tis a hovel," Mr. Keith groused. "A lady of your stature should be in a grand castle."

"Hogwash," Helen said. "This is exactly what I need whilst awaiting word from His Holiness."

They rode into the clearing and dismounted. "There is a burn about fifty paces to the south," Gyllis said. "And the water is pure and sweet."

"Lovely." Helen inhaled the scent of pine and wildflowers with a smile.

Mr. Keith tied the horses. "I'll set to unpacking the mule."

"My thanks." Helen looked to Gyllis. "Shall we?"

"It isn't a keep, but you and Maggie will want for nothing." Gyllis pulled down the latch and opened the door.

As soon as Helen stepped inside the cottage, she was rapt. Though Gyllis hadn't exaggerated about it being rustic, the hideaway had distinct charm. A large stone hearth consumed much of the far end wall with a brushed sheepskin rug before it. Cast iron cooking utensils hung from iron pegs and a grill had been installed over the fire for easy use. In front of the hearth were two wooden chairs—one was a delightful rocker with a cushioned seat.

Helen pointed. "I intend to spend my evenings rocking Maggie in that chair, singing lullabies until the bairn falls asleep."

"You do have a beautiful voice for ballads." Gyllis grinned. "Maggie will slip into slumber in no time."

With a smile, Helen looked to the center of the chamber. A long table consumed the space, with benches on either side. Helen imagined Sir Sean and his men would roast venison and eat like kings whilst embellishing tales of their hunting expeditions. And being a hunting cottage, bows and quivers of arrows hung near the threshold.

Gyllis gestured to an open door across the chamber from the hearth. "Follow me."

Helen crossed the floor to find a small bedchamber. It held a large bed, covered by a down-filled comforter and nearly consumed the entire space. "This is simply perfect."

The Lady of Dunollie cleared her throat. "I daresay Anna was conceived in this bed."

"Gyllis." Helen gaped. "That is scandalous."

Always the most daring of the Campbell sisters, Gyllis laughed. "Aye, but it was fun."

Helen glanced outside the doorway to ensure Mr. Keith hadn't overheard. "I cannot believe you speak so freely of such personal matters."

"Only to you." Gyllis bit her bottom lip. "Though given the circumstances, I should have held my tongue."

Heat flooded Helen's cheeks right down to her toes. God forbid she would never utter a word about her unpleasant experiences in the bedchamber.

Thank heavens Mr. Keith stepped across the threshold with his arms laden. "All the parcels are unpacked." He set them on the table. "Is there anything else you need, m'lady?"

Helen surveyed the abundance of stores, still unable to believe her fortune. "I think not. Thank you ever so much for your fealty. You will have a place in my employ as long as you should require it."

He bowed. "'Tis my pleasure, m'lady."

"And you will carry my message to Sir Eoin and let him know exactly what has happened?"

"Aye." Mr. Keith narrowed his eyes. "You are certain we can trust him?"

"Sir Eoin is a most dear friend of the family," Gyllis said.

Helen had to agree. "And he carried my missive to His Worship. He will help us for certain."

"Then I shall meet with him discreetly." The guard bowed.

"Thank you." Helen walked them outside and bid good day, anxious to move on with a new chapter in her life.

# Chapter Twenty-One

As usual, after he'd reported news of the MacDonald galleys mooring alongside Dunyveig on the Isle of Islay, things hadn't moved fast enough for Eoin.

They'd been at Tabert Castle for a sennight, and yet their tenure wasn't near long enough for the king. And Eoin didn't argue in the assembly when all the nobles agreed that the longer they remained hidden, the more confident the MacDonalds would grow. Everyone seemed to be content to remain idle except Eoin.

This morn while they were breaking their fast, he'd had a gut full of listening to Aleck boast about how the MacIain Clan fended off Alexander MacDonald's attack, and how Aleck wanted the bastard's head served on a platter. To hear the Chieftain of Ardnamurchan tell it, he and his men were all Scotland needed to bring the isles in order.

Eoin wanted to upend the table and shove Aleck's face in a bowl of scalding porridge. He made eye contact with Duncan sitting opposite. Though he was MacIain's brother-in-law, the Lord of Glenorchy rolled his gaze to the ceiling and shook his head. Duncan could be an arse about some things, but the man knew when he was being fed a pile of shite—unlike the young king who appeared to be lapping up MacIain's every word.

Well, Eoin had enough. He beckoned his men and headed to the wharf.

Fergus hurried beside him. "I thought we had orders to stay away from Islay."

"Did I say we were sailing to Islay?" Eoin couldn't very well tell his men he'd reached his limit of pompous nobles blowing flatulence out their arse-holes, instead he scowled and gestured for the men to follow. "We have rigging to tend and I want to inspect the hull. A sea captain is a dead man if he sails into battle with a galley that's about to sink."

Eoin's boat was in top condition, but presently he'd do anything for some fresh air. God's bones, it had only been three sennights since he'd seen John…*His Worship*. How the devil would Eoin be able to wait another month or more? And now that the whole goddamned Scottish army was stationed in Tabert, how would Eoin come up with an excuse to visit Lady Helen once he'd received word from the Pope?

A small birlinn tacked toward the wharf, flying the MacDougall colors. Eoin paid it no mind and started his daily inspection of the hull. "Fergus, make a note. The port side timbers need pitch."

"Again?" The henchman sounded a tad astounded.

"If we do not—"

"Stay on top of it, the timbers will rot without us being the wiser." Fergus looked to the skies. "I ken. You needn't tell me."

"Ahoy the shore," someone yelled from the MacDougall galley.

Eoin pointed toward the castle. "Sir Sean is in the great hall with the rest of the nobles."

After mooring the boat, sailors jumped over the side, their feet clomping on the wooden wharf. One

MacDougall wore a great helm and mail and kept himself apart from the others.

Eoin watched him out of the corner of his eye. He never trusted any man who completely hid his face—especially on the battlefield.

The helmed man held back, as if waiting for the others to leave.

Eoin pretended to inspect the rigging, while fingering his dirk.

The man stepped forward. "Sir Eoin. May I have a word?" he whispered. "'Tis in regard to Lady Helen."

***

Safely tucked away deep in the woods of Fearnoch Forest, Helen's first two nights in the cottage had been heavenly. Though Gyllis had practically packed half the household, Helen found no cradle for Maggie, and had lined a wooden crate with soft woolen blankets, and the bairn slept soundly.

Helen couldn't remember ever being so happy. For the first time since she'd married Aleck, she felt as though she could be herself. No affected, serene smiles, no clamping her insides taut to keep from blurting out something that might send Sir Aleck into a rage. True, she had no chambermaid in attendance, and no cook to prepare her meals, but she'd learned enough from Peter to be able to make her own food, and wearing simple kirtles with her stays tied in the front, dressing was easy too.

She had plenty of milk for Maggie, and Gyllis promised to deliver a fresh pitcher twice a week, along with other foodstuffs.

Maggie lay on her tummy atop the sheepskin rug in front of the hearth. Helen held up snipped pieces of cloth she'd found. Sitting beside the bairn, she took Maggie's wee palm and slid it over the first piece of fabric. "This is silk."

Maggie gave a gummy grin.

Helen picked up a coarse textured piece. "This is sackcloth worn by the pious when paying their penance. 'Tis made of goat's fur and very uncomfortable."

Maggie's eyes popped wide and she gave a wee gasp, clearly enjoying the new tactile sensations. Shifting the bairn's palm to the plush wool, Helen grinned. "But I'd wager you like sheep's wool the best."

Maggie squealed with delight.

Helen threw back her head and laughed. "Och aye, we two will have so much fun together. There's no keep to run, no malignant rules to follow, no lemans shooting me hateful glares." Helen snapped a hand over her mouth. Though Maggie did not yet understand everything she said, Helen must not speak out against the bairn's father. She'd not err again.

Before dusk, Helen set to preparing the evening meal of boiled mutton pottage and kettle scones. Maggie entertained herself, rolling back and forth over the rug and pushing up with her arms, and, on occasion, sticking a wooden spoon in her mouth and chewing. Teeth were about to come in, no doubt.

As the kettle began a rolling boil, Helen scooped a dollop of pottage with a large ladle. She blew on the steamy liquid and sipped. *A bit bland.*

She'd seen some houseleek outside. Surely a few sprigs would add flavor. Stepping outside for a mere moment, she strode to the overgrown garden and broke off a handful.

A twig snapped.

An eerie silence blanketed the clearing.

Helen held her breath, but the hammering of her heart roared in her hears. Mr. Keith should be away bearing her message for Eoin and Gyllis wouldn't approach at this hour. Had it been a deer? She wasn't about to wander into the woods to find out. Grasping her skirts, she ran for the door.

The unmistakable sound of horse hooves grew near—not at a gallop, but in the cadence of a fast trot.

Helen dashed inside and grabbed the bow and an arrow from its peg beside the door. Her hands trembled as she loaded the arrow. Only God knew who was out there. *With luck, they'll pass by unawares. Goodness, Gyllis told me there hadn't been any outlaws holed up in this forest in years.*

She moved to the window and cracked open the shutter, sliding the arrow through. Helen's heart flew to her throat. At the edge of the clearing, the rider, clad in a black cloak, reined his horse to a stop.

Helen pulled back the bowstring, willing her hands to steady.

The rider dismounted. When he pushed the hood from his head, he stared straight at the cottage.

Helen's stomach flittered all the way up to her throat. *Blessed be the saints!* She tossed her weapons aside and dashed to the door. "Sir Eoin! How on earth did you find me so quickly?"

His eyes sparkled with his incredibly attractive grin. "Mr. Keith delivered your missive late this morn."

"And you came all the way from Tabert? In one day?"

"Aye." He gave her a wink. "We had a good wind."

"I'll say." She glanced at the horse behind him. "And a young steed."

He gestured to the gelding. "Lady Gyllis offered me the best in her stable."

Helen could have swooned where she stood. *My stars 'tis good to see him.* "Did she now?"

After tying his horse, Eoin stepped up to the threshold and Helen craned her neck to gaze upon his handsome face. *Lord in heaven, how on earth did he grow more beautiful in the brief time since I've last seen him?* She stood there like a young maid and stared.

The corner of his mouth ticked up while his gaze trailed from her eyes to her lips. His Adam's apple bobbed and he brushed the back of his knuckle along her jaw. Gooseflesh rose across her skin.

"Ah, Lady Helen," he hoarsely whispered. "I raced here like a madman just to see you, and I have so much to tell, I've no idea where to start."

Rising to her toes, she cupped his cheek with the palm of her hand. Oh yes, she could gaze into those blue eyes for an eternity. "I'm ever so glad to see you."

He covered her hand and slid it to his lips. Closing his eyes, he kissed her fingers, plying them with full and tender lips. "To see your face is like opening a window to a valley of primrose on a spring morn."

Och, she wanted to wrap her arms around him and hold on for dear life. *If only it were proper.* Helen stepped aside and gestured toward the hearth. "You're in luck. I've put on a pottage, and once the leek has time to steep, we shall be ready to sup. I trust you will not be in such a hurry you won't stay for the evening meal."

"I've no reason to haste away." He inhaled deeply. "It smells far too good to decline your generous invitation."

She chuckled. "'Tis a bit bland, but I've a batch of kettle scones baking to liven it up."

Eoin stepped inside and closed the door. "You never cease to amaze me, Lady Helen. Where did you learn to cook?"

"Mother made sure we learned the basics, and then Peter at Mingary taught me the rest. I may not have been the one to stir the pot, but I most certainly oversaw the ingredients and their measurement."

Maggie chortled from her place on the sheepskin rug.

Eoin smiled in the babe's direction. "How is the bairn settling in?"

Helen's breast swelled with her smile. "She's unscathed by the whole ordeal. We've been playing a game of touching different textures. She's quite enjoyed it."

Eoin sauntered over and picked up the square of silk. "Would this be her favorite?"

"Oh no, she prefers the plush wool beneath her—let out a right royal laugh when she sunk her wee fingers into it."

He scooped Maggie into his arms. "And what say you, little one? Do you like sheepskin?"

Maggie reached up with both hands and clapped his face.

He chuckled. "Or is it a man's stubbled chin?"

The bairn threw her head back with a gummy grin, then bobbled upright, squealing with delight.

Helen tapped her fingers to her chest. "I think she's taken a liking to you."

"That's a good thing." Eoin rubbed his nose against Maggie's cheek. "She's the bonniest bairn I've ever seen."

Helen couldn't disagree. Standing completely still, she watched how Eoin handled the babe, his large hands cradling her securely, but ever so gently. And Maggie stared up at him with wide eyes, as if she adored the man.

Helen broke the houseleek into bits and tossed it in the pottage. Then she held a twig in the coals and lit the tallow candle on the table. Her hands tremored a bit, anticipating he'd say something about her plight. She then picked up the spoon and stirred. Eoin hadn't yet uttered a word about his visit to Iona either. Waiting made her fidgety and she clanged the spoon on the side of the pot. *Just ask him.* "Were you able to meet with my brother, John?"

When he didn't respond right away, Helen regarded him over her shoulder.

"Forgive me. I was so enamored with Maggie, I neglected to tell you." His expression was far kinder than a brawny man's should be. "And that is the main reason for my visit."

Eoin took a seat on one of the benches at the table and propped Maggie on his knee. "The bishop has already left for Rome."

"John is carrying the missive himself?" Helen turned from the hearth and faced him, covering her mouth with her palm. "Truly?" Her eyes stung with tears. Would she finally be freed from Aleck's oppressive yoke?

"He left for a meeting in Rome the day after I delivered your letter. I must say, the timing was ideal."

Her throat closed. Could she finally hope? "To think at last I'll be free."

"Aye, lass." Eoin bounced the bairn on his knee. "But you must remain hidden. John warned the Pope rarely approves an annulment when petitioned by the wife."

Helen didn't care for the sound of that. "Dear Lord. I will stay tucked away in this cottage for the rest of my life if His Holiness doesn't grant it." She clutched her hand around her throat. "After you left, Aleck interned me into the dungeon."

"'Tis criminal." He stopped rocking and his expression grew dark. "Mr. Keith mentioned as much when he met me at Tabert. I still cannot understand MacIain's brutality toward you."

She nodded and swiped a tear away. "For days I sat locked in the cold dark cavern. My crime? Asking Mary to tend the pigs and the chickens whilst Aleck charged to Sunart with the clansmen."

Maggie whimpered and Eoin resumed bouncing. "First he abandons you with a handful of aging guards, and then he punishes you for taking charge?"

"I'm afraid so." Helen nodded. "Worse, Glenda said she overheard him tell Mary that I would perish right there in the dungeon whilst birthing a bairn."

"God's teeth." Eoin looked toward the window, a tic twitching in his jaw. "A-are you with child?" he whispered with cutting tension in his voice.

Her stomach twisted. *How poorly I must appraise in his eyes.* "That is what I cannot understand. Aleck hasn't visited my bedchamber since I conceived Maggie."

"Christ." Eoin lowered his gaze and stared at Maggie for a moment. "What in God's name was he scheming?"

"Deep in my heart, I know he was planning my death." She drew in a stuttered breath. "He told me he'd been in love with Mary even before our wedding. She was his leman the entire time I lived at Mingary."

He simply shook his head. "How awful for you."

Helen's problems came flooding back tenfold as silence cut through the cottage with the weight of five hundred stone.

Her whole sordid marriage looked like a farce performed by players at the king's court. But still, now the ugliness was in the open, Helen desperately needed to confess her deepest secret—the one *no one* knew.

Licking her lips, she wrung her hands. "He didn't visit my bedchamber often and when he did it was *insufferable*."

Eoin again looked away, his face unreadable. Helen was well aware that a lady shouldn't speak of such matters to anyone. But Aleck's behavior had always confused her. She'd seen couples in love before. Invariably, they acted as if they were mad for one another.

*I'll wager Sir Eoin now thinks me frigid just as Aleck did.*

Helen cringed and returned her attention to the hearth. *I shouldn't have told him.* Her palms moist with perspiration, she reached for a cloth and folded it over. Then she used it to lift the lid from the kettle scones. "These are ready," she said softly.

Food was a nice diversion from their present conversation.

"Smells delicious."

Helen kept her gaze lowered as she set the table and scooped the scones onto a trencher.

"Is Maggie eating with us?" he asked, running his palm over the sleepy bairn's crown.

"Nay. She's already supped." Helen held out her arms. "I'll put her down, she missed her afternoon nap."

Eoin strolled in behind Helen and looked at the makeshift crate. "Now that's clever."

With a chuckle, she placed Maggie inside and covered her with a soft blanket. "'Tis the only thing I could find to suffice for a cradle."

"It appears as if she hasn't noticed the difference."

"I daresay she hasn't." Helen gazed upon her daughter. The babe sighed and closed her eyes. Indeed, she was ready for sleep.

Eoin pointed to a jug on the table. "Is that wine?"

"Aye."

"I'll pour us some."

Helen served up the pottage as Eoin collected two wooden cups from the shelf beside the hearth. There weren't many dishes, but enough to make do. "What news of the rebellion?" Helen asked.

He filled her cup and then his. "We'll be sailing into battle soon, I've no doubt."

She hated the idea of Eoin being embroiled in more fighting. "Why is the king waiting?"

"They are outfitting all the galleys with cannons, but the work's nearly done."

She pressed her hand to her abdomen. "You'll be expected back soon, then?"

"Aye." He gave her a sheepish grimace. "Actually, no one kens I've left aside from my men, and *they* are awaiting me at Dunollie."

"Oh heavens." Her gaze shot to the door. "Do they ken I'm here?"

"Nay." He patted her shoulder with a gentle hand. "Mr. Keith stressed how important it is to keep your location a secret and I most certainly agree."

Helen sat on the bench across from where he stood. As proper, he followed suit and took his seat, then raised his cup. "To you, Lady Helen. The bravest woman I know."

Goodness, he had an endearing way of making her feel important—respected. "You are very kind to say so, sir knight." She sipped her wine. The fruity, oaken flavor enlivened her palette. "Thank you for coming. I am ever so happy to see you," she added in a whisper.

"Lady Helen." Eoin reached across the table and touched his fingers to her cheek. Though his pads were rough, his touch was feather light. Closing her eyes, she leaned into his hand. Kindness from a man was something she knew little of.

His gaze grew dark and intense. "I would have sailed around the world just to see you if only for a moment."

A bit of her heart melted.

They'd never talked about what might happen after the annulment was granted—if it was granted. And if it was not, Helen could find herself at Aleck MacIain's mercy. Perhaps that's why she avoided thinking about her future.

She picked up her spoon and took a bite.

Eoin did the same. Through the entire meal, he held her gaze, staring at her with those intense blue eyes while the candlelight flickered amber across his sun-weathered skin.

Helen couldn't remember ever gazing upon a man more ruggedly handsome. Moreover, merely with a look he expressed his love—his strength. With Eoin near, she needn't fear. If only this eve would last forever.

# Chapter Twenty-Two

The moment Mr. Keith had arrived and told of Helen's incarceration and escape, Eoin had set sail for Dunollie with fury pulsing through his veins. Blast it all, he hadn't been able to protect her from Aleck's sordid treatment.

Without considering the consequences, he rushed to her to ensure she was safe and unharmed. At least that's what he told himself.

But chatting with Helen over simple fare and sweet wine was like being sent to heaven. She'd changed since he'd last seen her. Aye, she'd dropped a few pounds which she could ill afford, but Helen carried her shoulders with more ease. Her mouth wasn't pulled tight at the corners. Even her neck appeared longer. The stresses at Mingary most certainly had her wound tighter than a spring, but out there in the middle of the forest, she'd already relaxed some. She again looked like the winsome lass he'd fallen in love with so long ago.

Eoin listened thoughtfully to her banter, enraptured with the sultry lilt of Helen's voice. Had she no idea of the extent of her allure? He swirled his second helping of wine and sipped. He held the cup to his lips for a time, watching her from behind it, hiding his smile. By God, her beauty surpassed anything he'd seen in all his travels.

At the cottage, she'd left her tresses uncovered and unbound. Her hair hung past her waist in waves of honey. Eoin's fingers twitched. He reached across the table and grasped a lock. Ah, yes. It was spun of pure silk. "You should never cover your hair." Gruff with longing, he hardly recognized his voice.

Helen's hands flew to her crown. "My heavens. I've been in the forest for two days and already I'm forgetting propriety."

"Not at all. It pleases me that you're comfortable without a veil." He held the lock to his nose and inhaled. "Mm. Purer than a bar of rose-scented soap."

A nervous chuckle slid through Helen's lips. "'Tis just my wily mop of hair."

He lowered his chin and deliberately stared. "I beg to differ."

She fanned her face. "My, the wine is making me flush."

Eoin would wager the adorable blush blossoming in her cheeks wasn't caused by the wine. He'd been willfully staring at her since arriving.

"'Tis growing late," she said. "Are your men expecting you?"

So enraptured was he, that he hadn't blinked in some time, nor did he want to close his eyes for even a fraction of a moment. "On the morrow."

Helen's gaze shot to the bedchamber, then her exquisite pink tongue slipped out and moistened her bottom lip. "Eoin, I—"

He couldn't allow her to say it. Standing, he strolled around the table and grasped her hand. "Come here."

A wee gasp caught in her throat as she dipped her gaze to their hands, her dainty palm cradled in his. Watching, Eoin didn't hurry her. She raised her chin and met his gaze—those sky blue eyes turning the shade of midnight. Hot, raw desire thrummed through his manhood.

With a slight tug, he pulled her into his arms. Brushing a lock of hair from her face his chest swelled. "I want to gaze upon your beauty."

Without a word she smiled and slowly slid her hands around his waist until their bodies touched.

Damnation, she molded to him like she'd always been meant to be in his arms. He was so damned hard. He'd been hard since she'd opened the door to the cottage. There were no words to express the intensity of the love bursting from his chest. He wanted so much to protect her—to cherish her—to show her just how deeply a woman could be loved.

Her eyes watched him with a combination of fear and trust.

Eoin dipped his gaze to her lips—still moist. Searing need swirled in his groin. Heaven help him, but he wanted her. He'd wanted her every day of his life. Though he'd searched, he hadn't found another woman who could reach his soul like Helen Campbell, and now he held the object of his passion in his arms. Before she could utter another word, he claimed her mouth. Since the day he'd kissed her in the shed, he'd relived that glorious moment over and over. Greedy for more, he slipped his tongue between her lips forcing himself to be gentle, reverent.

As they joined, Helen sighed into his mouth—her response not pensive as it had been before. She yielded to him, slipping her arms up his back and pulling him closer. Her mouth was silky, hot and wet. Eoin pressed the length of his body against her, but it wasn't enough. He skimmed his hands down to her buttocks and tugged her hips flush against his all-demanding, mind-consuming erection.

Helen shuddered and softened her kiss until she pulled her lips away. Eoin leaned toward her, desperate for more.

"We mustn't," she said, her trembling voice barely audible.

He brushed the back of his finger along her cheek. She was as radiant as Aphrodite. "You have already left him."

Her inhale stuttered. "But I have not yet been granted an annulment."

"Will a slip of parchment make you want me all-the-more?" How could he allay her fears? *Her kisses declared her love—if only she would give in to her desire.*

Helen took in a deep breath. "I'm so afraid. Aleck could kill us both."

Eoin's jaw tensed. "That man can never touch us. I will protect you with my life. Never again will I allow him to harm you or Miss Maggie."

"Dear Lord." She pressed praying fingers to her lips. "I hate that I have brought you into this mess."

"I would not have you suffer this alone." He drew his eyebrows together. "I am here because there is no place I'd rather be. At Mingary, I made a vow that I would be your guardian knight and I will stand by that promise until I draw my last breath."

"Your kindness exceeds all expectations." She pressed her palm over his heart. "But I cannot rely upon you to push aside your life and hide as I am."

"Problems have a way of finding resolve." Eoin brushed a wisp of hair away from her face. "I ken you care for me."

"Och," she groaned, resuming her grip around his waist and resting her head on his chest. "I love you more than life itself. I've always loved you."

"Ah, mo leannan." He kissed her forehead. "My love for you runs deeper than the sea."

"I cannot tell you how much your words make my heart soar. But we cannot risk being caught. Aleck would see me hanged."

Eoin bristled at the mention of that bastard's name. "No, lass. I will never allow him to harm you again. He has treated you with more disdain than any woman could be expected to tolerate from her spouse. Moreover, no one, save Gyllis and Mr. Keith, kens where we are."

She raised her chin and met his gaze. "And your men suspect nothing?"

"I saw no need to tell them of your misfortune. For all they know, I've ridden to Kilchurn. Unless Mr. Keith says something."

Helen shook her head. "The noble guard spirited me away. I trust him almost as much as I trust my sister."

"True, he is indeed an ardently loyal servant."

Helen rested against him. "I've grown so tired of living in fear."

Eoin smoothed his hand over Helen's hair and cradled her head to his heart. "I ken, my love. You are such a giving person, you deserve to be happy. You deserve to know what it's like to be treasured." He pressed his lips against her forehead and closed his eyes. "I love you, Helen. I meant what I said. I have always loved *you.* I want to be the man to protect you, to stand beside you throughout this lifetime, to be a father for Maggie and for children to come."

"Mm. Your words are like a minstrel's ballad. You have no idea how long I've yenned to hear it." She took his hand and kissed his palm. "But what if—"

"There is no what if. There is only *us.*" Eoin scooped her into his arms and started for the bedchamber.

Helen pointed behind them. "But Maggie."

"She's sleeping." He covered her mouth with a swirling kiss, drawing away all her doubt. She looped her arms around his neck and gave in to their passion as he crossed the threshold.

Gently, Eoin set her on the bed. Faint light from the candles in the main chamber cast flickering ochre shadows through the room. "How many years have passed since we first met?" he asked.

"Since you arrived at Kilchurn for your fostering?"

"Aye."

She pulled the laces on his shirt, but like a timid maid, Helen released her grasp before she fully untied it. "I'd say it has been just shy of a score of years."

"Then that is how long I've loved you."

She chuckled. "Surely not when I was a child?"

"Even then." He leaned in and nuzzled her ear. "I remember watching you when I first arrived. Your skin was flawless, your eyes blue as the sky above, and your hair reminded me of gilded thread used only to stitch royal garments."

She twirled his shirt lace around her finger. "You thought all that at the age of four and ten?"

"I did." Leaning in, he trailed kisses down her neck. "I've always wanted you for my own, Lady Helen."

***

She shuddered right down to her toes. Aleck had never made her tremor with want, had never made the gooseflesh rise across her arms. But the deep rumble of Eoin's voice caused her insides to swarm with flutters of desire. Her body came alive with need, but yet she still feared so many things.

Eoin tugged the lace of her kirtle. Helen gasped and slid away from him. He reached out for her hands and pulled her back. "You've nothing to fear from me. I promise."

She nodded and looked down. Though copulation had never been enjoyable for her in the past, she trusted Eoin. Even more confounding, she craved his touch.

He fingered her kirtle laces. "Are you all right?"

"Aye," she whispered, allowing him to pull her to her feet.

As if he were honing the fine edge of his blade, he unlaced every eyelet of her kirtle. Bending down, he ran fluttering kisses over the top of her bodice as he slid it from her shoulders. "Your skin is finer than pure silk," he purred.

Helen's knees turned to boneless mollusks as he removed her stays. All the while, the scent of spicy male sent her insides aflutter with anticipation. Aleck had never fussed with removing her clothing. But now Helen's breath became labored as she allowed Eoin to undress her. She wanted him to see her naked, moreover, she hungered to see all of him.

Once Eoin stripped her down to nothing but her linen shift, she grew bold. Reaching up, she pushed the quilted arming doublet from his shoulders and let it cascade to the floor.

He grasped the skirt of her shift, but she placed the palm of her hand on his chest. "You first."

With a chuckle, he kicked off his boots, then pulled the shirt over his head and cast it aside.

Aye, she'd seen him shirtless before, but watching him now in the privacy of the tiny bedchamber brought on a longing so intense, her very skin coursed with anticipation.

Eoin's eyes darkened and his devilish grin turned up at one corner of his mouth while he loosened his belt and dropped his breeks. His need pushed out against his linen braies. With a flick of his fingers, he untied the knot holding them up and let them fall.

Standing naked as God intended, Helen never in her life imagined such virile beauty in a man. No piece of art or statue reflected Eoin's magnificence. Head to toe, and halfway back up again, Helen drank him in…all of him.

Trying to breathe, Helen traced the fine, chiseled muscles of his chest. She gasped. Though his skin was incredibly warm, it was as hard as iron. A powerful need deep within her core coiled like the winding of a spring. She swirled her fingers through the downy hair on his chest before trailing her hand down the center of his rock-hard abdomen.

Eoin's moan rumbled with basal desire.

His erection jutted from a nest of tight mahogany curls. Helen's need scorched her insides and she licked her lips while her fingers twitched, not daring to go further.

Rocking his hips forward, the tip of his manhood touched her finger. She gasped.

So did he.

Meeting his gaze, Eoin nodded and lowered his lashes, telling her what he wanted simply with a look.

Her lips parted as she gradually wrapped her hand around him and stroked. Letting out a belabored breath, Eoin pulled her into his arms and pressed himself against her.

His hardness made her head swoon. Helen rocked her hips toward him, craving friction.

"I cannot hold back much longer," he growled, tugging up her shift and pulling it over her head.

Completely naked, Helen slid back onto the bed and wrapped her arms around her knees—totally at a loss for what she should do. "I want you to join with me. And believe me when I say I've never uttered such words before. I feel like a virgin."

"Then I shall be all the more gentle with you." His voice rumbled like distant thunder.

Tugging her arms open, he crawled over her, and levered himself between her thighs. Helen could not drag her eyes away. The thick column of his erection pointed straight at her nether parts. With a stuttered inhale, Helen prepared herself for a jolt of pain—one she would welcome from Eoin MacGregor.

But he did something completely unexpected.

Rocking back on his haunches, he ran the pad of his thumb down her sex and swirled it through her moisture. "You're so wet for me."

"'Tis a good thing?" she asked with a tremor in her voice.

His deep chuckle rolled through her chest. "Aye, a very good thing."

Helen closed her eyes and moved her hips in tandem with his caresses. Gently, he slipped a finger inside her. In and out—oh, how unbearably tantalizing his touch. Helen's breathing sped. Never would she have believed she could feel this completely aroused. Only her deep love for Eoin could allow such unabashed intimacy. She opened her eyes and drank in his manhood while Eoin tempted her with his feather-light strokes.

Gasping, she could manage one syllable. "Now."

Eoin grinned and shifted his hips forward while guiding his erection to her entrance. Helen spread her legs wider. His tip filled her, stretched her taut, yet it felt amazing. She braced herself for the pain.

He took his weight onto his elbows and lay atop her without crushing. Rocking his hips forward, he slid deeper inside while covering her mouth and entwining her tongue with his. Completely and utterly alive, Helen gave in to the most thrilling experience of her life. Devoid of pain, her insides were slick with moisture, and welcomed him, as if telling her this had always been the man with whom she should be joined.

Together their breathing sped as they united in a glorious dance between a man and a woman who'd spent most of their lives suppressing their affection for one another.

Helen closed her eyes and gave in to the amazing merging her body and soul with the only man she had ever loved. The years apart only made their lovemaking all the more enjoyable. Just when she thought the pleasure could not grow better, her body shuddered on a pinnacle of pure ecstasy. Losing complete control, she cried out, bursting into magnificent spasms around him.

Eoin pressed up with his palms and thrust deep and fast. With a basal, shuddering moan, he pulled away and found his release.

Helen smoothed her fingers up and down his back, soothing him while his entire body tremored above her.

Gradually his breathing stilled and he kissed her with a passion more fervent than their first kiss in the shed on that rainy day.

Helen's heart squeezed tight while a tear moistened the corner of her eye. "I had no idea it could be like this."

# Chapter Twenty-Three

Helen's eyes flew open at the sound of Maggie's cries. Beside her, Eoin's body was so warm, she hated to slip out of bed into the chilly morning air. But her daughter needed tending, and through God's grace, she was now the only person to provide that care. She found her shift in the mussed pile of garments on the floor, and pulled it over her head, then wrapped a woolen blanket around her shoulders. Shuffling to the makeshift cradle, Maggie stopped crying as soon as Helen peered over the edge.

"Are you hungry, lassie?"

Secured by her swaddling clothes, Maggie wiggled and grinned.

"Let us change out these linens first." Though it was common practice to remove the swaddling linens and dry them by the hearth, Helen found the odor too strong, and she washed them after each use. The bairn seemed to think Helen's idea was splendid as well, because as soon as the swaddling bands were released, she kicked her legs and gurgled.

"I rather think she likes it when she's not bound so tight," Eoin said, leaning against the doorjamb to the bedchamber with a plaid tucked low around his hips. His dark hair mussed and a shadow peppered his face. He stared at Helen with a halfcocked grin, his heavy-lidded eyes reminding her of the unbelievable night they'd shared.

*I know I'll burn in hell for thinking it, but I could stare at that well-muscled chest all day.*

She smiled, then returned her attention to tying the coif atop Maggie's head. "I've some oats for porridge. I'll set a kettle to boil as soon as I've finished here."

"Not to worry, I'll set to rekindling the fire and making the porridge. A man's got to fend for himself when on the trail—I'm no stranger to mixing up a kettle of oats."

"My heavens, that's even more surprising than my ability to cook." Helen wound the long length of linen fabric around Maggie and refastened the swaddling bands. The babe wriggled and fussed.

"How much longer will you swaddle her?" Eoin asked.

"They say four to nine months. Though, Maggie is clearly preferring it when she has free movement."

"You could swaddle her from the waist down to catch the drippings. If it were up to me, I'd use oiled doeskin over the linen to keep her bedclothes dry. But who would ever listen to a bachelor?"

"What a good idea." Helen glanced around the sparsely appointed chamber. "Have you a length of soft leather?"

The fire crackled to life. "Nay. I must remember to bring some on my next visit."

A welcomed warmth spread through Helen's chest. She liked that he was planning to return. She poured some milk into a bowl and sat at the table with Maggie in her lap. "When will that be? Your return, that is," she asked, spooning a bit of milk into the bairn's mouth. The distraction of her task kept the anxiety from building up too much.

"I wish I knew." Pots clanged. "MacDonald surveillance up and down the coast has been keeping us running. I'm certain things will come to a head soon, but only God knows how long the fighting will last."

Helen's stomach tensed. If only he could stay with her. "I hate to think of you being embroiled in the midst of harm."

"'Tis not me I'm worried about."

"Oh?"

"I do not like the thought of leaving you here alone."

"You're worried about me when you're the one riding into battle?" She offered a reassuring smile. "I'll be fine. Besides, Gyllis and Mr. Keith will be watching out for me."

Eoin picked up a cast iron kettle and headed toward the door. "I ken. But 'tis dangerous and will be more so when Aleck discovers you're missing. We cannot risk anyone finding you until the annulment is granted. I'd prefer to remain here with you."

After Eoin opened the door, a cold wind chilled Helen to the bone. When would Aleck discover she had escaped? If the men were running sorties, he could learn of it any day. The chill made her shudder as she remembered his threat… *If you attempt to take my daughter from Mingary, I will hunt you down and kill you…It won't be an easy death. I'll make sure you suffer for a very long time.*

She must have had a terrified look on her face, because when Eoin returned with the kettle filled with water, he hastened to set it down and dashed to her side. "What is it?"

"Please, do not let him find us."

He gathered her in his arms. "I'll never let that man harm you again." He cradled her face in his palms. "Duncan never should have arranged your marriage to MacIain and, further, I should have stopped it at the time.

I will spend the rest of my life making up for your past five years of suffering."

"No, you mustn't carry the burden of my past upon your shoulders." Helen slid her arms around him and clung tight. "I only wish you could stay."

***

Nearly a month passed before Eoin could slip away to see Helen again. Even now, he should be patrolling with MacIain, but when Aleck's galley was forced into dry dock for repairs at Tabert, Eoin took advantage of his window of time. *I told the braggart to clear those damn mussels from his hull ages ago.* Eoin chuckled. *Lucky for me he didn't listen.*

Before he sailed off with a small crew, Eoin had given Duncan the excuse he needed to take care of Clan Gregor business and would return within a sennight. Duncan didn't like it, but the baron had no grounds on which to argue. The Lord of Glenorchy had made two visits to Kilchurn Castle during the past month.

As the boat tacked into the pier at Taynuilt, Fergus grinned like a wet-eared lad. "Me missus will be happy to see us."

Eoin winked. "You'll make her a happy woman, I've no doubt. Go on ahead with the men and I'll meet you back here in a sennight."

Fergus snorted. "You're not going with us?"

"Nay, I've business to the south."

"Bloody hell, m'laird. Every time we cast ashore for a moment's rest, you ride off on some clandestine mission."

Sometimes Eoin's membership in the Highland Enforcers came in handy. "You ken how it is when carrying a message for the king. The more who ken my whereabouts, the more dangerous it is."

Fergus gave a knowing nod. "Well, do not count on seeing me for a sennight, then. I aim to keep my woman warm and make up for all the time we've been away."

"Good to hear." Eoin slapped the henchman's shoulder then turned his attention to the mooring. Sailing into the small fishing village of Taynuilt, no one at Dunollie Castle would be aware of Eoin's visit this time, and since his men had no idea what he was up to, Helen's hiding place was safe from discovery.

After procuring a horse from the local stable, he made his way south into Fearnoch Forest, ever so anxious to see her again.

Approaching the cottage, he slowed his horse to a walk. A gentle hum sailed through the air—Helen's voice. Gooseflesh rose across Eoin's skin. Oh how he adored the melodic sound of her singing. He drew near enough to glimpse his lady through the trees.

Her honeyed locks swung forward while she raised her skirts and stepped into the wooden washbasin. "Oh my, the water is cold," she squealed.

Maggie's infant voice giggled on the breeze. The bairn rested against pillows atop on a plaid, watching her mother as Lady Helen stomped on the washing like Eoin had seen washerwomen do countless times.

He marveled at the industriousness of a woman used to being catered to by servants. *She's so willing to do anything necessary to keep her house in order.*

He tapped his heels into the horse's barrel and started forward.

A twig snapped with a crack.

Helen's head jerked up. Hopping out of the basin, she dropped her skirts while her fists flew under her chin. "Who's there?"

"'Tis only me," Eoin said, riding into the clearing.

She planted those fists on her hips, her initial expression of fear turning angry. "Eoin MacGregor, you said you would visit me as soon as you could get away.

Do you realize I've been beside myself for the past fortnight because I have received no word from you?"

"Forgive me, m'lady." Eoin hastened to dismount and bowed deeply. "There have been continuous skirmishes up and down the seaboard. My men and I haven't had a moment's rest."

"Not even to send a missive to Lady Gyllis? How much time does it take to dispatch a letter to Dunollie?"

Eoin smacked his forehead with the heel of his hand. "I was hesitant to write because of the importance of keeping your whereabouts hidden. But I should have penned a missive to Gyllis."

She shook her finger. "Yes, you should have."

He tossed the reins around the post outside the door. "Please accept my deepest apology. The thought didn't cross my feeble mind."

"Did I say how worried I have been?"

He nodded. "Aye." Then he tried to reach for her. "It was wrong of me to allow so much time to pass without sending word."

She clasped her hands behind her back as if not yet ready to make amends. Then she looked away, her bottom lip trembling. "The last time you were here, everything was so heavenly, so perfect…a-and I knew you had to go away, but anxiously awaited your return. And then when you didn't come for *sennights*, I began to think of awful things." She gasped "Anything could have happened. Your galley could have sunk, you could have been severely injured in the fighting—or killed." Helen wrung her hands. "I do not think I could have survived if something horrible had happened to you."

A tear dribbled from her eye and streamed down her lovely cheek.

Eoin's heart twisted. The lass was so fragile. He pulled her into his arms. "My God, Helen, I'm so sorry. I thought I was doing the right thing by not sending a missive, but seeing you so distraught, I realize how mistaken I was."

She squeezed her eyes shut. "Do not ever do that to me again."

"I promise I will not." He held her at arm's length and wiped away her tears with the pad of his thumb. "But you are aware I am oft required on the king's business. At times, such work can take me away for a month or more."

She nodded. "I hate to think of ever being without you."

He pulled her into his chest and cradled her head to his heart. "I know my love. I feel the same."

Taking in a staccato inhale, Helen leaned into him. "Once I am out of hiding, I must tell Duncan he cannot require you to spend so much time away from your home and your family."

Eoin liked the sound of that. At long last, he would have a family of his own—sharing his life with the woman of his dreams. "I daresay if anyone can persuade Duncan to her will, it is you."

Maggie blubbered behind them, like she was trying to talk.

He glanced over his shoulder. "She's awfully chatty."

"Aye, making new noises every day." Helen started to pull away.

Moving quickly, Eoin captured her face between his palms. "I'd feel so much better if you'd kiss me first."

Her eyes glistened with her smile. Yes, she might have been worried and angry, but sliding her hands around his waist and tugging him into her supple body, Eoin knew she loved him. Dipping his head, his lips met hers as her soft, sweet breath whooshed. When he held Helen Campbell in his arms, nothing in this world could deter him.

As the kiss ended, she emitted a long sigh. "I need to finish the washing."

He inclined his head toward the bairn. "Let me say hello to Miss Maggie, then I'll help you."

"I'm nearly done."

"'Tis good to hear, because I have other plans about what I want to do with you." Eoin scooped Maggie into his arms and gave her a kiss on her chubby cheek. "And how are you, miss? Giving your mother strife?"

The bairn threw her head back and laughed from her belly.

Eoin couldn't help but chuckle. "And you seem awfully happy about it, too."

"I think she's missed you," Helen said while raising her hem and resuming her stomping.

He regarded the child now tugging at his shirt laces. "I missed you too." Then he stared at Helen, her bare calves glistening with streaks of water. "Not a moment passed when you weren't on my mind."

She looked up and smiled, her cheeks taking on a blush. "Will you be able to stay long?"

"A sennight. If I remain away much longer, your brother will pronounce me dead and assume my lands due to my lack of an heir."

"He wouldn't dream of pushing out Clan Gregor."

"Nay?"

"Absolutely not." Helen stepped out of the basin and rung out the linens.

Eoin set Maggie on her blanket and stepped beside Helen. "I'll dump the water."

She straightened and brushed off her hands. "I'd almost forgotten how nice it was to have a brawny knight in attendance." Looking at her palms, she blew over them. "Though I'm rather proud of these new calluses."

Returning with the empty basin, he examined Helen's hands. "Your palms look like they've been shredded."

She closed her fists. "'Tis not that bad."

"What have you been doing?"

"Nothing more than fetching water…and cooking…and chopping wood. You ken, things a woman must do when fending for herself in the wild."

"God's teeth, I should be here to do those things for you. The thought of your noble hands set to labor goes against every knightly code."

"You mustn't look at it that way. I certainly do not." She picked up Maggie and balanced the bairn on her hip. "I see it as my liberation from helpless lady to independence."

He placed his arm around them both and escorted them into the cottage. "It pleases me that your independence makes you happy…as long as you still need me."

Helen stretched up and kissed his cheek. "I will always need you, sir knight."

***

The sennight with Eoin flew past in a blur. Though half worried out of her mind, Helen couldn't remain angry with her handsome knight. And having him to share the chores, gave them more time in the evenings after Maggie drifted off to sleep. She and Eoin shared tenderness so deep, she never could have guessed a man and a woman could harbor such powerful love.

Now Eoin had but one night before he must leave again.

After Maggie fell asleep for her midday nap, the sound of an ax chopping wood came from outside. Helen moved to the shutter and peered through the gap.

In one fluid motion, Eoin swung the axe in an arc. With a crack, the log split on contact. Helen shook her head. She would have had to whack that big piece of wood four or five times to achieve the same result.

He worked tirelessly to build up a pile of wood, every swing of his ax cutting deep. Stopping for a moment, he wiped his brow with his sleeve. Then he pulled his shirt over his head.

Helen gasped and touched a hand to her chest. Autumn had begun to turn the leaves golden, and with it came cooler temperatures, though the perspiration glistening across Eoin's skin testified to the exertion he made.

As he resumed chopping, the muscles in his arms flexed like iron gauntlets. The sunlight highlighted the contours in his back, while every movement rippled with masculine vitality.

A bead of sweat dripped from his hair and slid down his spine. He seemed not to notice, wielding his ax like a well-oiled machine. Simply by watching him, Helen worked up a thirst. She hastened to the bowl, doused a cloth with water, and then she poured two cups of watered wine and headed out the door.

With a crack, wood splinters darted through the air.

She inclined her head toward the wood stack. "Look at all you have accomplished, and in short order."

Eoin lowered his ax and turned. "I'll not be having you chop another stick of wood, m'lady."

She handed him a cup. "You do take care of me."

He rested his ax on the woodheap and held up his watered wine. "'Tis a responsibility I embrace."

They tapped their wooden cups together and drank.

"Mm," Eoin said. "'Twas just what I needed to quell my thirst."

Helen licked her lips and stepped into him. She smoothed the damp cloth over his shoulders and chest. "Maggie's asleep."

A deep chuckle rumbled through his throat and he slid his hand around her neck, plying her mouth with a kiss. "That sounds like a promise."

"Aye." She chuckled. "I thought that might draw your attention."

He grasped her waist and pressed his hips against hers. "Always."

Blessed desire gripped her nether parts as her passion inflamed. Helen shamelessly rocked her hips from side to side. "My, you have turned me into a wanton woman."

"And that's a bad thing?" His voice grew deeper with each word.

She emitted a seductive hum. "Perhaps not when we're alone."

Helen loved the look of desire on Eoin's face when he gazed upon her with a fervent hunger through half-lidded eyes. Their bodies entwined while their lips joined in a languid dance. Warm and enticing, his mouth invited her to sail uncharted waters with him, and after a sennight of passion, Helen's excitement grew. Every blessed joining brought a new adventure.

Eoin's hand slid down her thigh and grasped her skirts. Her heart fluttered. Would he take her there, outside with a cold breeze caressing their skin? Anticipation of a new path to pleasure heightened her hunger.

Helen slipped her fingers into the top of his breeks and pulled on the cord holding them up.

An infant's cry squealed from inside the cottage.

Eoin touched his forehead to hers and chuckled. "It appears we timed things a bit late."

Helen took in a ragged breath. "Will you remember where we are until we're alone this eve?"

He nuzzled against her ear. "I'll be thinking of it every moment until then."

Maggie's cries rose until they bordered on panic-stricken.

Helen gave him one last kiss. "Then I shall hold you to it."

# Chapter Twenty-Four

At long last the king had decided to deploy his forces—not a few galleys at a time to quell skirmishes, but the entire armada King James had amassed set sail on course to capture Alexander MacDonald once and for all. It was a chilly October day when Eoin stood manning the tiller of his galley, wearing his helm and hauberk. He and Aleck MacIain flanked each side of the V formation, with Duncan's three galleys taking the lead, followed by five of the king's royal galleys.

Finally, they would confront the MacDonald marauders. Eoin only hoped this grand sortie would put an end to the unpredictable MacDonald raids up and down the coast as well as end Alexander's outrageous claim to the Earldom of Ross.

Manning the cannon, Fergus and Willy stood upon the platform Eoin had built at the stern. With luck, they'd sink a MacDonald galley or two before they ran aground and alighted for the battle. The more MacDonald men they could dispatch now, the better their chances for a swift victory.

Before they approached the shore, he saw a MacDonald ship on the horizon. Eoin watched it change course. Anyone within miles would spot the king's armada. Aleck's galley veered off course and headed toward the distant ship.

*Bloody hell, he's splitting our forces.* Groaning, Eoin had no choice but to follow. All the boats were paired to ensure strength of numbers—and Eoin would make certain Aleck didn't have a sudden change of heart and swap sides.

The MacDonald galley's sail picked up the wind, speeding to the southwest.

"After them. Due south," Eoin bellowed the order and countered with pull of the rudder, putting his ship on a direct course to intercept the galley. Aleck's boat adjusted too, but not as fast. Picking up a hearty gust, Eoin's men quickly overtook MacIain, gaining on the MacDonald ship.

Once in range of the cannon, Eoin bellowed, "Set your sights, Fergus. I'll not watch this MacDonald vessel slip away from our clutches."

The henchman touched the flame to the cannon's fuse and the big gun blasted with deafening force. The gun recoiled so violently, it trundled to the length of its anchoring chain before Eoin blinked. A resounding splash indicated a miss.

"Raise your sights and blast again," Eoin yelled, though he could scarcely hear his own voice due to the ringing in his ears.

Willy labored to turn the crank while Fergus used the ramming iron to stoke the barrel with black powder.

Eoin held the rudder steady. The galley rose and fell as it cut through the waves at a steady tack. "We need a direct hit this time, men."

When the cannon again boomed, the wheels screeched as the barrel recoiled and rolled back until the chains bolted to the hull stopped it from smashing through the other side. The cannonball whistled away and Eoin peered through the thick smoke, praying.

A crash roared across the sea. Eoin ran to the side of his galley, peering through the sulfur cloud. His gut squeezed. The MacDonald galley's mast was down. Her oars slid out and the boat turned south.

Eoin blinked and wiped his eyes. *They're heading straight for the Isle of Oronsay.* "We'll finish it on land, lads," he yelled while muscling the rudder.

Eoin's blood coursed faster as their sail picked up the gale and they gained on the crippled galley. MacIain wasn't far behind. Good, they would make quick work of these scoundrels and then they'd rejoin the king's fight on Colonsay. "Heave to," Eoin gave the command to slow as they approached the shore. The men worked quickly to furl the sail and man the oars—a maneuver every man could perform in his sleep.

Ahead, the MacDonald galley groaned and scraped as she ran aground, then listed to port.

Eoin expertly sailed his boat and stopped just as the hull met with sand. "Drop anchor," he yelled. "Draw your weapons and prepare for battle!"

The MacDonald men scrambled over the side of the crippled boat and Eoin wasn't about to wait for them to regroup. Clan Gregor warriors splashed into the thigh-deep surf. Eoin pulled his sword as he rushed ahead and led the charge.

Surrounding a man protectively, three burly henchmen moved up the beach. Fighting off a scoundrel with a poleax, Eoin tried to make out the man's face. As the MacDonalds sped toward his men, Eoin chanced another glimpse at the mysterious lord. One of the big men stepped around a rock, revealing a glimpse of Alexander MacDonald. Bloody Christmas, they'd chased after the scoundrel himself.

Bellowing his war cry, Eoin surged forward. A battleax came from nowhere and swung at his knees. Leaping in the nick of time, the ax hissed beneath him. A lance came from the side. Eoin deflected with a backward slash of his blade. On he fought while Alexander MacDonald and his henchmen raced for the scrub beyond the beach.

Out of the corner of his eye, Eoin caught sight of MacIain charging after them with Grant in his wake. "MacDonald," Aleck roared. "Stand and fight, you milk-livered coward!"

With a thrust of his sword, Eoin cut down the man with the battleax. The other soldier lunged with his lance. Eoin dodged to the side. The man stumbled forward and Eoin pummeled him on the back of the head with the hilt of his sword.

Finally free to run ahead, Eoin challenged two of the henchman while Aleck circled with Alexander MacDonald. Though Eoin wouldn't lose any sleep if the MacDonald Chieftain won the fight, his duty was to capture the man and, if possible, keep him alive to stand trial in Edinburgh.

Together Grant and Eoin fought the henchmen while Aleck and Alexander clashed in a battle of strength.

Eoin quickly bested his attackers and spun, ready for his next opponent. On the beach, Fergus and the MacGregor army had already taken control and were binding the surviving enemies' wrists and ankles as MacDonald soldiers lay on their bellies. Off the shore, most of the MacIain men still watched the battle from the safety of their galley. *Milksops, the lot of them.*

They'd chased down Alexander MacDonald and not ended up on a wild goose chase, even though Aleck MacIain had driven them away from the armada. Perhaps the chieftain recognized the galley? It mattered not why.

Capture of the MacDonald Chieftain meant Eoin would soon part company with the Ardnamurchan Clan and never need see them again.

Eoin knocked Grant's opponent in the back with the pommel of his sword. Spinning, Grant used his hips to gain an advantage and cut down his foe. The MacIain henchman readied his weapon and started toward Aleck, but Eoin grasped the younger man's shoulder. "Let Sir Aleck have his vengeance."

The MacGregor guard joined them, encircling the fighting nobles. Sweat streaked from Aleck's brow, his breathing labored. Between bouts, he balanced his great sword on the sand to catch his breath—but doing the same, Alexander was every bit as exhausted.

Though the two proved to be equally matched, Eoin stood ready to pounce if MacDonald gained the upper hand.

He watched as a battle between love and duty warred inside him. Eoin himself yenned to face Aleck MacIain in a fight of swords and brawn, but Alexander MacDonald's crimes against the crown must not pass by unpunished. If only Eoin and his men had taken control of the beach before Aleck had arrived.

The contenders faced each other, bleeding and haggard, each one barely able to lift his weapon. Aleck sneered with blood staining his teeth. He dropped his sword and staggered forward while shaking his left arm at his side—the one he'd broken.

A dagger dropped from Aleck's sleeve into the blighter's palm. "You will never attempt to take my lands again," he growled, slashing the knife across Alexander's throat.

Eoin clenched his fists.

The MacDonald Chieftain, descended from the Lord of the Isles, stood for a moment. A stunned look stilled his features as blood flowed down his iron breastplate. Without uttering a word, he crumpled to the sand in a heap.

Aleck swayed on his feet and smirked at Eoin.

Behind them, Duncan and the king strode up the beach.

Aleck raised his dagger in the air. "The usurper has been vanquished by my hand."

Eoin gaped at the bastard in disbelief.

With a hearty laugh, the king marched straight to MacIain and placed a hand on his shoulder. "You have done Scotland a great service." King James raised his palms in triumph and walked in a circle. "This day, we have quashed the rebellion against Scotland and I am very pleased."

Aleck slid his dagger back into his shirtsleeve and grinned.

The young king faced the miserable blackguard. "Sir Aleck, I bequeath to you lands on the former MacDonald Islands of Jura and Islay, for you are the true hero of this battle."

Aleck puffed out his chest like a strutting peacock, then bowed deeply. "I am forever in your debt, your Grace."

The king slapped his shoulder. "You are and I caution you to nay forget it."

Eoin could have taken his dirk and stabbed himself. No doubt the land on Islay included one of the MacDonald castles.

Duncan stepped beside him. "What really happened here?"

Eoin pulled his friend aside. "MacIain had a feud to solve with the MacDonald, so I allowed him to fight." Eoin thumbed his finger at the MacIain men who were still watching from the safety of their galley. "Half the

MacIain cowards are trembling in their boat, while my men have battle wounds to tend. What do you think happened?"

Duncan shrugged. "No matter. The lands will all remain in the family."

"*Your* family, aye."

"Of which your clan is a part."

Eoin bristled. He dearly loved Duncan Campbell, but the man had no idea what it was like to be a Clan Chieftain and owe fealty to another. The Lord of Glenorchy owned lands and castles far greater than anything Eoin could ever hope for.

He summoned his men and headed for his galley. He'd endured just about enough of battles for one season and there was another place he'd much rather be.

# Chapter Twenty-Five

"This cider is delicious," Helen said, taking another heavenly sip while balancing Maggie on her lap.

"I knew you would enjoy it." Gyllis sat across the table, enjoying a cup as well. "And I filled two satchels with apples."

"Thank you so much. I love the harvest. Everything is so fresh." Helen glanced at the book on the table and chuckled. "I'm ever so grateful that you brought a book as well. I've missed reading."

Gyllis smoothed her hand over the worn leather volume. "*The Wedding of Sir Gawain and Dame Ragnelle & other Romantic Tales*," she recited. "Do you remember when Mother sent this to me at Ardchattan Priory?"

"Aye, I'm the one who picked it out, lest you would have ended up with a copy of The Holy Bible for your entertainment."

Gyllis chuckled. "I'd always thought it was awfully bold of Mother to send a romantic book. I must thank you. Enduring the monks day and night whilst I suffered with paralysis was penance enough."

Helen hated to think of all the pain and suffering her sister had borne. "I knew it at the time. I worried about you ever so much."

Gyllis sat quietly for a moment, as if recalling something sad. "And then you paid a far greater penance than I, suffering the ire of Aleck MacIain for so many years."

Helen gulped. "Let us pray those years are now behind me." She lowered the cup to Maggie and the bairn helped guide it to her mouth with her tiny hands.

Gyllis watched them while a smile spread across her lips. "Every time I visit, she's doing something new."

Helen looked up. "Was it that way with your two?"

"Aye, the first year always has the most changes. And then they start thinking about walking. That's when things really become interesting."

"I'll be happy when she can talk and tell me what's wrong."

"I agree with you there. Why God saw fit for us to bring helpless bairns into the world, I'll never understand. Wee chicks can walk and eat, even puppies are up and around in a few days."

Helen gave Maggie a squeeze. "I don't think I'd have it any other way. This little miss is ever so interesting to watch. I wouldn't want her to forgo a moment of her childhood."

"No parent would care to miss it." Gyllis looked away, biting her lower lip. "'Tis unfortunate some do not see it that way."

Helen took a sip of cider and thoughtfully swirled the tart liquid around her mouth. She knew exactly what Gyllis implied. "I only hope I'm doing right for her."

"Of course you are. In my opinion, Aleck MacIain has no honor."

"I daresay I agree." Helen stood and held Maggie out to Gyllis. "Would you hold her for a moment? I'd like to take a cup of cider out to Mr. Keith."

"Och aye, you should. He's been ever so kind. Why not invite him in as well? 'Tis chilly outside."

"Very well." Helen pattered across the floor and opened the door.

She jolted so violently, cider splashed over her hand.

Eoin's knuckles were raised as if he were about to knock. "You look surprised to see me." His deep voice flowed like thick treacle.

"Thrilled is more like it." She offered her hand, inclining her head toward Gyllis.

Eoin nodded his understanding and graciously accepted her offering, bent over her hand, and plied it with a kiss.

"Shut the door you two, you're letting all the heat escape," Gyllis complained from the table.

Helen beckoned Mr. Keith. "Won't you come in and join us in a cup of cider? I'm afraid the one I poured for you has sloshed all over my sleeve."

The guard blew on his hands and rubbed them. "Thank you, m'lady."

Eoin stepped inside and removed his cloak while Mr. Keith did the same.

Helen gestured to the table. "Please sit."

Gyllis greeted Eoin with a smile. "How goes the battle?"

"Alexander MacDonald was killed by Sir Aleck at Oronsay."

"Honestly?" Helen kept her surprise hidden as she poured for the men. "Does that mean the rebellion is quashed?"

"Aye." Eoin raised his cup. "It also means everyone's headed home for St. Crispin's Day. I've sent my men to their wives in Glen Strae as well."

Gyllis clapped a hand over her mouth. "Sean might already be at Dunollie?"

Eoin picked up his cup and gave her a nod. "If he's not there now, he will be. I left him and Lord Duncan standing on the shores of Oronsay with King James."

"You left them?" Helen asked, worried that he might have been remiss.

Eoin shrugged. "I figured they no longer needed my services—at least not in the next sennight anyway, given the holiday and the fact we'd finally stopped Clan Donald from razing half of Scotland." He looked to Helen and waggled his brows. "I've some good news to share."

Could she allow herself to hope? "Aye?"

Eoin looked to Gyllis and Mr. Keith. "I'd wager you both can keep a secret."

The elderly guardsman placed his hand over his heart. "You ken I'd protect her ladyship with my life."

Helen inched to the edge of the bench. "We've nary a secret amongst ourselves."

"Very well, then." Eoin removed a missive from inside his quilted doublet, his big grin stretching his features made Helen's insides swarm with butterflies. "After we stopped Alexander MacDonald, I sailed to Iona on my way back here. Your brother had returned from Rome only two days prior."

Gyllis cleared her throat.

Eoin's gaze darted to Mr. Keith. "M'lady," he added hastily. After all, certain formalities could not be cast aside when in the presence of others.

Helen's fingers trembled. "Is that missive for me?"

Eoin nodded and held it out.

After she took it, Helen could scarcely hold the velum steady enough to run her finger under the wax seal.

"What does it say?" Gyllis asked before Helen even had the missive opened.

"A moment." Helen took in a calming breath and read. A tear spilled from her eye and streamed down her cheek. "Praise the heavens."

"The Pope approved?" Gyllis snatched the parchment from Helen's hands.

"Aye. My marriage has been annulled." She stared at Eoin in disbelief. Though her toes touched the floorboards, she felt light enough to float up to the rafters.

Eoin reached out as if to give her a squeeze, but that wouldn't appear proper in front of Mr. Keith and he drew his hand away. "The bishop advised we…uh…you should continue to remain hidden. He's dispatched a messenger to Mingary and it would be best if Aleck didn't know your whereabouts until he's had time to adjust to the idea."

"Do you think he'll try to lash out?" Gyllis asked.

Mr. Keith held up his cup of cider. "If I know Sir Aleck MacIain, he'll be in a rage for a month or more."

Helen couldn't have put a damper on her giddiness if the sky had fallen. "I don't mind staying here all winter if that's what it takes."

"You shouldn't need to hide that long." Eoin moved his palm over her hand—a simple enough gesture. "Also, John intends on visiting Duncan after St. Crispin's Day to personally explain."

"Bless him. Bless both of my brothers." Helen stared at Eoin, wishing they were alone. Oh, how much she wanted him to pull her into his arms and never let go.

"My, look how low the sun is in the western sky. I do believe the day has drawn away from us." Gyllis, ever so good at taking her cue, stood and placed Maggie on the sheepskin rug. "We'd best be heading back, Mr. Keith. And pray Sir Sean hasn't yet arrived home. I'll want to be on the shore watching his galley sail to the embankment."

Mr. Keith gulped down his cider. "Thank you for the tot, Lady Helen. 'Twas good to see you as always."

Helen's insides still quavered with the news, but she managed to bow her head to the guard. "Thank you for your service, Mr. Keith. I shall never forget your selfless kindness."

"Nor shall I." Eoin held out his hand.

Mr. Keith glanced at Helen before he shook the MacGregor Chieftain's hand. Though they already considered each other man and wife, the rest of the world had yet to be advised, including Mr. Keith *and* the clergy.

Eoin bowed his head respectfully. "I hope to have the pleasure of meeting you again soon."

Helen and Eoin stood together and watched as Gyllis and Mr. Keith rode into the woods, until they disappeared into the foliage. Eoin placed his arm around her shoulder. "I believe I gave the guard a bit of a surprise."

"I daresay you did—though he does know you are the one who appealed to John on my behalf. I hope he doesn't think badly of us."

Eoin shrugged. "It is not his place to have an opinion. Besides, he's sworn fealty to you, and should want for your happiness." He pulled her into the cottage and shut the door, grinning with feral desire. Before she could say a word, he wrapped her in his embrace. "I've missed you ever so much."

Helen rose up on her toes and met his lips with a kiss. "I'm ever so glad you're here."

"And how is Miss Maggie? Well, I pray?"

"Aye, she's sitting up now."

Eoin grinned and looked at the bairn who was indeed sitting on the sheepskin. "Och, the lassie is growing stronger by the day." He crossed the floor in four easy strides and pulled Maggie into his arms. She squealed as he spun her in a circle. "You are growing as bonny as your mother."

Helen set to preparing the evening meal while Eoin told of the events of Alexander MacDonald's end. She ground her teeth when Eoin described how he'd held the men back and allowed Aleck to fight, and then detailed his bravado afterward.

"You mean the king granted Sir Aleck lands without asking for the full story? And half the MacIain men watched the fighting from the safety of their galley?"

"My men had the skirmish in hand." Eoin's shoulder ticked up. "And as for the king, Sir Aleck was standing over MacDonald's body with a bloody dagger in his hand. 'Twas obvious he'd done the killing."

"But you and your men made it possible."

"Duncan knows that."

"Aye, but does the king?"

Eoin slid his hand across her waist and nuzzled into her ear. "Does it matter?"

Helen sighed. "I suppose not. You've land a plenty and are aligned with one of the strongest clans in Scotland."

Eoin's gaze narrowed and he stepped away. A sudden coolness coursed over Helen's skin. Had she misspoken?

He heaved a troubled sigh. "I've no castle to give you, Lady Helen."

"Riches, a grand keep?" She drew her brows together. "After all this time we've spent together, you think I want a castle?"

Taking another step back, he spread his hands to his sides. "But you have lived in opulence all your life."

She gestured to the walls of the meager hunting cottage. "Aside from the past three months. And to be perfectly honest, I've been happier here than any place I've ever lived."

His chin ticked up as he took a step closer this time. "Clan Gregor is a proud people. Our blood runs thick. Honor runs deep with us."

"As it does throughout the Highlands." Helen stepped within inches of Eoin and grasped his hand. "Are you worried I'll be unhappy if I haven't dozens of servants to direct?"

That twitch returned to his jaw. "Helen, I look at you standing over the cooking fire and I ken you were bred for a better life."

"But I enjoy cooking. I enjoy staying busy."

"Then as we've discussed, you will consider becoming Lady MacGregor?" The tension in his jaw eased.

"Given our…" She glanced toward the bedchamber. "*Interludes*, I assumed it would go without saying."

Eoin grinned and tugged her into his arms. "I give you my solemn vow you will never go without. And you will have servants to cook and clean."

"As long as I am by your side, I should want for nothing."

He captured her lips with a kiss. Slowly plying her mouth with languid strokes of his tongue, Helen melted like butter in the sun.

Maggie squealed.

Helen forced herself to pull away and hold Eoin at arm's length. "She's hungry."

He licked his lips. "As am I."

***

With his belly full and his mind eased with the effects of Helen's fruity wine, Eoin watched as she put Maggie down for the night. Helen wore a white linen apron atop her woolen kirtle. Though a simple ensemble, she still looked like a queen. Eoin grinned at the way her bottom curved against the skirts when she bent forward.

He had a notion to cross the floor and sink his fingers into those womanly hips. Helen bent further and kissed the bairn's forehead.

Eoin growled. It would be so easy to lift her skirts and slide into her from behind. But *Lady* Helen would be mortified. He swiped a hand across his eyes to change his train of thought. He would never do anything that would make her uncomfortable. She'd endured far too much.

Now that Eoin had earned her love, he would do nothing to jeopardize it. But before his mind caught up with his body, he'd crossed the floor and placed his hands on those irresistible hips.

Helen glanced back and smiled, touching her finger to her lips.

He looked around her. The bairn's eyes were already closed.

After one last tuck of the bedclothes, Helen straightened and took a step back, pressing her alluring buttocks against him. *Aye, this must be heaven.* He rubbed his cock between the crease of her bottom. "I've missed you," he whispered in a low growl.

She turned and grasped his hand. "Come."

All too willingly, Eoin followed her into the bedchamber.

Helen smoothed her palms over his chest. "I know not what's come over me. Every day I think about doing this." She ran her finger over the hard ridge of his manhood. Her hands trembled as she unfastened his belt. They worked quickly to untie laces, with clothes cascading to the floor until they both stood completely naked.

The image of her hips as she bent over consumed his mind. He dared ask, "Do you trust me?"

"Aye. I trust you with my life."

He placed his hands on her shoulders and turned her back to him. Then he reached around and slid his hand down between her breasts, over her abdomen and stopped at the apex of her sex.

She released a gasp.

Ever so gently, he pushed his finger between her folds and caressed her. Oh, how much he loved being completely naked with this woman.

Helen rested her head against him. "You ken how to make me ravenous with need."

"No more than you do to me." He worked more of his hand between her thighs. "Open for me."

Her head shot up. "Here? N-not on the bed?"

He chuckled. "I think you'll enjoy what I have in mind." Maintaining a steady motion, he caressed her inner thighs. "We'll only proceed as long as you're comfortable," he whispered in her ear. "I'll not encourage you to do anything that doesn't feel right."

She gave him a shy grin and parted her legs. How she could bring him to his knees with her demure mien. He made love to her with the fingers of his right hand, while swirling his thumb around her nipple with his left. Helen responded to his advances with seductive churning of her hips.

Her provocative movement made a bit of his seed leak from the tip of his cock. Bending his knees, he slid himself between her buttocks, her slick moisture spreading along his manhood. Helen arched her back and her delectable bottom pressed against him. "What are you doing?"

He rocked his hips to show her what he wanted, while he continued to finger that taut button that was driving her mad. "I'd like to try to enter you from behind. But only if it pleases you."

She rolled her hips atop him. "Is that possible?"

"If you have an adventurous spirit." He slipped his hand away from her breast and smoothed it down her spine. On the way back up, he encouraged her to lean forward. "Place your hands on the bed."

She glanced at him over her shoulder with a seductive grin. "Being adventurous is new for me—and a bit scary."

"And 'tis my duty to ensure you enjoy it." He grasped his cock and guided himself to the edge of her opening.

Helen moaned.

Holding on to her hips he watched himself disappear inside her. Then he reached forward and swirled his finger around her mons. "Does it feel good for you?"

"Mm." She ground her hips into him, taking him deeper. "I like your idea of trying new things." Her words came out breathless.

His thighs shuddered as he watched himself slide in and out, maintaining himself on the ragged edge of control.

Eoin focused on Helen's passion until her breathing sped and her buttocks shook against his legs. Her mewls made his heartbeat race. As she gasped, nearing her peak, he let himself go and increased his thrusts. Working his finger faster, Helen cried out and arched her back.

Her quavering insides milked him until he no longer had control. Thrusting, watching her naked bottom spread open to him with her back arched, his seed erupted from his body with a bellowing roar.

# Chapter Twenty-Six

Helen lay in Eoin's arms content and satiated, like she imagined a woman should always be when at rest with her man. With Maggie sound asleep in her crate, and her annulment granted, Helen hadn't a care. "The only thing I miss is my lute," she whispered. "I love music."

"Me as well. I love to listen to you play…and sing. The last time I heard you, I could have sworn you could contend with the king's minstrels."

She wiggled against him. "I wouldn't go that far." Though he exaggerated, Helen did enjoy hearing his compliment.

"I don't lie," he continued. "I would have been quite happy to have reclined in my seat and listened to you all evening."

"Och, that's very nice of you to say." She craned her neck and looked at him. His face was peppered by the dark shadow of a new beard, giving him a rather devilish look. "I remember you played the pipes rather well. Do you oft have a chance to play them of late?"

He picked up a lock of her hair and drew it across his nose, as if he couldn't get enough of her scent. "Definitely not as of late—the occasional fete or funeral is about all I can manage. Bagpipes are a bit clumsy to tote around on the back on my horse."

She chuckled. "I remember when you and Duncan used to practice in the hall at Kilchurn."

He trumpeted out his nose. "Don't remind me. We sounded like a pack of howling cats."

She rolled with laughter at the memory of it. "Especially Duncan. I don't think he ever got the hang of it."

"Nay, piping didn't have enough action for him. He'd make every excuse not to practice."

"Then why did you become so good at it?"

Eoin smirked stared off across the chamber. "I guess when I think about my days of fostering with so many talented lads, piping was something I could do better than the others. Duncan, Sean, your brother, John, and I were quite a foursome, and very competitive. But not a one could touch me when it came to the bagpipes and knowing that made me want to practice all the more."

"Funny, but I always thought you were the best at everything. You were the only one who could give Duncan a walloping in the sparring ring."

"Och, believe me, he doled out plenty. If I had to choose a victor after all our years of clashing swords, I'd say we were pretty evenly matched. But he's a year older than I. That made a difference in the beginning." Eoin held up his finger. "Though not with the piping."

Helen threaded her fingers through Eoin's and marveled at how much larger he was than her—in every way. His hands were enormous and made hers appear almost childlike. Odd, but she couldn't even recall what Aleck's hands looked like, or whether they were large or small. Most certainly, she hadn't ever shared such a tender moment with him. *Such a pity. And I will stop thinking about that vile man from here out.*

"What else do you like to do?" Eoin asked.

Helen blinked, drawing herself back to the enjoyment of the moment. "I love to read. Mother always said if she didn't find something for me to do, I would spend every waking hour with my nose in a book."

"If only there were a plethora of books available for such an endeavor."

"My sentiments exactly." She brushed her fingers along the fine dark hairs on his arm. "I must have read every book in Kilchurn's library dozens of times."

"My word, you do love to read."

"Aye. Gyllis brought a book for me to read just the other day—a romantic tale."

"Now that sounds interesting." He kissed her temple. "Would you read to me?"

"You wouldn't grow bored?"

"Not if you were reading, my love."

Helen slipped off the bed, tiptoed into the main chamber and retrieved the book from the table. When she returned, Eoin had situated the candelabra to provide good light, and arranged the pillows for comfort.

How wonderful it was to be with a man who actually cared enough to do simple things like fluffing the pillows.

He opened his arms and beckoned her to him. "Come and tell me what this story's about."

"It would be my pleasure, sir knight." Helen climbed up and snuggled into his arms. She opened the cover and read the title. "*The Wedding of Sir Gawain and Dame Ragnelle*." She looked at Eoin and grinned. "The story begins when the mystical knight, Sir Gromer Somer Joure, challenges King Arthur to discover what women desire most, or face *dire* consequences."

He rested his chin on her shoulder and peered at the pages. "You have me entranced already."

"Oh, believe me, it gets so much more riveting."

As Helen read, Eoin listened to every word as if he were captivated by the fairy tale. How a rugged and powerful warrior such as the Chieftain of Clan Gregor could be completely enthralled by one of her books amazed her. He suited her in every way. He treated her respectfully and he loved Maggie. He'd shown her what it was like for a man and a woman who were truly in love to express their feelings in the joining of their bodies. When she lay with Eoin it was not sinful. Their love was a gift from heaven and she would cherish every moment they shared for the rest of their days.

***

The following day was too cold for a bath outside and Helen asked Eoin to bring the wooden basin inside. "Miss Maggie's skin is chafing. I know they say 'tis bad to bathe a bairn more than once a month, but where Maggie's concerned, her skin always looks better after a bath."

"I say do whatever is best for the lass." Eoin put the big basin beside the fire and picked up a bucket. "I'll go to the burn and fill this."

"Thank you." Helen looked in the kettle suspended over the fire. "The water's nearly boiled."

From her rug, Maggie clapped her hands.

"Are you looking forward to the bath?"

"Babababababababa."

"I agree." Helen lifted the babe into her arms. "I rather enjoy a tub of warm water, myself."

The wind whipped through the door before Eoin stepped inside. "My oath, I think we may have our first snow soon."

Helen shivered. "Oh no. We cannot weather a harsh winter this year."

"'Tis still early." He strode across the floorboards and dumped the bucket of water into the basin. "If we do see snow, it should only be a dusting and will be gone by the morrow."

"I suppose it is God's will, whatever happens." Helen inclined her head toward the kettle. "Would you please pour in the hot water as well?"

"My pleasure m'lady."

Once the bath was filled, Eoin swirled his hand in the water. "'Tis nice and warm. Perhaps I should set another kettle to boiling in case…ah…" The brawny Highlander could make her melt with a single arch of his eyebrow.

Helen chuckled. "I don't suppose it would be proper to bathe in front of the wee one."

"Are you jesting? I doubt she'd mind."

Helen set the bairn in the tub while Eoin headed outside with the kettle. "He's a bit brazen to suggest each of us strip down and bare our nether parts in the main chamber."

Maggie bubbled and splashed her hands in the water.

"You seem to think there's nothing wrong with that idea in the slightest." Helen reached for a cake of soap. "I'll tell you, nothing of the like would have been allowed at Kilchurn Castle. Why, if one of my mother's daughters so much as left her chamber wearing but a shift, she would be sorely punished."

"Bubub," Maggie replied, reaching for the soap.

Helen held it out. The bairn squeezed the cake with both hands. The blasted think slipped up and hit Helen between the eyes. "You little rascal."

Maggie chirped with laughter.

Eoin pushed through the door and hastened to the hearth. "I'll just add a couple of logs to the fire. 'Tis really starting to blow a gale."

Helen used a cloth to finish bathing Maggie and avoid further incidents with the soap.

Eoin finished his task and sat across from her. A rolling laugh snorted through his nose. "What happened to you?"

Helen touched her fingers to her forehead and wiped off a blob of soap. "You think that's funny do you?"

Maggie splashed her hands and water sloshed across Eoin's shirt. He gaped at the bairn. "So now you're after me are you?" He dipped his fingers in the water and flicked it at Helen. "I think Miss Maggie rather enjoys getting us wet."

As if on cue, Maggie clapped both hands in the water and, with rolling laughter, doused them both.

"Look at this." Helen gestured to her soaked apron with a snort. "I do believe the wee lass wants us to join her whether 'tis proper or nay."

# Chapter Twenty-Seven

Aleck had wasted no time establishing his rule over his new lands on the Isle of Islay. Only after he'd felt confident there would be no retribution by the locals did he finally head for home to celebrate his victory at Mingary. Everything had fallen into place for him in the past month. Aleck threw his head back and laughed. He cared not what his men might think. He'd put up with Eoin MacGregor's contemptuous attitude for six months, but who had come out the champion? Eoin was a lowly chieftain who paid fealty to the Campbells of Glenorchy. The smug bastard didn't even own a castle and Aleck doubted he could afford to pay a mason to build one.

Aleck laughed again. Oh, how he'd used the MacGregors to fight off Alexander MacDonald's men. The greatest ruse? Eoin had made it all possible. He and Sir Grant had fought off the henchmen while Aleck raced ahead and challenged Alexander himself. God bless Grant, he was a good hand.

And Eoin had stood aside and allowed Aleck to claim victory. *The onion-eyed milksop. He'll never amount to anything.*

Heavy clouds rolled in and the calm seas turned into angry swells, but Aleck wouldn't allow that minor inconvenience to darken his mood. He'd move Mary to the castle on Islay where she could take charge of the servants. He'd winter with the widow in his arms, but Mingary would always be his primary estate.

He again chuckled. Now that he had won the king's favor, he needn't worry about Duncan Campbell. Many women died in childbirth. With his excuse for Helen's death, she would no longer cause Aleck consternation. Perhaps he could make an alliance with the house of Stewart with Maggie's hand. God, he hated the name Maggie. The sooner he sent Helen's bitch away from his lands, the better. At least he would profit from a formidable alliance first, and now that he'd been granted additional lands, he could use a small portion for the child's dowry to entice the right suitor.

*Mayhap the king will be so kind as to grant me an earldom?*

By the time Mingary Castle appeared as a grey speck on the horizon, Aleck had convinced himself that, for the rest of his life, Scotland would be his oyster. He would continue to impress the king and continue to gain lands owned by his now distant and disowned relations, the MacDonalds. By the time they laid him to rest, he would be the most powerful man in Scotland, second only to the king himself.

As they approached the fortress, a small birlinn bobbed in the waves, moored near the sea gate. Aleck didn't recognize the boat and wondered who on earth would pay Mingary a visit so close to St. Crispin's Day.

Something unpleasant needled at the back of his neck. He glanced at Grant. "Do you recognize that birlinn?"

"Nay." The henchman frowned and scratched his chin. "Perhaps Lady Helen's mother has come to call."

Aleck narrowed his gaze. At times he believed his henchman a bit soft-hearted, especially in matters where Helen was involved. Aleck had frequently reminded Grant that it behooved him to remember who paid his wages—and kept *his* mother fed. "Hold your tongue and your insolence. The next time you make such an untoward statement, I shall cut that useless thing out."

"Forgive me, m'lord. I couldn't help but wonder how Lady Helen has fared during the lengthy duration of our absence." Grant bowed his head and moved toward the stern.

*Blast him, and blast any man who has a soft spot for that woman.* Aleck expected to receive word of the birth of his son any day and then he would finally be free to dispose of Helen.

Aleck's heart twisted. Was that birlinn from Duntulm Castle, bringing word that Mary had delivered his son? Of course. Why shouldn't his good fortune continue?

Once the galley pulled onto the shore, Aleck hastened toward the keep.

An old guard fell in step beside him. "Welcome back m'laird. I…um…there's something I should t-tell you."

Aleck dismissed him with a flick of his wrist. "I see we have guests. I trust it is a messenger from Duntulm." He walked into the great hall with purpose.

A monk wearing a brown habit stood and bowed. "Sir Aleck MacIain, I presume?"

"Aye." That his uncle opted to send a cleric struck him as odd. "And what news have you for me?"

"I've a missive from the Pope—was told I could deliver it only to you. I've been here for a fortnight."

The grey-haired guard stood in the doorway and wrung his hands, his gaze trailing to the stairwell.

Aleck frowned at the monk. "What the devil would the Pope want with me?"

"I am merely a messenger of God—not of the Devil."

Plucking the missive from the holy man's fingers, Aleck examined the stamp. Indeed, it bore the seal of His Holiness. He slid his finger under the wax and shook open the folded velum.

His blood boiled.

He didn't care if Mary birthed a toad, he would kill Helen for her finch-brained madness. He glared at the nervous sentry. "Did you know about this?"

"T-to what are you referring, m'laird?" Samuel asked with all color draining from his face.

"Did you know Lady Helen applied to the Pope for an annulment?"

"L-lady Helen did that?"

"No, you dull-witted imbecile. She requested to be interred as a saint." Aleck marched up to the soldier and grabbed him by the scruff of the neck.

"I-I've been trying to tell you…" Samuel shot a panicked look to the monk. "Lady Helen escaped three months ago."

"Excuse me? My wife escaped three months past and this is the first I've heard of it? Why in God's name did I not receive a missive with such disturbing news?" Aleck shook the guard and pushed him away.

Samuel stumbled. "I—"

The monk hastened across the floor. "In using the term 'escaped', I can think of nothing else but you were holding your, now annulled wife, *prisoner*?" The man crossed himself as though he'd uttered blasphemy.

Aleck glared. If he weren't a holy emissary in the service of the Pope, he'd run the dull-witted swine through. "You, sir, should mind your own affairs." He pointed in the direction of the sea gate. "You've delivered your missive, now be gone with you."

"Very well, but first I require your signature and seal to recognize your marriage has been dissolved in the eyes of God, and you henceforth have no claim over the Lady Helen of Glenorchy."

With his nostrils flaring, Aleck drew his dirk from his belt. "I will acknowledge no such thing and I shall cut your tongue out for uttering such ungodly accusations. In fact, I deem your missive a forgery of the most disturbing nature."

The cleric drew back. "I assure you, I am in the services of His Holiness, Pope Alexander VI, and any actions against me will be considered an act against the Pontiff, the church, and Almighty God himself!"

Aleck raised his dirk and lunged. "Be gone with you afore I make good my threat."

The monk hastened to the door. "You will be severely punished for this come the Day of Judgment."

With a bellowing roar, Aleck started after the bumbling magpie.

Some errant cur grabbed his arm and stopped him. Blindly, MacIain reeled around with a fist.

Sir Grant blocked the blow and clamped his fingers tighter around Aleck's wrist, making the dirk drop to the floorboards. "All your good deeds will be for naught if the king hears you've attacked a Benedictine monk who delivered a document from the Pope."

Aleck jerked his arm away and rubbed it. "I'd like to wrestle that bastard to the floor and cut out his tongue."

"Aye, and I'm sure you'd do it to any other man," Grant said. The damned henchman always had a way with words.

Aleck shook his head. Though he'd never admit it aloud, he knew full well Helen's brother, John, was the Bishop of the Isles and wielded the power to secure her annulment. He should have seen this coming. Leaving her here with a handful of worthless guards would have only served to empower her to persuade them to assist her.

He pointed to Grant. "Bring the old guards to me. I will discover where she's fled, even if I have to hang every last one."

The henchman eyes flickered sidewise. “Straight away, m’laird.”

Aleck sauntered forward. “Loyalty before family, aye, Grant?”

“As you’ve taught, sir. Loyalty before family.”

“I shall have words with your mother as well.”

“Aye, m’laird.” Grant turned and nodded to the guards flanking him. “Assemble the men in the great hall. I’ll fetch my ma.”

Aleck slapped the flat side of his dirk in his palm. “If I find anyone in my service has withheld information from me, they will endure a slow and painful death.”

# Chapter Twenty-Eight

None of the Aleck's men knew a goddamn thing about Helen's whereabouts. No one saw or heard a thing. The only nugget of information that could be of any help at all was that Mr. Keith had turned backstabber. He was gone and there was little doubt he'd been the culprit who'd helped her.

Sitting with his elbow on the armrest, Aleck balanced his chin on his fist and watched Grant usher his mother forward. Aleck could bet the old crow knew something, even though she made a good show of wringing her hands and appearing distraught.

When they reached the foot of the dais, Grant stepped away and left Glenda standing alone with her hands tightly clasped before her. She didn't look up.

Aleck stared at her for a moment, well aware of the power of his steely gaze. He'd made many a man quake with a look. Such was the benefit of being an ugly cur. Sick to death with the ineptitude of his kin, he had no mind for pleasantries. "What do you know about Lady Helen's disappearance?"

"Me, m'laird?"

He spread his palms. "There's nay other soul standing before me."

"The first I heard of it was when Miss Sarah came to me and told me the bairn was missing—taken straight from her cradle, Miss Sarah said."

"And where is Sarah now? I understand she went missing shortly before I returned." At least that tidbit of information had been easy to wrest from the men.

The old woman hunched her shoulders. "I've no idea. But she…" Glenda glanced at Grant.

The guard rolled his hand forward, encouraging her to go on.

"Miss Sarah took a fancy to one of the MacGregor men."

Aleck cast his gaze to the rafters. "A MacGregor? God save the lass if she's chasing after that worthless mob of heathens."

Glenda's eyes flashed wide, then she quickly looked at the floor.

Aleck sat forward. "I take it you disagree with me."

She shook her head. "No, m'laird."

Aleck stood and glared at the cowering woman. "I think you do know to where Lady Helen absconded with *my* child."

"Honestly." She crossed herself. "I know not. They must have stolen away in the night. I heard nary a sound."

The outer door opened and a messenger walked inside. "I've a missive for Sir Aleck MacIain."

*Another bloody missive?* "From?" he demanded.

"Duntulm Castle. Mistress Mary has birthed a girl, m'lord."

Glenda snorted and clapped a hand over her mouth.

For a moment, Aleck's vision failed him. Mistress Mary was supposed to have birthed a lad. He clenched his fists. Were all his plans to be thwarted? He focused his gaze on Glenda. "Do you think this news is humorous?"

"No, m'laird."

He clomped down the steps and towered over her. "You laughed. I heard you."

"No, simply blew out my nose a bit too hard." She curtseyed. "Forgive me m'laird."

"You're a liar." Striking like a whip, Aleck backhanded the mouthy wench.

Glenda stumbled backward, snapping her hands to her face.

Grant stepped forward and pulled his mother behind him.

"Do not touch her," Aleck roared. "I've not yet completed my inquisition."

Grant faced him. "Leave her be, she confided to me she was as shocked about Lady Helen's disappearance as everyone else."

Aleck pointed to the door. "You may wait outside."

Grant took one step back, then folded his arms. "You ken I'd give you my life, but my mother is old. I'll take any punishment you choose to inflict upon her."

Glenda stepped around him. "No, son."

Aleck stepped toward the woman, ready to issue another strike.

Grant stepped in front of the woman, his jaw set. "I mean what I say. I'll not stand by whilst you raise a hand against my mother."

Narrowing his eyes, Aleck gnashed his teeth and balled his fist. With a bray, he delivered the hardest punch he'd ever thrown—right across the insolent henchman's jaw. Jesus Christ, his knuckles stung, but he wouldn't let on about it. "Leave my sight and there'll be no meals for either of you for a day."

The damned chivalrous guard grasped his mother by the elbow and helped her to the stairwell.

Across the hall the sniveling messenger cleared his throat and held up the missive. "I was told to await a reply, m'laird."

Aleck snatched it from the imbecile's hand and read. "God's teeth, Mary named the bairn Fiona. What kind of name is that?"

"Sir?"

Aleck could have smacked the messenger too. "Tell Mistress Mary there's been a delay."

The man bowed. "Thank you, m'laird."

"Haste ye to your boat, else you'll feel the cold steel of my hospitality."

Aleck stormed to the courtyard. "If there's anyone left in this godforsaken castle whom I can trust, prepare to set sail forthwith."

"Where to, m'laird?" Robert asked with a bit too much delight.

"Kilchurn Castle."

"What will you do when you find Lady Helen?" The sadist jailer rubbed his hands.

"I'll kill her."

Robert licked his lips. "At Kilchurn? In the presence of her family?"

Aleck swatted the ignoramus on the back of the head. "We sail within the hour."

He stomped back inside. *A man's supposed to celebrate when the king has just granted him lands. But no. My inept guard allowed my useless wife to escape and now I've no choice but to hunt her down.*

***

Helen took a bite of pheasant. "Mm." She closed her eyes and savored the roasted meat. "We are truly blessed this St. Crispin's Day."

"I agree." Eoin smiled from across the table holding Maggie on his lap. "Even her ladyship agrees." He placed a sliver of meat into her upstretched hands.

Helen chuckled. "I do believe she is enamored with you."

"She had better be. I just gave her the most succulent part."

The bairn seemed to approve, as she gnawed on the meat with drool wetting her apron.

Helen watched Eoin feed her and himself, playing a game of hide-and-seek, which Maggie found outrageously funny.

*If only we could hide here forever.*

Eoin caught her staring and held her gaze. "You look deep in thought."

Helen stretched her arms forward. "I suppose I am."

"And…?"

"I was just wishing we could stay here and allow the rest of the world to pass us by."

"Aye, we could try. No doubt Duncan would be the first to lead a search party." Eoin reached across the table and placed his hand atop hers. His hands were always so warm. "I need to return to my clan soon and I intend to do so with you beside me."

Helen bit her bottom lip. "Do you think Aleck knows yet?"

"John said he'd dispatch a monk to Mingary with a missive." Eoin gave Maggie another morsel of meat. "There's no reason to think Aleck has not received it."

Helen slipped her fingers out from under Eoin's palm and wrung her hands. "I hope he accepts the Pope's decree without causing a row."

"Oh, he'll act out, all right. I only pray that once he's had a chance to mull it over, he'll realize an annulment is for the best."

Helen refilled his cup with wine. "Gyllis will let us know any news."

"I'm sure she will. But we cannot tarry here much longer, else Duncan will have all of Argyllshire searching for us."

Though she knew Eoin was right, she hated to think of it. "What if we stayed another month? Surely Duncan can live without your services for that long. Besides, winter is nearly upon us."

"Exactly. We'll see our first snow soon. This wee cottage isn't equipped for us to survive the entire winter. I need to take you to Glen Strae where we've supplies built up for the season."

Helen looked away. With the hearth at her back, she suddenly grew overwarm.

"There's something else bothering you," Eoin said.

"Aye."

"We can harbor no secrets."

She crossed her arms and hugged her shoulders. "I'd like to visit Kilchurn and reconcile with my mother, if not Duncan as well. This news will be upsetting."

"I agree." But Eoin didn't want to approach the Lord of Glenorchy too soon. "We should pay a visit after His Worship has had a chance to talk to them."

Helen cringed. "I don't think Duncan will ever forgive me."

"When he learns of Aleck MacIain's treatment of you, it will be difficult to prevent him from launching an attack on the blackguard."

"But that would further ruin the alliance between our families." She tsked her tongue. "That's why Duncan contracted with him in the first place."

"If it is an alliance with MacIain he needs so badly, I suggest we let Duncan figure out how to maintain favorable relations." Eoin reached out and smoothed his hand over her hair. "His love for you will not be diminished over this. I'm sure of it."

"I hope you are right. And…"

He leaned in and arched his eyebrow. "Aaaand?"

It wasn't her place to be anxious about taking their nuptials, but she had to say something. He had, after all, asked her to become Lady MacGregor. He just hadn't mentioned *when* that might happen. She hung her head. "I am now a marked woman—a disgrace to society."

Eoin stood and placed Maggie on the sheepskin. Then he sat beside Helen on the bench and slid his arm around her shoulders. "M'lady." He kissed her cheek. "We must rectify that first and foremost. We can be wedded by the priest as soon as we leave this cottage."

Helen nodded. "I will not be allowed to be married in a church."

"A church isn't the only hallowed ground on this earth." He grasped her hand and kissed it. "We shall ask the first cleric we find to marry us."

"Thank you."

"Are you happy?"

A satiated chuckle rolled through her insides. "I am happier now than I've ever been in five and twenty years."

# Chapter Twenty-Nine

Duncan Campbell, Lord of Glenorchy, enjoyed the music and ale while celebrating St. Crispin's Day with his clan in the great hall of Kilchurn Castle. It was a pleasant respite to be home amongst his family after so many months fighting the MacDonalds. His wife, Lady Meg, sat to his right, and his mother, Lady Margaret, on his left. The high table presented an elaborately dressed array of meats, vegetables and breads to rival the king's fare.

Meg speared a tidbit of venison with her eating knife. "I do believe we shall have a festive Yule this year. I can hardly wait to green the castle."

Duncan blessed the day he'd rescued Meg from the clutches the Earl of Northumberland a hundred times over. If he hadn't been the man in charge of the mission to infiltrate Alnwick Castle, he may have never met the fiery, redheaded lass. He grinned at their progeny sitting across the table—at the age of seven, the twins Colin and Elizabeth both sported their mother's ginger hair. Archibald, seated beside his sister, was blessed with Duncan's black locks. He grinned at the likeness. Black tresses had served him well—made him look fiercer—a characteristic useful for a land baron in the Highlands.

Duncan tucked an errant curl under his wife's veil. "Mayhap in a few years' time you'll be greening our new castle on Loch Tay."

Her eyes popped wide. "Pardon me?"

Duncan had only decided it was time to build during his tour with the king. He hadn't had a chance to discuss it with his wife as of yet. "The king has seen fit to grant me lands, I'd best build suitable accommodations for our visits."

Lady Margaret sat straight, looking directly at him with alarm etched in the lines of her careworn face. "But Kilchurn is the seat of the Campbells of Glenorchy."

Duncan had expected his stepmother's initial shock. "Of course it is mother, but with more lands comes added responsibility. My cousin, the Earl of Argyll, has three castles, and my father, your husband, was responsible for building one of them."

She pursed her lips. "As long as the family seat remains in Glen Orchy, I have no qualms against your expanding the family dynasty."

He patted her hand. "I knew your enterprising spirit would see reason." He held up his tankard. "Now shall we all drink to our growing success?"

Meg smiled broadly and raised her drink. "Sláinte!"

Everyone followed suit, even Archibald at the tender age of four.

A commotion erupted at the far end of the hall and a man's voice rose above the throng. Duncan pushed back his chair and stood.

"I care not if a feast is underway, I shall gain an audience with Lord Glenorchy now!" Aleck MacIain pushed his way through the crowd.

Duncan moved to the front of the dais and met Aleck at the steps. "MacIain? What on earth are you doing away from your family on St. Crispin's? You should be home celebrating your grant of lands."

"Aye? I've no family with whom to celebrate." Aleck held up a missive. "I was met by one of your brother's monks and given this."

When MacIain shoved the parchment into his chest, Duncan had no recourse but to grasp it. He glanced back at his family. "I shall be but a moment, please excuse me."

He ushered the uncouth chieftain to the small antechamber at the back of the hall. Once inside, he examined the broken seal. "This is from His Holiness, the Pope."

"Bloody oath it is, and your sister conspired with your brother—*His Worship*, the venerated Bishop of the Isles, no less—to destroy my marriage."

Duncan opened the letter and read. A tight ball formed in his chest. "This accuses you of beating your wife, as reported witnessed by bruising noted on her person on more than one occasion."

The chieftain's face flushed red. "I assure you, any disciplinary action taken by me was necessary to maintain order in my household."

"Helen?" Duncan stared at the cad, completely dumbfounded. "You mean to tell me you had to resort to force to control my most good-natured sister?"

"She turned bad, m'lord." MacIain shot a quick glance to the closed door. "Is she not here? I should like to take her home forthwith."

"Lady Helen is not at Kilchurn, nor has she been." Duncan folded the missive and faced the hearth. *Did she and John truly contrive this scheme together? It isn't like my brother to do anything untoward—or Helen for that matter. Does her claim have merits? If so, why did she not approach me? I am the Lord of Glenorchy, surely she would know I would protect her if she had a founded claim.* A piece of lead sank to the pit of Duncan's stomach. *Her fears must be grave if they took this matter all the way to Rome.*

Duncan glanced over his shoulder and regarded MacIain. *The man has a mean streak, no doubt. But abuse his wife? Surely he would know raising a hand against Helen would put a grave strain on our alliance. An annulment granted by the Pope? Why in God's name was I not consulted?*

Duncan needed to dig to the bottom of this quandary. He faced the Ardnamurchan chieftain. "Your news is disturbing indeed. I shall take immediate steps to seek a resolution and inform you of my findings. Please, 'tis St. Crispin's Day. Sit at the high table and enjoy the feast. On the morrow, you can return to Ardnamurchan."

The man's face grew even redder. "Do you think I'm planning to tuck my tail and head back to Mingary on the morrow?"

After folding the velum, Duncan slipped it inside his doublet. "I suggest that's exactly what you should do. Dealings with *my* family are best left in my hands."

The bald-headed chieftain moved his fists to his hips, forgetting who was lord of this castle. "Are you planning to pay a visit to the Bishop of the Isles? Because he's next on my list, and I'll not be as pleasant with him."

Every bit as tall as the over-stuffed codfish, Duncan stared him in the eye, nose to nose. "Are you threatening to raise a hand against my brother, *His Worship*, the most revered holy man in the Highlands?"

Aleck's tongue shot across his bottom lip. "He secretly obtained an annulment for your sister under false pretenses."

*The more I think on it, the more I doubt Helen's claims are unfounded.*

"I will uncover the truth." Duncan pointed to the door. "I suggest you do as I say and find a place in the hall. Your accusations against my family are not taken lightly and will not be treated as such if I discover the assertions in that missive are true."

Aleck narrowed his steely eyes for a moment, and then held his palms up. That he'd just exercised restraint was obvious. Had he lashed out, it would have been the action Duncan needed to take the man to his knees. But five years ago, he'd made an alliance with MacIain, and that pact had proved fruitful in bringing the MacDonald uprising to an end. This situation with Helen needed to be investigated before relations grew worse.

Duncan bowed and gestured to the door. "If you please."

He waited until MacIain had made his way to the dais. God bless Meg, she welcomed the bastard with outstretched arms and summoned the servants to tend him at once. Duncan gestured to Mevan, the old man-at-arms who had been loyal to the Campbells since the early days. "Ride to Glen Strae and fetch Eoin MacGregor at once. Tell him his presence is needed urgently."

"Straight away, m'lord."

"We'll leave for Dunollie at dawn. I shall have a word with Lady Gyllis before proceeding on to Iona. Perhaps she's seen Lady Helen"

***

Duncan rose early and gathered his retinue by the stables. God's teeth, there wasn't a bloody MacGregor man in sight, yet the Kilchurn man-at-arms sat on a barrel and watched the men ready their horses. "Mevan, where the blazes is Eoin?"

"He's not in Glen Strae, m'lord."

What more would go wrong with this unsettling news? "Are you sure? He left Oronsay before any of us."

"Aye, but he moored his galley at Taynult and sent his men home—they said he took a horse and headed south."

"God on the cross, what business did he have south?"

Mevan looked like he'd swallowed a bitter tonic. "I-I didn't ask."

"Never mind. When he returns, tell him I've gone to Dunollie and then to Iona. I need his help in locating Lady Helen. MacGregor has the sharpest nose for tracking in all of Scotland."

The old man-at-arms always remained behind to take charge of the castle guard in Duncan's absence. "I will, m'lord."

Duncan grabbed his horse's reins and mounted. "Come lads, we've no time to waste."

He led them through the yard to the main trail that would take them twenty miles to the west coast.

They'd been moving a steady trot for a good while when Aleck MacIain and his men galloped up behind them. "I had a change of mind this morn."

Duncan urged his horse a bit faster. "I thought I told you to return to Mingary."

The bastard kept pace like a pesky fly. "You did, but my galley is moored at Dunstaffnage."

"Very well, we'll part ways at the V in the road."

"Why are you so anxious to be rid of me?" Aleck growled, far too disrespectful for a chieftain who was not a peer.

"Must I remind you of your station? I will take pause with your tone, make no bones about it." He glanced at MacIain out of the corner of his eye. "I *will* speak to my siblings alone. If you are present with that beef-headed demeanor, they may not be inclined to speak frankly."

The man blubbered a guffaw. "You don't even trust your own kin?"

"'Tis not my kin that concerns me."

Aleck thumped his chest. "So it's me you do not trust?"

"Bloody hell, MacIain. Must everything be a battle with you? You came to me and requested my help." Duncan pointed his gloved finger to the trail ahead. "At your request, I've spurred into action without hesitation. All I ask is that you allow me to discuss Lady Helen's disappearance with Lady Gyllis and the Bishop of the Isles *my* way."

The chieftain jumped his horse over a fallen log. "If you wish me to stay away whilst you speak to your kin, I'll grant you that. But I will not tuck tail and head for home. Helen took my daughter as well."

Duncan growled under his breath. The missive from the Pope indicated one of the criteria for granting the annulment was that Aleck refused to acknowledge the child, Margaret Alice MacIain as his only heir. But thinking of the bairn gave him an idea. He shot a sideways glance at MacIain. "What's her second name?"

"Helen Flora," Aleck said with overzealous annoyance in his tone.

"No, I was referring to your bairn, Margaret. What's her second name?" Duncan asked again.

"Helen calls her Maggie."

*Wrong.* Duncan tightened his fist around the reins. He would dig to the bottom of this.

***

About two miles out from Dunollie, Duncan and his men, including the uninvited band of MacIain upstarts, came across the MacDougall patrol. Duncan reined his horse to a stop and addressed Sir Sean's man, Angus. "Good morrow. I hope all is quiet on Dunollie lands this day."

"Good morrow, m'lord." Sitting his horse, Angus dipped his helmed head. "Things are quiet, indeed. In fact, we've had almost no problem with outlaws since Sir Sean stopped Alan MacCoul near five year' ago."

"'Tis good to hear. I need a word with my sister. Is she at home?"

Angus threw his thumb over his shoulder in the direction of the castle. "Aye, about to bid good day to the bishop—your brother."

Duncan shot a startled glance at MacIain.

The man certainly wasn't deaf. Aleck gathered up his reins. "We'd best make haste." He dug in his heels, but then pulled the horse to a stop. He leaned over the gelding's neck and eyed the soldier at the rear of the retinue.

Duncan followed Aleck's line of sight. The man kept his face averted.

Aleck grabbed a poleax from one of the guards and rode straight toward the man. "Well, well. Hello, Mr. Keith. I thought I might find you here."

Before Duncan had time to react, Aleck slammed the guard in the chest with the shaft of the poleax. The force lifted the guard from his saddle and sent him crashing to the ground flat on his back.

Drawing his sword, Duncan dismounted. Horses skittered aside as he dashed to the fallen guard.

Moving fast for a large man, Aleck hopped from his mount. Baring his teeth, he crouched over the guard, levering a dirk against his neck. "Where is my wife, you mule-brained backstabber?"

The guard clutched at his chest, gasping for air.

The back of Duncan's neck burned. "How do you know this man?"

"He's the very guard who helped Helen escape." Aleck sneered. "Keith's his name."

The chieftain used that *escape* word again. Duncan bristled.

Aleck fisted the hilt of his dirk and struck the guard across the mouth. "I can see it in your eyes. You know where she is."

Mr. Keith continued to gasp. Aleck hit him again. When he drew his fist back for another blow, Duncan caught MacIain's elbow. "Can you not see he's lost his air from the fall?"

"He's a traitor and a backstabber."

"Yet you said yourself he knows where Lady Helen is." Duncan shoved Aleck aside and kneeled beside the guard. "Are you in my sister's confidence?"

His gasps becoming slower, the man held Duncan's gaze and gave a single nod.

Shoving Duncan aside, Aleck jumped atop the guard. With a snarl, he again held his blade to Keith's neck. "I'll not ask you again. Where is Lady Helen?"

The guard's eyes shifted east to the forest.

Aleck looked toward the trees, then smirked. "MacDougall's hunting cottage? I should have known." Growling, the chieftain took one last swing at Mr. Keith's head, leaving a welt spreading under his eyes.

Duncan knew the cottage well. Worse, last summer a hunting party camped there with MacIain. *Ballocks.*

Aleck hastened to his horse and mounted. "This way, men."

Duncan had no recourse but to follow. He pointed at Angus. "Ride to Dunollie and tell Sir Sean to meet us at the cottage straight away."

Duncan spurred his mount ahead. If MacIain unleashed his violent temper on his sister, she'd not survive to reveal the truth.

# Chapter Thirty

Gyllis was ever so happy to have her husband at home. Yesterday, her brother, John, had come to celebrate the holiday feast with them, and now the family sat upon the dais for their nooning before John returned to Iona.

Sean MacDougall and John had been boyhood friends and they had served together with the Highland Enforcers. The retinue had originally been established by Gyllis's father, Colin Campbell by order of King James III to maintain order in the Scottish Highlands. Now the enforcers had a new leader and Scotland had a new king. Such was the succession. As far as Gyllis knew, bringing peace to the Highlands was still their primary responsibility, though the king used them when necessary to help maintain order along the borders as well.

Half the time, Gyllis had no idea where her husband was, but today she didn't want to think about that. Two of her favorite men were seated at the high table in Dunollie's great hall. Sean, dressed in plaid with a black leather doublet, looked like a powerful land-owning chieftain and John appeared so incredibly official in his purple damask chasuble. Gyllis was proud of her brother's achievements after he'd left the enforcers to join the priesthood. A second son, he had become a powerful man in his own right—*The Bishop of the Isles.*

"How was your visit to Rome?" Sean asked.

John dabbed the corners of his lips with his fingers—ever so proper of him. "The channel crossing was smooth, thank the good Lord. As usual, however, there was no time to venture outside the Vatican."

"And what news have you from His Holiness?" Gyllis asked.

"A great concern consumed most of our time." John glanced between them. "Ferdinand and Isabella of Spain commissioned a rather mysterious character, Christopher Columbus, to undertake a seafaring venture to discover worlds not following our Lord, Jesus Christ."

"New worlds?" Sean's eyes lit up. "I thought we'd discovered all the land our world has to offer."

"As did all of Christendom, but the captain returned with the most disturbing information."

"Truly?" Sean broke his bread and spread cream over one half. "Tell us."

"The peoples he discovered were reported as going unclothed and the Christian religion is completely unknown to them."

Gyllis reached for the remaining half of bread. "But is it not our duty to deliver the word of God to those who have not yet been saved?"

"Yes, and that is exactly what the Pope Alexander communicated to Spain in a rather pointed letter."

Both Gyllis and Sean looked at the bishop expectantly.

Pursing his lips, John assumed the stern countenance one would associate with his position. "Under penalty of excommunication, all persons in Christendom are forbidden to trade with these uncharted worlds, lest they be struck down by the wrath of God. Only missionaries of the faith will be allowed entry with the sole purpose of bringing the Catholic religion to their inhabitants."

Gyllis studied her brother and covered her smile with the tips of her fingers. "And clothing, I'd surmise."

John gave her a sober nod. "Most definitely."

*Goodness, when did my brother become so inordinately serious?*

Sean reached for the pitcher of ale. "What else can you tell us about these new lands? Run by naked savages? How will they know how to use their God-given resources?"

John held up a finger. "Let there be no question. His Holiness has decreed that any trade—including resource exploitation with heathen nations will be dealt with severely."

"But why?" Sean asked. "Wouldn't it be a way for good men, perhaps second sons like yourself, to gain lands and riches?"

"I'll pretend I didn't hear you utter such blasphemy. The souls of the savages you referred to are of paramount importance." John turned to Gyllis and cleared his throat. "Now, we've more important things to discuss. You haven't said a word about Helen. How is our sister faring?"

Gyllis placed her hand atop her husband's and gave him a clench-toothed grin. "Sean hasn't been home long enough for me to tell him. Lady Helen has obtained an annulment from His Holiness."

Sean looked surprised, though not cross. "Interesting. And Aleck MacIain went along with this news? He doesn't seem like the type…"

John brushed his hands over the front of his chasuble. "*He* didn't have a choice in the matter, once I discovered dear Helen had been battered, I agreed to represent her plea to the Pope."

Sean clenched his fist around the handle of his tankard. "That bastard raised a hand against my sister-in-law? My God, the very thing knights fight against was happening in our own family?"

"Mind your vulgar tongue, my dear." Gyllis rested a reassuring palm atop her husband's arm. "Besides, we've spirited her away for now, until we're certain 'tis safe."

Sean pulled his arm away. "You've done all this without me?"

Gyllis planted her fists on her hips. "Forgive me if the world doesn't come to a halt whilst you're away enforcing the king's orders."

"I—"

"M'laird." Angus hastened into the great hall. "Lord Duncan and the Chieftain of Ardnamurchan intercepted us on the trail from Glen Orchy. His lordship asked me to have you meet him at the hunting cottage at once."

Behind Angus, two guards helped a battered Mr. Keith to a bench.

"Goodness gracious." Gyllis gasped. "What did my brother do to Lady Helen's guard?"

"It wasn't Lord Duncan. His lordship tried to step in, but Sir Aleck grew enraged."

Rising to his feet, Sean snatched his sword belt from the back of the chair. "Angus, summon the guard. We ride at once."

The henchman pointed. "They're already mounted and waiting, m'laird."

Sean bounded toward the door with long strides. "Then we must make haste."

Gyllis dashed to Mr. Keith. His face was bloodied with one eye swollen shut. "What on earth happened?"

"Sir Aleck saw me riding patrol with the men." The elderly man coughed. "He knocked me off my horse, then pummeled my face. I swear I didn't tell him where Lady Helen is—but he figured it out all the same."

"My word." Gyllis wrung her hands. "I fear that man is evil beyond saving."

Mr. Keith grasped Gyllis's wrist. "He's the worst sort."

"I must go to her."

He struggled to stand. "Not without a guard, m'lady."

***

Helen and Eoin sat on the rug before the hearth with Maggie. Eoin had made a ball out of a piece of leather and swung it from a thong while the wee one tried to catch it. Every time she stopped the ball between her palms, she let out a squeal.

Helen threw her head back and laughed. The bairn seemed much happier in the cabin with Eoin there as well. It was so incredibly warm and homey—even happier than her childhood had been. Though she knew he would have to return to Glen Strae on the morrow, Eoin would be back as soon as his spies reported Aleck's whereabouts—and if the man had made threats against her life. She closed her eyes and shook her head. Now away from that horrid situation, her time at Mingary seemed like a passing nightmare.

All of a sudden, Eoin stopped laughing and froze. His eyes darted to the door.

"What—?"

He sliced his hand through the air and listened. Springing to his feet, he pointed to the door. "Take Maggie to the bedchamber."

Helen gasped.

Eoin reached for his sword belt and swung it around his hips. "Now."

Helen pulled the bairn into her arms. Before she reached the chamber, she heard the horse hooves thumping the ground outside the cottage. *How on earth did Eoin hear them so much sooner than I?*

Trembling from her head to her toes, she dashed inside, wrapped Maggie in a blanket and hid her under the bed. But the babe launched into an earsplitting wail. Helen knelt down and smoothed a hand over Maggie's crown. "Wheesht, darling."

The door burst open and with it blew a gale that sapped the heat straight out of the bedchamber.

"MacGregor," Aleck's gravelly voice rumbled. "I should have known you'd be here, living in sin with my wife."

"Lady Helen is no longer your concern or your wife," Eoin growled.

"MacGregor?" Duncan's voice rose in astonishment. "What in God's name are you doing here?"

*Duncan? Have mercy.*

Helen moved so she could peer around the door. Behind her, Maggie started to wail.

Red in the face, Aleck looked as if he were about to kill Eoin. "He's debauched Helen. Turned her against me."

"I have done nothing of the sort." Eoin lowered his sword and looked to Duncan. "Lady Helen was abused by—"

Aleck drew his dirk. With a deep bellow, he launched himself at Eoin.

Taking in a sharp gasp, Helen's heartbeat raced.

With a flick of his wrist, Eoin deflected the attack and sent the blackguard stumbling toward the hearth. Then Eoin faced him and raised his weapon. Aleck reached for his sword. It hissed from its scabbard as the two men circled.

Helen rushed forward and grabbed Duncan's arm. "Stop them!"

"How could you degrade yourself, keeping company alone in the forest with a *man*?" He drew his arm away. "You are ruined. Your daughter is ruined. I cannot believe your behavior—something I would never expect from *you*, above all."

Helen backed away in horror whilst Maggie's cries grew louder. Duncan's bitter words were far more painful than any blow delivered by Aleck's slap.

Clutching her fists beneath her chin, she watched in horror as Eoin and Aleck crashed into the table as it screeched across the floorboards. Each man's eyes filled with hate, they brandished their swords like wild men. Behind her, Maggie's wails pierced through the mayhem.

Duncan stood with his fists on his hips and watched with a scowl, doing nothing to stop the fight.

Eoin moved like lightning—so fast, Helen didn't see exactly how it happened, but Aleck was disarmed of his sword, and Eoin had her estranged husband flat on his back in a stranglehold.

Duncan stepped forward. "I'll have words—"

Helen dashed in front of her brother and cut him off. "With me!" She jabbed her finger into his sternum. "How could you marry me off to a tyrant—a man who thinks nothing of beating me—a man who refuses to see his own daughter because he wanted a lad—a vile braggart who locks his wife in the dungeon for sennights because I asked his leman to tend the pigs and chickens when the villagers sought refuge in Mingary Castle?" She stamped her foot. "Whilst said tyrant rode off to secure his lands in Sunart, leaving me *alone* to defend to the keep against a MacDonald sea attack." She took in a deep breath, hardly able to believe she'd uttered the entire repugnant affair in one outpouring.

Duncan's mouth dropped open.

But Helen was only starting. She threw a finger Aleck's direction. "If I am ruined because I allowed Sir Eoin to assist me and carry my missive to Iona so that I could seek safety, not only for me, but for my daughter, then I choose complete and utter ruination."

Duncan threw a heated glare toward Aleck. "Are these accusations true?"

The scoundrel's feet squirmed while Eoin maintained his grip. "Get this mule-brained boar off me," Aleck garbled.

Eoin's knuckles grew white and he flashed Duncan a quick look. "I saw the bruises on Lady Helen's face, and witnessed MacIain's untoward hostility toward his wife—when she *was* married to the slobbering weasel."

Sir Sean pushed through the door. Behind him Gyllis marched inside, dragging a battered looking Mr. Keith in her wake. "This man can testify on Helen's behalf."

The old guard cringed, giving Helen a hesitant grimace.

"Go on," Gyllis urged.

"M'lord." Mr. Keith bowed to Duncan. "I released Lady Helen from the dungeon at Mingary where she'd been incarcerated for two sennights with orders that no one see her. At her request, I rowed a skiff all the way to Dunollie where Lady Gyllis graciously gave her refuge."

"You *rowed* from Mingary?" Duncan asked.

"Someone had to do something. Sooner or later she would have succumbed to the violent hand of the chieftain."

"You lie!" Aleck garbled from the floor, kicking his feet while Maggie continued to howl in the back room.

Gyllis disappeared into the bedchamber.

"Silence, you whoreson." Eoin's grip strengthened. "I witnessed your tyranny myself."

"But you have been caught, MacGregor. Your word bears no witness here. Regardless, I intend to uncover the truth." Duncan turned to Mr. Keith. "Were you aware of any scandalous action by Eoin MacGregor before the annulment was granted?"

Mr. Keith scratched his beard and looked to Helen.

*Please say no.* She slowly shook her head as Gyllis stepped beside her, cradling the bairn. Goodness, Helen hadn't even realized the crying had stopped.

"I can testify to your question." Thank the heavens, His Worship stepped into the cottage. John marched straight to Duncan. "I asked Sir Eoin the very same when he came to me with Helen's missive requesting help."

Helen shot a panicked look to Eoin. He gave her a reassuring wink.

"We talked about his fondness for our sister, but he swore to *me*, the Bishop of the Isles, that he had not compromised the sanctity of marriage."

"Mr. Keith," Duncan squared his shoulders. "When did you become aware of Sir Eoin's affection for her ladyship?"

Helen's knees wobbled.

"Not until a month past. I kent he helped her ladyship, but I swear on my mother's grave there was no impropriety between them. Honestly, it surprised me when he came to visit with the missive from the Pope. He'd always been a bit stand-offish, good at training the guard, mind you, but he never sat with the men at Mingary and drank ale—you ken, he kept to himself." Mr. Keith looked to Aleck, still gasping in Eoin's stranglehold. "Ah, if the lordship will also allow me, I must bear witness to the fact that Sir Aleck was openly affectionate with the widow, Mary."

"Openly?" Duncan asked.

"Aye, there was no question what went on above stairs, if you know what I mean." Mr. Keith pointed to the door. "In fact, before we came in, one of the MacIain lads told me news had arrived that Mary birthed a lass—Sir Aleck's illegitimate daughter."

Duncan crossed the floor. "Is this true?"

MacIain spat. "Call off your dog."

It took but a flash for Duncan to pull dirk and place the point a hair's breadth from Aleck's eye. "I'll ask one more time. Is it true?"

"Aye," Aleck growled. "A man needs to take a leman when he has a fickle wife."

"That's a lie." Helen stamped her foot. "I pleaded with you to come to my bed after Maggie's birth so that I could give you a son, but since the day she was born, you have shunned us both."

Gyllis stepped forward. "And Helen told me in confidence that Sir Aleck had been unfaithful throughout the duration of their marriage."

John steepled his fingers in front of the cross on his chasuble. "I'm afraid, brother, a higher order has made a decision on this matter. His Holiness the Pope has annulled this marriage and Aleck MacIain is no longer our brother-in-law."

Duncan drew his dirk away from Aleck's eye and sheathed it. "You heard the words straight from His Worship, MacIain. Take your men back to Mingary now and leave my sister in peace. If I hear you have ever again acted against a decree from His Holiness the Pope, I will personally preside over your hanging."

"Not if I get there first." Eoin released his grip and stood back.

Aleck sat up, coughing and rubbing his throat. "You're taking her word?"

"Aye." Gathering the bairn from Gyllis, Helen hugged Maggie to her breast. "I'll not be seeing my daughter traded for lands when she's still but a babe. She will mature into a fully grown woman before she weds." Helen glared directly at Duncan. "And when she does marry, it will be to someone of her choosing."

***

After Aleck and his retinue rode away, Duncan rapped Eoin on the shoulder. "Come, take a walk with me."

Eoin knew what was coming. He looked like a goddamned fool hiding out in the cottage with Helen. If Mr. Keith and John had not arrived, who knew what the outcome of that altercation would have been. Most likely, Duncan would have killed Eoin and discovered the truth later.

Stepping outside, the autumn air was cold and a thick mist hung above the clearing, but Eoin's blood was still running too hot to feel it.

Duncan wasn't smiling. In fact he was red in the face and looked like he wanted to hit something. *Perhaps my nose*. Every muscle in Eoin's body tensed. He followed as the Lord of Glenorchy marched along the path like an ogre. They'd gone about a quarter mile when Duncan stopped and grasped Eoin by the shoulders. "I thought better of you, MacGregor."

Eoin clenched his fists and shrugged away. Must Duncan always jump to conclusions? "I—"

"You ken you have ruined my sister *and* her daughter."

Bowing obsequiously, Eoin spread his arms. "Only if you declare it to be so."

"Have you gone completely mad? How many people know your whereabouts? I'd wager half of Argyllshire is aware of your indiscretion by now."

"Perhaps, but *you* can make it right." Eoin licked his lips. "I offer for Lady Helen's hand. I love her. Always have."

"Love?" Duncan threw up his hands. "How that notion has a way of putting men in a world of strife."

"I seem to recall you had a similar situation with Lady Meg's brother when he marched his army to Kilchurn and nearly blasted her walls down with his shiny new cannons."

Duncan raked his fingers through his black hair. "Christ, don't remind me how foolish I was."

Had Eoin found a slight fissure in Glenorchy's anger? Regardless, he wasn't about to let it pass. "I remember that day well—I even cautioned you, *m'lord.* But off you went, the courageous knight stepping out alone to meet the Earl of Angus and his troops. What did you say to him after you convinced him to follow you into the antechamber? Did you declare your love for Lady Meg as I have for Lady Helen?"

Duncan crossed his arms—a clear sign Eoin was wearing him down. "My situation was entirely different." Oh yes, the Lord of Glenorchy could be smug.

"Was it now? Exactly how did you arrive at such a remarkable conclusion?" Eoin stepped in, gaining confidence. "I watched Lady Helen grow from a lass into a woman. Out of respect for you and your family, I kept my feelings in check all these years. Why should we not be married as you and Lady Meg were?"

"First of all, Lady Meg wasn't married prior to my meeting with Lord Arthur. Secondly, Helen's dowry has already been lost…"" Duncan resumed his wary scowl. "What were you doing staying with *my sister* in a cabin in the woods?"

"I—she—" Eoin expected to be hammered with this argument first. *Damn him for attacking with a devious blow.*

"Do you have any idea how disgraceful your actions appear?"

Eoin kicked the dirt. "I was planning to approach you this day, as a matter of fact."

"But we beat you to it. That doesn't bode well for you, MacGregor."

"I didn't think anyone knew where we were, aside from Lady Gyllis."

"And Mr. Keith."

Eoin had to agree there. "The guard pledged fealty to Lady Helen."

"You should know he didn't turn backstabber. He gave you away with a mere shift of his eyes."

"I could never blame him—only myself for this bungle." Eoin stepped in and placed his hand on Duncan's shoulder. "Please, you are my closest friend and ally. I'll take good care of Lady Helen. She'll never want for anything, and I swear on my father's grave, she will never fear being struck by a man again."

Duncan winced, then he stepped away and turned his back, as if finding something he needed to study in the trees. "In light of your indiscretion before speaking to me, I will not be able to offer you a farthing for her maintenance."

Eoin's stomach performed a backflip. "Do you think I want your coin? After all these years of riding in your shadow, supporting you and your father, how can you not know that your respect is what I covet most?"

Duncan swiveled around and one corner of his mouth turned up. "So nothing's changed, then?"

"Of course nothing has changed…except now you know I've been in love with your sister since I was four and ten."

Duncan gestured toward the path leading back to the cottage. "Four and ten? Honestly?"

"Aye."

"Bloody hell, why did you not say something when I was arranging her marriage to that monster?"

Eoin had a plethora of responses to that question, including his own ill-founded feelings of inadequacy for such a gem as Lady Helen. Instead, he shrugged. "You seemed so intent on making the alliance. I didn't want to stand in your way." That was true as well and it didn't make him out to be less of a man. He may not be lord of a castle, but Eoin was chieftain of a powerful and feared clan. He would always be proud of his parentage.

Duncan slapped him on the back. "And the bairn. You will raise Maggie as your own?"

"Who wouldn't adore a lass as bonny as she? Of course, I will see to her care in every way."

His lordship pulled away and narrowed his eyes. "What is Maggie's middle name?"

Eoin remembered the first time Helen had said the name. She'd been so proud. "Alice. Helen named her Alice after her younger sister."

A big grin parted Duncan's lips. "I kent you wouldn't cross me."

"Never."

# Chapter Thirty-One

When the door opened, Helen handed Maggie to Gyllis and faced Duncan and Eoin, hands clasped, ready to wage war with her brother. She would do and say whatever was necessary not to lose Eoin again. They had pledged their love, and though Duncan was their lord and master, he would not deny her happiness for the rest of her life.

Duncan eyed Helen with a stern countenance. Eoin, however, grinned like he'd just won the grand prize at the Highland games. Gyllis, Mr. Keith, Sean and John stood behind her, not only their presence, but their support bolstered Helen's nerves. She would not fail.

Duncan tipped his chin up.

Helen decided to allow him to speak first. After all, her brother *was* the Lord of Glenorchy, even if she would defy him this day.

But he did something Helen did not expect. He gestured to Eoin. "The Chieftain of Clan Gregor has something he'd like to say."

Eoin stepped forward. "Forgive me for conducting this proposal in public, but in light of all that has transpired, I want everyone present to hear." He took Helen's hands in his ever-warm palms and kneeled. "Lady Helen, I ask your forgiveness. I should not have behaved so rashly when I discovered you had been spirited to this cottage. I should have insisted on a chaperone at all times to ensure your virtue was never brought into question." He bowed his head. "Will you please find it in your heart to forgive me?"

Helen glanced to Duncan who was looking on with his usual dour frown. Generally a man on bended knee meant only one thing, but Sir Eoin was begging an apology. And he had nothing to apologize for. She knew better than to say so, especially not when they had an audience.

"Sir Eoin, you acted gallantly on my behalf, delivering my missive to my brother, John, Bishop of the Isles, and pleading my case, given the precarious circumstances. On threat of death by my annulled husband, I was unable to personally seek John's assistance. Afterward, the security you provided whilst I hid in this domicile was greatly appreciated by my person and cannot go without expressing my sincere gratitude." Praise God her tongue had not failed as she delivered her oration. She even managed to maintain the serene expression she'd mastered after so many years of hiding her emotions.

Eoin raised his head and grinned at her. His blue eyes crinkled at the corners, telling her she chose exactly the right words. And then the look in his eyes took on a deeper meaning, one that she'd seen in the bedchamber, one that made her insides swarm with a maelstrom of desire. Helen took in a deep breath and held that gaze. Though she loved him to his toes, she would not permit Eoin MacGregor to disarm her resolve in this hour.

He squeezed his fingers tighter. "With your acceptance of my apology, I would ask you something else."

Helen's insides became weightless, like she'd just leapt from a cliff. "Aye?" she whispered, almost afraid to speak.

Eoin cleared his throat, but his eyes never wavered from her face. "Lady Helen, I haven't a keep encircled with bailey and curtain to offer you, but I can say this: You will have the protection of Clan Gregor, the fiercest force in all the Highlands. You will preside as lady over the clan, and have servants to attend your every need. But moreover, I pledge to you my unfaltering love, my life, my sword, my honor and my heart, if you will agree to be my wife."

By the time he'd finished, tears streamed down Helen's face. A smile stretched her lips and, at first, all she managed was a nod. When finally she found her voice, she said, "Aye. I will marry you, Sir Eoin MacGregor."

He stood and wrapped her in his arms. Oh how wonderful his body felt pressed against her bosom, knowing that he would be hers for all eternity.

Duncan grasped Eoin's shoulder and pulled them apart. "You'll not be touching my sister again until you are properly wed." He reached for Helen's left arm. "And you will go home with me."

Eoin grasped his lady's right hand. "Oh no, I'm finished with waiting."

Duncan scowled. "Pardon me, but—"

"If you would allow me to explain." Eoin tugged Helen behind him to shield her from Glenorchy. "We have The Most Illustrious and Most Reverend Lord, His Worship the Bishop of the Isles, in our midst. Who better to marry us than your brother?"

Duncan blinked rapidly. "But Mother will have one of her spells and tie me up by my thumbs." Such an admonition sounded trite coming from the most powerful man east of Inveraray.

Gyllis cleared her throat from beside the hearth where she cradled Maggie. "Please, Duncan, the spoiled laddie pout no longer suits you."

"Then Mother will have to live with our decision." Moving from behind Eoin, Helen took up his hand. "I will marry the Chieftain of Clan Gregor this day if John will be so kind as to do us the honor."

John thoughtfully stepped forward with praying fingertips touched to his lips. "Though this situation is rather untoward, it is my opinion than an expeditious marriage would be the best for both Lady Helen and Sir Eoin." He eyed Duncan. "And the least damaging to our sister's reputation. Mother will have to understand."

"She will," Gyllis said.

"'Tis settled then." John stepped into the center of the room.

Duncan moved beside him. "I do believe I have been usurped by my siblings." He cleared his throat with a sheepish dip to his chin. "And presently I'm feeling a bit the heel. Helen, I wanted to wait until we returned to Kilchurn to say this, but I believe now is more appropriate. Please forgive my harsh words. I spoke before I had uncovered all the facts."

Yet another weight lifted from her shoulders. "Thank you. You've no idea how much it means to have your blessing."

"Aaaand, though I said differently, I do believe a wee dowry is appropriate." He looked to Eoin. "I grant you three hundred acres north of the River Orchy."

Eoin bowed. "Your generosity is very much appreciated, m'lord."

Duncan nodded and gestured to John. "Well then, shall we move on with this marriage?"

Beckoning both Helen and Eoin to step forward, he grasped each by the wrist. "Come forward and allow me to join your hands by binding them together with the holy stole of Christ Jesus our Lord."

Helen's skin tingled with gooseflesh as she faced her dearest friend and lover. At long last the dreams of marrying her hero had arrived. She had eyes for no one else but Eoin as John wrapped his stole around their wrists while chanting the Latin mass for Holy Matrimony.

Behind them, Maggie cooed as if she approved of this union.

While she gazed into Eoin's loving eyes, Helen had found happiness at last. She would live out her days with the only man she had ever loved. Finally, her heart's desire would be fulfilled.

# *Epilogue*

*Two years later*

Before the altar in Kilchurn Chapel, Helen cradled her son, Alasdair. Eoin stood beside her, holding Maggie's hand. The wee lass wore a blue damask gown with a square neckline and a matching coif atop her head. The darling grinned up at her wee brother. Och aye, Alasdair's elder sister looked incredibly grown up for a child of two-and-a-half.

Wearing an ivory mitre atop his head, the Bishop of the Isles posed an impressive sight as he consecrated the holy water in the baptismal font. The Latin recitations rolled off John's tongue as if it were his native language.

Helen glanced over her shoulder and regarded her family standing in the front row. How Duncan and Gyllis's grins reminded her of the day she and Eoin had wed. Shortly after the ceremony in the cottage, the retinue had ridden to Kilchurn Castle to announce the news of their marriage. Helen's mother, Lady Margaret, had been elated to hear that Helen and Maggie had not been ruined—aye, the news of Duncan discovering Eoin and Helen in the cottage indeed had reached Kilchurn before Helen's arrival on that day. It may have been a good thing, however, because Mother's look of horror changed to rapture when Duncan delivered the news that Helen had wed Eoin, one of Lady Margaret's favorite knights in the Highland Enforcers. Without a moment's hesitation, the Dowager Lady of Glenorchy had welcomed their marriage with open arms.

While John continued with his prayers, Helen smiled at Duncan and Lady Meg. They stood with their three children. And beside them, Mother held young Colin's hand. In the second pew were Gyllis and Sean with their two youngsters.

Across the aisle, Alice and Marion, Helen's twin sisters were joined by their spouses. Even Iain, the First Lord of Lawers and Helen's youngest brother, had come for the baptism. Throughout the chapel, the pews were filled with the proud people of Clan Gregor. In the past two years, she had grown to love each and every soul. The clan had accepted her with open arms. After all, the Campbells of Glenorchy and the MacGregors were the closest allies in the Highlands. Why should they not be united by marriage?

Though Helen had not given her former husband a lad, in her heart she'd always known she was capable of producing an heir. And by the grace of God, Eoin had given her that opportunity.

He grinned at her, his blue eyes reflecting the brilliant hues from the stained glass above the altar. Oh, how she loved him. Alasdair squeaked out a wee cry. Eoin pressed his lips to the bairn's crown of chestnut locks and settled the lad directly. Such a potent man, Eoin was surprisingly gentle with children, and they loved him in return.

After John asked for the bairn, Helen removed his coif and, supporting Alasdair's neck, the bishop ladled water over the babe's head to baptize him into the Catholic faith.

Eoin placed his arm around Helen's shoulders and whispered in her ear. "Let us pray for his long life."

Helen inclined her head toward Eoin's shoulder. "Long life and good health for all."

"Agreed. I'll need considerable more time on this earth because I haven't had anywhere near my fill of you, bonny Helen."

"Nor I of you. I will love you and our children for the rest of my days."

*The End.*

# Author's Note

Thank you for joining me for Lady Helen and Sir Eoin's adventure. Eoin is also listed in some genealogy records as Iain MacEwin McAlaster MacGregor, of Glen Strae, $7^{th}$ Chief of Clan Gregor. I even found a record that interchangeably used Iain and Eoin and, as an author, I found it too confusing to have a hero named Iain put up against an antagonist named MacIain. Interestingly, Eoin did not inherit his title, but received it through more sinister means.

Helen is also an interesting heroine. Her first husband was indeed Alexander MacIain MacDonald $7^{th}$ and last Chief of Ardnamurchan (not to be confused with Alexander [aka John] MacDonald who vied for the Lordship of the Isles). Legend has it that Alexander MacIain died, leaving Helen a widow, but MacIain's genealogy chart shows him living a long life. Thus I took literary license and created the annulment, which allowed me to include a cameo appearance by the Bishop of the Isles, John Campbell, who has appeared in all the Highland Dynasty books.

Also for the record, Lady Helen wedded Iain Og MacLaine, $5^{th}$ of Lochbuie for a time, with whom she had two sons, which I chose to omit from this story.

Her relationship with Eoin could have been rather tenuous. The legend reflects: "*The 7th chief ravished her and afterwards Lady Helen, widow of two other Highland chiefs, and daughter of Colin Campbell of Glenorchy, which relationship was no doubt the reason why the Campbells advanced him to the chieftainship.*" *(website ref: MacFarlane Clan & Families Genealogy: Helen Campbell.)* Evidently, the ravishing of Lady Helen is still a bone of contention between the clans, but Helen and Eoin were married and bore three sons: John (Iain) MacGregor (who must have died in infancy), Alasdair Ruadh MacGregor, 8th Chief of Clan Gregor, and Gregor MacGregor.

The Campbells and the MacGregors were fast allies during the medieval period. It was in the sixteenth century that feuds began to arise between these two great clans. Perhaps the scandal created by Sir Eoin's ravishing of Lady Helen could have been the spark that started it all.

This has been a fun series to write. Presently, I'm off writing other Scottish historical romances, but hope to soon return and continue building on the Highland Dynasty Series.

## *Other Books by Amy Jarecki:*

Highland Force Series:
*Captured by the Pirate Laird*
*The Highland Henchman*
*Beauty and the Barbarian*
*Return of the Highland Laird (A Highland Force Novella)*

Highland Dynasty Series:
*Knight in Highland Armor*
*A Highland Knight's Desire*
*A Highland Knight to Remember*

Pict/Roman Romances:
*Rescued by the Celtic Warrior*
*Celtic Maid*

Visit Amy's web site & sign up to receive newsletter updates of new releases and giveaways exclusive to newsletter followers: www.amyjarecki.com
Follow on Facebook: amyjarecki
Follow on Twitter: @amyjarecki

If you enjoyed *A Highland Knight to Remember*, we would be honored if you would consider leaving a review.
*~Thank you!*

## *About the Author*

A descendant of an ancient Lowland clan, Amy adores Scotland. Though she now resides in southwest Utah, she received her MBA from Heriot-Watt University in Edinburgh. Winning multiple writing awards, she found her niche in the genre of Scottish historical romance. Amy loves hearing from her readers and can be contacted through her website at www.amyjarecki.com.

Amy also recommends books by three of her favorite historical romance authors. Have a look at these talented author's Amazon pages:

Monica McCarty
Tessa Dare
Grace Burrowes